PRAISE FOR THE DI EMI

'A gritty, fast-paced police procedural'
Jennie Ensor

'[This book] will keep you gripped and guessing until the end'
Amanda Gussin

'A great crime thriller that had me hooked throughout'
Julie Lacey

'A gripping, twisty thriller with an intricate plot and fascinating, flawed characters'
Katy Johnson

'Chilling'
Livia Sbarbaro

'[A] great read that sucks you in and keeps you turning the pages'
Rose McClelland

'Written deftly with marvellous characterisation, a pacy plot and a compelling and often darkly humorous narrative . . . The female lead provides a hugely engaging antagonist'
InTheAmazone

'Well-written and intriguing to the end'
S. J. Butler

FORTRESS

THE NIGHTHAWK

LOUISE MULLINS

Published in 2025 by Fortress.

Y Bwthyn
Ringland,
Newport,
Wales.

Text copyright © 2025 Louise Mullins

Cover Design: Jamie Curtis

Cover Photography: Canva

The moral right of Louise Mullins to be identified as the author of this work has been asserted in accordance with the Copyright, Designs and Patents Act 1988.

All rights reserved, including the right to reproduce this book, or portions thereof in any form. No part of this text may be reproduced, transmitted, downloaded, decompiled, reverse engineered, stored, or introduced into any information storage and retrieval system by any means, whether electronic or mechanical without the express written permission of the author.

This is a work of fiction. Names, characters, places, incidents and dialogues are products of the author's imagination or are used fictitiously. Any resemblance to actual people, living or dead, events or locales is entirely coincidental.

A CIP catalogue record for this book is available from the British Library.

ISBN (eBook): B0D158KX3W
ISBN (Paperback): 979-8-3063-2215-5

CONTENTS

DEDICATION

DAY ONE OF THE INVESTIGATION

DI LOCKE

PS TOMOS

KERRY-ANN

DI LOCKE

PS TOMOS

KERRY-ANN

DI LOCKE

PS TOMOS

KERRY-ANN

DI LOCKE

PS TOMOS

KERRY-ANN

DI LOCKE

PS TOMOS

KERRY-ANN

DI LOCKE

PS TOMOS

KERRY-ANN

DI LOCKE

PS TOMOS

KERRY-ANN

DI LOCKE

PS TOMOS

KERRY-ANN

DAY TWO OF THE INVESTIGATION

DI LOCKE

PS TOMOS

KERRY-ANN

DI LOCKE

PS TOMOS

KERRY-ANN

DI LOCKE

PS TOMOS

KERRY-ANN

DI LOCKE

PS TOMOS

KERRY-ANN

DI LOCKE

PS TOMOS

KERRY-ANN

DI LOCKE

PS TOMOS

KERRY-ANN

DAY THREE OF THE INVESTIGATION

DI LOCKE

PS TOMOS

KERRY-ANN

DI LOCKE

PS TOMOS

KERRY-ANN

DI LOCKE

PS TOMOS

KERRY-ANN

DI LOCKE

PS TOMOS

KERRY-ANN

DI LOCKE

PS TOMOS

KERRY-ANN

DI LOCKE

PS TOMOS

KERRY-ANN

SIX MONTHS LATER

DI LOCKE

DS TOMOS

KERRY-ANN

SIX MONTHS BEFORE

DI LOCKE

PS TOMOS

KERRY-ANN

DI LOCKE

PS TOMOS

KERRY-ANN

DI LOCKE

PS TOMOS

KERRY-ANN

DI LOCKE

PS TOMOS

KERRY-ANN

DI LOCKE

PS TOMOS

KERRY-ANN

DI LOCKE

PS TOMOS

KERRY-ANN

DI LOCKE

PS TOMOS

KERRY-ANN

SIX MONTHS LATER

DI LOCKE

DS TOMOS

KERRY-ANN

SIX MONTHS BEFORE

DI LOCKE

PS TOMOS

KERRY-ANN

DI LOCKE

PS TOMOS

KERRY-ANN

SIX MONTHS LATER

DI LOCKE

DS TOMOS

KERRY-ANN

The Next to Die, DI Emma Locke: Book 5 coming soon!

CONTACT NUMBERS

AUTHOR'S NOTE

ALSO BY LOUISE MULLINS

ACKNOWLEDGEMENTS

DEDICATION

To Rosco and Starla, my best friends.

CHAPTER ONE

The young woman stood on the pavement waving at him, signalling for him to pull over. A bicycle lay on the concrete beside her. He indicated onto the forecourt of the petrol station – closed now – stopping the maroon-coloured car a few yards behind the derelict building, the pumps gone, the shop windows boarded up. As he exited the vehicle she ran towards him, grinning. He rolled down the window. It squeaked as it came down.

'Boy, am I glad to see you.'

He stared, vacantly, back at her.

'I got a puncture,' she said, indicating to the lilac Raleigh on the ground.

'Nice wheels.'

He had a southern accent and wore a parka buttoned up to his neck.

'Thanks. I don't suppose you've got an air pump in your boot?'

'No.'

'Uh, where are you heading?'

'Home.'

'Don't suppose you could take me with you? Give me a lift I mean. My dad can repair the bike.'

'Sure.' He shrugged.

'Thanks.'

She turned, knelt, lifted the bicycle, and walked it round to the back of the car.

~1~

The Nighthawk	Alys Wynn

'I don't know what I'd have done if you hadn't come along. It's so hot today, and who knows how long I'd have been waiting for someone to pass. Ya know I haven't seen another soul in,' she glanced down at her wrist, 'an hour.'

When she looked back up, she saw that his eyes were still focused on her bare thigh, where her watchstrap had left an indentation.

***

As they drove away, the Nighthawk's first victim may have felt the warm air comb through her hair, smelt the oceanic tang in the mid-summer breeze, and was likely grateful for the ride back to the house she lived in with her parents.

She couldn't have known she'd been picked up by a sadistic lunatic with murder on his mind.

DAY ONE OF THE INVESTIGATION

MG 11(T)

RESTRICTED (when complete)

WITNESS STATEMENT
(CJ Act 1967, s.9; MC Act 1980, ss.5A(3) (a) and 5B: Criminal Procedure Rules 2005, Rule 27.1)

Statement of: <u>Ms Demelza Boyde</u>
Age if under 18: <u>Over 18</u> (if over 18 insert 'over 18')
Occupation: <u>Independent Mortgage Advisor</u>

This statement (consisting of page(s) each signed by me) is true to the best of my knowledge and belief and I make it knowing that, if it is tendered in evidence, I shall be liable to prosecution if I have wilfully stated in it, anything which I know to be false or do not believe to be true.

Signature: <u>Ms D. Boyde</u> Date: <u>21st November 2022</u>

Tick if witness evidence is visually recorded: ☐ (supply witness details on rear)

My name is Ms Demelza Boyde, a mortgage advisor, of Cliff Hill, Penarth. I have recently separated from my husband, Geraint, who I reported missing shortly after he left our house at 4 p.m.

Signature: Ms D. Boyde
Signature witnessed by: PC Warner

Continuation of statement of: Ms D. Boyde

Geraint has been behaving in a fearful and paranoid manner for several weeks, becoming obsessed with home security and taking whispered phone calls late at night, which he dismisses as misdials when confronted, claiming the person has rung the wrong number. He has also displayed erratic emotional responses that do not correlate with the situation, such as laughing or crying in circumstances that warrant the opposite. Our relationship broke down as a result and we agreed to separate four weeks ago. Our separation has been amicable, and we have been co-parenting our twin daughters, civilly.

Today, as is usual, he came to see the children after school. However, before he entered the house, I noticed that he appeared agitated, as though he were in a hurry, and he kept glancing over his shoulder as he stood on the doorstep. He briefly saw the children, but the visit was awkward, and before he left, he asked to speak with me alone. He said he would not be returning and that this would be the last time he saw the children. I asked what he meant but he wouldn't tell me. As this was so out of character, I became concerned for his wellbeing.

Signature: Ms D. Boyde
Signature witnessed by: PC Warner

Continuation of statement of: Ms D. Boyde

As soon as he left, I called his mum, Lorraine, and asked her to stop by the flat he's been renting on Glebe Street since we separated and check in on him. I was concerned he might be considering suicide. She did not get a response from his flat, so called his landlord and asked if he'd let her in. He said he couldn't because the lease was dealt with by an estate agency who had the only spare set of keys. She rang them but they refused to grant her access to the property, so she called the police.

Signature: Ms Boyde
Signature witnessed by: PC Warner

DI LOCKE

PRESENT

My feet hurt as I pound the pavement. The houses I pass are a blur in my peripheral, my attention homed in on my assailant; at least ten years younger than me and a tad slimmer she's far fitter than I am. But no matter how out of breath I've become, nor how much the distance between us has grown, I'm not going to lose sight of her.

I can't.

If I fail my yearly fitness test, I'll have to undergo a medical assessment to prove my physical competency.

She rounds the corner, and I duck beneath the overgrown hedge of a nearby garden, chasing her along the pavement like my life depends on it.

Bleep.

My timer is up.

I stop the running machine, the video footage on the built-in screen freezes. The computer-generated suspect I'm pretending to hunt pauses mid-run.

'What's the score?' I ask my instructor, breathlessly. I should really hit the gym.

'Five point four. You've passed.'

Just.

I remove the sweatband from my forehead and grab

the face towel from the handlebar, dabbing at my damp face and neck.

Thirty minutes later, I'm exiting the car in the direction of the school where my son, Jaxon, and my mate's kid, Ethan – who's been living with us for the past two months – should be standing beside their prospective teachers, waiting to be collected. Only I can't reach the playground for the fire engines parked in front of the building, which is ablaze.

FIND MY DEVICE DATA TRACKER REPORT

PING statistics for: 07********* (**OS:** Android Version 13; **Network:** EE)
Wi-Fi MAC ADDRESS: 3c:07:fe:f4:ae
Reply from: (IP) fe98:c7c:2a02:baff:fed700:drd
Data: (ID) 8685>open GPS
Bytes= 22
Time= 51ms
Packets: Sent= 4, Received= 4, Lost= 0 (0%)
Approximate round trip times in milliseconds: Minimum= 46, Maximum= 54, Average= 51

PS TOMOS

PRESENT

Flames and shrapnel litter the road. Dust fills the air creating a mist that's so thick I can barely breathe. I choke out a command but find my mouth desert dry.

The loud roaring of an RAF helicopter thundering through the sky jolts me awake. The ground vibrates as it lands.

I sit bolt upright and tear myself away from the duvet, slipping and tripping into the safety of my wife's arms.

'Alright, Dafydd, it's just the vacuum.'

'Bloody hell I thought it was Bloody Friday. Can we buy something that makes less noise?'

'Not unless you get a promotion.'

I extricate myself from her grip and shake off the memory of the blasts. 'I suppose I'm stuck in eighties Belfast every time you decide to do the housework then.'

'It's not that loud. You're just being melodramatic.'

'Maybe you're losing your hearing.'

She grabs a pillow from the bed and lobs it at me. I catch it and fling it back at her and we fight it out until we're both panting, exhausted.

'No . . . more,' Sarah says. 'Can't . . . catch . . . my . . .

breath.'

'Do you give in?' I taunt.

She pulls the white pillowcase free and waves it in the air like a flag.

If only the IRA had surrendered before I'd been sent to Northern Ireland all those years ago.

Has it really been almost three decades?

I'm getting old.

I laugh, lean over Sarah, wrap an arm round her shoulders and squeeze her into a hug before giving her a smacker to the cheek.

She wipes her face and kisses me back, on the lips.

I note the time on the bedside clock behind her.

'I've gotta go.'

'No rest for the wicked, eh?'

'I can't wait to get wicked with you tonight.' I wink.

She reverses her wheelchair from the door, allowing me to exit, and I pretend she's rolled it over my foot, pulling a face and limping while she cracks me across the ass with the flat of her palm.

'Feisty.'

'You love it.'

'Love you more.'

'Bugger off, you soppy git.'

And bugger off I do, towards the centre of the city half an hour before I'm due to start my 8 a.m. shift.

PENTRITH MEDICAL

Patient Record Summary

Patient: Mr Geraint Fford
Date of Birth: 12th January 1974
Address: Flat 27a Glebe Street, Penarth.

Repeat Medication(s):
Sertraline (100mg)
Propranolol (40mg)

Recent Consultations:

(20/9/22) Acute Depressive Episode – Patient experiencing severe insomnia and anxiety relating to work-related stress and childhood aversity. Suggested referral to in-clinic Cognitive Behavioural Therapist. Prescribed anti-depressant medication, with review in one month.

(16/9/22) Stress – Patient experiencing work-related tension. Suggested referral to in-clinic Stress Management Therapist.

(8/9/22) Insomnia – Patient re-experiencing anxiety related to childhood adversity, which is causing trouble sleeping. Suggested use of lavender oil on pillow and use of guided visualisation/meditation exercises before bed to aid relaxation.

(24/8/22) IBS – Increase in symptoms relating to Inflammatory Bowel Disease. Prescribed course of Prednisolone at 25mg for five days.

(9/8/22) Tension headache – Suggested practising relaxation exercises.

KERRY-ANN

PAST

I slammed back my coffee, threw the paper cup into the bin beside the lift and was just about to sit in the waiting area facing the floor-to-ceiling window overlooking the city when my editor called me into her office.

'Kerry-Ann, it's so good to see you. How are you keeping?'

I didn't know how to reply. It had been less than twenty-four hours since I'd unpacked my grandmother's things, the items that had been bestowed to me after she'd passed away just a few weeks ago. I'd just been getting my head around the fact that she would no longer be at the end of the phone for our weekly catch-up, when I'd found the note bearing my biological father's name while sifting through her belongings. Finding out who he was, was a shock I didn't quite know what I felt about yet. And then I'd received the call from my publisher. This meeting couldn't have come at a better time. I'd never done well in my own head and have always thrived on busyness. Having a project to occupy myself with was a welcome distraction.

'Good, considering...'

She tilted her head and said, 'A death in the family is always difficult, but you were close to your grandmother, weren't you?'

'Irene brought me up.'

'She was from Wales, wasn't she?'

'Penarth.'

Something unreadable flashed across her eyes for just a second, but it was enough to suggest that I might not like whatever it was that she was about to impart. 'Why don't you take a seat. Would you like a coffee?'

'No, thanks, I've just had one.'

She sat opposite me, the desk between us. It was slim-legged and matched the rest of the modern décor that filled the room. A circular red rug was parked between the bookcase and a triangular-shaped floor lamp that consisted of just a light bulb attached to a metal frame. The single painting that hung on the wall to my left was some impressionist art that looked vaguely like a sunset over mountainous terrain but could just as easily have been a bloodied corpse bobbing along the sea. The look was one of cold simplicity and nothing at all like anything I'd choose to adorn the rooms of my own home with, but it worked well and suited her hard exterior perfectly.

She seemed hesitant to talk, and I wondered briefly if she was about to release me of my contract, but then she spoke. The assignment she was proposing might just give my career the lift I needed.

'You've heard of the Nighthawk?'

'I think everyone from Cardiff to Tenby has.'

'You know the case well?'

'He was a serial killer who terrorised South Wales in the eighties. Lured women back to the cattle shed he'd insulated and turned into a torture chamber where he held them captive, beating and raping them repeatedly until they starved to death.'

She appeared to want to say something else but a knock on the door interrupted us.

Leah's publishing assistant put her head round the open door and gave me a smile. 'Hi, Kerry-Ann.' She turned to Leah and said, 'Here,' handing her a book. 'You left it in the conference room.'

Leah took it and placed it on her desk. I recognised the title and the author's name on the spine.

She waited until her assistant had left the room before she continued. 'Alys Wynn has been given a few months to live. Cancer. Not only will this give the author the opportunity to voice her own story, but it'll allow you to use the skills you've honed throughout your career on something much longer. What do you think, would you like to write her memoir?'

Thinking back, somewhere in the spaces between her words she was asking me if I felt able to go back there, to the place of my birth, but I had no idea then that she knew anything about my father, and what he'd done. Even if I had known, I wouldn't have been able to pass on the opportunity to interview Alys Wynn, the prolific true crime author whose instant bestseller made her the Welsh equivalent of Kathryn Casey.

As I stood up to go, Leah passed me the book that her assistant had given her.

'Read it before you leave Cornwall.'

Google

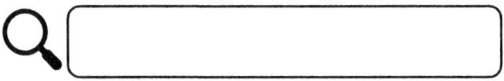

All   Images   Videos   News   Maps

WALES ONLINE
https://www.walesonline>
POLICE APPEAL FOR INFORMATION IN HUNT FOR MISSING CARDIFF MAN
Scott Chamberlain left work on the 3rd of June 2018 and failed to return home . . .

SOUTH WALES ARGUS
https://www.southwalesargus>
BODY FOUND IN HUNT FOR MISSING BRIDGEND MAN
New father, Lee Porter disappeared after a night out with friends in Swansea . . .

WALES ONLINE
htttps://www.walesonline>
INQUEST INTO DEATH OF MAN WHO WENT MISSING FROM HIS HOME IN BARRY
Stephen Crowley went missing in October 2019. His body was recovered two weeks later . . .

BBC NEWS
https://www.bbcnews>
SHOCKING FIGURES SHOW RECORD NUMBER OF SUICIDES IN WALES
There are collectively more suicides in Wales than in England, and the majority of those are men . . .

WALES ONLINE
https://www.walesonline>
SUICIDES IN SOUTH WALES REACH HIGHEST LEVEL IN FOUR DECADES
Documentary exploring the prevalence of male suicide in Wales will be aired tonight . . .

SKY NEWS
https://www.skynews>
MALE SUICIDE RATES IN WALES A NATIONAL EMERGENCY
The Welsh government has published preventative strategies after a report reveals 278 men took their lives in 2017. Glamorgan being the epicentre . . .

DI LOCKE

PRESENT

I awake gasping for air and looking like one of the undead from an apocalyptic zombie film I throw the quilt off my slick skin and crawl from the bed to thunder from the room and into the bathroom, where I moan as the pin-sharp needles of ice-cold tap water stab at my flesh as I splash my face with it.

    The boys have not come to any harm. I tell myself it was just a nightmare, my subconscious playing my fears in videographic format while I manage some shuteye. The worst kind. Because since I was forced to confront my best mate, Craig, over his drinking, after his return to the bottle, his son has become my sole responsibility. And since they were both living under my roof when he fell off the wagon and the boy's mother is not able to care for him, I promised to bring up Ethan alongside my stepson for as long as necessary should he relapse. So now I have not one, but two children to worry about.

    I tear myself away from the mirror before I can catch the hollow-eyed face reflected at me. With two active kids under eight who both exhibit additional needs vastly different to one another's, and who both struggle to nod off, and whose nocturnal patterns differ by hours, it's not surprising I'm losing sleep. But how much longer I can get away with it I've no idea.

I know it's not likely my nightmare of losing both the boys will come to fruition, but it sits at the back of my mind like a dark cloud overcasting an outdoor photoshoot as I dress and make them their breakfast.

I watch them eat it, half-dazed, sipping a hot strong coffee, praying it'll wake me up.

Johnno plants a kiss on my forehead, sniffing as he retracts, and says, 'I think your toast is burnt.'

I glide some butter on the blackened bread as I watch him leave, to meet with the photographer who's accompanying him to whoever it is he's interviewing this morning. He's done with freelancing and has got himself a job with the local newspaper.

I stare at the empty bowls on the table. I'll deal with them later.

With one arm through the sleeve of my coat, I hand the boys each their lunchboxes, slam the front door behind us, and escort them to the car.

The drive to the school passes in a blur of sleep deprivation and worry. How are we going to be able to afford to continue feeding and clothing Ethan with our incomes stretched so much already? Will his father turn up to my place of work drunk, demanding I hand him back, despite being the one who begged me to look after him? Is it possible to survive on four hours sleep a night indefinitely?

I pull up in front of the school, note the desolate playground, and hurry the boys towards their classrooms. Praise the Lord they're next door to each other! And though I'm late to work, nobody mentions it. Which is one of the perks of being a senior officer, I suppose.

In Situ Initial Examination (Case No. IC1MOUO224) completed on iPad

Home Office Pathologist: Lucy Griffin.
Date: Friday 25th November 2022.
Time: 10.42 a.m. (found 7.57 a.m. by coastguard, secured 8.36 a.m. by SWP, ID'd preliminarily by CSI at 9.21 a.m.)
Location: Swanbridge Bay, Lavernock.
Appearance: Bloated, blackened skin, post-mortem abrasions, two bullet wounds penetrating: 1) small intestine (no exit wound); 2) cranium, through occipital bone, perforating cerebellum.
Cause of death: Gunshot to brain.

PS TOMOS

PRESENT

I tap the steering wheel to the sound of the late icon Tina Turner's *The Best* that emanates from the speakers. It reminds me of the dance hall where I used to take Sarah, when she was still on her feet. Before that drunken idiot got in his car. Before the accident. Before the wheelchair. That there's a whole radio station dedicated to the music of our youth reminds me how much time has passed and makes me feel old.

I pull up outside Gregg's on Commercial Street and head inside to order my usual: bacon roll and a doughnut. I'm a walking talking cliché.

The wife thinks I'm still adhering to the vegan diet she put me on after the doctor told me my cholesterol was almost as high as my BMI, but I'll tell her I've cheated. There are no secrets between us.

I stuff my face while seated in the car, watching the entrance to the charity shop next door, where a man is attempting to resurrect his tent. The homelessness in Newport is staggering.

The passenger door opens, allowing a blast of cold air to enter the cabin, and before we've exchanged a word Jonesy, as I've nicknamed him, has applied his seatbelt. Then he leans over the centre console and snatches the paper-bagged doughnut from my hand before I have the chance to take a bite.

'Cheers.'

I open my mouth to say something, but I'm disrupted by the buzz of the phone strapped to my vest.

Image No. 2

Description:
Discharged cartridge found two feet from corpse on snow-covered grass. Frosted around the case. Blood and cadaver tissue visible on bullet.

Materials:
Copper-tipped, brass cartridge case with full metal jacket over steel core projectile.

Dimesnsions:
9mm calibre diameter, 19mm length.

Ballistic assessment:
Extractor head shape and groove depth consistent with parabellum bullet used in:
- Glock 17/19/26

- Sig Sauer P226/P228/P210
- Smith & Wesson SD9/SW1911/M&P9
- Springfield XD-M/XD-S
- Ruger LC-R/LC-9/SR-9
- Beretta 92-FS/M9/PX-4
- Taurus PT-111-G2/1911B-9/PT709

KERRY-ANN

PAST

Home was wherever I felt safe. It always had been. And wrapped in a blanket with the cat on my lap, a cup of hot sugary tea in one hand, Alys' open book in my other, I acknowledged my position of privilege. I probably wasn't going to die today, and if I did it was unlikely to be at the hands of a man.

As I began reading, I noticed immediately *The Nighthawk* was written in a way that included the author's own experiences of the locality that would forever be haunted by the despicable acts of the man who had been dubbed by that very same name and was not dissimilar to the way I write.

To what extent did Alys Wynn's own feelings and experiences colour her writing on the subject?

One passage described the route I'd be taking so vividly that I was able to get a feel for the geography of the place as if I had already been there. You see, despite having been born and brought up so close to Lavernock I'd never gone further afield than Cardiff, where I studied journalism.

In celebration of passing my degree I took the train to Newquay for a music festival with three of my college friends, where I met Amélie. A few weeks later, having said adios to my mates, we were living together in a camper van in a field owned by a guy who offered us work cleaning the statics on the holiday park adjoining it in exchange for rent. Things didn't work out between us, but I chose to stay, cleaning caravans in the adjoining holiday village or picking daffodils and potatoes on the farm the guy's father owned during the tourist season.

I grew biceps as wide as a weightlifter hoisting those boxes of harvested goods to the truck I was taught to drive in, often entering the camper too exhausted to cook, shoulders aching so much I could barely lift my arms. By the end of each balmy summer day my clothes were ripped and dirty, and I stank of sweat, but I'd saved enough money to see me through the winter.

I was crossing the field on my way back to the camper van when I got the call to say that my grandfather had died. Cardiac arrest. Unexpected but not unavoidable. I came home on the next available train. Two actually, I had to change over in Bristol. My grandmother accosted me at the funeral, told me they'd released the equity from the house she and Stanley had brought me up in.

'We'd planned to buy a narrowboat. Stan wanted to live on the canal.'

It was worth double anything I could afford with a mortgage, not that I would have been able to get one with just a cash-in-hand job.

'I'm alright on your grandfather's pension. And I get to stay in the house until it's my time to meet our maker. I want you to have it.'

She was adamant I use the money to buy myself somewhere to live.

'I don't like thinking of you all alone in that rickety camper van on that windy clifftop, especially during these cold, dark nights.'

One of the lasting effects of the Nighthawk's crimes was that she'd developed an overprotective instinct. If I was ever a few minutes late calling her she'd ring me in a panic. It didn't matter that the serial killer had been apprehended, convicted, and imprisoned long before I'd been born.

By spring I'd passed my driving test, bought a second-hand Seat Leon, had enrolled on an MA in Writing, and had secured a job at the *Plymouth Herald* covering reader's stories and reviewing literature.

Now here I was fifteen years later, the proud owner of a two-bedroom cottage where I was facing another night in on my own, as Natalia, my girlfriend, was hitting the clubs later tonight with her work colleagues after her shift at the restaurant.

What was it that led creatives to each other?

I ended my self-reflection by dipping a biscuit into my cup and sucking the sweet liquid off it as I turned the page, diving right back into the book on my lap. It wasn't exactly bedtime material, but I couldn't very well go and interview the author without having read her debut bestseller, could I?

Newport MIT <dtvcstallen@nptmit.gov.uk>
To: **dtvsgtdavidsmith@nptmit.gov.uk**

📎   1 attachment   Fri, 25 Nov 2022 11:53

Re: Geraint Fford

Smithy,

Looks like our victim was given an Osman Warning (attached). Awaiting report from Intelligence Analyst as to whom it involved.

DC Allen.

Geraint Fford,

We are in possession of intelligence which indicates that your life is in immediate danger.

South Wales Police have a duty to ensure that you are told about this information which we predict poses a serious threat.

Although we are taking steps to minimise the risk to your personal safety and that of your extended family members, who we identify as being at potential risk by association with you, we suggest you take such remedial action as you see fit to increase your own safety: change daily routines; always walk with an associate; do not meet with anyone related to your job outside the workplace, alone; carry a mobile phone at all times; install a house burglar alarm; install a domestic CCTV door guard system, increase house security measures (locks and bolts on windows, doors, and gates etc.).

It may be that you decide that it is more appropriate to move out of the area for the foreseeable future. That is a matter for you to decide.

Detective Inspector, Bridges.

DI LOCKE

PRESENT

A nighthawk croaked nasally as he swooped down on his long slender wings to capture a moth mid-flight. His mate trilled eerily from below, where she guarded the ground-nest beside a sprig of adder's tongue ferns that were sprayed with blood.

The bullet lay in the long-stemmed grass, hidden from view of the passing trawler. The lights on its bow lit a path towards the mainland across the moon-dappled sea. Waves crested on the ocean floor. The tide slapped against the sandstone cliffs and sprayed against the salt-encrusted spleenwort that sprouted between the shore-lined rocks.

The boat lurched on the tide as the skipper steered it portside around the island to avoid becoming stranded on the mudstone, the loamy wind strong and ice-cold.

Snow fell, glittering the tarmac in a blanket of white and dusting over tyre tracks and a set of footprints that led from the isle to the mainland, across the road that lined the bay, and along the pavement to where a row of oak and ash trees provided an awning, protecting the single imprint of the executioner's shoe from the elements.

Further up the road, where it grew steep, the trees were replaced with an overgrown hedge covered in thorns and thistles, beyond which snow blanketed the field that was split in two by a narrow dirt track that led to a wrought iron gate painted black.

Two gargoyles stood sentry atop the brick walls at either side of it, guarding the occupant of the idling car parked in front of the porch. She was not long home, ferrying shopping bags filled with groceries from the boot and into the house when PC Amanda Kelly trod up the path to begin her house-to-house enquiries. She was tasked with finding out what, if anything, the few nearby residents had witnessed.

The owner claimed not to have been home around the time the manager of The Captain's Wife heard what he believed was a car backfiring, which may have been the same evening one of the holidaymakers from the campsite on the clifftop overlooking the cove reckoned she saw someone wearing a hoodie running the length of the public footpath that borders the campsite from the coastal defence lookout. Whoever it was might be the same individual captured on a CCTV camera fronting the gated entrance to the campsite at 6.57 p.m. exiting the area in a black Vauxhall Astra. Which unfortunately, due to the darkness and the position of the lens the vehicle's registration was not visible.

The rooms within the Edwardian property were in a state of disrepair and the land surrounding it far too much for a widow to cope with alone. Which is why, thirty years ago, Celyn's late husband had hired a groundskeeper and housemaid. The two had fallen in love and they might have lived happily ever after if the groundsman hadn't gone on to murder their employer.

PC Kelly learned this when running a PNC check on the inhabitant of the property, the address instantly flagged up as the scene of a grisly crime. She regales this to me as she hops from foot-to-foot and rubs her pocketed hands together in an attempt to keep warm.

I'd just pulled away from the kerb, the school still visible in my rearview mirror, when I'd got the call informing me that a body had been found bobbing up and down on the surface of the sea a few hours ago, and that the deceased had been killed.

He isn't a fresh corpse then, was my first thought. Not if he can float.

My flat shoes sink into the water-logged sand and the silt gathers around my ankles like it's trying to weigh me down as I wend my way towards the foamy curled waves.

The lifeboat is being lapped at by the tide where it's stationed a few metres inland, on the shale, several feet away from the white tent that has been erected to contain the deceased. One of the RNLI personnel reaches into the rescue boat and withdraws a plastic bag, like the kind used to collect evidence in. Containing something that fell from the deceased's trouser pocket? A wallet? Phone? Another of the volunteers uses a gloved hand to retrieve it.

'What's goin' on 'ere?' a female voice asks, barely audible above the howling wind.

'They've found someone,' another bellows from somewhere within the crowd of people that are stood behind me on the paved verge.

'Probably one of those paddleboarders got caught up and swept out to sea,' a man replies, older and with a scratchy voice like he's got a twenty a day smoking habit.

'Nah, it'll be that bloke who went missing.'

'The fisherman?'

'No, that solicitor.'

'I can't keep track of them all. There are so many of them. Men that is. Who disappear. And most of them end up in the sea if not on the tracks.'

'His mum's been putting posters up all over town. Dunno how you could miss 'em, they're everywhere.'

I don't let on that I can hear them, or that I'm tuned in to what they're saying while my gaze is absorbed in the goings-on ahead of us.

'Tis the tides,' the man says. 'They're some of the most dangerous on the isle.'

'No,' the woman says confidently, shaking her head. 'It's the seawomen.'

'Seawomen?'

'Mermaids. Sirens. Whatever you want to call 'em, singing sea shanties, calling out to fishermen, and seducing them from their vessels. Tis the wife of one who haunts the isle. Waited three days she did for her husband's return, but he never did.'

'That's just the tides,' the man says incredulously, shaking his head. 'Their bodies don't return cos of the direction of the current.'

'His did,' she says, pointing to a piece of exposed tarpaulin that the rescuers flopped the deceased man onto, and which is too wide to cover completely with the crime scene tent, causing it to peek out of the entrance. The shadows of two Crime Scene Investigators are visible from the blue-tinged light of a lamp situated somewhere within the tent, in preparation for an initial examination by the on-scene pathologist.

The crime scene manager spots me stood fronting the huddle of onlookers and I raise my hand in a wave. We tread towards one another and meet several yards away from the gathering of locals. She hands me the clear plastic Ziplock bag in her nitrile-gloved hand, so I can see the driver's licence inside it that's slipped from the sleeve of the conker-brown leather wallet.

The name written on it will go some way towards

identifying the man who was captured in the photograph his wife gave to South Wales Police four days ago.

HOLMES 2 DATABASE

File	searches	Tools	Help

CONTACT
Officer(s): Garda Kenny Ward
Arrest time and date: 8.15 a.m., 12/06/1989
Caution: Wounding with Intent
Report(s): Arrested on suspicion of bombing a pub called The Stallion, in Belfast, in 1978, which resulted in the injury of a patron.
Convicted offences: Terrorism

PERSONAL
Name: Fergal McGinty
DOB: 06/04/51
POB: Belfast, Ireland
Race: Caucasian
Ethnicity: Irish
Religion: Catholic
Sex: Male
Gender: Male
Skin colour: IC1
Build: Medium
Height: 6'2
Weight: 18st
Hair colour: Brown
Eye colour: Blue
Scars/Marks: Birthmark below right elbow
Tattoos: Celtic symbol inside cross on right bicep; lily inside closed fist on left bicep; one-inch scar beneath right earlobe

IDENTIFICATION
NINO: NX 84 ▮▮▮
Birth certificate number: YH 79 ▮▮
Driver's License no: FERGM90406 ▮▮
Passport Number: 799 ▮▮▮

IMAGES

📁

ADDRESSES
Contact: N/A
Residence: Gleann na Sióg, Castel Park, Coast Road, County Antrim, Ireland.
Business: N/A

VEHICLE
Year: 1986
Make: Ford
Model: Transit
Style: Tipper
Colour: White
Reg Year: 1986
Fuel: Diesel
Reg Plate: JD 18 ▮▮
VIN: UNUT ▮▮▮ ▮▮
Occupation: Builder

PHONES
Residence: 028 (94) ▮▮▮
Business: N/A

PS TOMOS

PRESENT

Two months ago, I worked a missing persons case that led to the discovery of a body and resulted in a short secondment with the Murder Investigation Team at the Criminal Investigation Department in Cwmbran. My request to join the department so that I could use my three-decade long career supervising serious and complex cases – which for the last ten years has been focused mainly on missing and vulnerable persons within the Public Protection Unit – was accepted immediately based on my skillset, and for the past five days I've been on attachment, shadowed by DS Dylan Jones who just stole my iced doughnut as part of my initiation.

Since Monday I've successfully located a suspect in Scotland, led a team who found a suspected murder victim on a landfill site, and another who discovered a reused murder weapon that had links to an organised crime network, which we've handed over to the Major Crime Unit. All necessary ticks on my portfolio checklist and will assist my study towards the National Investigators' Exam that Detective Inspector Emma Locke, my superior, has agreed for me to take. Telling me I'll 'smash it'.

Jonesy wears a smug grin as he chomps on *my* doughnut while I drive us through the gridlocked roads, comprising morning traffic – both human and vehicular commuters – to HQ, where I slam my butt down on the first seat I can find and log on to the computer parked in front of it using my new passcode as an official member of CID.

The call from Emma was to let me know she was with the murdered man who South Wales Police had been searching for since he'd been reported missing. Now the investigation has become a murder inquiry, I've been tasked with reading through the documentation that was uploaded onto the HOLMES 2 database when Geraint was still considered a misper. The information acquired had originally seemed to suggest that he'd likely taken his own life, there were several lines of enquiry and a few leads which appeared to have led nowhere, and that I'd have to reconsider now that his body has been found.

His ex-wife had used the 'Find My Device' tracker available free of charge via Google prior to calling the police. Whenever the service is used the PING is recorded. South Wales Police were able to provide us with the location by requesting the securely filed data record, not accessible to the public.

> DigiFcs were unable to triangulate the mobile phone belonging to the victim as it was disconnected from the Vodafone network within a quarter mile radius of ID 8685 (Penarth train station). The last hit from open Wi-Fi GPS signals that the IP address belongs to an Italian restaurant called Romeo's, situated thirty-seven yards from the yacht club. Prior to this there is no

cellular data available for this mobile phone.

The time stamp provided by the Digital Forensic Technician suggests the phone was switched off or disabled approximately fifteen minutes after Geraint left his wife's house on Cliff Hill, which also happens to be the only GPS location that's ever been picked up by the network and indicates that before the day he went missing Geraint was using a VPN.

Did he 'allow tracking' on his mobile phone for the first time that day because he wanted a digital record of his whereabouts in case things went south with whomever he met on Sully Island? Is the person he met the last individual to have seen him alive?

2022-11-21 09:04.18	07*******	029********	BT	00:06:03	Cardiff
2022-11-21 10:23.29	07*********	07*******	Vodafone	00:01:14	Penarth
2022-11-21 10:26.47	07*********	07*******	Vodafone	00:00:51	Penarth
2022-11-21 11:17.35	07*******	01633******	Virgin	00:22:09	Newport
2022-11-21 12:32.26	07*********	07*******	Vodafone	00:00:36	Penarth
2022-11-21 13:40.54	07*******	01656******	TalkTalk	00:09:05	Porthcawl
2022-11-21 15:49	07*******	1792******	Sky	00:07:36	Swansea
2022-11-21 16:31	07*******	029********	BT	00:12:48	Cardiff

KERRY-ANN

PAST

I used the note I'd found in the shoebox beneath my grandmother's bed to mark the page I was on. I read it again before I closed the book.

Your father's name is Roderick Penrose

I'd only seen my mother, Nancy, a handful of times throughout my childhood. She spent the majority of her life in and out of psychiatric hospitals. My grandparents unofficially adopted me when I was five. After my grandfather, Stanley's, death, Irene explained what it was that haunted Nancy. 'She was a sensitive child, easily led, the perfect prey for bullies. As she grew older, she became more confident, louder. Then she became with child, and you lit up her whole world. But some women don't cope very well on their own. She suffered awfully from depression, was struggling to cope. We did what we thought was right, offered to take care of you, give her time to heal what ailed her. We had no idea how bad things were.'

I'd always been under the impression that my father had left, and that him walking out on us had been the catalyst for her suicide attempt, which ultimately led to her first admission to Whitchurch Hospital. But after finding that note I googled my father's name and discovered that Nancy's stay in the psychiatric hospital almost immediately followed her husband's arrest.

I don't blame my grandmother for lying to me. She was protecting me from the truth. I can't fault my mother either. She was weak-minded. Neither of the times I'd seen her were appropriate for her to discuss my heritage or the fact that my father was a murderer. But now I had the perfect excuse to investigate both while writing Alys' memoir. I could squeeze in a few extra-curricular activities between interviews.

My all-expenses paid trip would begin Monday. There was no deadline, but Alys wasn't expected to make it to spring, the cancer had spread from her womb to her colon, and into her bones, so I had three months, tops, to get everything I needed. The cancer would soon be in her marrow, her blood. She'd just finished her final course of radiation therapy and was now, in her own words, 'waiting for God'.

I couldn't fathom spending so long away from the home I'd built in Cornwall, my cat, and the support network I'd created for myself. But having recently watched my grandmother's coffin being lowered into the ground, the thought of being in Alys' position forced me to acknowledge the fragility of life. The memoir, published in memorandum with no specific set release date, would be her legacy. It also raised the question of what mine would be. Something I thought about a lot now that my last living relative had died.

Call Handler: Martin G.
Date: Tuesday 22nd November 2022.

Call Log

Time: 7.17 a.m. (029 **** ****).
Caller name: ***** ******.
Report: TWOC of vehicle reg no. CA 19 ▆.
At: 28 Clive House, Redlands Road, Penarth.
Action: Handover to PC Hughes (FIN: ****).

Time: 7.28 a.m. (07*********).
Caller name: ***** ******.
Report: Illegal fishing.
At: Cosmeston Lakes Country Park, Penarth.
Action: Handover to PCSO Merrick.

Time: 7.31 a.m. (01633 ******).
Caller name: ****** *******.
Report: Requesting welfare check on ****** *****. Neighbour fell off kerb and injured head while crossing road yesterday. No answer when knocking on door this morning.
At: 333 Clos Yr Erw, Penarth, CA64 3R▆.
Action: Emergency Response by PC Randall (FIN: ****).

Time: 7.36 a.m. (07*********).
Caller name: ******* *********.
Report: Info re. case no. IC1MOUO224.
At: The Elms, Porlock Drive, Sully CA64 5Q▆.
Action: Handover to PS Saunders (FIN: ****).

Telephone conversation, audio recorded between: Esmerelda Le Fay (caller) and PC Patel (receiver) of Heddlu De Cwmru (South Wales Police: Missing Persons Unit).

On: November 22nd, 2022

At: 7.47 a.m.

Operator: Transferring call to 101 from 07███████ relating to Case Number: IC1MOUO224

PS U: South Wales Police

E LF: Hello?

PS U: Who am I speaking to?

E LF: Esmerelda Le Fay. But please, call me Esme.

PS U: Can I take your address?

E LF: Yes, it's The Elms, Porlock Drive, Sully CA64 5Q█.

PS U: And what is it you'd like to tell us?

E LF: I was on the beach yesterday morning where that man was found, the missing lawyer, and I thought you should know that I saw him, before he died. He gave a woman a stack of cash.

PS U: When was this?

E LF: Yesterday morning.

PS U: You saw him yesterday morning?

E LF: On the beach. He looked just like that picture used on those Missing posters someone's sellotaped to the lampposts in town.

PS U: Can you describe what the woman looked like?

E LF: Blonde, about five foot five, slim, in her late forties. She wore a light-coloured top and a pair of jeans. Not sure what shoes she wore, I think they were white.

PS U: And the man?

E LF: His name's Geraint. He asked me not to tell anyone.

PS U: He spoke to you?

E LF: Well, not him, of course, his spirit. He put his finger to his mouth, asking me to be quiet, so it must have been a secret. Whatever that money was for he didn't want anyone to know about it.

PS U: You said you were on the beach yesterday morning. What time was that?

E LF: About nine-ish. I was collecting sea glass. I saw the tent and the CSI van. Crime Scene Investigation it said on the side of it. You asked us to leave. There were some others see, gawping. He waited until we were alone before he came to talk to me.

PS U: We'll send an officer to take your statement. Are you at home?

E LF: No. I'm visiting my sister. I won't be back until Saturday.

PS U: I can send a local officer to you. Where are you stay—?

Call ended. No response at callback, voicemail stated phone was switched off.

DI LOCKE

PRESENT

The death knock is the worst part of the job for me and no matter how many times I do it, it never gets any easier, but as I'm going to be leading the homicide investigation, I feel it's important I be the one to do it. The family have already been notified that the body of a man has been discovered during the search for Mr Fford, but no amount of preparation can ever really be enough to override the hope that your missing loved one will be found safe and well.

Demelza, who is going by her maiden surname: Boyde, lives in a cream-painted two up two down opposite the pier in Penarth. DC Banks – who only returned to the office yesterday after having taken three days off to complete his mandatory Authorised Firearms Officer refresher course in Waterton – meets me at the door of the seafront property with a sugarless cappuccino made with oat milk in a takeaway cup. I thank him and he gives me a tight-lipped smile. The Family Liaison Officer, DC Burtenshaw, is visibly consoling the wife of our victim on the Chesterfield in the living room. The curtains are pulled back, giving me a view of the woman through the window.

'How're things inside?'

He lowers his voice to a whisper to maintain privacy as the next-door neighbour treads down the path towards her car that's parked on the road. 'No booze bottles in the recycling box, no smell of bleach inside the house, no scuffmarks on the walls or holes punched in the doors, no prescribed medication in the kitchen or bloodied clothes stuffed into the wash basket inside the utility room, and according to the FLO, Demelza is acting every bit the concerned wife.'

'Soon-to-be ex. They're separated.'

The house is almost as frosty inside as it is out, but I expect that when your husband's missing turning the heating on is the last thing on your mind.

I enter the seafront property after DC Banks who nods to a tall, slim, dark-haired woman. The wife according to the framed wedding photograph of Geraint and Demelza which is parked beside a joint school picture of, it appears, their daughters Holly and Daisy.

The house is tidy, but not worryingly so. There are no signs of a clean-up. The kids are quiet, but they watch me with curiosity not fear.

Demelza, who was worried enough to report her husband missing, is visibly calm, hovering by the door that leads from the wide hallway and into the lounge. Does she know what we're about to impart?

She looks upset at my arrival, and expectant, but it could just be due to the mere fact of our presence.

The doorbell chimes the moment I enter the room and Demelza goes to open it, rigid-limbed, looking dazed. The girls – the same age as my stepson and godson, who's currently living with us, each wearing matching dresses, tights, and bows in their hair – bolt from the sofa in close pursuit.

I step out into the hall and watch an older woman

close the front door behind her, take one of Daisy's hands in hers and give it a squeeze while stroking Holly's overgrown fringe from her eyes and placing it behind her ear which she shakes back into place after she's pulled away. Clearly considering herself to be too old to permit public displays of affection.

'Carol,' she says, introducing herself and looking slightly bewildered.

'Nan!' Daisy squeals, bouncing, oblivious to the trauma her mother is feeling. 'He's dead.'

Carol shoots me a startled look that evaporates the moment Daisy tugs on her hand and adds, 'The snowman.'

Demelza shakes her head slowly and Carol's temporary relief is obvious when she places a hand to her heart and blinks slowly.

Holly's face remains still as she follows her sister and grandmother down the hall, through the kitchen and out the back door and into the garden to salvage their headless snowman.

I mirror Demelza's stance and remain standing while DC Banks leaves the room to use the bathroom, though I know he's really having a nosy around upstairs.

Now that we're alone Demelza allows herself to cry. Brushing off the tears falling down her nose with the heel of a shaky hand.

I wait until the rear door is closed on the kids and their nan before I speak, not wanting them to overhear.

I show Ms Boyde my ID card. 'Detective Inspector Emma Locke.'

'Gwent CID?'

'Your husband is a registered duty solicitor who works from time to time from the central custody suite in Bridgend. It was deemed a conflict of interest for South Wales Police to investigate his—'

'You've found him,' she says, a statement not a question.

She's calm when I tell her his body was discovered in the sea this morning, and replies confidently, 'He killed himself,' then is visibly distressed when I say, 'No, I'm very sorry to have to tell you that he's been murdered.'

'What!? How?'

'He was shot.'

She slaps her hands over her face, tears slipping through her fingers. 'Ohmygod.'

I open the travel packet of tissues I have in my pocket and offer them to her.

She takes one.

'And there's no way he could have done it himself?'

'Going by the angle and proximity it's highly unlikely.'

'Who did it, do you know?' she sobs.

'Not yet.'

She takes a deep breath and asks, 'How will I tell the girls?'

'Detective Constable Burtenshaw here will help you to figure out how to broach the subject and what to say.'

She nods mutely and wipes her eyes with the sleeve of her jumper.

'Who would . . . do this?'

'Can you think of anyone who may have held a grudge against your husband, wanted to harm him?'

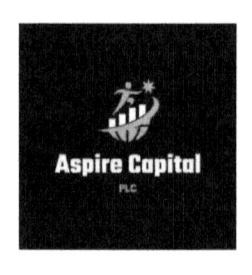

Aspire Capital PLC
Current Account

1 November – 25 November 2022

Mr Geraint Fford

Sort Code 20-70-
Account no. 5395
SWIFTBIC UKB
IBAN GB59 BUKG 2070

Mr G Fford
Flat 27a Glebe Street
Penarth
South Wales
CF64 1EE

DATE	DESCRIPTION	MONEY IN	MONEY OUT	BALANCE
1 Nov	Start Balance			£24,456.87
1 Nov	Transfer from Sort Code 20 70 Account 0810	£3,200.00		£27,656.87
1 Nov	Optima Group		£39.99	£27,616.88

1 Nov	CC Benedict		£601.00	£27,015.00
1 Nov	Tesco Superstore Terra Nova Way Penarth		£40.02	£26,974.98
1 Nov	BGas		£89.00	£26,885.98
1 Nov	Direct Debit to Vodafone		£9.00	£26,876.98
2 Nov	The Beach Hut Penarth		£34.80	£26,842.18
2 Nov	The Rock Shop Penarth		£12.20	£26,829.98
3 Nov	SWW Water		£31.00	£26,798.98
5 Nov	Sainsbury's Local Windsor Road Penarth		£157.85	£26,641.13
8 Nov	Vale Bedwear		£21.00	£26,620.13
11 Nov	Tesco Petrol Station Brewery Lane Bridgend		£60.09	£26,560.04
19 Nov	Transfer to Sort Code 20-18-■ Account 0306■		£600.00	£25,960.04

21 Nov	Cash Withdrawal timed at 9.14		£10,000.00	£15,960.04
21 Nov	End Balance			£15,960.04

PS TOMOS

PRESENT

Having scoured roadside cameras DC Watkins was able to locate footage of Geraint walking past the Mint and Mustard Indian restaurant at 5.09 p.m. A female who we have yet to identify is walking several yards behind him. The same woman was spotted exiting Alexandra Park shortly after Geraint, on CCTV, ten minutes later. Despite a plea for information having been circulated to the media three days ago nobody has come forward claiming to be or to know the woman who appears to have been stalking him. Although it did ignite interest from a lot of the usual nutcases, including a psychic who reckoned his spirit had told her he'd handed a fair-haired maiden a stack of cash. 'Notes,' she said during her telephone conversation with a call handler at Crimestoppers. 'Several grand' by all accounts.

Speaking of which.

'Chapman?'

'Yes, er, sarge.'

'Can you get in touch with Geraint's bank? Looks like the warrant South Wales Police applied for yesterday to go through our victim's financial records has been issued.'

It wasn't a particular priority when Geraint was a missing person, and it is still only standard procedure now that his body has been found, by chance of a passing search and rescue team training one of their newest RNLI recruits, but it might help us to answer some questions.

'Yes ... sir.'

'Just call me Dafydd if it pains you to consider me your superior.'

'It's not that, it's just we're a bit formal here. We tend to address people by their surnames.'

'Well, where I'm from we're on first name terms, and for the next thirteen weeks I want you to use whatever makes you feel comfortable.'

'Yes, sir.'

I dip my head so he can't see me roll my eyes as I take a gander at the transcribed audio recorded telephone conversation between PS Kumar and Geraint's senior partner, Liam.

Transcribed informal interview, audio and visually recorded in: Cardiff Bay Police Station, James Street, South Wales.

Between: Liam Bailey of 2 Elin Gardens, Porthkerry, Rhoose, Barry CF62 3█ & Police Sergeant Surjit Kumar, of: the Missing Persons Unit (MPU), South Wales.

On: November 23rd, 2022

At: 9.08 a.m.

S K: Thank you for coming in to speak to us today. Before we start, I must inform you that we're recording this conversation.

L B: Of course. No Problem. How can I help?

S K: As you know we're investigating the disappearance of your business partner, Geraint Fford. During our inquiries we came across some information we're hoping you might be able to clarify for us.

L B: I'll do my best.

S K: We appreciate it. What do you know about his disappearance?

L B: Demelza called me the evening she reported him missing. I told her what I told the police when they called me later that night. I didn't know where he was and had no idea why he'd want to disappear. I couldn't sleep so I drove over to the office early the following morning, to see if there was anything that might help us all to figure out where he might have gone. Our online diaries are synced, so we're aware of each other's commitments. It helps if our legal assistants know where we are, so they don't book us an appointment with a client when we're in court. There were no anomalies as far as I could see. We schedule our own TEAMS meetings, though we share a channel. There wasn't anything suspicious on there, though I wasn't expecting there to be. However, I did notice that he's had a lot of 'out of town' meetings in the last few weeks that don't seem to have resulted in any follow-ups. Which is what we term wasted visits, something that generally only occurs in cases involving a hostile witness. Client confidentiality prohibits me from accessing such information myself but if you were to get a warrant then you'd be able to find out who those clients are and in what capacity they are instructing Geraint.

S K: We'll let you know if that becomes necessary. How well do you know Geraint, on a personal level?

L B: He and his wife were guests at my wedding last year, though I wouldn't say we were especially close.

S K: How long have you known Geraint?

L B: I met him at a conference in 2010. We've been working together since he joined the office back in 2012. I knew his previous boss. Good fella he was, but when he died there was nobody to fill his shoes as he was the sole director, so Geraint needed a job. My father passed away in 2018, so I asked if he'd partner with me as a senior. But I'd say that since I've known him, we've retained a friendship that somewhat surpasses that of a colleague.

S K: Would Geraint confide in you then if he had a problem?

L B: I wouldn't have thought so, he never has done.

S K: How has Geraint seemed to you in the last few months?

L B: If you're asking if I know what's been going on in his head then I'm afraid I can't help you. He's been . . . withdrawn, quick to lose his temper, not himself at all. But I couldn't tell you why.

S K: Has Geraint sustained any injuries that you're aware of?

L B: If you're alluding to domestic abuse then no, I can't imagine Demelza hurting him in any way. Especially not physically. She's the last person I could envision becoming aggressive, least likely violent with anyone, from what I know of her.

S K: What do you think of their relationship?

L B: They adore each other. Which is why it was a shock when he told me they'd separated.

S K: What reason did he give you for their separation?

L B: He said they'd begun arguing and that it had caused a lot of tension at home. He's never dealt well with confrontation, hence why he never joined the Bar, so I'd assumed he'd been the one to make the decision to leave and that it was just a temporary thing. I'd never expected her to file for a divorce. But his reason for their separation seemed flimsy to me. I'd certainly never witnessed anything to suggest they were anything but a united front. I didn't believe his reasoning then, and I still don't. It seemed like an excuse, a fabrication even, so he wouldn't have to divulge the real reason.

S K: Why do you think they separated?

L B: It probably has no relevance whatsoever, and I'd also like to stress that I've never seen or heard anything to suggest Geraint was anything but faithful to his wife, but Xavier, my partner, told me something that made me question the veracity of Geraint's explanation for the separation. You see, Xavier had kept his suspicions to himself. But when he came home Monday, and I told him Geraint had gone missing, he confided in me that he believed Geraint was having an affair. Apparently about a week before, Xavier saw Geraint in a car with a blonde woman. They seemed – body-language-wise – intimate. He thought that perhaps Demelza had found out about them and kicked him out, but in case she didn't know, or he'd misinterpreted it he decided to keep it to himself.

S K: What do you think?

L B: I can't imagine Geraint cheating on Demelza but one thing I learned early on in my career is that even the most loyal, honest, civilised, and respectful people can surprise you with what they're capable of. Being a lawyer doesn't make you infallible.

S K: How is Geraint finding work, at the moment?

L B: There are no problems that I'm aware of.

S K: Has Geraint ever expressed to you an additional interest in a particular case that either he or you took on?

L B: Not that I can think of. Why, is he looking up our clients on his personal laptop or something? I suppose it's not that unusual. We get a lot of walk-ins and people ringing up asking for advice about all sorts. Only a small proportion of what we do, believe it or not, involves advocacy. We have to vet everyone. To sift out the cranks, to put it bluntly. Sometimes we go over work hours. Maybe he ran out of time and needed to complete some background at home.

S K: Do you ever discuss each other's clients?

L B: Rarely. But we do have access to one another's computers. We share passcodes in case an emergency situation requires us urgent access. I wouldn't be comfortable logging into his computer though, without his knowledge, which is why I haven't done so, as tempting as it is.

S K: Has Geraint ever spoken to you about any clients that have raised any concerns for him?

L B: No. Not that I can think of. Why? Is someone bothering him?

S K: Not that we're aware of.

L B: I see. I mean he's covered some high-profile cases throughout his career, and of course you can't win them all, but surely if someone was harbouring any resentment it would be towards the prosecution, not the defence team?

S K: We're just covering all angles.

L B: I see.

S K: Have any of the clients you've represented caused friction between you?

L B: Not really, though there are some cases Geraint refuses to take on whomever the client, and which he'll inevitably hand over to me. That has caused some . . . differences of opinion, shall we say.

S K: What kinds of cases?

L B: Anything involving child abuse.

S K: Has he ever explained why?

L B: No, but if I were to hazard a guess, I'd say it probably had something to do with his stepfather.

S K: How so?

L B: His mother divorced the man a couple of years ago. Until then Geraint hadn't spoken to her since he left home. Though where home was, I don't know. Geraint doesn't speak about the past, in any capacity, so I couldn't tell you where he was born or where he grew up.

S K: His stepfather, is he still around?

L B: He's still alive if that's what you mean, despite almost being killed in prison twelve months ago. Someone trapped him in his cell and kicked his head in. Whoever did it got away with it because none of the inmates would snitch on him, not one of the four prison officers who found him unconscious caught anyone entering or leaving through the cell door, and neither of the four cameras trained on the floor captured anything suspicious.

Odd that, don't you think? I mean, to me, it looks like the incident was planned, perhaps by someone with insider knowledge.

S K: Do you know what he's in for?

L B: GBH. Pub brawl.

KERRY-ANN

PAST

The shoebox in which I'd found the note bearing my father's name had also contained newspaper clippings, photographs, and a letter meant for Roderick that as far as I could see had never been sent. I hadn't read them until I'd scanned through every online article that I could find concerning his conviction.

    He and my mother weren't married at the time that my birth was registered either, but I soon learned that Roderick's name wasn't on my birth certificate because he was in prison when I was born. I had suspected Nancy had chosen not to add his name because she was ashamed of what he'd done, but it turns out to have been a legal requirement for the father to be present during the registration of a birth. And, of course, he wasn't there; he was serving a life sentence.

    I can only assume that Irene chose not to tell me my father's name or explain his absence from my life because she didn't want the criminal actions of his past to have any impact on my future. But I had grown up thinking I had been born out of wedlock as the result of a fling, I had no idea my parent's relationship was serious and that they'd lived together as though they were husband and wife or that they had planned to get married.

My mother's handwriting was neat and cursive and the love she obviously still felt for my father poured off the paper.

In her letter, dated shortly after the trial, she wrote:

My darling,

My heart aches to know that we will be parted from each other for so long.

I will wait for you my love, until we can be together once more.

Our girl is a quiet little bundle of beauty, and I cannot wait for you to meet her.

Any news on the visiting order?

I look forward to seeing you soon.

Yours always,
Nancy. x

I wondered if she'd taken me to see him, imagined what that must have been like for her, how my grandparents had reacted to the news of her fiancé's incarceration.

Had she even told them?

Then I'd tried to guess what might have happened that would have ended their engagement and led her to stop bringing me to visit him, because they had obviously continued to communicate for some time after Roderick's conviction.

That was something I hoped to be able to discover from the man himself. Which was why I'd contacted the Prisoner's Family Support Service's 'Find a Prisoner' department.

Case No. IC1MOUO224

Summary of files (contained within this digital folder) extracted from hard drive of Apple laptop, IP address: 989.■■.■.■, registered to Mr Geraint Fford of: 27a Glebe Street, Penarth, South Wales, CF64 1EB, seized for investigatory purposes on 22nd November 2022:

- Email exchange between 'Ant' and 'Caz' dated Tuesday 6 September 2022, at 7.14 p.m.
- Search history (backdated three months)
- Deleted files from 'archive', which include:
  1) Screenshot pages of Facebook Profile for Charlotte (Lottie) Lettes, AKA Charlie, realtor of Andrew Lettes Real Estate, Alabama, United States
  2) Research titled 'Investigatory Files' which includes:
     a) Public information easily accessible online for property being sold in Alabama, US
     b) NDA between Sandra Dean and Geoffrey Goldsborough
     c) Contact details for Cassandra (Cass) Newton, AKA Cassie

👤 Ant
beyondthedeepbluesea@gmail.com

It was great to talk to you today. How do you feel about meeting face-to-face?

🐈 Caz & Jaz
cazandjazhairandnails@gmail.com

Thank you for listening. It seems like the logical next step. When and where?

👤 Ant
beyondthedeepbluesea@gmail.com

Do you know the Duck and Orange?

🐈 Caz & Jaz
cazandjazhairandnails@gmail.com

I love that place! I'm on annual leave next week.

👤 Ant
beyondthedeepbluesea@gmail.com

Me too, they do a fantastic roast lamb. Are you available Monday?

🐈 Caz & Jaz
cazandjazhairandnails@gmail.com

I have to take the cat to the vet in the morning, but I'm free lunchtime onwards.

👤 Ant
beyondthedeepbluesea@gmail.com

Midday?

🐈 Caz & Jaz
cazandjazhairandnails@gmail.com

Purrfect.

History

🔍 ✕

Clear browsing data…

· ·

Today — 3 Nov 2022

🔒 Locked Items ✕
password protected

🗃 Archive ✕
background>research>casenotes>deansandra>clientlist>home>fileexplorer

📁 Folder ✕
deanwotton>documents>home>file explorer

☁ Cloud Storage ✕
onedrive>save>nda.pdf

⬇ Downloads ✕
nda.pdf>download>attachment>emails

✉ Fford and Bailey ✕
to: gf.solicitor@ffordandbailey.co.uk ←
from: charanddrewlettes@gmail.com

🗑 Trash ✕
permanently>delete

🖼 Image ✕
delete>image1774>downloaded>today>recent>downloads

🖼 Images ✕
downloaded>images

🐦 Twitter – Profile ✕
0results>ffiontownsend>search>www.twitter.com>twitter>google

G Twitter – Google Search ✕
www.google.com

📷 Instagram ✕
0results>ffiontownsend>search>www.instagram.com>instagram>google

G Instagram – Google Search ✕
www.google.com

f Facebook ✕
0results>ffiontownsend>search>www.facebook.com>facebook>google

G Facebook – Google Search ✕
www.google.com

💼 LinkedIn – Profile ✕
ffion.townsend/www.linkedin.com>journalistffiontownsend>2results>search>www.linkedin.com>linkedin>google

LinkedIn – Google Search
www.google.com   ×

Google Maps   ×
satnav>sync>directions

Google Maps – Google Search   ×
www.google.com

TEAMS   ×

from: gf.solicitor@ffordandbailey.co.uk ↻
to: newton.cass7619@gmail.com

f Search Facebook

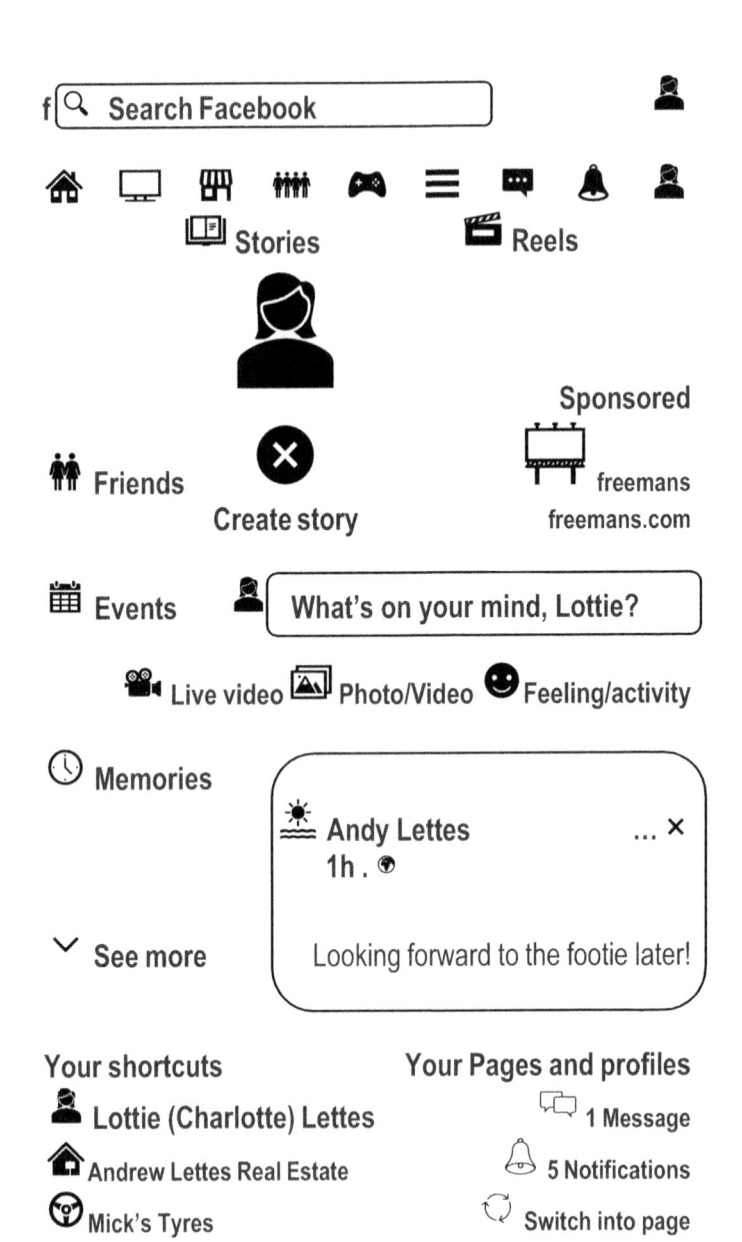

Stories   Reels

Friends

Create story

Sponsored

freemans
freemans.com

Events   What's on your mind, Lottie?

Live video   Photo/Video   Feeling/activity

Memories

Andy Lettes   ... ✕
1h . 👁

Looking forward to the footie later!

∨ See more

Your shortcuts
Lottie (Charlotte) Lettes
Andrew Lettes Real Estate
Mick's Tyres

Your Pages and profiles
1 Message
5 Notifications
Switch into page

◁ **Create promotion**

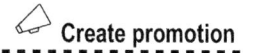

Friend requests   See All

Investigatory files

4-bedroom, 3-bathroom, 2,200 square foot suburban property in 1104 Sherwood Drive, Huntsville, Alabama, AL35, which according to a report on 'The Best Places to Live in America 2022', cited in Forbes Magazine, was voted one of the Best (and Cheapest) Places to Live in the US.

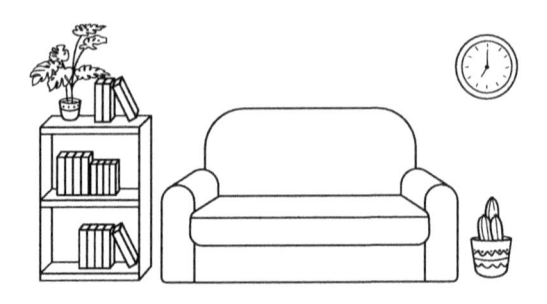

Spacious living room opposite open-plan kitchen-diner.

Downstairs office that extends from large hall, opposite stairwell.

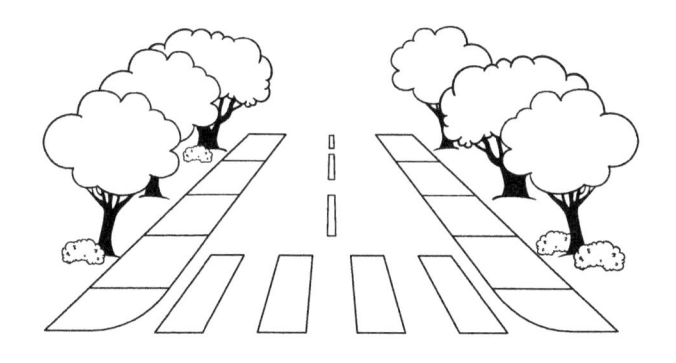

Close to schools and local amenities.

Book your viewing today with Charlie.

Call: 251-515-
Email: Charlie.b.@alettesrealty.com
Address: Andrew Lettes Realty, 365 Coast Road, W Beach Blvd, Gulf Shores, AL 36542

Charlie has thirteen years' experience in the real estate business and has sold more than 400 properties across the southern state of Alabama. Born in the UK, Charlie gave up the corporate world to pursue her dream, crossing the Atlantic from a small town in Wales. She lives on the Gulf coast in West Beach Boulevard with her husband, adopted son, and dog.

Non-Disclosure Agreement

I <u>Sandra Dean</u> of <u>204 Fairview Crescent, Chepstow, NP16</u> agree to be contractually obliged not to communicate, verbally or in writing, using handwritten or typewritten text, what was discussed between <u>Doctor Geoffrey Goldsborough</u> and I, in the presence of <u>Howard Young</u> of <u>Watson and Young solicitors</u> on this day of <u>4th April 1996</u> in order to execute this contract regarding accusations I made against the Head of Women's Mental Health Services at <u>Wotton Dean Psychiatric Hospital, Gloucestershire, Doctor Geoffrey Goldsborough,</u> concerning events I alleged took place between <u>11th July and 5th December 1989</u>, while I was a patient undergoing treatment for psychiatric illness, for which I wish to formally revoke.

Signed by <u>Sandra Dean</u>
With agreement by <u>Geoffrey Goldsborough</u>
Witnessed by <u>Howard Young</u>

findpeopleuk.com
People • Businesses • Places

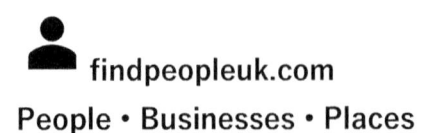

Electoral roll search

Search results for C. Newton, Wales...

Who?
Cassandra Newton, age 52

Where?
91 Nottage Park Road, Porthcawl, South Wales

DI LOCKE

PRESENT

There's an audible creak of a floorboard above our heads which causes Demelza to pause and glance up at the ceiling before she replies.

DC Banks must be in the bathroom. I noted the overflow pipe is directly above the side of the house as I stood gazing at the exterior.

'Geraint and I separated five weeks ago,' she says, mouth quivering. 'He moved out and into a flat on Glebe Street above The Tea and Biscuit café in town. He drops by most weekdays to see the girls as he finishes work at 5 p.m. And he takes them out Saturdays. He can't have them overnight because the flat he's renting has only one bedroom. We've been amicable, for the kids. But when he called round Monday, he was acting weird.'

'Weird how?'

'Anxious, paranoid, talking about the past. It started about three months ago.'

'Did anything significant occur around that time?'

She hesitates before replying, 'No.'

'Is there anything you can think of that might have caused a change in your husband's behaviour?'

She shakes her head, her eyes briefly skirting the

tiled floor and failing to return to mine.

She's lying. Why?

'You told the attending officer that Geraint had been the one to ask for a divorce and had chosen to leave the family home. Can you tell me more about that?'

She hesitates and begins to fidget.

Is she being obtrusive because she doesn't want to know who killed her husband or because she does know who killed him?

'Anything you tell us could help us uncover a motive which we can use to find out who took your husband's life.'

'I thought he'd taken his own life.'

'Why?'

'He started taking anti-depressants for work-related stress.'

'And the beta-blockers?'

'He suffers from celiac disease which stops his stomach absorbing vitamin B12, which causes severe anaemia, which causes cardiac arrhythmia. It's an erratic heartbeat.'

The propranolol wasn't for anxiety then.

'When did he start taking the Sertraline?'

'About two months ago?'

'It's okay, we can verify the dates when we obtain his medical records.'

'I just thought the stress was making him paranoid. I didn't really think he was in danger.'

She pauses for breath.

'He said he had to leave to keep us all safe. He refused to explain why, but with the hushed phone calls I assumed he was being threatened. Though when I questioned him, he denied it.'

Or he was seeing someone else.

I keep that thought to myself for now, but if he was and she found out, that would be reason enough for her to want him dead.

'As a solicitor he's represented some high-profile criminals in South Wales over the past decade. Have any of his clients given him cause for concern?'

She shakes her head.

I'll have to get a warrant for a list of names from his senior partner.

She frowns. 'Why? Do you think his . . . death . . . had something to do with a client?'

'I'm afraid I can't answer that.' I say this in a way that suggests I don't know rather than because I'm not legally permitted to inform her about what I do know.

'What can you tell me about his family?'

We know he has no siblings. His parents are Welsh. His mother's from Holyhead. She's got one brother in Merseyside and another in Spain. Geraint's father was born in the valleys. Caerphilly to be exact. And like his son, is an only child.

'His dad's not around. From what I understand he's working abroad for king and country, though I don't know in what capacity. When I asked him why his dad couldn't attend our wedding, Geraint said he was unable to travel as he was on active duty, serving overseas. He's never visited or been in contact with us. Either to congratulate us on getting married or the twin's births. I don't think he was cut out to be a dad. I get the impression he's good for nothing.'

Or up to no good.

'Do you have any idea how we might be able to get hold of him?'

It's proving difficult because his exact whereabouts is classified information and divulging it is at the discretion of his superior.

'No, sorry, I don't.'

'And his friends?'

'Geraint doesn't see much of his mates anymore,

not since the twins were born. Those he has kept in touch with he isn't particularly close to. His grandparents are dead. He's not sporty, which was a bone of contention between Geraint and his stepfather.'

'How so?'

'He was competitive. Used to be a boxer. Geraint's not . . .' she stumbles over the present tense.

I need to keep her talking. I can't afford for her to close up now.

'What about *your* family and friends?' Any problems there?

'Mine?' She shifts uncomfortably. 'My dad comes from a long line of lobster trappers. My mum's a courier. She works for a chain of restaurants. I've got a few mates I've acquired throughout the years, from college, work etcetera, a pen-pal I met on holiday . . . I started out in sales myself. Following the family tree you could say.'

'How'd you meet Geraint?'

'We were staying in the same hotel. There was a party. Some meet and greet black tie thing. We were both pretty smashed. Got talking at the bar. We swapped numbers. And the rest, as they say, is history.'

She smiles at the memory while fresh tears spill down her cheeks.

'When can I see him?' she asks, wiping them away with the sleeve of her jumper.

'I'm afraid that won't be possible.'

'Oh, but won't you need me to identify him?'

'We can use his dental records and DNA to test against the oral mouth swab his mother provided to the responding officer.'

'Sounds very . . . scientific.'

'You're an independent mortgage advisor.'

I find throwing questions at the grieving stops them

lingering on their turmoil, which helps us get quicker answers as opposed to waiting until their grief has taken a fuller hold.'

'Yes.'

'I know you've already told the officers who took your statement, but we have to approach everything with fresh eyes now that—'

'My husband's dead.'

'Now that we're taking over the investigation.'

'Right.' She stares at the floor as though seeking a hole to swallow her up.

'What does an independent mortgage advisor do that's different to say one working from within a bank?'

'I can provide a more individualised service. One with far less limitation. For example, I don't just find the best lender for someone based on their affordability, I assess their finances before they choose a property, then advise them on the products available to them from across the whole of the market.'

'Do you charge a flat fee, or do you make a commission once a lender has been secured?'

'A fixed rate, brokerage fee, plus commission once the paperwork is completed. It works out to be around £3,000 on average.'

She'd only need to secure a mortgage for one client a month to earn a liveable wage.

'Have you had any issues with your clients? Have any of them been refused a mortgage for example?'

'Other than the usual, being non-payment or the refusal of credit by a lender, no,' she replies, sitting on the chesterfield leaning against the wall below the bay window. 'I mean, in my line of work it's not uncommon for people to try it on. I've seen it all, fake bank statements, falsified share values, I've even dealt with a borrower planning to purchase a property development that didn't exist. Dodgy real estate agents inflating prices and bankers on the fiddle are rare but not unexpected, to an extent. Investment brokers and even conveyancing lawyers aren't immune to a little bit of fraud either. There was even this one man who wanted to borrow against his own house. Remortgage it basically. Only he'd just paid it off, in full, using his savings. Because the value of the property had gone up by two hundred grand, so he could lend a larger chunk of money. Bizarre, but not illegal.'

'You reported these instances, where necessary, to the Financial Conduct Authority?'

'Of course.'

'Have any of your clients been party to any criminal proceedings?'

She blinks a smidgen too long. 'Not that I'm aware of.'

Why do I get the feeling she's lying?

NOTICE TO CEASE AND DESIST

From
Blackwater and Son Lawyers, Tooley Street, Southwark, London, SE1 2█ (on behalf of:)
Doctors Abroad, Pheonix Place, Marshalsea Drive, Southwark, Camberwell, London, SE1 1█

Date
18/10/2022

Re: Notice to Cease and Desist for Specific Activity

Dear
Geraint Fford (of:) Fford and Bailey Solicitors, Hickman Road, Penarth, Wales, CF64 2█.

This notice is served upon <u>Geraint Fford</u> due to your harassment of our client in the form of typewritten letters, in an attempt to gather information concerning their finances from their administrative department, despite having been warned prior to this, both verbally and by mail, against further contact ("Activity").

<u>If you do not cease the aforementioned Activity a lawsuit will be commenced against you.</u>

If the Activity continues, we will immediately seek a temporary restraining order in the District Court against you and any accomplices in this matter. We will also seek monetary damages to be proved at trial. Hopefully this recourse is not necessary, we have our own interests to protect and will vigorously do so.

You will not receive another warning letter. If you do not confirm in writing to us by the 1st day of <u>November, 2022</u> that you will cease violating our Agreement a lawsuit will be commenced immediately.

Sincerely,
Verity Blackwater (LLP)

PS TOMOS

PRESENT

The incident room is as full as I suspect the magazine was that the bullet which killed our victim sprang from. One entering the stomach where it remains lodged, the other to the forehead. There are no prizes for guessing which shot was fatal.

In the interests of the investigation, and respecting Data Protection Legislation, we have retrieved a list of named individuals that are in the public domain who Geraint has represented. The problem we've got is not a lack of potential motives, witnesses, or evidence (bar forensic). In fact, we have far more leads than any inquiry I've been involved in so far, to date. But sifting through all the people who wanted Geraint dead and narrowing down our list of suspects is proving tricky, considering it's grown almost twice the size since Detective Constable's Chapman and Winters began organising their names into order of relevance.

'Execution style,' a familiar voice from the doorway states, as I'm shrugging off my coat.

I assisted Emma on an assignment in September, staying on the case until I caught our wanted woman whose murderous exploits were linked to a cold missing persons investigation. When her boss, DCI

Evans, told me he was in the process of setting up a taskforce dedicated specifically to combine the knowledge formed from both the Homicide Division and the Missing Persons Unit – since many of their largescale investigations of the last couple of years had involved both departments – I jumped at the chance of a potential future promotion and requested a temporary transfer. But I feel like I've been thrown in at the deep end with this one.

'The two entry wounds had different goals though. The shot to the stomach was likely aimed at incapacitating him, which may have been to ask him something before taking his life.'

'Carrying out the hit, you mean,' Emma says.

'This screams gangland.'

'Or the marksperson missed while aiming for his head,' Emma says.

'Whoever the trigger-puller was knew Geraint would be on the island at that time, which means they either arranged the meeting or know who did.'

'Someone with links to an organised crime network perhaps,' Emma says. 'Which is why South Wales Police thought McGinty might have had something to do with Geraint's disappearance.'

'This is the chap who they had intelligence on that suggested he wanted Geraint dead?'

'Yeah. The Osman Warning was only sent to him eight weeks ago,' Emma says. 'Which is why his disappearance was escalated to an amber alert so quickly, not because his ex-wife thought he'd topped himself as the local news stations reported.'

'And this McGinty fella's a name in the underworld?'

'We suspect Colm's got dealings in a drug distribution ring who are running heroin into the UK from Dublin. The NCA nabbed several members of the faction in the summer, though we haven't yet been able to stick anything on him. His father, Fergal, was convicted for terrorism offences during the early nineties. His appeal was refused in 2008, so he died in prison two months ago, a guilty man. Right around the same time Demelza says Geraint developed a sudden personality change.'

'I'm assuming by the Irish connection we're talking IRA and not ISIS.'

'I'd usually remind someone assuming such a thing that biases can only fuck things up but in this instance you're correct.'

'What's his link to our victim?'

'Geraint failed to secure a pardon for Colm McGinty's father, as part of a petition made by him and several former inmates of HMP Maze, to have their criminal records wiped by the British government. They claimed that their republican attachments were in the past and they no longer wanted their association with the paramilitary organisation to hinder their future opportunities. They argued that quashing their convictions supported the Good Friday agreement made in 1998 between the UK and Northern Ireland.'

Her words strike a little too close to home for comfort. She knows I worked for the British Army in Ulster during the Troubles, but she doesn't know in what capacity or the extent of my involvement.

'Just out of interest, what was his father's connection to the republicans?'

'Fergal was given a life sentence for his affiliation with a paramilitary group who bombed a meeting hub for the Ulster Defence Association,' Emma replies.

My mouth goes dry, and my pulse begins to rise. I stare at her, unblinking, as I'm transported back to the fateful day when I lost my friend Mohammad in that very same place all those years ago.

She's not talking about the very explosion that killed him, is she?

I take a few seconds too long to respond and when I do there's a nervous inflection to my voice, which I'm certain Emma can hear. 'So South Wales Police thought McGinty murdered his lawyer to avenge his father's death, because he failed to get him and his pals exonerated, until they learned he was in the nick.'

'Yeah. He was imprisoned for Grievous Bodily Harm with Intent last month, so he can't have been the one to shoot Geraint. Though that doesn't mean he didn't put a hit on his head and order someone else to do it, which is why South Wales Police started looking at his associates, and that's how they came across Paddy Daly,' Emma says.

Where have I heard that name before?

Intelligence Report

Name: Rohan Cooper, (Lead Investigator, Organised Crime Command – National Crime Agency)

Received from: Dean Harper (Intelligence Analyst, TARIAN – Regional Organised Crime Unit of Southern Wales)

Reference: Operation Thoroughbred

Person of Interest: Patrick 'Paddy' Daly

Intelligence: Information concerning the above-named individual has come to our attention through the work of both the Regional Investigation Unit and the Regional Intelligence Unit regarding the largescale sale of horses, several of which have gone on to race at Royal Ascot and taken part in the Grand National. The individuals buying the horses are known associates of criminals who are involved in the distribution of drugs within the UK. We have acquired intelligence from an informant that the proceeds have been used to obtain horses for training in order to race them, to both create long-term investment as well as to immediately spend the cash derived from the sale of heroin. Some of which, according to our covert operatives, has been chemically traced to the same concentration of compounds that we've been able to directly connect to county line suppliers operating in London, Birmingham, Liverpool, Manchester, Glasgow, Bristol, and Cardiff. Though these investigations are ongoing we have reasonable suspicion to believe that the horses bred by the above-named individual were bought using laundered money and as such can be seized according to the Proceeds of Crime Act 2022.

KERRY-ANN

PAST

While I waited to hear from the Prisoner's Family Support Service, I did some digging into my mother's background. I knew I wouldn't be able to visit the hospital itself until I travelled up to Cardiff, but I did a walkabout of the area using Google Maps which is how I discovered the place had been shut down.

I skim-read the Wikipedia entry for Whitchurch Hospital that told me at its most populated the building accommodated seven hundred and fifty patients and clicked onto a link to an article on the Whitchurch Hospital Historical Society website, which I read while sipping the coffee I'd just made.

My mother had more or less lived in Whitchurch hospital from the point of her diagnosis in 1997 until she was transferred from the red brick building nineteen years later to the residential care home that she'd died in.

The imposing water tower that stands sentry over what had once been a psychiatric community looks like a prison now it's been gated off from curious tourists, bored kids, and paranormal investigators. But it once housed an entire village within its walls: butchers, bakers, grocers, florist, launderette, café, hair salon, gym, dentist, library, dance hall, cinema, bowling alley, and farm. Which not only provided food but also jobs for the patients. The bandstand where the article says that the choir practiced in the garden every summer is visible in the photograph supplied.

Whitchurch hospital was known to be one of the most progressive psychiatric establishments in Wales. Even during its term as a lunatic asylum in the first half of the century the building was considered to be modern and the nursing practices forward-thinking. But still, I can only imagine how my mother felt being transported to the facility on Park Road, entering the estate beneath the ominous archway and being escorted into a dormitory alongside far worse affected patients where she would reside until she was considered mentally fit enough to return home.

I wonder how she felt when she learned she'd lost her council house, and her mother had been given custody of her daughter.

Had that been what had triggered her stay to lengthen, almost indefinitely?

I'd often thought about who fathered me too, what he looked like, whether I took after him in features or personality. I could see I'd inherited his pointed nose and thin lips from the photographs provided by the more recent newspaper reports, which these days are thankfully online and are therefore much easier to find. They spoke about his upcoming parole hearing, hence how I'd come to understand he'd been jailed.

He was first imprisoned in HMP Cardiff and resided there until his victim's widow appealed for him to be moved out of the area.

How ironic, I thought, that as I'd knelt on my mattress with my elbows leaning against the headboard, gazing up at the sky above the valley from my bedroom window, consumed with a desire for a male figurehead so strong it burnt me out, that my dad was just six miles south of my grandmother's. And a mere nine miles east from where my mother was institutionalised.

Had he ever written me a birthday card? Sent me a self-crafted present to go under the Christmas tree?

***

'What's that you're reading?' Natalia asked, flicking the cover of the book and jolting me back to the present.

'Research.' I glanced up and saw that she was wearing the thigh-high camouflage dress I'd bought her. 'You look nice.'

'So do you,' she said, bending down to kiss me.

'What time are you leaving?'

'As soon as the lads get here.' She gave me a sympathetic smile. 'You sure you don't wanna come?'

'I've got to finish this book over the weekend.'

She gave me a quick hug then headed out the room. Shiloh stood, stretched, and followed her to the door where she stopped in the doorway at the sight of my roller case, coated in a thin layer of dust, parked beside the sofa.

I hadn't yet had a chance to tell her about my assignment.

'Where are you going?'

'Home.'

'Wales?'

'Yes.'

'When will you be back?'

'April?'

'You're leaving me for three months!?'

I gave her the backstory, and told her about the contract, the advance.

'It's a big thing this then?'

'It is.'

She winked. 'I'm proud of you.'

'I'm going to miss you.' She leaned down and collected Shiloh from the floor and nuzzled her furry face. The cat purred and licked her cheek. 'Shiloh's gonna miss you too.'

'I'll drive down when I can, stay the weekend.'

She nodded, pressed her lips together in concentration, then said, 'I'll see if I can take some time off work, and come up to visit you too.'

'We'll make it work.'

'We always do.' She smiled.

I watched her retreating form through watery eyes.

WOTTON DEAN: INSIDE INNOVATIVE PSYCHIATRIC HOSPITAL

South Wales Argus
Wednesday 21 March 2003
By Julie Montgomery (Senior Reporter)

Wotton Dean Psychiatric Hospital (Image: Aled Walsh)

The former Gloucestershire County Lunatic Asylum has gone through a lot of changes since it was built in 1845 by the same architectural designer responsible for some of the most stunning stonemasonry to be found in the southwest. The building work, funded by the Council, took four years and once complete could house up to two hundred patients, until the addition of wings to treat injured war veterans at the start of the twentieth century increased its capacity to three hundred. In 1962 further renovations provided the room for another fifty beds allowing the entire main building to be used for the isolation of smallpox during the Welsh endemic. Today, however, Wotton Dean is a sleek modern establishment used to facilitate the recovery of both inpatients and outpatients with specialist services for addiction, eating disorders, and wellbeing support groups, which include: 'managing stress', 'grieving positively', and 'living with anxiety'.

Despite its historical association with lobotomies, cold baths, and bloodletting, the treatments provided by the psychiatric hospital these days focus on rest and recuperation with an emphasis on talking therapies.

DI LOCKE

PRESENT

Having described our victim to the room, briefly summarising his disappearance and subsequent murder, I draw everyone's attention from the photograph of Geraint's face that fills the screen of the sixty-inch flatscreen TV attached to the wall to the enlarged image of Colm McGinty's newly acquired dormer bungalow, which he'd just inherited from his father Fergal.

'Nice isn't it. It's called Gleann na Sióg. It means Fairy Glen in Gaelic. The owner is the son of a former resident of HMP Maze and a former IRA member who adamantly denied any association with or sympathy for the terrorist organisation right up until his death in September. He lost his first appeal for a royal pardon in 1999 and was refused release in 2008 when the UK government exonerated over two hundred other inmates serving time for terrorism offences relating to IRA membership. Our victim, Mr Geraint Fford, represented him.'

I swipe the screen of my mobile phone which I've linked up to the TV via Bluetooth, replacing the image of the property with a screenshot from Google Maps. The faces of two of the PCs seated nearest the screen turn blue from the projection of the sea. 'He lives here in a coastal area of County Antrim.' I glance from the inlet fronting his abode to DC Winters when she comments, 'Nice gaff.'

'Having looked through some of the press clippings and court records that are held in the public domain it seems that at the time of the trial some of McGinty's associates were thought to have been assisted out of the country. One of whom was a Mr Douglas Daly, whose son, Patrick, just so happens to have made several calls to Geraint the day he was reported missing. Although his phone has not been found and is – reasonably, I think – believed to have entered the sea on his person, digital forensics were able to figure out its last known location was three point one miles from where Geraint's body was discovered, which suggests it may have been switched off or possibly lost prior to him walking to the island and entering the water.'

'The battery could have died,' DC Bishop adds.

'Or his phone was stolen,' DC Chapman says.

'He could have tossed the phone from the pier or deposited it somewhere else for safekeeping or even to get rid of it,' DC Banks says.

'He might have been ordered to do so by the person he met up with,' DC Chapman adds.

'You've been watching too many narco films,' DC Winters says, snickering.

'What, then forced him to walk along the coastal path without anyone noticing he had a gun to his back?' DC Bishop says in disbelief.

'Or the person he met up with on the island took it from him there,' DC Banks adds. 'That's if he *did* meet someone, of course.'

'DC Banks, you used to live in Penarth. What's around that way?'

He glances up at me from his swivel chair as though

startled and I wonder where his head has been. 'The path begins just past the pier, a short way up the road, on the bough of the hill, past a row of houses. It cuts through some bushes then takes you down the slope along by the holiday camp towards the bay.'

'A PC Priddy working for South Wales Police searched the bin in front of the gift shop, aptly named Shore, which is just a few yards from where it last pinged, and came away empty-handed,' DC Chapman says, 'but there are plenty of other places he could have left it.'

'Wasn't his ex-wife the one who pinged his phone?' DC Banks asks.

'Yes, but only South Wales Police were able to extract an exact location from the data,' DC Winters replies.

'Still, she knew where he was after he left her gaff. And though she wouldn't have had time to follow him and kill him before calling us, she could have rung someone and told them which direction he was taking,' DC Chapman says.

'Okay guys and gals, while I appreciate and acknowledge these ideas, we can't afford to speculate, so I'd like to bring your attention back to Dougie's son, Paddy. He's never come up on *our* radar before, but we all know how appearances can be deceptive. I've asked PS Tomos to go visit him at the pub he runs and lives above in Usk once we're done here.'

'So what's up with this Paddy then?' Dafydd asks. 'The first time I met him, two months' ago now. I was there to meet with a retired detective to discuss a former case of his that had gone cold then heat up again when the missing woman's daughter showed up wandering the street alone at night. He seemed a bit shifty, but I couldn't put my finger on why.'

'Paddy bred some horses TIRIAN reckon were sold

to associates of a gang supplying heroin to dealers operating in seven UK cities. Though we don't yet know how the drugs are entering the country we can reasonably suspect the money used to buy them is intended to wash the drug money, which is why the ROCU are working closely with the NCA to figure out who the trainers bought them from. If they find the original owners of the horses, they'll be able to put the breeders under surveillance and work out how they're financing their business. In such cases, as you well know, it's imperative to "follow the money" as the saying goes.'

'Wait! So they think the breeders as well as the buyers are involved in this drug dealing operation?'

'They don't know, which is why they're covering both ends of the production line.'

I pause for a moment to allow that information to set in before continuing.

'Another point of interest is that the attending officer responding to the initial report of Geraint's disappearance was approached by his neighbour as he was entering the premises. She said she'd seen him in town a couple of days ago and claims he kept glancing over his shoulder as if he believed he was being followed. As well as this, prior to their separation, he returned home from work one evening agitated and informed his wife he was moving out to "keep them safe", though when pressed he refused to elaborate. She convinced him to stay but told us she regretted it because he was "never the same man" from that day onwards. She says he received a lot of phone calls in the lead-up to their separation which he left the room to answer, and often at odd times of the day and night.'

Had Colm McGinty sent one of his heavies – Paddy Daly perhaps – after the lawyer, who'd failed to prevent his father's continued incarceration by being unable to secure a pardon, because he'd died in prison a convicted man? Or was Geraint, rightly or wrongly, suffering from some form of paranoia?

'Is there anything you've been able to uncover about the dynamics of the couple's relationship or their lifestyle that you think is relevant?' DC Winters asks.

'Neither Geraint nor his wife have criminal records. They're not even on the system having ever reported a crime. One of their daughters is a bit... quiet.'

'In what way?' DC Chapman asks.

'Uncommunicative.'

'Teenager?' DC Banks asks.

'They're both ten. Very different personalities though. One's an introvert, the other's a little... wild.'

DC Banks nods. 'Noted.'

Though girls do tend to mature quicker than boys, so it *could* be hormonal.

'The girl's – Holly and Daisy – grandparents are friends. In fact, everyone's amicable since the split. None of their relatives appear to be drug users or abusers. Geraint's mum, Lorraine, was proactive, printing off posters. Demelza's mother, Caroline, too, organised a search party by some of her biker friends. Though the family all expressed concern for the state of Geraint's mental health from the off, hence why they were adamant he'd taken his own life, which was a theory held by South Wales Police too. That was, of course, until they discovered the Osman Warning concerning Colm McGinty, which led them to Paddy Daly, his dad's, long-dead mate Dougie's son.'

'Backpedalling a bit here, boss, but what do we know about the parents?' DC Bishop asks, aiming his question at the entire team.

'Whose, Geraint's?' DC Banks replies.

'Both,' DC Bishop suggests.

'Not a lot to be honest, though not for lack of trying. I just don't think they air their dirty laundry in public.'

'No social media?'

'Demelza's mum and dad have.'

'Okay, well, let's start with them.'

'There isn't really much to say. They don't regularly post updates, and when they do it's to share "Save The Donkey" charity links or to ask their followers to donate to a JustGiving page.'

'And what about his?'

'His mum's got a bit of money, inherited from her father. Doesn't act it though, if you get what I mean. Comes across as really down-to-earth. Ed – his dad – is not around. Being an army wife wasn't his mother's cup of tea. Moving around all the time, the way you decorate your house scrutinised by the MOD, having to seek approval if you want to add a bit of decking to your garden.'

'Where is he based?'

'He last did a stint in Qatar.'

'What section?'

'Adjudicator...?'

'Adjutant General's Corps,' DC Bishop replies. 'The administration department.'

No access to guns then.

There is a collective 'ah' by those of us who otherwise would have no idea what it means.

'Any enemies?'

'Not that we know of.'

'What about witnesses?' DC Banks asks.

'Just getting to that.'

I swipe the screen once more and the waterside fronting Colm McGinty's property is replaced with the still image captured from the camera footage South Wales Police acquired of the woman who was twice seen following Geraint the very day he went missing.

'There've been no leads as to whom this woman is, but considering Geraint withdrew ten grand that same morning we can't discount the possibility that he was being blackmailed.'

'He could have been having an affair with her,' DC Chapman suggests. 'What if he slept with the woman and she found out that he was married, then demanded he pay her in exchange for her silence?'

'Or Demelza suspected he was cheating on her and hired an agency to collect evidence of his unfaithfulness?' DC Winters adds. 'What if the woman was a private investigator?'

'You wouldn't be one for very long if you acted that conspicuously,' DC Banks says, with a snort.

'We know the woman following him wasn't Caz, with whom he was exchanging emails as recently as a week ago,' DC Bishop says, 'because South Wales Police paid her a visit. She refused to discuss the contents of their conversations, but despite how familiar their exchange appeared to be, she was adamant that her relationship with Geraint was purely professional, that of legal counsel and client. They were able to link "Caz's" emails to Geraint to those used for the TEAMS call under the name of Cassandra Newton by her IP address. Caz, AKA Cass, also known as Cassie, was born Cassandra Dean. She used the name Sandra when she signed the Non-Disclosure Agreement, perhaps thinking it would make it nil and void and would allow her to speak out at some point in the future if she chose to use a variation of her legal name.'

'Weren't those emails recovered by South Wales Police only when they fit the black box to his laptop?' DC Winters asks.

'Yes, because they'd been deleted, which suggests he didn't want anyone finding them.'

'Perhaps Demelza had a habit of going through his

things, or he at least was concerned enough to think that she might,' DC Chapman suggests.

'Believing your husband is shagging someone else is certainly motive enough to root through his belongings,' DC Banks says.

'And finding out that your husband has been adulterous could be a good enough excuse for wanting him dead,' DC Bishop adds.

We know she didn't shoot him herself because Geraint left the family home – where Demelza remained with their twin daughters – prior to being captured on CCTV being followed by the blonde woman. But then again, a hired killer wouldn't be stupid enough to put themselves – in this case, literally, – in the frame.

'Geraint's Senior Partner at the law firm *was* told by his husband that he'd seen Geraint in a precarious position a few weeks ago. Apparently, Xavier told Liam, he'd seen Geraint sitting in his car talking to a blonde woman.'

'Wasn't the woman that psychic saw through her third eye handing Geraint a wad of notes also blonde?' Dylan asks, smirking.

'Apparently. Though she was ruled out fairly quickly as a quack when digital forensics found a thread on an obscure site discussing how she used information gleaned online to scam vulnerable people with claims of having spoken to their missing or deceased loved ones.'

'A real-life Oda Mae Brown then,' Dylan says. He gets a few confused looks from several younger members of the team and adds, 'Whoopi Goldberg plays a fake psychic in the film *Ghost*.'

'Yeah, but like Oda Mae, maybe Esmerelda isn't aware she actually possesses some psychic abilities,' DC Winters says.

'You're not into all that mumbo-jumbo, are you?' DC Chapman asks, incredulously.

'All I'm saying is there must be something in what she claims to have been told by Geraint's spirit. How else could she know about the money, or the woman?' DC Winters replies.

'Inside knowledge,' DC Bishop says, with a nod.

'Police intel?' DC Banks asks.

'You think South Wales Police have a leak,' DC Chapman replies.

'That's a strong accusation to make.'

'There is another explanation,' Dylan says. Everyone's heads turn towards him. 'She knew Geraint and he told her, while he was alive.'

'Well, thanks to the fact she called us from a landline we have her home address. Will you go on over to the assisted living facility she resides in and speak to her this afternoon? Find out how she came about the information? She said she'd be back from her sister's today and we still need to substantiate and corroborate her alibi for the day Geraint was murdered, if only to eliminate her from our enquiries.'

'Yes, boss.'

I swipe the glass of my Motorola, and the image of Wotton Dean replaces the previous. 'Among the files South Wales Police recovered from an archived folder on Geraint's personal laptop, and which were deleted, there were some items of interest that led them here. Namely a LinkedIn profile for a reporter named Ffion Townsend, who lives in Bridgend. Satnav directions to her property were also located within the folder. Amongst the deleted files there was an empty password protected folder titled "Case Notes – Dean Sandra", pertaining to a woman, which is why South Wales Police initially thought "Dean Wotton" was a man. There was also a single contact for "Cass Newton" saved in TEAMS, which is where they found evidence of a meeting/call or whatever you call them between her and Geraint. There were several emails, too, between Geraint and "Charlie Lettes", AKA Charlotte, also known as Lottie, a realtor living in Alabama, concerning a home he was interested in viewing, as he was "seeking to relocate for work" which she discovered was a lie, likely by searching online and discovering he was a UK-based solicitor with shares in the company. In one of her emails, she confronted him and told him: "I do not want to talk to a lawyer. I've put that ordeal behind me. Not even my husband knows about any of that". Make of that what you will but maybe she's another one of Geoffrey Goldsborough's victims.'

'They can't pursue a criminal conviction against him though, can they?' DS Llyons says. 'I mean he's dead.'

'Murdered. Two-and-a-half decades ago. Geraint defended the man convicted of killing him. Of course, the man responsible has a very good alibi for the last twenty-five years so we can rule him out as a suspect regarding Geraint's homicide.'

'What motivated Geraint to look into those allegations?' DC Banks asks.

'See what you can dig up.'

He gives me a salute.

I tap the table in a faux drumroll. 'And . . . there was a photograph of an unknown woman who looks identical to the blonde captured on CCTV, but which could not be verified. Reverse image searches of both the photograph and the still image of the blonde woman captured on CCTV resulted in no matches.'

I pause for a second, allowing everyone to absorb this information. I know it's a lot, and we're only halfway through the day.

I scroll down the screen of my phone from the black and white photograph of Wotton Dean to the text printed below it. 'A quick search online brought up this news article about the psychiatric hospital in Gloucestershire. If Caz and Charlie were victims of something Geoffrey Goldsborough did there may very well be a discernible link between the women Geraint was looking up, and Wotton Dean Psychiatric Hospital, so South Wales Police applied for a warrant to search Geraint's office at Fford and Bailey. They believed Geraint was working on something involving historic allegations. They found a stamped addressed envelope dated October of this year inside his desk, within which contained a Cease-and-Desist Notice from the lawyer of a UK-based organisation who provide roles to doctors who wish to volunteer abroad.'

I swipe the screen again, revealing the final image.

'It was enough evidence to suggest Geraint had been undertaking some kind of investigation that somebody didn't want him to pursue, allowing South Wales Police to retrieve his office computer. On it, digital forensics found this, an email sent to Geraint from his legal secretary, Theodore Andrews. When an officer spoke to Theo, he told them Geraint had tasked him with tracing records concerning an individual he suspected had volunteered for a charity in Ghana, and shortly afterwards the organisation that had arranged the role began sponsoring the charity. Geraint wanted to know what had pre-empted the monthly donation, and when Theo was unable to obtain the information, Geraint enlisted the help of a private investigator. The consultancy service had been used by the law firm before and when we spoke to them it became apparent that they regularly assisted law firms, including Fford and Bailey, with both criminal and civil lawsuits, so their involvement wasn't unusual. They weren't able to provide South Wales Police with the identity of the doctor who Geraint believed had volunteered for the Ghanian charity due to confidentiality clauses, but the individual could easily have been the late Head of Women's Mental Health Services of Wotton Dean Psychiatric Hospital, Geoffrey Goldsborough. And rather than an act of altruism the organisation's regular payments to the charity might in fact be hush money.'

'To find out what for we need to speak to Caz,' DC Winters says.

'Will you do that?'

'Yes, ma'am,' DC Winters replies.

'But to be able to match her allegations against something we're going to need to speak to the charity,' DC Chapman adds. 'I doubt the volunteering organisation is going to want their reputation tarnished and it'd show our hand too soon if we were to approach them before making more covert enquiries.'

'I agree. Would you follow that up?'

'Gladly,' DC Chapman replies.

'I'd like someone to have a word with the Private Investigators too.'

'I will,' DC Bishop says enthusiastically.

I give him an affirmative nod. 'Find out who was put in charge of investigating the donor and see if you can get them to open up as to why without the need for a costly trip to the Magistrates for a warrant. My budget is tight this month.'

They might be more willing to speak to us if they learn of Geraint's demise.

'We're short on staff too, so DS Llyons will you head on over to Bridgend and speak to Ffion Townsend, find out what reason Geraint had for visiting her and whether in fact he did?'

'No problem.'

'PC Meyer, will you give DC Burtenshaw a call, ask our FLO to question Demelza about Geraint's fidelity, and whether she suspected or indeed knew he'd been unfaithful. I'm just not buying the reason for their separation.'

Geraint was emailing Caz using his personal laptop which he kept at home, and he was arranging to meet her while still living with his wife. If Demelza suspected he was having an affair, she might also suspect that if he was it put her in the frame when he went missing. Which would have been a good enough reason to withhold her suspicion from the police once she learned he'd been killed.

'Hands up who wants to ask Geraint's mum about his relationship with his stepfather? Lorraine might be able to fill in some gaps to help us understand her son's state of mind at the time of his murder, and we have to consider the insinuation Liam made as to his "adverse childhood".'

'I'll go, boss,' PC Coulter volunteers.

'Thank you.'

'I'll hold the fort while you're all out there, obviously.'

I get a few nods and a couple of mumbled 'boss's'.

'Now last but by no means least, I want you all to go home as soon as your shifts finish today. I don't want to see you back inside this building until the morning, no matter what you discover. Unless of course it involves the name of the person who stole our victim's life. Is that understood?'

A collective murmur follows.

'I'll see you all back in here at the usual time for a full briefing if I don't hear from you before. Though my phone is always on, I'd prefer not to be disturbed after 6 p.m. unless it's urgent.'

While everyone's occupied and with a few minutes to spare I spend it googling Demelza's business. I'm unable to find anything related to her personally except on the second results page of the worldwide web my search brings up mention of her business in relation to a transaction that led to a dispute between a buyer and a bank regarding the sale of a barber shop on a Newport high street. On closer inspection it appears to be a case of local residents getting pissy over Billy Big Bollocks from London buying out small businesses the locals can't afford and have no interest in owning anyway, resulting in a purchasing delay.

But you never know. People have killed for far less than a simple difference of opinion.

Case No. IC1MOU0224

Summary of files (contained within this digital folder) extracted from hard drive of HP laptop, IP address: 797.███.█.██, used by Mr Geraint Fford, registered to Fford and Bailey Solicitors of: Hickman Road, Penarth, Wales, CF64 2AJ, seized for investigatory purposes on 24th November 2022:

- Email exchange between 'Ant' and 'Theo' dated Thursday 17 November 2022, at 3.22 p.m. which includes attached email between Theodore 'Theo' Andrews and Doctors Abroad.
- Search history (backdated three months) which includes:
  1) Webpage from search for Juniper Consultancy Services, Private Investigators
  2) Downloaded PDF format Women of Christ Community Initiation Fund e-newsletter, dated April 2022

Fford and Bailey Solicitors
<ta.legal@ffordandbailey.co.uk>

To: **gf.solicitor@ffordandbailey.co.uk**

Thurs, 17 Nov 2022 15:22

Ant,

I was able to obtain the information you requested. I have forwarded you the email I have just received from the director of the charity.

Theo (Legal Secretary)

Theo Andrews <ta.legal@ffordandbailey.co.uk>
To: gf.solicitor@ffordandbailey.co.uk

↓ Hide original message

-----forwarded message-----
From: "Doctors Abroad" <freddiemurdoch@doctorsabroad.co.uk>
To: "Theo Andrews" <ta.legal@ffordandbailey.co.uk>
Sent: Thursday, 17 Nov 2022 at 15:22:11 BMT
Subject: information request

Mr Theodore Andrews,

Thank you for your recent enquiry concerning our sponsorship of the Women of Christ Community Initiation Fund (WCCIF).

Doctors Abroad is a UK registered charity providing volunteer opportunities overseas by qualified doctors living and working in the United Kingdom. In exchange for their time and skills, we cover living and travel expenses for the duration of their stay. We cover these costs through donations. We receive state and private funding through the British Government, The National Lottery Fund, and anonymous donors. Due to data protection legislation, I cannot divulge where individual sponsorships come from. However, I can confirm that we do ourselves, as a non-profit, sponsor a range of enterprises throughout the world, including the WCCIF, using any excess funds. This is to cover the continued costs associated with this organisation which provides volunteer opportunities to our list of registered doctors (current members are categorised by professionalism and specialism and are named on our website).

A record of former members is kept for legal purposes, but I cannot disclose this information to you without a subpoena.

Regards,
Frederick Murdoch (Director)

-----HOME-----

Juniper Consultancy Services
24/7 Phone Number 020 ▇▇▇ ▇▇▇

One of the UK's Top Rated Private Investigation Agency's.

We cover Fraud, Spouse, and Online Investigations.

We are experts in helping both commercial and private clients seeking the truth.

Our investigators are professional, affordable, have an outstanding success rate, have a global reach, and have five-star reviews on Trustpilot.

Book your discrete consultation via our online form **HERE.**

WOMEN OF CHRIST COMMUNITY INITIATION FUND

NEWSLETTER

April 2022

What is happening this month?
Local News
Church Times
Celebrations
Praise
Topic of the Month: Our Climate
Volunteer Opportunities

NEWS
Two Ebola cases have been confirmed in central Ghanan city, Kumasi. People are being warned to look out for the symptoms which include:
- Fever
- Pain in head/body
- Weakness
- Tiredness
- Sore throat
- Stomach cramps
- Vomiting
- diarrhoea
- Bleeding or bruising

Ebolavirus is spread through contact with body fluid (urine, saliva, sweat, blood, faeces, vomit, breast milk, amniotic fluid, and semen). Contaminated bedding, clothes, and medical equipment. And through giving medical care to or having sex with an infected person.

You can protect yourself by avoiding contact with infected persons, and do not have sex with recovered persons. Do not share clothes or medical equipment. Do not touch the body of an infected person during burial.

CHURCH
Ghanian Community Assembly
Prayers: Daily – morning (8-9 a.m.) and evening (6-7 p.m.)
Service: Sunday morning (8-10 a.m.)

CELEBRATIONS
Celebrating their union, two of our volunteers, Amari and Nia, were married last week. The ceremony took place in their native city of Koforidua. Congratulations! We wish you both health, fertility, and prosperity.

Congratulations to Issa Afolabi, one of our shop volunteers, and her husband Yazid on the birth of their first child. We wish your baby daughter a long and happy life!

PRAISE
Praise be to Kamau, who has been teaching reading and writing skills to some of the community's most disadvantaged children, including within our own orphanages. Kamau's wife received health care from one of our nurses after a cancer diagnosis in 2016 because she could not afford medical insurance. Her devoted husband offered to volunteer his skills after her death three years later, and we'd like to say a very big thank you!

TOPIC OF THE MONTH: OUR CLIMATE

A major cause of the droughts we are experiencing this year is the result of changes to our climate. Our community has been especially affected by global warming due to the area being so rural. Without rain our crops cannot grow, we have no running water to drink, our toilets do not flush, our power supplies burn out from the heat, and diseases spread due to a lack of sanitation. Impoverished families suffer the most. In the villages surrounding our town there are many people who cannot access or afford transportation, which means they are unable to get to work or reach a hospital when they are sick. Many of these people feel isolated and because of their location it is difficult for them to access help when they need it, which is why it is so important to minister to the elderly, frail, and poorly advantaged. Our volunteers trek for miles to provide our services to them, free of charge, but this is only possible with your help. You can donate money to us directly, or anonymously. An alarmed donation box is attached to the front of the building.

VOLUNTEER OPPORTUNITIES

The Women of Christ Community Initiation Fund is a Non-Governmental Organisation based in Ghana. Our aim is to guide, support, and nourish the financial independence of women by providing funding to assist with the development of projects to increase job opportunities or to cover the cost of setting up a business. We also provide grants for necessary medical treatment and provide safe spaces where women can socialise within their communities.

The WCCIF was founded by Christian Minister Adeleke and his wife Rosa Owusu, who set up the charity from their small rural home on the outskirts of Mampong, twenty-seven years ago. Originally intended to provide emergency medical treatment and emotional support to female victims of gender-based trauma, often resulting from domestic or war crimes, we now provide accommodation, food, and work, as well as health checks and counselling to all women regardless of whether they've experienced violence in their lifetime.

Many of our financial sponsors have previously gifted us their time and skills, from helping us to grow food to vaccinating our most vulnerable members of society. Volunteers travel from all over the world to assist us as part of our international ministerial programme.

We currently have a range of vacancies: from handing out food parcels to sewing garments to sell at our market stall. Speak to Jabari Chinua Achebe, Volunteer Co-ordinator, for more information.

Prayers and blessings.

Our Sponsors:
The Christian Fellowship (local – Ghana)
The Mensah Foundation (national – Africa)
United in Prayer (international – US)
Doctors Abroad (international – UK)

PS TOMOS

PRESENT

The pub's a traditional one. The hoppy smell of ale hits me as I enter. There is lots of carved dark oak, and sketches of local landmarks drawn by some unknown artist during the previous century adorn the walls. A group of tall, muscled men with shaved heads stand muttering under their breath at one end of the bar. The man behind the counter, leaning between them, indicating my arrival with a nod of his head – to one of his heavies I imagine – is the man I've come to speak to. Paddy Daly. Son of a former member of the IRA, and regular resident of various buildings owned by Her Majesty's Prison service – which I'm assuming since the recent death of the Queen will now be retitled *His* Majesty's Prison Service? – mostly for assault, Actual and Grievous Bodily Harm, until five years ago when he bought the premises he owns today. He reckons he's a reformed character now though, at least that's what he said the first and last time we spoke.

'What can I get you, good man?' he asks. 'Locally brewed beer?'

'Next time. I'm here on official business so it's more than my job's worth to begin drinking before lunchtime.'

I reach beneath my shirt and raise the lanyard hidden under my vest to display the ID card that touts my credentials, alongside an unflattering photograph taken before I lost the final few threads of hair from my crown, eleven months ago. It's almost time to get a new one snapped. Something I'm not looking forward to, considering I now have a timeline of identification cards that fill the left-hand side of my sock drawer, which display my hair loss in chronological order.

'Out the back,' he motions towards the door. 'Don't wanna put the punters off.'

He informs a woman he tells me is the bar manager, who looks like a very close relation – perhaps his daughter? – to hold the fort for fifteen minutes and I assume that's because he doesn't want to give me any more time than that. Passing through the door into the hall I come face-to-face with a short, overly made-up underage bride.

'My youngest. It's her first holy communion in an hour. I don't have long to piss about, so let's get this over with, huh?'

If white's the symbolic colour of innocence is his choice of a black V-neck polo shirt a subconscious sign of guilt?

He doesn't wait for me to reply, just escorts me with a firm hand between my shoulder blades, into a room to the left of the front door, closing it behind us and sitting on the chair closest to my only exit, forcing me to take the sofa opposite, in front of the window.

'Who am I supposed to have hit now, Sergeant?'

'You remember me?'

'You were here two months ago.'

I take my phone from the pocket of my suit jacket and turn it round to show him the picture I'd left on the screen so I wouldn't have to search through my storage to find it.

'Nice dag.'

I frown and flip it over, finding a picture of my late American Bulldog filling the screen.

'Screensaver, sorry. Here, this one. He ring any bells?'

'No. Never seen him before in my life.'

'Funny that. Cos you rang him a week ago. Three times in fact. What did you speak to him about?'

'I don't remember.'

'Might it jog your memory if I escort you to the station for a formal interview? It'd be a shame if you were unable to accompany your wife and children to the church.'

'This and that.'

'The kind of "this and that" that might get a man killed?'

'He's dead?'

'Murdered.'

'I didn't kill him.'

'Do you know who did?'

'No. But if I had that information, I wouldn't tell you.'

His honesty takes me by surprise.

'We think Geraint was . . . involved in something.'

My hope is that by adding that ambiguous snippet of information Paddy might question whether whatever it was might have led to his death and concern him enough to worry about his own mortality, maybe even get him to tell me what he discussed with Geraint.

Case No. GBRP459601   12 Pages

HEDDLU DE CWMRU
(SOUTH WALES POLICE)

HOMICIDE CASE FILE

FULL NAME	JOB DESCRIPTION	DATE RETRIEVED	TIME
Martin Collins	Detective Superintendent	22/8/2022	9.05 a.m.
Ayisha Sharma	Detective Chief Inspector	24/10/2022	11.44 a.m.
Frankie Pritchard	Detective Inspector	9/11/2022	2.17 p.m.

CONTENTS:
Page 1 - Crime Scene Investigation Report
Page 2 – Image 2 (Crowbar)
Page 3 – Image 3 (Blood Spatter)
Page 4 – Image 4 (Bloodied Fingerprint)
Page 5 – Autopsy Report
Page 6 – School Attendance Record
Page 7 – CV
Page 8 – Pre-Trial Evaluation
Page 9 – List of Staff
Page 10 – Party Invitation
Page 11 – Birth Certificate
Page 12 – Medical Report

Investigator Name: Caryn Williams
Case #GBRP459601
Crime Scene Location: (Living room) Penrith House, Fort Road, Lavernock, South Wales, CF64 5UL

Crime Scene Investigation Report

Did the death take place where the body was discovered or was it moved?
This appears to be the primary murder scene.

Was there any attempt to alter the scene?
There is no obvious sign that anyone has tried to clean up, tidy away, or remove evidence.

Is the cause of death clearly apparent?
The visible wounds on the male victim appear to have been caused by blunt force trauma, due to repeatedly striking the head with a large, heavy, metallic implement, consistent with the weapon found beside the body.

Are there sufficient clues (physical evidence to indicate how the crime occurred, and where the victim and perpetrator were in relation to each other during the crime)?
The body lies in front of the fireplace on a rug which is saturated with blood that has pooled around the victim's head. The blood spatter is sprayed up the stone hearth and onto the wall. Brain matter is visible on the weapon suggesting some force was used to strike the victim. The physical evidence is consistent with the use of the weapon by an individual of approximately five foot five inches to six feet tall.

Image #2

Description:
Crowbar found beside body, upon which blood and brain matter was visible.

Material:
Forged steel, painted black, chisel end and swan neck.

Dimensions:
36'/915mm long, 1 inch wide.

Weight:
2 kilograms.

Image #3

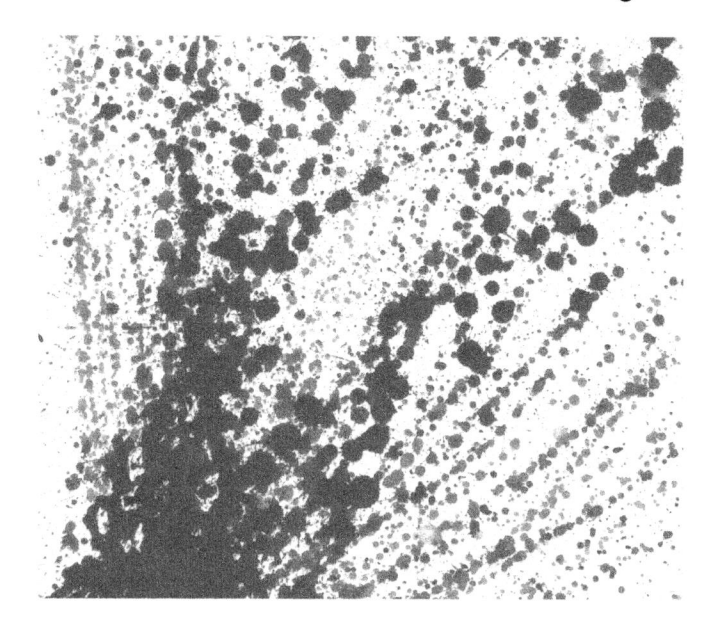

Description:
Blood spatter on wall beside fireplace, suggestive of initial strike with weapon.

Dimensions:
47/1193.8mm

Pattern:
In-line staining suggests victim was alive and standing at full height when the initial blow occurred. Elongated staining suggests the victim was struck at close impact with a heavy object. Medium velocity spatter with four-foot total cast-off suggests victim was struck with the weapon located at the scene. Parent drops with satellite spatters and spines with smooth edges suggest the perpetrator was standing in front of and slightly to the right of the victim, nearest the painted wall, at the point of first impact. The falling droplets upon the

decreasing angles of staining suggest the victim was struck with a left-sided blow, consistent with an individual of a similar height to the victim and who is right-handed.

Image #4

Description:
Bloodied thumbprint retrieved four inches from chiselled end of crowbar.

Biometric Dimensions:
2.2cm length x 1.6cm width

Identifiable characteristics:
Looped Non-Tented Arch without a Whorl, and four friction ridges

Features:
*Ridge ending: The abrupt end of a ridge (2)
*Bifurcation: A single ridge dividing in two (2)
*Short or independent ridge: A ridge that commences, travels a short distance and then ends (2)
*Island or dot: A single small ridge inside a short ridge or ridge ending

that is not connected to all other ridges (4)
*Lake or ridge enclosure: A single ridge that bifurcates and reunites shortly afterward to continue as a single ridge (0)
*Spur: A bifurcation with a short ridge branching off a longer ridge (0)
*Bridge or crossover: A short ridge that runs between two parallel ridges (0)
*Delta: A Y-shaped ridge meeting (1)
*Core: A circle in the ridge pattern (8)

Numerator/Denominator: (a 1 is added to both top and bottom, to exclude any possibility of division by zero): Rt (16 + 8 + 4 + 2 + 0 + 1/1) / (2 + 2 + 2 + 4 + 0 + 0 + 0 + 1 + 8 + 1/1)

Resulting Calculation: 31/20 (Finger Number 6)

Pathologist Name: Dr. Kevin Crocker
Case #GBRP459601

Autopsy Report

Who is the deceased?
Name: Geoffrey Goldsborough
Age: 37
Sex: Male
Address: Penrith House, Fort Road
City, County, Postcode: Lavernock, South Wales, CF64 5UL
Phone #029 2021 ▮

Race	Length	Weight	Eyes	Hair	Identifiable Features
Caucasian	6'0	252lbs	Blue	Brown	Beard

Blood type	Contents in blood	Rigor Mortis	Liver mortis
A+	**RBC Morphology:** Normal **Toxicological compounds present:** 0 **Vitamin/mineral levels:** Normal	Present in eyelids, jaw, and central body, suggestive of 2-5 hours post-mortem	Lividity consistent with rigor mortis (1-3 hrs)

Marks and Wounds	Description
	Open head injury (2'x3mm deep laceration to skin, with skull fracture, swelling, bleeding, and clotting.
	Lacerations (superficial)
	Fractured cheek
	Fractured eye socket
	Fractured nasal cavity
	Fractured jaw
	Fractured teeth

Probable Cause of Death
Brain injury

Date of Autopsy	Location of Autopsy
6/9/1995	Cardiff Vale Forensic Services, South Wales

Conclusion

The wound most likely caused by the initial blow is to the left side of the victim's head, one inch to the right of and one centimetre below the temple, fracturing the skull and causing swelling of the brain, blood loss and clotting. The impact would have been enough to incapacitate the victim. Further impact would not have been necessary but occurred to the face and head nine more times, while the victim lay upon the rug, which is where he died. In my estimation it was the initial blow which caused the victim's death; it is possible death resulted from blood loss, just as it could also have occurred as a consequence of the swelling and blood clotting resulting from the injury.

Address/Cyberia:
Saint David's High School (Welsh Medium), Bishop Street, Cardiff.

Ysgol Uwchradd Dewi Sant (Cyfrwng Cymraeg), Stryd yr Esgob, Caerdydd.

Name/Enw: Roderick Penrose
Date of Attendance/Dyddiad Presenoldeb: Sept 1982- Sept 1987

Qualifications/Cymwysterau:
Welsh/Cymreig – D
Literacy Foundation/Sefydliad Llythrennedd – D
Numeracy Foundation/Sefydliad Rhifedd – E
Science Foundation/Sefydliad Gwyddoniaeth – E
Religious Education/Addysg Grefyddol – D
History/Hanes – D
Geography/Daearyddiaeth – E
Art/Celfyddyd – C

Attendance/Presenoldeb:
Total Absences/Cyfanswm Absenoldebau – 207
Average Per Year/Cyfartaledd y Flwyddyn – 51

<u>Curriculum Vitae</u>

Name: Roderick Penrose
Date of Birth: 9/6/1971

Work History:
Newspaper Distributor – Gerry Warner Newsagents (1985-1987)
Mobile Car Washer – Self-employed (1987-1989)
Mobile Window Cleaner – Self-employed (1988-1989)
Mobile Home Repairs – Self-employed (1989-1990)
Gardner/Landscaper – Self-employed (1990-1992)

Current Employment:
Groundskeeper – Dr Geoffrey Goldsborough (1992-ongoing)

Pre-trial evaluation

Psychiatrist Name: Dr Niall Griffiths (Doc. ForPsych: MBPS, MHPC, MRCPych, GMCmBPS)
Patient Name: Roderick Penrose
Date: 05/01/1996

Childhood:
Roderick is an only child to a mother (Y) who raised him single-handedly. His birth was the result of child rape and as such he has had no contact with his biological father and his mother has had no interest in men for the duration of his childhood. He was brought up in what he considers a safe, loving environment.

Family:
His Uncle Billy (William) has been a supportive influence throughout his life, both emotionally and financially.

Health:
Possibly as a result of Y's experiences of child sexual abuse she was over-protective and wouldn't allow Roderick to play with other children outside of the home. As a consequence, Roderick often felt suffocated and lonely, so he began to use food as a way to fill the void. Overeating became a problem during his teenage years as being kept indoors didn't allow him to get the adequate exercise he required and as such he became overweight. This led to bullying in school and resulted in a high level of absence.

Adverse Childhood Event(s):
Y developed the lung disorder (COPD) from exposure to Mundic Block damp/black mould, which meant that she tired easily during physical exertion, restricting her movements and therefore also Roderick's.

Notable Information:
Y died (on the sofa in the living room while Roderick played with his toy cars on the floor in front of the television) as a consequence of her health problems, in 1981, when he was ten years old. A neighbour, wondering why she hadn't seen Y in a few days, knocked on the door to enquire on her wellbeing. A police call was made to 999 from the neighbour who stated that Roderick had told the woman, 'You can't speak to her because she's dead', in what the woman described as a monosyllabic tone. After Y's death Roderick went to live with his uncle Billy and aunt, which is where he learned who his father was and how he'd been conceived.

Y and Billy were separated from their parents during the Second World War when they were evacuated to Cornwall. They lived in a large house owned by a single man who physically abused Billy and sexually abused Y. They were largely ignored by the governess (nanny/au pair) paid to care for them and were mostly left to occupy themselves within the grounds. Though both siblings knew how to read and write neither were given the opportunity to, nor were they schooled for the duration of their stay, which ended after a fire broke out, leading to the death of the master, and the house became so badly burned that it had to be raised to the ground. When the children returned home to Bristol, they discovered that their father had been killed on duty and their mother had become withdrawn and would often take to her bed. Y gave birth to Roderick – her first and only child – four months later, at the age of sixteen. Y and Billy's mother – Roderick's grandmother – took her own life shortly afterwards.

Billy studied on the job as an apprentice while Y took care of the baby and the flat that he rented out for them both. When Billy met his wife and eventually married her, they moved into a home of their own. Y began working, but her lack of qualifications and experience affected her job opportunities and led to long-term poverty, and eventually homelessness, which resulted in her having to seek emergency accommodation from the council, which is how she and Roderick came to be living in social housing.

Formulative Assessment:
Roderick exhibits moderate Dyslexia, which is likely the reason he has found it easier to find and retain employment of a physical variety.

Y found it hard to connect to Roderick, on a deeper than superficial level, which may have impacted how Roderick was able to express his feelings, though it does not appear to have prevented him from being able to bond with people.

It's possible that Roderick displayed such a blasé attitude to his mother's death because he did not know how to communicate with the outside world and through lack of teaching about emergency procedures rather than as a result of having any psychological deficit.

Conclusion:
Roderick is able to articulate his thoughts and feelings adequately. He displays emotional intelligence when responding to questions and expresses an age-appropriate understanding of his crime. Using cognitive, behavioural, and personality tests I was able to conclude that Roderick's neurological functioning is within typical parameters. Though he stated he did not want to discuss the offence for which he has been accused, he was aware of the legal ramifications and acknowledged responsibility for having committed it. When prompted, however, he did not want to discuss his motivations and has shown no remorse.

LIST OF STAFF

Beatrice Zielińska – Nanny/Au Pair
David 'Dai' Beckman – Chef
Charlie Radthorne – Chauffer
Nancy Pascoe – Housekeeper
Peter Smyth – Handyman
Mark Troy – Stable Master/Head Groom
Roderick Penrose – Groundskeeper/Gardener

Geoffrey & Celyn

CORDIALLY INVITE ROD
& NANCY TO OUR
10TH WEDDING
ANNIVERSARY SOIRÉE

Saturday | 18 June, 1994 | At 6 pm

Wenvoe Castle Golf Club

CERTIFIED COPY OF AN ENTRY BBU 479526	
Pursuant to Births and Deaths Registration	
Birth	**Entry No. 15**
Registration district Cardiff Subdistrict South Wales	
Child	
1. Date and Place of Birth May 4 1996	Cardiff Royal Hospital South Wales
2. Name and Surname Kerry-Ann Pascoe	3. Sex Female
Father	
4. Name and Surname Unknown	
5. Place of Birth Unknown	6. Occupation Unknown
Mother	
7. Name and Surname Nancy Penrose	
8. (a) Place of Birth Cardiff, South Wales	8. (b) Occupation Unemployed
9. (a) Maiden Surname Pascoe	9. (b) Surname at Marriage if Different from Maiden Surname Penrose
10. Usual Adress (if different from place of child's birth) Whitchurch Psychiatric Hospital Park Road Cardiff CF14 7XB	
Informant	12. Qualification
11. Name and surname (if not the mother or father)	Mother
13. Usual address (if different from that in 10 above) 49 Forrest Road Penarth CF64 5BT	
14. I certify that the particulars entered above are true to the best of my knowledge and belief Nancy Pascoe Signature of informant	
15. Date of registration May 7 1996	16. Signature of registrar *D. Flood*
17. Name given after registration and surname	

Certified to be a true copy of an entry in a register in my custody.
D. Flood   { *Deputy* *Superintendent* *Registrar   Date *May 7th 1996*
*Strike out whichever does not apply

System no. 50919481

CAUTION: THERE ARE OFFENCES RELATING TO FALSIFYING OR ALTERING A CERTIFICATE AND USING AND POSSESSING A FALSE CERTIFICATE

WARNING: A CERTIFICATE IS NOT EVIDENCE OF IDENTITY

PRISON SERVICE

MEDICAL REPORT

Date 13/10/2021 **Time** 11.05 a.m.
Patient name Roderick Penrose (**if prisoner what's their prisoner number?**) 59358109
Male/Female Male
Date of birth 9/6/1971
Details Patient developed symptoms of Covid-19 6/10/2021 and was isolated from other prisoners. Test confirmed positive 8/10/2021. Patient referred to nurse 9/10/2021. Blood oxygen levels low. Ambulance called.

Illness/injury Infectious Disease
Does patient require hospital/physician Yes X No
Hospital name University Hospital of Wales
Address Heath Park Cardiff CF14 4XW
Hospital phone number(s) 029 2074 7747
Patient signature R. Penrose **Date** 9/10/2021
Important notes and instructions
Prisoner has no Next of Kin, no living family or friends to notify of his admission.

Signed Katrina Riley (Nurse)

KERRY-ANN

PAST

Natalia and I had met in the restaurant where she'd begun waiting tables before she'd left to pursue a college degree, at the end of which she'd secured a job as assistant chef. The place was owned by the Greek friend of her mother's ex-partner, the man I was there to interview. We'd shared a few surreptitious glances across the dimly lit heads of the diners, and a smile when one of the customers shared a joke a little too loudly, but it wasn't until I'd caught the grief-stricken look on her face as she exited the bathroom holding her phone in one shaky hand while I was entering it that we exchanged our first words.

It turned out that her cat, who she thought had run away, slipping between her legs, and bolting out of the front door the moment she opened it that morning, had been found a couple of streets away by her neighbour, who was walking his dog. She appeared to have been hit by a car, an accident from which she'd hoped the cat had died instantly.

I instinctually reached out to embrace her and she'd fallen into my arms, weeping against my shoulder. When she pulled away, I grabbed some tissue from one of the toilet cubicles, rolled it up, and handed it to her.

We didn't exchange numbers; I hadn't even asked her name when I returned the next day carrying Shiloh.

Her face lit up at the sight of her cuteness and she held out her hands for a cuddle.

'What's her name?'

'She hasn't got one.'

'Shiloh,' she said.

'That's nice. What's yours?'

'Natalia.'

'That's nice. Mine's Kerry-Ann.'

Her boss leaned out of the serving hatch and said, 'You'd better get that cat out of here before one of the punters calls Trading Standards.'

Natalia reluctantly handed Shiloh back to me, grazing her face against her silky soft fur as she did.

'What time do you finish your shift?'

'I'm on a late one. I probably won't get out of here until gone midnight.'

'I'll wait for you, outside, in the car.'

'Will you now?'

'Well, you'll want to take her with you, won't you?'

'Will I?'

'She's yours.'

'What!?' She took a step back.

'Shiloh is yours.'

'You got her for me?'

'I did.'

'You're serious?'

'I know what it's like to lose someone you love.'

She grinned, said, 'Nobody's ever done anything like that for me before,' then gripped me by the shoulders and pressed her mouth against my forehead, making a smacking sound as she retracted as though the action was normal, as if we were long-time friends. 'Thank you.'

DI LOCKE

PRESENT

The sky is beginning to darken as I read the update on the HOLMES 2 database provided by the technical team while stuffing my face with a cheese and pickle sandwich.

Patrick Daly's Range Rover was flagged up on an ANPR camera west of Cardiff City football ground on the night of Geraint's disappearance.

It doesn't mean he was in it though, or that he didn't put a contract out on Geraint.
After becoming lost in translation during an international phone call to the Ghanian charity, DC Chapman was informed by an administrative assistant working for the WCCIF that Geoffrey was their first and last UK volunteer through the Doctors Abroad scheme. The potential relevance of this information didn't become apparent, however, until DC Bishop managed to get put through to *the* Private Investigator who was under Geraint's employ when he called Juniper Consultancy Services. The call operator transferred him directly to the man who refused to cooperate stating that client confidentiality continued

even after death, but when he was told the information that we needed didn't directly involve Geraint, who we knew had been murdered, he openly admitted to fearing Geraint was killed to muzzle him and freely stated he had secured evidence of what I can only describe as extortion, because Doctors Abroad have been paying WCCIF £1,000 a month since Dr Goldsborough's one and only placement.

'Hush money perhaps?' DC Knowles says, leering over my shoulder at the screen of my computer while he removes his coat and throws it over the back of his chair.

'Maybe.'

'Urgh,' DC Leech says, gazing down at the sandwich in my hand with a disgusted look on his face as he passes my office on his way to his desk.

'You don't have to eat it.'

'Thank god for that,' he replies, sitting on his swivel chair so fast that it skids away from him, and he lands on his backside with a thud just as my phone rings to the tune of *Bad Boys* by Inner Circle.

I pick it up and put it to my ear, while trying not to laugh.

'This had better be important. It's home time.'

'Says the inspector who's still seated at her desk.'

'How do you know where I am?'

'You're almost as predictable as the Welsh weather,' Dafydd replies.

'What did Paddy have to say?'

'The usual. Once I implied Geraint was party to something and hinted that it might have given someone cause to end his life, he revealed he'd been receiving legal counsel from Geraint. Though he shut down when I asked him what for. I can't blame him. Legal professional privilege doesn't end after the death of client or lawyer. I can only imagine it might have had something to do with those horses.'

'Which significantly widens rather than narrows our suspect list,' PC Meyer sighs, when after I've ended the call, I reiterate my conversation with Dafydd.

'What about the psychic?' DC Bishop asks.

'Asserted herself into the investigation from the off,' PC Meyer adds.

'She rang us with information shortly after the first news report regarding Geraint's disappearance and was on the beach when his body was recovered from the sea,' DC Bishop says, with a shudder. 'Bit of a coincidence, no?'

'DS Jones has headed over to her cottage to have a word with her. Let's see what she has to say for herself.'

We shouldn't judge her behaviour before she's given us her side of the story, but it wouldn't be the first time a murderer had presented themselves as helpful and volunteered to assist us with our enquiries in the hope of finding out how the investigation into their crime was progressing, allowing them to concoct a story in preparation for when they're caught for having committed it.

As I put the phone down, I catch sight of something in my peripheral. I glance up in time to see a shadow flit past the incident room. I jump up off my chair to investigate, reaching the doorway where I spot a familiar-shaped form dart down the corridor.

'DS Jones?' I cross my arms and lean against the doorframe.

A couple of beats later he walks backwards wearing a sheepish look on his face.

'The nightshift has started to arrive.'

'I left my ... um ...'

I raise my chin. 'Cut the crap.'

'Why haven't *you* left yet?' he asks me.

'Same reason you've yet to go home. How did it go with Esmé?'

'She's psychic,' Dylan replies, stuffing his hand into the pocket of his trousers and withdrawing a handful of loose change.

'So she says.'

'She knew my girlfriend's name began with D,' he says, dropping two coins into the vending machine.

'What else did she predict?'

He hesitates a moment before replying. 'That we were going to have a baby in Easter, but that's close enough.'

Something heavy tumbles down the shoot and into the pocket so loudly that I wonder for a second if I've misheard him.

'You're what!?'

'Dempsey's pregnant,' he confirms with a shit-eating grin.

My stomach twists. 'That's—'

'Sudden, I know, but we're serious.' He kneels and reaches into the pocket and retrieves an ice-cold bottle of water.

'Actually, I was going to say, that's great news. Congratulations.'

'Thanks,' he says, twisting the cap and downing a sip of the liquid. 'It's still early days,' he adds through wet lips, looking shifty. He screws the cap back on. 'We've got our first maternity appointment booked in for tomorrow evening. I can cancel it if you need me here?'

'I'm sure we'll survive.'

'Thanks.'

He knows I'm physically unable to conceive a child of my own.

'Did she read your palm?'

'Tea leaves actually,' he replies, wiping his mouth

with the back of his hand.

'I sent you there to talk to her.'

'And an interesting conversation it was.'

'What did she have to say?'

'I'm going to have a windfall soon. Which with the soaring cost of bills and the increase in our food consumption now that my girlfriend is expecting is more than welcome.'

'That's lovely for you. But I meant how did she explain her presence on the beach the very day we recovered Geraint's body? Who she just happens to have visualised handing over a huge wad of cash "to a fair-haired maiden" shortly before he died.'

'She was collecting sea glass.'

'Right.'

Nutcase then.

'She couldn't stop and chat for long. Said she had to go and charge her crystals under the light of the moon.'

'Don't tell me you believe in all that hocus pocus?'

'Hear me out Miss Marple.'

'I take offence to that. I'm not much older than you.'

He ignores me and continues. 'Forensic accounting told us Geraint withdrew a large sum of money the morning he was reported missing.'

'Yeah, but it was found in his flat.'

'We still haven't worked out why he took it out though.'

'But you have an idea.'

'It was as I sat down to eat my cod and chips.'

'It's alright for some isn't it?'

'Nice little country pub. You'd have liked it.'

'Thanks for the invite.'

He ignores my sarcasm and continues as if we haven't gone off-piste. 'What if we're looking at this the wrong way round?'

'What do you mean?'

'How much is a gun these days? A clean one, I mean?'

New. Unused.

'I dunno. I'd say a fair few grand, at least.'

'Must cost a lot to get it through customs, no? And then there's the risk the procurer carries.'

Unless it's already in the country, but I get what he means.

'Spit it out, it's been a long day.'

'Well, let's say Geraint wasn't being blackmailed and didn't withdraw ten thousand pounds to pay someone, what if he planned to use the money to *buy something*.'

'We've no evidence Geraint was into anything shady.'

'No, we don't. But he dealt with a lot of shady characters. And we know he was being followed. It's not a huge leap to imagine he intended to buy the gun for protection and that whoever he was meeting on the island to purchase it from instead turned it on him.'

He has a point. The on-scene pathologist stated in her preliminary report that Geraint's body was covered in what she termed 'post-mortem abrasions' but there may have been some pre-mortem cuts and bruises from a scuffle prior to his death.

'I'm attending the autopsy in the morning, so we'll be able to determine then whether Geraint fought with anyone before he was shot.'

PS TOMOS

PRESENT

The sky is indigo-grey when I leave the building, and sleet falls down the back of my coat as I skip inelegantly over puddles of sludgy mud that fill the dips in the tarmac on the way to my car. The drive from Cwmbran CID to Newport takes ten minutes longer as they've closed part of the A48 for road repairs. I arrive home just off the Southern Distributor Road, known locally as the SDR, to find our neighbour's car parked so close to our driveway that I narrowly miss scratching their rear bumper with my front one. The path is slick with clumps of wet moss that birds have flicked out of the guttering and onto the concrete, so I have to avoid slipping on it as I tread down the path to the front door where the sound of gruff barking from next door's dog greets me.

    I enter the house to a warning look from Sarah, who glances down at the mat indicating for me to wipe my feet before proceeding into the house, as she crosses the tiled floor of the kitchen past the doorway.

    'Chris not here yet?'

    It's a rhetorical question because if he was, we'd have definitely heard him.

    She stops what she's doing to glance at the digital

clock on the cooker. 'He's late,' she says, narrowing her eyes in thought.

I remove my shoes, replace them with the slippers she bought me for my birthday (vegan suede and organically procured lambswool), hang my coat on the hook, dump my phone on the dining table, and follow the scent of cooked food until I'm standing over the oven hob.

'Need a hand?'

'Nope. Just sit your arse down,' Sarah replies.

I take a seat at the table, and she plonks a glass onto the coaster in front of me, a fresh-from-the-fridge bottle of Mexican beer beside it, and then turns to retrieve the bottle opener from the drawer.

I widen my eyes. 'Special occasion?'

She raises her elbow and jabs me lightly in the hip as I pull out a chair to sit.

'Want some garlic bread?' Sarah asks, handing me the foil plate.

I take two slices and dip them into the tomato sauce that's sitting on top of the spaghetti on my plate, blow on them and take a huge bite of both, just as my phone buzzes from the centre of the table.

Sarah rolls her eyes but doesn't say anything as she places a bowl of tangy grated cheddar in front of me.

She's a good 'n. Never complains about the early mornings or disturbed nights, just gets on with it. I wish I had half her patience.

I see the caller's name lit up on the screen before answering.

'Chris? How's it going?'

'Dad!?'

He sounds pained. A jolt of fear grips me by the throat as I stand on instinct to rush to whatever emergency is awaiting me, knocking over the crisp, cool pint of beer Sarah's just poured me.

'What's wrong?'
'It's Eva.'
His girlfriend.
'She's . . .' His voice breaks.
I dread to hear his reply, but I have to ask. 'What's happened?'
'She's gone.'
'What do you mean, *gone*?'
'Missing. The police were here. They said she hasn't been home.'
'Call her parents.'
'I have. I just spoke to her mum. Nobody's seen or heard from her since she left here this morning.'
'What time was that?'
'Early hours. About one, two o'clock?'
'You don't know?'
'I can't be sure, I was drinking. We *all* were.'
I sense some hostility.
'I was nineteen once, ya know. I'm not suggesting you can't get pissed-up on a Friday night. How did she get home?'
'She walked.'
'On her own?'
'It's what, three hundred yards max from one end of Halls to the other.'
'I'm not criticising you. Women should be allowed to walk anywhere on their own, day or night, and not have to worry about their personal safety.'
'I should have walked her back to her room.'
'It's not your fault.' I continue. 'So she was on the university's grounds, and as far as you're aware there's no reason for her to have left?'
'No.'
'How did you find out she was missing?'
'Gen called Eva's mum at around three, four o'clock this morning to tell her she hadn't returned after

leaving my room. Her mum rang the police. They checked in with Millie, but she was with Tarquin last night. Gen was with Lucas, Sparrow, and Amelia in some nightclub in town.'

'Had Eva been drinking?'

'Of course, she was.'

'How did she seem to you?'

'She wasn't drunk if that's what you're insinuating. Tipsy maybe.'

'Was she on her phone while she was with you?'

'She wasn't planning to meet anyone, Dad.'

'There are security lights and CCTV all over the building. The police will be able to get some idea of where she went from the footage. If she left the area there'll be cameras on the high street. The campus is central so someone in the city is bound to have seen her.'

'I should have kept my phone charged. She always sends me a text to let me know she's made it back home alright, but I lost my charger, my battery died, and I forgot to check it until this morning.'

'You're not to blame.'

'What if the police think I am?'

KERRY-ANN

PAST

I made cheese toasties, nibbling at them as I sipped a sweet, dry white. I wasn't a big drinker, but occasionally liked to drink a glass of wine while I watched a film. I couldn't concentrate on the plot though, there were far too many characters, and I couldn't remember their relationships with each other, so I switched it off and returned to *The Nighthawk*, which I was now midway through reading.

The book described the killer's childhood, how his upbringing may have contributed to his warped beliefs and lack of morals. He'd been abused.

Had his experiences led him to commit such despicable acts of cruelty against the female sex?

I shivered.

There was a draught.

I straightened my spine and flexed my muscles as I walked across the room to turn the dial up on the thermostat.

Those poor women whom the Nighthawk had captured and imprisoned for his own depraved sexual urges weren't given the luxury. They were bound naked inside a cattle shed for months.

DI LOCKE

PRESENT

The house is surprisingly quiet by the time I get home, carrying two shopping bags filled with supermarket produce I grabbed and threw into the basket on my way round the aisles. I'm not entirely sure if any of it will go together but I was craving cheese and chocolate and so my stomach led my movements all the way to the till.

'Where are the boys?'

It's not yet 8 p.m.

'Bed,' he replies. Then, lowering his voice he adds, 'Which is where I plan on getting you very soon.'

He grabs me by the waist and pulls me towards him, so that I can feel his erection digging into my thigh. I tilt my head back against his chest, turn to face him, and raise my chin, allowing him to devour my mouth.

He pulls away at the sound of a screech of happiness.

'Later. They're still awake.'

'You're letting them play games on the console?'

'It seemed like a good incentive.'

Bargaining tool more like.

I don't criticise his parenting. I know they can be a

handful *and* how tempting it is to just let them stare at a screen for an hour to get some peace, but I'd put my foot down if it started to become a habit.

He scurries off to the kitchen, returning a minute later with a warm plate of vegetable lasagna while I'm hefting off my shoes and flexing my toes to reignite the circulation lost sitting opposite DCI Evans for the final hour of my shift trying to convince my superior additional expenses are necessary for us to locate our unsub and within budget while clicking 'refresh' on the evidence database.

I eat while Johnno unpacks the shopping, voicing aloud each item as he puts it away. 'Double chocolate fudge cake . . . olives . . . farmhouse cheddar . . . crusty white bread . . . chicken nuggets . . . French fries . . . strawberry iced doughnuts . . .'

The second my backside lands on the sofa Johnno's hands are on my shoulders, squeezing them. I lean back as he kneads away the tension that's been building in my muscles since I arrived at the scene of the crime this morning.

Was it really only eleven hours ago?

My eyes almost roll back in my head as I relax into his embrace. 'Mmm, you should have been a masseuse.'

'I prefer telling stories,' Johnno says. Which makes sense because he's a journalist.

'Talking of which, it's your turn to read to Ethan and tuck Jaxon in.'

He growls like a tiger as if the effort is too much for him, but then lowering his voice to a whisper says, 'Sure, but I'd rather be tucking *you* into bed.'

Ethan's not adjusting well to not having his dad – his one single constant – around, so has latched onto me like a limpet to a rock, so I'm trying to get him used to spending time with another man who does not share his DNA.

Ethan's bedtime routine requires a bath and a few chapters of a story book, whereas Jaxon goes down better without either. Thank God they both sleep with night lights on because I don't know what I'd do if they had to have their own bedrooms. We can't afford to move.

It's almost 9 p.m. by the time Johnno treads down the stairs, the boys having settled down. He finds me curled up on the sofa in my pyjamas flicking through TV channels for something to stream. He likes to watch crime dramas; I prefer to leave work where it belongs. We agree on a mockumentary, but he falls asleep with my head resting on his chest within ten minutes of clicking *play*. A blanket covering our legs to keep out the chill that's crept under the doorway and into the living room, which I leave stealthily, creeping down the hall and into the kitchen to boil the kettle to pour myself a coffee. I'm a night owl so it's unlikely to turn midnight before I wake my husband and we head upstairs to the warmth of our king-size, so the caffeine won't matter.

A PNC check by South Wales Police brought nothing up on Geraint when he was a missing person except the usual: his full legal name, address, the names on the deed reported by land registry, his wife's name, and the fact neither of them have been charged for having committed a criminal offence. Neither did anything interesting about his friends and family turn up either.

His wife was the obvious suspect, having been the last person to have seen him until CCTV footage proved he'd been alive and well shortly after leaving the family home to return to his own flat. Inside, police found empty pill packets and a stack of money, suggesting he'd swallowed the tablets and withdrawn enough cash to cover the cost of his funeral.

But once his body had been discovered and the fact that he'd been murdered in what appeared to have been a hit became apparent, we had to consider the possibility that his work on the frontline of criminal law might have had something to do with his death. We had to look closely at those recent cases lost and won, the families left behind after a loved one had been killed or locked up.

A simple Google search had produced little in the way of evidential value but what DS Llyons discovered concerning Ffion Townsend was interesting.

I didn't get a chance to read the news article he updated HOLMES 2 with before I left CID, but I find it easily online now that I know what I'm looking for.

South Wales News, *August 29, 2022*
Written by Ffion Townsend

LOCAL-BORN FOOTBALLER ON TRIAL FOR RAPE

The trial of local-born footballer, Oscar Goldsborough, 36, of Porthkerry, begins today at Cardiff Crown Court. Oscar is charged with the rape of a woman he met in a nightclub in celebration of scoring the winning goal of the championship during a match against a rival team that led his own to the premier league.

Oscar is the son of the late renowned psychiatrist and former Head of Women's Mental Health Services of Wotton Dean Psychiatric Hospital, Geoffrey Goldsborough, who was murdered in 1995 by his groundsman, Roderick Penrose.

PS TOMOS

PRESENT

I read the text message Emma sent me as I lie in bed unable to sleep, because my youngest son's girlfriend has gone AWOL and he's the last person to have seen her alive which makes him – for now at least – suspect numero uno.

I shift the duvet slowly and climb out of bed, stepping over the creaky floorboard, believing I've made it onto the landing without waking Sarah, only realising I haven't when she croaks, 'Try not to stay up past midnight. You know how tiredness can set off the flashbacks.'

Aside from the therapist I consulted for two straight years immediately after my discharge, Sarah is the only one who knows the impact my time spent working for the Special Air Service has had on my mental health. And I intend to keep it that way. But even to this day she thinks I was a covert surveillance operative and has no idea what I actually did. I signed a declaration when I joined that forbid me to speak about my job and although it's been many years since I was given my orders to leave, I continue to take my promise to protect the country seriously enough not to.

I head into the kitchen to boil the kettle, and two minutes later I'm slurping a steaming hot, sweet sugary tea as I read the comments section of the second online article relating to the trial of Oscar Goldsborough, that was published by *South Wales News* on October 6, when the judge decided the premier league footballer couldn't be tried, after the defence successfully submitted a 'no case to answer' application, resulting in the case being dismissed.

@Tallulah76 (Tue, 9.01 a.m.)
Like father like son.

@MarkeyBoi (Tue, 10.08 a.m.)
What do you mean?

@Tallulah76 (Tue, 11.06 a.m.)
https://www.Facebook.com/Groups/SilentNoMore:TheVictimsOfWottonDean

I log in to Facebook using one of my many alias accounts, which come in handy for most investigations, and type the name of the Facebook Group into the search bar. It's been made public, which makes my job much easier; I don't have to infiltrate the group to find out what the allegations are. There are a lot of accusers. All women. Including one by the name of Ronnie Sykes. Who just happens to be the administrator.

I notice the time on my phone and make a mental note to follow up on the lead in the morning once I've had some shuteye. If I manage any at all that is.

It shouldn't be difficult to find the woman who started the campaign against the man they're accusing of having abused the trust of vulnerable female patients while they were under his care.

KERRY-ANN

PAST

With nothing else to do to occupy my time and my eyelids growing heavy with the weight of the words I was absorbing I closed the book and put it down then trod along the hall and grabbed the vacuum to suck up all the sand from inside the roller case.

Next, I began rooting through my wardrobe in search of things to pack. I folded my clothes into neat piles and stacked them inside the case next to my slippers and toiletry bag.

I was sat on it, trying to zip it shut when I heard the clacking of heels alongside the house, followed by the sound of Natalia struggling to fit the key in the lock and turn it.

I reached the front door in time to catch her before she face-planted the floor, steered her up the stairs, and tucked her up beside me with a blanket.

She hooked her arms round my neck and kissed me. Her lips were sticky, and she tasted of cigarettes and Bacardi.

I lay on my back staring at the ceiling, twisting my grandmother's sapphire ring around my finger. She'd given it to me long before I was old enough for it to fit.

She survived three years a widow, that was long

enough for her. It was a stroke that killed her, causing irreparable damage to her cerebellum, the part of her brain responsible for regulating her heartrate and blood pressure. She'd never regained consciousness.

Her death was as sudden as my grandfather's; I hadn't got to say goodbye to either of them.

I'd rung her every day after I'd left home, and right up until she was buried – *if you cremate me, I'll haunt you*,' she'd said jokingly, often enough that I knew she meant it.

The last time I boiled the kettle and picked up the phone to call her at our usual pre-arranged time, remembering the landline had been cut off only when I'd gone to tap in her number, I sat and cried. A wave of realisation washed over me; Irene had been my last living relative, and with her gone, I was now on my own.

I think that's why I'd invited Natalia to move in with me.

I turned to face the back of her head nestled snugly against the pillow that bore the faint scent of the coconut and lime shampoo she wore. I closed my eyes and tried to block out the noise of her snoring, but I was jolted awake without feeling as if I'd slept by her clumsy attempt to climb back into bed carrying a glass of water as a bird began its dawn chorus in front of the bedroom window.

A moment later, an elbow jabbed me in the ribs, and I turned in time to find Natalia about to headbutt the nightstand as she tried to claw the quilt up to her chin.

I snaked my arm around her waist and pulled her towards me. She sighed in contentment and burrowed her face into my neck, her breath hot on my skin.

Her bare leg slid between mine, and I bit my lip to stop myself from gasping aloud as her hand drifted down to my thigh.

I wanted nothing more than to glide her tight vest-top over her head and to peel her lace-edged cotton knickers down past the swell of her buttocks, but she seemed to be comfortable enough spooned against me.

I gave up on the idea of sleep when my phone lit up with a notification.

I read the text message as I slipped from Natalia's embrace, closed the bedroom door behind me, and headed downstairs.

> Bang on the living room window if I don't answer your knock, in case I'm having a nap when you arrive.

I'd be taking mid-afternoon catnaps too if I got up as early as she did every morning.

I tapped out a reply as I dropped a pod into the coffee machine.

It was 6 a.m. when I settled down in front of the morning news; muted and with the subtitles on to avoid waking Sleeping Beauty.

Shiloh purred, stretched, then hopped onto my lap, before curling into a ball, and falling asleep.

The espresso I'd slammed back hit me just as Natalia appeared at the bottom of the staircase.

'G' morning, blue eyes.'

She yawned and nodded at the roller case parked beside the front door. 'What time are you planning to hit the road?'

'Before rush hour.'

'I'm gonna miss you.'

'Not as much as I'm going to miss you.'

DAY TWO OF THE INVESTIGATION

DI LOCKE

PRESENT

I open one of the double doors of the Edwardian building that contains the mortuary attached to Cardiff University's Institute of Forensic Medicine and DC Banks steps aside, allowing me to enter ahead of him.

The artistically styled frontage bearing the year of completion is however, inside, sleekly designed with modern décor. The white-painted walls and wide windows overlooking the car park give the place a light and airy feel.

At the end of the corridor is an open-plan, forensic laboratory. The coroner greets us from behind his desk partitioned off to create an office space. His computer monitor sits upon it, sidelong, allowing me to see the coat of arms that's being used as a screensaver; regal and denoting authority. Six doors extend from the corridor into rooms, one of which houses deceased Forty-eight-year-old Geraint Fford. Which is where we're shown after our introductions.

DC Banks takes a seat beside the filing cabinet, and I notice, out of sight of Geraint's torso when Dr Parekh stands in front of him.

The pathologist is preparing to assess the body that

is swollen and discoloured and lying on the steel gurney inside a black watertight bag, which he unzips with care and consideration. His assistant takes notes as he informs the audio-recording device of his every action.

'What the on-site pathologist initially thought during her in-situ examination were post-mortem abrasions "typically associated with a body impacting rocky debris in the sea" appear to me to be pre-mortem scars that include a recent cut on the left wrist, which may be self-inflicted.'

Dr Parekh retains the same level of concentration by the end as at the start of the two-hour-long process. Having removed and weighed the organs, withdrawn blood for toxicology tests, swabbed the inside of the deceased's cheek for saliva and taken prints of his fingertips, he ends the procedure by thanking Geraint for his time as though he is a patient undergoing a minor operation, while sewing up the Y-shaped incision that extends from his waist to his chest.

The skin cell fragments, saliva, and fingerprints taken from Geraint will be compared to the DNA extracted from the items police seized during the search of his flat, which include an eighteen-pronged plastic tortoiseshell comb, a blue Oral-B electric toothbrush, a half-full glass of water, and a sage green pillowcase, in order to officially confirm his identity. A legal formality that must occur as well as a dental match by a forensic odontologist.

With the obligations out of the way, however, Dr Parekh asks me to catch him up on the outcome of the last autopsy I attended here with him present, just a fortnight ago.

'There's going to be an inquiry into the deaths of three more people who've overdosed on heroin laced with fentanyl within the last month.'

He didn't complete their autopsies, so wouldn't have known about the others otherwise.

'All in Newport?' he asks.

'Yeah. We think they sourced it there too.'

He nods. 'Whoever is putting it on the streets is indirectly responsible for four deaths.'

'I wish we could do them for manslaughter,' I affirm.

'The drug squad can charge them for drug offences though,' Dr Parekh says.

'If they find them,' DC Banks replies, unable to disguise his pessimistic sigh.

We leave Dr Parekh who is about to begin his assessment of the body of a refugee who'd been put up in a Travelodge where she'd passed away in her sleep before her starving dog, who'd remained by her side, whining too quietly for anyone to hear, mauled her corpse. A member of the housekeeping staff found their female guest during their routine weekly clean.

I can only imagine the horror they must have felt walking in on *that*.

PS TOMOS

PRESENT

DC Banks shuffles over and slumps into his chair to my right looking paler than usual and with a wheeze suggestive of a twenty-a-day smoking habit, though I've never seen him with a cigarette. While DC Bishop hurries towards the water dispenser and fills a plastic cup which he downs in seconds, gasping and wiping his mouth with the back of his hand as he heads in my direction. He lands on the chair to my left with a thud.

The incident room smells of spicy tomato cuppa-soup and coffee. I slurp the hot sugary tea from my paper cup as Emma enters the room and perches herself onto the edge of the desk nearest the door, clapping her hands to get our attention.

'Let's have a catch-up, see where we're all at,' she says, pausing to swallow a mouthful of the cappuccino I know she's filled her refillable lidded cup with.

Emma starts by telling us what the pathologist uncovered during the autopsy, the report of which is yet to be added to the database. 'The abrasions Geraint sustained were acquired before his death and appear to be self-inflicted. Now while this goes some way in aiding our understanding of Geraint's state of mind at the time of his disappearance it also serves to demonstrate a possible motive for Geraint wanting to pursue his investigation into Wotton Dean. At least if we consider what Liam told us about Geraint's poor relationship with his stepfather, his refusal to defend cases involving child abuse, and what PC Coulter learned from Geraint's mum.' She indicates for him to take over.

'But isn't there some ethical boundary Geraint crossed, having previously been on the defence team for the man who killed the psychiatrist who was working at the psychiatric hospital?' I ask.

'Probably. Though that's not our problem,' she replies, not seemingly bothered by my interjection.

PC Coulter speaks with a deep baritone voice. 'If there was animosity between Geraint and his stepfather, and he self-harmed, it's not a giant leap to assume the two correlate, especially when Lorraine told me he was a bit of a bully in and out of the ring, always trying to "toughen Geraint up, get him to spar with him". Even dragging him to the local amateur boxing club despite him having never taken an interest in the sport. Though that wasn't the reason she kicked Geraint's stepdad out of the house. Apparently, he had some unsavoury friends. One of whom was a regular visitor to the house until he was caught grooming a boy online by Paedo-Hunters. It was for beating the man up that his stepfather was imprisoned. We don't know if anything happened between him and Geraint, but we do know he was around when Geraint was small, so it's probable. I was able to confirm that the man was given a suspended sentence – first offence – for obtaining indecent images of children on the laptop police confiscated and black-boxed as a result of the citizen's arrest made by the bloke whose online persona is The Spider. Presumably as he catches predators on the web. Unfortunately, The Spider filmed the confrontation and uploaded it to TikTok, which resulted in him being arrested for obstructing an ongoing investigation . . .' He leaves his words hanging, allowing us to digest them.

I'm all for members of the public assisting us but there are ways and means of doing it that don't impede our investigations.

Emma cuts through the uncomfortable silence by updating us on what PC Meyer was able to ascertain from DC Burtenshaw, who is acting as the FLO and has spent every day with Demelza and the girls since Geraint was reported missing. 'She confirmed at least one of our theories. Demelza admitted to thinking her husband was being unfaithful.'

She indicates for PC Meyer to describe her findings, who says, 'Demelza broke down and told the FLO that she'd gone through Geraint's phone and found some, what she believed were compromising text messages, between him and another woman arranging to meet out of town.'

Two of the PCs seated at the far end of the room ask simultaneously: 'Who was this woman?' and 'Have we seen those messages?'

'She went by the name of Jules, according to Demelza,' PC Meyer replies. 'And no. Demelza threw the phone across the room in a rage. He heard her screaming and walked into the room to find his phone smashed on the floor. They had a blazing row by all accounts. He accused her of being paranoid and snooping, she alleged he was trying to gaslight her. She reckons the incident was the catalyst for their break-up. He swapped SD cards over when she replaced his phone, and he dropped the broken one off to one of those recycling bins. And of course, Geraint had the new one on his person, so it likely went into the sea with him, hence why we haven't been able to locate it since the day he went missing. Which according to the pathologist is the day he died.'

'Which one?' one of the civilian administrators asks from her chair next to the filing cabinet. 'Recycling bin I mean?'

'Tesco, I think she said,' PC Meyer replies. 'Why?'

'Text messages are saved to individual phones not memory cards,' she replies.

I retrieve my Samsung from the pocket of my trousers and google phone + recycling + Penarth. The superstore Geraint visited on the 1st of November, according to his bank statement, is listed at the top of the search results. 'Terra Nova Way.'

'Those places don't collect until they have a full bin,' DC Winters says.

'Which means it could be there for months,' DC Chapman adds.

'So who wants to go down there and have a look-see?' Emma asks between a lengthy gulp of her drink.

PC Meyer volunteers to do the deed.

We hear from the intelligence team who've been sifting through the eyewitness accounts that have been trickling in since we released a picture of the blonde woman to the public. Several people have contacted us via social media claiming to have recognised her based on her likeness to 'so-and-so across the street' or 'that Karen who's always complaining about the neighbours' or that 'Council Estate Queen who's often found yelling at her kids in the park' but our prospect of identifying her is looking about as good as the exposure from the image we captured, if that's all we have to rely on.

We move onto DC Winters then, who has spoken to Caz, and who, having been informed of his murder was far more inclined to discuss why she was in regular contact with Geraint. 'She claims to have been seeking legal counsel from him because she intended to sue Wotton Dean. Though we'll have to deduce why ourselves as she wouldn't tell me. But if we consider the hostile reception DC Banks got from the psychiatric hospital when he went to speak to the current managing director of adult services . . . well, perhaps it'll be better if he told you himself.'

DC Banks turns in his chair to address the room. 'He called a lawyer while I was there and "no commented" every question I asked as if he was being interrogated".'

'What has he got to hide?' DC Bishop asks.

'Exactly,' DC Chapman replies.

'I think it's fair to say that whatever it is has something to do with Geoffrey Goldsborough,' I add.

'I'm assuming you've all read the information that PS Tomos updated HOLMES 2 with this morning?' Emma asks.

Everyone responds with a nod or a 'yes', a 'yeah', or a 'yep'.

'Well, to explain how we got there I'll hand you over to him,' Emma says.

I lean back in my chair and cross one foot over the other before I begin. 'Ffion Townsend is a journalist working as a crime reporter for *South Wales News*. We know Geraint checked out her LinkedIn profile using his personal laptop, and that he drove to Bridgend on the eleventh of November thanks to the receipt for fuel we found in his car, which he bought from a garage on route using his debit card. And, he not only typed in her address, but according to the history on his Satnav, it notified him of an alternative route to take due to roadworks midway, so it appears he at least left the fuel station heading in the direction of her property. But what we don't know is why. She wasn't home when DS Lyons went to speak to her to ask her what they discussed when Geraint travelled there, but he didn't waste any time in looking her up when he found that she wasn't in, and it turns out that in April of this year she wrote an article about the trial of Geoffrey's son, Oscar, who was recently charged for rape. The case was dropped by the CPS due to insufficient evidence because the woman chose not to testify in court and without her testimony there is no case for him to answer. Which of course has no bearing on whether he's innocent. But beneath the article I read last night I saw some comments, one of which contained a link to a Facebook Group titled: Silent No More, dedicated to "The Victims of Wotton Dean". Which got me thinking. What if Caz, and perhaps Lottie, aren't the only ones alleging to have been abused at the hospital. So I took a gander and found that the group was viewable to the public.'

'Providing you have a Facebook account,' Jonesy comments.

'It's private and has been authorised by the boss,' I respond quickly so as not to lose my train of thought.

'There are sixteen women in all, of various ages and physical characteristics, openly accusing Wotton Dean of "indirectly aiding and abetting their mistreatment by covering it up and then silencing them". And though their accusations range in severity they all concern their inpatient stays during Geoffrey Goldsborough's tenure. Though none of them name the individual(s) to whom their complaints concern, possibly due to advice not to libel themselves, which if they were consulting a lawyer they may have been warned not to do. The information they've provided, however, is disturbing. They mention bed restraints, cold baths, enforced Electro-Convulsive Therapy, and being locked in what they describe as "blackout cells" as part of a "reign of terror" used "solely against female patients as part of the psychiatrist's (singular) experiments"'

'It sounds like something from the Victorian era,' PC Coulter says.

'Isn't it possible there were other staff members involved?' DS Lyons asks.

'Absolutely,' PC Meyer replies. 'I mean they haven't named anyone.'

'Don't you think the women consulted the same lawyer as a collective?'

Emma nods, then says to me, 'Can you list those names from that Facebook Group? We'll need to speak to them all. One of them might be the blonde woman.'

DS Lyons cuts in then. 'When you examine what DCs Chapman and Bishop found out regarding the grand a month Doctor's Aboard started paying the WCCIF from the moment Geoffrey returned to UK soil, it doesn't take a genius to put two and two together and figure that something happened in Ghana that neither organisation wanted anyone to know about. And, given the information we've gathered concerning the isolation rooms and ECT, I think it's reasonable to suspect it involved some form of physical harm.'

Emma opens her mouth to speak but closes it again the moment Jonesy says, 'I agree.'

'Maybe that's where he began practising his so-called "experimental treatments",' DC Bishop says.

Emma appears to want to say something but then seems to think better of it and sits back and folds her arms.

'Success can only be achieved through failure,' DC Banks wheezes.

I've noticed his staggered breath today and I don't like the sound of it. I make a mental note to check in with him when this is over.

'Honing his skills through trial and error, you mean?' Chapman asks.

'So . . . something went wrong, someone got hurt, and it was serious enough to cause a company worth millions to pay a foreign charity to keep quiet about it, for what, twenty-six years!?' DC Winters exclaims.

'I doubt there's any way we'll find out who or what it involved if there's a gagging order in place,' DS Lyons says.

Emma's eyes skate from person to person looking smug.

'You think Doctor's Aboard would have been plugging the charity with money all this time if there was?' Emma says, with a twinkle in her eye.

'Well, now you put it like that,' DS Lyons replies.

'With respect boss, what do you suggest we do to get it out of them?' Jonesy asks.

'It hit me when I learned how Geraint's stepfather's mate was exposed,' Emma replies.

'Praise be to the power of the internet,' one of the digital forensic technicians says.

'You think like the Victims of Wotton Dean there might be a thread in some discussion forum somewhere containing the testimony of a Ghanian woman who was harmed by Geoffrey Goldsborough during his voluntary placement?' a PC who is usually mouse-quiet asks from the back row.

'No, I don't,' Emma replies confidently. 'Because she died.'

There is a collective silence that fills the room like an ice blast, which Emma quickly fills by introducing us to a man named Kojo who she's had on standby and who waves at us from the screen of her phone, before she links it up to the TV.

We greet him then we listen intently as he explains who he is and his connection to the woman who died of brain damage. Something the woman's husband holds 'Mr Gold' responsible for.

Had Geoffrey Goldsborough shortened his surname to avoid detection by the UK authorities? Or was the moniker given him by the man because he couldn't pronounce his name in full?

'Merci was expecting a baby. Contraception here is expensive and in West African culture birth control is still viewed as immoral. She had experienced low moods throughout the pregnancy. The infant died shortly after he'd been born. She became sad and was unable to care for her other children. She was already receiving weekly food parcels from the charity to help feed her family when they offered to provide her with pastoral support. Mr Gold was working there at the time, as a counsellor. His methods were not unusual. Talking therapies had been used for a few years then and he was very skilled at getting people to open up. Merci appeared to be recovering.'

Kojo goes on to tell us that Geoffrey Goldsborough prescribed medication – antidepressants – which her husband made it clear he didn't want her to take. 'He refused to collect them from the pharmacy or hid them so she'd go days without them, and her behaviour would fluctuate between calm and elated. One day she felt admired and believed herself to be a voodoo priestess, the next she refused to eat, claiming her husband was poisoning her. It was that kind of irrational thinking which led to the accident.'

One morning Merci's husband awoke to find her side of the bed empty. His sister watched over their children while he searched for his wife. He found her in bushland miles from their home, delirious with a fever. A nurse from a neighbouring village came to her aid and diagnosed Typhoid.

'Her psychological symptoms had been misdiagnosed. The loss of appetite, elation, and confusion was due to damage to her central nervous system.'

She was driven home and treated with antibiotics but was left with permanent neurological complications due to the delay in medical care.

'Merci had been experiencing hallucinations and delusions prior to being medicated. But weeks later she had developed convulsions and was unable to sleep. Dr Gold insisted she take sleeping tablets and anti-epileptics, but her husband complained, and Mr Gold left.'

As her guardian Merci's husband was left to decide on her fate. Without the involvement of the psychiatrist or any need for charitable assistance he isolated his wife from outside influence, choosing instead to care for her in the only way he knew how.

'He sought the help of a religious leader, who prayed day and night over her bedside to restore Merci to the good health God had provided her with. But when this didn't work, he advised a local Chief who practised spirit exorcisms. It's not uncommon in Africa to blame medical complaints on witchcraft.'

My stomach does a backflip when I realise with a heavy sense of dread where this story is going. I want to tune out, but that wouldn't make me a very good cop, would it? Instead, I remain seated, listening to Merci's tale of woe from none other than her brother.

Kojo goes on to explain how Merci – terrified into a seizure was exorcised of the demons that were thought to possess her – for hours, leaving her hungry and exhausted, which are two of the precursors known to exasperate convulsive episodes. The Chief ordered her husband not to let her sleep, stating that was when she was most vulnerable to spiritual attack.

'He gave him a wooden stick and told him to lightly tap her with it to rouse her if she closed her eyes.'

Did he beat his wife to death?

It's like a car crash. I want to look away but like the rest of my colleagues I'm in thrall by the sheer horror of this macabre story.

'A group of villagers heard screams. They followed the noise to a hut where they found Merci wild-eyed, making ungodly sounds, body contorting.'

He goes on to detail what I consider the very definition of a lynching.

'Merci's husband adored his wife and had strong Christian beliefs. He was left bloodied and bruised as he tried to stop the men and women from carrying his wife away. In the struggle she obtained a spinal injury.'

Paralysed from the waist down she became wheelchair dependent.

This really hits home.

'In a cruel twist Merci was now considered blessed. The villagers flocked to her to receive healing. A child, a girl of about ten years old, liked to push her in circles and sing gospels.'

The girl was hyperactive and would probably be diagnosed with ADHD if she'd been born in the Western hemisphere. She got carried away. Ran too fast and fell, and along with her Merci, chairbound.

'It severed her spinal cord and tore through her brainstem. Her death was instant.'

I look up the name Merci when we're done. It means tolerance. And I can't think of a word more fitting for a woman who tolerated so much. The loss of her child, and the psychological impact of such grief. The neurological impact of a disease that children in Africa are now routinely vaccinated against. The initial pain of her physical injury and the subsequent lack of function and feeling in her extremities that ultimately led to her sudden and violent death.

KERRY-ANN

PAST

There's no motorway in Cornwall, the M5 begins in Exeter, so I spent the first half of my trip traversing narrow winding roads before hitting the A30 from St. Agnes, a small fishing town that was once a tin mining village, on the coastline.

I stopped at a service station in Plymouth for a rest and something to eat, zipped through my emails as I slurped a vending machine coffee, hit the M4 from Bristol before lunchtime. And once over the Prince of Wales bridge, navigated my way along the A4106 to the Welsh coast, slowing outside the four-storey, stark-looking, white-painted building on the corner of Summerville Street, overlooking the ocean.

I parked close to the entrance and exited the vehicle. When I stepped outside, I was hit by the briny scent of the sea on the roaring wind. I stood for a moment staring out at the lapping waves caressing the soft sand. The only sound, apart from my feet treading the gritty slush covering the concrete, was the gulls squawking to one another as they hovered over the clifftops in search of food.

The two-hundred-and-twenty-mile drive to southern Porthcawl was uneventful. Though the four-hour journey to Wales had left me feeling so tired that now I was standing outside Alys' West Drive home I was starting to wish I'd postponed my initial visit to the following morning.

It took her a while to open the door, and I was pleasantly surprised to find that she had a full head of hair and wore makeup so perfect it was hard to imagine she had less than twelve weeks left to live. She smiled as she tugged on the collar of my full-length coat, telling me to get inside out of the cold.

'I'll put the kettle on while you get out of those clodhoppers you've got on your feet.'

I looked down at my shoes and saw for the first time what she meant. They were wide-soled and made my legs appear longer and thinner than they actually were.

'I expect you're exhausted from all that driving.'

'Not half.'

She pointed to a door at the far end of the hall on the opposite side of a downstairs toilet. With it being slightly ajar I was able to peek inside at the driftwood hung above a small sink, the wall behind it a rich warming turquoise. 'Make yourself at home. There's a blanket through there. I don't use that room much, so I had the chimney swept yesterday in preparation for your visit. I lit the fire this morning. It should have warmed up nicely by now.'

She moved quicker than I'd expected, but then despite the lines on her face she wasn't much older than my grandmother had been when she'd died. Her death punched me fresh in the stomach as it often did at the strangest of times.

I watched Alys retreat down some steps and into a kitchen that wasn't as well-lit as I'd have expected it to be considering the skylight that offered up a view of the white sky.

I pushed open the stiff wooden door and could immediately feel the heat. I circled the room first, scanning the odd array of ornaments dotted about on the surfaces of furniture that instantly reminded me of the objects I'd given to the charity shop when I'd cleared out my grandmother's house that the equity release company who owned it wanted back as soon as possible after her death, barely giving me enough time to grieve or organise a funeral, and forced me to accept the help of her neighbour to remove everything she and my grandfather had once shared.

I took a seat beside the bay window, on a paisley patterned chair that had arms and legs made of engraved wood. It looked like something that might have survived the 1930s, though I knew rather than having been post-war era the style was colonial and had been crafted in the 1970s.

I leaned forward to get a better look at a black and white photograph that was held in a plastic frame and situated on top of a burnished oak-style cabinet whose drawer handles were rectangular.

Alys appeared then, carrying a tray. As she placed two cups on saucers onto the top-most tiered coffee table – round and in need of a good polish with some beeswax to disguise the scrapes and scratches from years of use – I noticed how thick and shiny her hair was and how there was not a grey strand in sight.

'It's a wig,' she said, handing me a small plate of biscuits.'

I realised, as she stood, that I'd been gawping at her and blushed.

'Lost my hair months ago,' she said, 'in the first round of chemo. Had to have half my teeth removed beforehand too, to counter any chance of infection. It lowers the immune system, see.'

'I'm sorry.'

'Don't be, dear.' She waved me off as though swatting a fly. 'It was getting far too long to manage.'

'Well, I think you look fabulous.'

She winked at me, and asked, 'Shall we get started?'

I nodded and she clapped. Then, opening a drawer inside a tall pine cabinet, causing the little bone china figurines on one of the shelves inside it to tremble, she withdrew a folder which she handed to me. It was thick and filled with typewritten pages, yellowed with age.

'Righto. Now first off, you've read the published version of *The Nighthawk*, haven't you?'

Not all of it, not yet, but I intended to, just as soon as I got to the Airbnb.

'Yes,' I lied, feeling guilty as I did.

'There's no room for supposition in true crime, you've got to stick to the facts. But even with credible sources and diligent research there were things that didn't quite add up to me. Things that suggested the Nighthawk didn't act alone. My editors wouldn't touch the manuscript unless such claims were removed from the final copy, in case it interfered with any potential future police inquiry, but I found it hard to believe him capable of doing what he did to all those women without help.'

I indicated to the stack of paper. 'Is that the uncensored version?'

She tapped the folder. 'This is the original copy. From this you'll be able to fill in the blanks. Maybe even figure out who he is.'

Alys had barely finished her sentence before she toppled slightly, steadying herself with a flat bony palm on my knee.

'Are you okay?'

'I'm as well as I'll ever be.' She snickered.

She didn't seem at all bothered by the fact her life

had been shortened. And I didn't think to question why, at the time. Though in hindsight, I should have.

DI LOCKE

PRESENT

With no more Automatic Number Plate Recognition, Closed Circuit Television or Ring Doorbell camera footage to view I've allocated each constable to locate and speak to two of the women from the list Dafydd wrote up before he left the incident room to head on over to Southgate to speak to the journalist, Ffion Townsend. Which just leaves a few PCs back at nerve station to continue sifting through call logs and other background material that might be relevant, while being distracted by pointless intelligence gathered from the phone lines by fame-seekers, curtain-twitchers, and bored housewives.

    DS Lyons has managed to get hold of Liam, Geraint's senior partner, who has agreed to speak with him at the solicitor's office before he leaves to meet with the barrister representing one of his clients in court this afternoon. We need to know if defending in cases involving child abuse ever caused problems between him and Geraint. Because although South Wales Police touched upon the subject during his interview, what with Lorraine's recent disclosure about his stepdad's mate I think it'd be a good idea for someone to speak to him a second time, since the knowledge that Geraint was murdered might give Liam further reason to cooperate. I really find it hard to believe Geraint attended his wedding but that they're not 'especially close'.

Dylan is attending a midwifery appointment with his girlfriend.

Which leaves me here to hold the fort.

Speaking of which . . .

Everyone's read the case file on Geoffrey Goldsborough's murder, which occurred inside his sprawling property on Fort Road. But nobody has questioned his widow, Celyn, who sold the mansion and moved to Gloucestershire, shortly after her husband was killed.

Talking to the former owner of the grand estate is a box we have to tick. From what I've seen of her in the news that was broadcasted at the time of Roderick's trial, she's so petit I can't imagine her being physically capable of raising a gun nor I doubt does she have the skills to use one, or indeed know where to get hold of one, but we can't eliminate her from our enquiries until we know for sure where she was at the time of Geraint's disappearance. Because Roderick Penrose was due for release from prison last week, which she strongly opposed at the parole hearing in the presence of the man who defended him. Which of course was successful and therefore gave her a very good reason for wanting him dead.

PS TOMOS

PRESENT

I exit the building ahead of DC Banks, who is halfway down the corridor. I slow my pace so he can catch up with me. I can see that his brow is dotted with sweat.

'You alright? You look a bit pale?'

He waves off my concern then stops to catch his breath. I don't push it, though all sorts of scenarios are scrambling around inside my skull.

My phone shrills as I catch sight of one of the constables that I vaguely recognise from the drugs squad upstairs. I watch him get behind the wheel of his car, reverse out of the space and turn onto the road as I press my phone to my ear.

'Dad?'

I stop in my tracks.

'Yes, Chris. What's happening?'

'I need a lawyer.'

'Where are you?'

'Newport.'

The central custody suite. Where until just a fortnight ago I'd been working for the last twenty-odd years.

I'm behind DC Banks when he stumbles on the step leading away from the automatic doors and onto the car park.

'What have they charged you with?'

He sobs.

'Chris?'

'Murder.'

It hits me like a punch to the stomach.

'Don't talk to anyone until your lawyer gets there.'

I drop my phone back into my pocket and hurry towards my car so that DC Banks is just a few feet away from me when he tilts sideways, allowing me to catch him before he hits the ground when he falls.

KERRY-ANN

PAST

I'd been under the impression my goal was to write about the life of the author who'd written of a crime in which the perpetrator had been apprehended, not delve into the evidence suggesting he had an accomplice who'd got away scot-free. No longer exhausted from travel, what Alys had told me had left me feeling energised. My mind was in a whirlwind when I trod down the path and onto the road to unlock my car, buoyed by coffee and sugar.

It was full dark now and along with the blizzard a mist had ascended from the channel, lowering my visibility as I reversed out of the parking space and turned a 180°.

This is how I die I thought, as I traversed the dual carriageway with only my fog lights glinting off the stark white snowdrifts lining the verges of the A4232 to light my way.

Every so often I hit a patch of newly formed ice and had to release the accelerator to allow the car to glide over it while repressing the urge to brake.

The snow that fell appeared to freeze almost the second it hit the windscreen, the wipers squeaking as they attempted to clear the glass. I'd so far managed to maintain control of the car, but I knew one turn of the steering wheel too quick, one patch of ice too wide to swerve and I'd lose it.

Against the backdrop of the news presenter discussing the discovery of the culprit responsible for several nearby home invasions and the continued investigation into the recent spate of stolen vehicles in the area a song from another station wove its way through the speakers.

I should have been seated on the couch beneath a blanket, sipping hot chocolate, my laptop on my thighs and my fingers tapping away at the keys, writing the introduction to Alys' memoir, but the inclement weather had thrown my self-imposed timescale completely out of whack. I'd held off leaving for as long as possible, waiting for the snow to subside, but it didn't seem to want to, and now it was coming down even harder than before.

The radio began to crackle.

It wasn't long before I passed the square of concrete where the abandoned Esso garage once stood, that was now being used as a HAND CAR WASH, according to the signage.

White noise replaced the radio presenter's voice that fell intermittently over broken music.

Here is where the Nighthawk abducted his first victim.

DI LOCKE

PRESENT

I make it halfway down the corridor to the tea caddy to top-up my caffeine and glucose levels before my phone shrills. I stare at the screen confused.

'PS Tomos?'

'Car park!'

I don't ask him why. The blunt way he greeted me tells me something is wrong. I swing round and head back towards the double fronted exit while Dafydd tells me what's happened.

'I'm fine,' DC Banks says, attempting to sit, as I hurry over to him, stuffing my phone back into my pocket, calf muscles aching from lack of use.

'You're not fine, you just collapsed,' Dafydd says.

'I fainted is all.'

'Well, I can't have you doing that in front of suspects,' I add.

'I'll be alright in a minute,' DC Banks replies.

'We'll see what the paramedics have to say.'

An ambulance arrives six minutes later. They give him a Covid test as a precaution. It's negative. We test ourselves every day, so I'm not surprised.

'138/88. Your heartrate is a bit high for my liking,' the paramedic says. She gives her colleague a nod and tells him to start the engine. 'And your blood oxygen level is a bit low. That'll explain why you fainted.'

I glance down at the oximeter she's pegged onto DC Banks' finger. It reads 92.

'Well, of course it is,' he says. 'I wake up on the ground surrounded by some of my colleagues to be told that I've passed out. And you're making me panic more with all this talk about hospitals. I hate those places. Full of sick people.'

'Well, you're going and I'm coming with to make sure you don't try and leg it the second they wheel you into there.'

'Charming, isn't she,' he says, sarcastically, gasping.

The paramedic taps him on the shoulder and says, 'You've got a good boss there.'

She doesn't give him the chance to reply. The second he opens his mouth to say something she's placed an oxygen mask over his face. It doesn't disguise his yelp though when she squeezes the pad of his thumb between two gloved fingers and pricks his skin, blotting the blood spot that forms with a device that checks his blood sugar levels.

'Low. When was the last time you ate?' she asks him.

'An hour ago.' His muffled voice steams up the mask.

She frowns. 'Looks like you're coming in with us.'

He goes to protest but Dafydd just shakes his head at him, and he huffs.

He catches me smirk as the other paramedic helps him up and escorts him into the back of the ambulance, where he's told to lie down on the trolly and keep still. I suspect it's so that she can test whether the lack of movement has any impact on the readings of the device still attached to his forefinger.

He doesn't notice I've joined him until the driver

has slid the door closed behind us. He turns towards me while I take a seat, and I notice the colour is starting to return to his face already.

I turn away while the medical assistant raises his polo-neck shirt to apply several paddles to his chest, to give him as much privacy as he can get in the small, enclosed space we're forced to share. I watch the monitor the ECG machine is linked up to blink on, then the zigzag line of his heartrate track along the screen. It doesn't appear to correlate with his pulse.

By the time we pull up outside the Accident and Emergency Department of The Grange, his cheeks have pinkened and he appears to have perked up. His blood pressure hasn't changed though, signalling that his heart might not be functioning properly.

***

The last time I was seated inside a hospital waiting room was just two months ago, where I learned the news that my childhood best friend – like so many of our peers – had slid into alcohol addiction, just as effortlessly. I'm practically perched on the edge of the hard-backed plastic chair when the doctor enters the communal area (no family room for me) to update me on DC Banks' condition, at his discretion.

'He said if I don't, you'll order food and get your husband to bring you in a blanket.'

I can't help but smile. 'What's the verdict then, doc?'

He sits opposite me and leans forward, resting his elbows on his knees. His stance worries me, but his blunt reply is oddly calming. 'Hypoglycaemia.'

'Diabetes?'

'Type Two. We need to get his blood sugar levels stable and his heartrate down before we can let him go. I hope this doesn't interfere in his job?'

'No. Gone are the days needing glasses to read or having a bit of arthritis prevents you from working in law enforcement.' But even as I'm saying this, I'm thinking how disappointed he'll be when he loses his firearms authorisation, what with him having recently completed his yearly retest.

'That's good to hear,' he says, turning his face and tapping his right ear to show me the barely visible, tiny, see-through hearing aid plugged into it.

'Nice one.'

'You're the first person who hasn't responded to my joke with an uncomfortable nod.'

'A gallows humour is a necessary component of the job.'

'Same ear,' he says.

And I can't help but smile.

'He's not going to be a happy chappie if he ends up on insulin.'

He gives me a questioning glance.

'His wife's diabetic, and he's always harping on at us about all the sweet treats he can't store in the house. His desk drawer is full of biscuits and cake. Everything he won't eat in front of her.'

'Mmm.'

'Yeah, I know. That's probably what caused it.'

I look over at the clock on the wall to check the time.

'I don't see any point in you hanging around. He's likely to be with us for the remainder of the day.'

I stand. 'Don't worry. I know when I'm not wanted.'

Though Dafydd should be in Southgate, talking to Ffion Towsend, I find him leaning against his car as I exit the hospital, phone in hand.

He looks across at me and slides his phone into the pocket of his trousers.

'What're you doing here?' I ask.

'Thought you might want a lift,' he replies.

'How'd you know I was going to be leaving now?' I ask.

I glance at the time on the screen of my Motorola and realise only forty minutes has passed. Which is certainly not long enough for him to have driven the sixty miles to and from Ffion Townsend's place.

'I followed the ambulance.'

'Why didn't you come inside?' I indicate the double doors of the hospital entrance.

'Had to make a call.'

'What's going on?'

'I'll tell you in the car.'

Before I make it towards the passenger door my phone pings with a text message from Sophie, Jaxon's biological mother, confirming that she'll be picking him up from the house at 4 p.m. to take him to the soft play centre in the trading estate, and promising to bring him home for 7 p.m.

Dafydd nudges my elbow and asks, 'Everything okay?'

'I'll tell you in the car.'

PS TOMOS

PRESENT

Emma tells me about her thoughts concerning Celyn and her intention to send someone to have a chat with her at home in Gloucestershire. And I agree. Roderick's agreed release from prison gives her a motive for wanting to kill the lawyer who was part of the legal team who advocated for his parole. 'But we have to consider other motives too. For example, whether it's possible Oscar was guilty of rape, as he wasn't exactly exonerated. I mean the trial was only a no-go due to the witness refusing to cooperate by retracting her statement, which is a mere technicality and so there may have been other victims, which could have been what Geraint intended to talk to Ffion about, and not, as we initially suspected, Geoffrey Goldsborough's alleged crimes at Wotton Dean. And if there *are* other women accusing Oscar of having raped them, Celyn had every reason to want to prevent Geraint blabbing and damaging the reputation of her own flesh and blood. And a gun to the head is a sure-fire way of doing that, if you'll pardon the pun.'

Emma nods, then says, 'We also know from the information that was gathered by South Wales Police around the time of Geoffrey Goldsborough's murder that he had friends in high places. Photocopied paperwork from inside the house that was reviewed to gather information about the family and their lifestyle showed us he was a member of the Freemasons, one of his golf buddies was a high-ranking police officer, another a judge. We can't dispute the possibility that had Celyn called in a favour from any one of them, either to silence someone or to prevent something already said from leaking, that they'd have done all they could to help her.'

I've still yet to speak to the journalist who wrote the article about Oscar, so I suggest we head to the sprawling mansion his mother bought with the sale of the Penrith estate after we visit Ffion, together, as we're already sharing a car.

Heading west towards the Brynglas tunnels as we exit Newport, I wonder aloud the knowledge of which crime came first.

'It doesn't really matter if Geraint was researching the allegations against Geoffrey Goldsborough and came across the article about his son while collating background or if the comments below it are what spurred him on to investigate Oscar's father, any threat to his sporting career gave him enough reason to kill Geraint.'

Which meant both Celyn and Oscar had motives to murder him.

Oscar has a water-tight alibi and as he was never remanded in custody, either after his initial arrest or before the date that had been set for the trial, his opportunity to obtain a contact from a cellmate to buy a gun from is nil. And there's no known association between Oscar and anyone on our radar who has any connection, even a loose one, to crime, organised or otherwise. Which lessens the possibility he put a contract out on Geraint's head. Though we can't dispute the fact he had the means to pay a killer for hire, what with him earning . . .

'What do professional footballers earn?'

'Before his arrest he was worth around thirty-five grand a year. But believe it or not, despite being arrested immediately after his team hit the big time, he's been getting paid the same as his teammates throughout his suspension, which according to Google is around sixty grand a week.'

'A week!?'

She nods, then says, 'I've dealt with cases involving hitmen who've killed for less than fifteen thousand pounds.'

Something about what she's said hits home, but I can't think why.

As she's 'dying' for a coffee I suggest we stop off for some pancakes that are advertised as being made from buttermilk on the road sign fronting an American-style diner midway between Port Talbot and Southgate, in Swansea. I gave her the lowdown on Chris' predicament in the car, but I didn't expand on it because she looked like she had something on her mind.

She told me about her stepson and his useless mother while I drove the long straight road, the snow tapping relentlessly against the bonnet and the flakes – growing larger and thicker by the minute – were swept off the windscreen by one wiper that staggered, and another that squealed in protest. I hate to say that about someone I don't know but the term in this instance seems fitting considering Sophie practically abandoned Jaxon as soon as he could walk.

I didn't try to convince Emma that he wouldn't hate her when he got older, or suggest she was worrying about nothing when she said she was concerned his mum might not bring Jaxon back after their first few hours alone together since the judge granted Sophie unsupervised access as per the order of CAFCASS. She knows as well as I do how common the occurrence is and what the ramifications are.

By the time we get to me and my problems Emma has slid the car into a space nearest the entrance of the diner, so we don't have far to walk.

'Out with it then,' Emma says, waiting for me to offload the moment the waitress has served us our order. 'What you told me about your son being implicated in the disappearance of his girlfriend isn't all of it, is it?'

I stare at the plate piled high with pancakes that sits between us, maple-syrup drizzled over the top so that it runs in rivulets down the sides and onto the fresh fruit framing them.

Sensing my hesitation, she plunges her fork into the soft stack and retrieves a mouthful from the bottom-most pancake, drawing my eyes towards her own. 'Start at the beginning.'

She retains an impassive expression as I tell her about my son's phone call earlier this morning, updating me on the investigation. But having now worked with her for several weeks, I know her hard exterior is a professional mask, and that underneath it there is a kind, caring, compassionate person with integrity and who is dedicated to solving crime. And I feel privileged to be one of the few people capable of penetrating the walls she's built up around herself.

'A student found Eva's body this morning in undergrowth bordering the university.'

'They think he killed her?'

'Chris was the last person to have seen her alive. The police found evidence she'd recently had sex with someone. They've got male DNA all over her.'

'No sign of sexual assault?' I flick a look of what-the-fuck at her, but she adds, 'In case her murder was sexually motivated.'

I've already considered this but hearing the information coming from her mouth makes me feel worse somehow.

'I don't know, they won't tell me, will they. Conflict of interest.'

'What else have they got?'

'CCTV footage puts them together shortly before the pathologist believes she was killed, and there are multiple eyewitnesses – fellow students – who claim they saw Chris entering Halls with her.'

If only someone had seen her leave, alone.

'So he was with her in his room that night?'

'Yeah,' I croak.

'Any idea when she left?'

'He says they were drinking, so he can't remember exactly, but reckons it was around midnight.'

'And there's nothing to back that up?'

'No.' I shake my head and sigh. 'He didn't do it.' I give her an imploring look, but she knows better than to accept my words as fact, and so do I.

'We'll have to report this to the Super.'

'I don't want to be thrown off this case. I haven't even been on secondment for a month!'

'You know the score. You have to disclose it if a close family member is placed under investigation for a crime.'

'I know.' I'm unable to disguise the defeat in my voice.

'This criminal defence lawyer who's representing him, is he any good?'

'I fucking hope so.'

KERRY-ANN

PAST

My journey to Swanbridge Bay was vastly different to the one narrated in Alys' book. She began writing it in the autumn, immediately after my father had been sentenced. In it she described the leaves falling from the oaks in hues of blood red and sunset gold. It had been so sticky that summer, according to Alys, that the wild grass sprouting around the trunks of the ash trees was brittle enough to turn to dust when trod on.

I turned off before Fort Road, so I didn't have to pass Penrith House.

It was a stifling afternoon, though it was not so bad as to cause a drought or lead to a hosepipe ban when Celyn returned from the book club hosted by one of her fellow members from that month's Women's Institute meeting to find herself a single parent. She found Geoffrey lying on his side atop the Persian rug fronting the fireplace, the poker used to end his life resting horizontal against the tiled hearth beside him, where it had been thrown after what police later described as a 'passionate frenzy'.

My father, by then of course, was long gone, his bloodied footprints leading down the grand hall to the front door.

I snaked the car along the single car-width dirt lane of West Drive towards the Airbnb.

By the time I reached the end of my increasingly perilous journey the snow had begun to thicken, landing fast and settling, leaving my tyres slicker against the tarmac.

I turned the radio off. Silence replaced the static.

I stopped the car at the end of the lane, parking sidelong to what turned out to be the rear gate.

Having spent half an hour inside the warm cabin, the cold snowflakes stung my face and hands the moment I got out. I carried my bags along the pitch-black footpath to the last house on the right. The ocean-facing cottage was exposed high up on the clifftop with no trees or shrubbery to shield it from the dry biting wind.

The sea was in a storm, the wind had begun to whip up the surf, but I'd made it to my beachfront abode – for about the next ninety days – safely.

Or so I thought.

DI LOCKE

PRESENT

Dafydd is trailing a few feet behind me. Every now and again he pauses mid-stride to view the steep slope down to the bay on our left, feet crunching through the thick snow. 'How long is this lane?' he pants.

I glance down at my phone. 'About another quarter of a mile according to Google Maps.'

He frowns.

I smile.

He wobbles as he attempts to hop over a rabbit warren and trips over his own foot.

I barely suppress a laugh when he skids several paces, almost landing on his arse.

'Are you sure we've got the right place?' he asks, righting himself. 'There's nothing here!'

I glance down at the red arrow on the map that fills the screen of my phone.

'Yes. It's just across from that field, past those trees.'

He sees where I'm pointing and rolls his eyes.

He's still moaning about having to leave the car on the road when we reach the gate to the footpath that leads us downhill to the converted shipping container.

There's a wooden sign on the drystone wall partitioning the homeowner's land from that which is owned by The National Trust that sates: Hunters Ridge. The wall is decorated with a string of solar-powered LED fairy lights that still glow faintly. Behind the property is a meadow that during the summer months is filled with bluebells and was used to film the scene of a romance that was popular in the nineties.

I looked the place up on Zoopla before we left the diner. Having never been to Southgate I wanted to know the geography of the land before we set off towards the little-known cove that's only a short drive from the tourist hotspot that is The Mumbles. The ruins of the castle that overlooks the marshes leading to the bay can be seen poking out of the earth several hundred feet below us.

The roof, made of corrugated sheeting, has six solar panels and a small wind turbine attached to it, which is spinning so fast that were I not staring at it so intensely, it would appear not to be moving at all.

The crack of bracken diverts my attention back to where Dafydd had been.

I follow his footfall and almost whack my jaw on his shoulder as I turn the corner. 'Fucking hell.'

'Sorry, boss,' he says. Then pausing to listen to something he mouths, 'Did you hear that?'

I nod and press on lightly.

He points to the door, the route to it clogged with brambles that fallen branches have nestled inside like nests, preventing access to the front of the property framed by an oak timbre wraparound porch.

I tread carefully round to the other side of the two-storey building where at the rear of the decking something stirs.

I glimpse the sway of a bough in my peripheral and stop and wait for further movement or the sound of a snapping twig but after a few beats nothing happens.

Aside from the sea breeze brushing against the tall

grass it's quiet here. Eerily so. Which is why when a man's voice cuts through the near silence, we both start.

'Can I help you?'

We jerk our heads north to the upstairs window he's peering down from.

'Aled Townsend?'

'Yes?'

I withdraw my ID card from beneath my coat that's buttoned to the neck, at the same time that Dafydd flashes the man his own.

'We'd like to speak to your wife.'

'She's out, foraging. She won't be long. There's a lot of wild herbs we can use out here.'

I nod in acknowledgement, not because I know a sprig of basil from a stinging nettle.

'You'd better come in. It's freezing out there.' Aled comes down the flight of eight steps from the mezzanine and directs us inside a quaint lounge. Everything from the blinds to the wallpaper to the cushions to the rug is striped or patterned and shouldn't match, but perhaps because of that fact they do.

'Would you like a drink while you wait?'

'No thanks.'

'Are you sure? We've got dandelion coffee, camomile tea, elderflower cordial—'

Ffion opens the front door then, shadowed in the gloom holding a small spade and carrying a handful of white-headed plants and some manky looking bulbs that smell of onion. Her hair is windblown, her skin appears dry and the freezing gale she brings with her – due to the heat emitted from the wood burning stove in the small space we occupy – feels colder than it did while we were walking in it just a couple of minutes ago.

Aled introduces us to his wife, who drops her goods onto the small square reclaimed dining table that has only two chairs drawn beneath it and with her back to us asks what we want in false joviality while shrugging off her coat.

'Geraint Fford.'

Her back goes rigid as she folds her coat and lays it flat on the table directly on top of the folder I saw as I walked in labelled 'Marshfield', then she turns slowly.

'We have reason to believe that he may have come here to meet with you on the eleventh of this month.'

'He did.'

'We'd like to know why.'

'You think it has something to do with his murder,' she says matter-of-factly. Then a look of concern washes over her, and she asks, 'Am I in danger?'

'We've no reason to suspect you are.'

She appears to be grappling between concealing and offloading something.

'If you know of any reason someone might have wanted him dead it's better you tell us now, because if we find out you've been withholding information that inhibits our investigation you could be charged for doing so.'

'Did it have anything to do with Oscar Goldsborough?' Dafydd asks. 'You wrote an article recently about his non-starter trial.'

'I'm not permitted to discuss it.'

The Editors' Code of Practice prohibits her.

'Is Oscar under journalistic investigation?' Dafydd asks.

'Not that I'm aware of,' Ffion replies, 'and certainly not by me, but then I'm not an investigative journalist, so how *would* I know? Though I had to do my research of course, and what I found out while conducting background prompted further examination.'

'Are you saying there are more allegations of rape against Oscar?'

There aren't as far as the police are aware. And had the CPS known about them the case wouldn't have been thrown out of court before it had even started.

'If there were I wouldn't be able to tell you.'

'You have to check the accuracy of your sources pre-publication,' I say. By way of explaining my knowledge I infer that my husband is a crime reporter too.

'Yes, but as you're aware, the Investigatory Powers Act 2016 prevents you from obtaining information that could identify who they are.'

'We don't need names. We don't even really need to know what you discovered during your inquiry. We just need to know if what you discussed with Geraint the day that he came here had anything to do with his murder, as it could help us to understand why he was killed and who by.'

'I can't answer that if it risks exposing someone's right to privacy. I have legal obligations too.'

I feel my shoulders sag with the weight of her words because she's right.

'Did your conversation have anything to do with the man who murdered Oscar's father, Geoffrey Goldsborough?'

She glances from me to Dafydd and says, 'I'm sorry, Detectives, but I can't help you.'

'Roderick was granted parole, wasn't he?' Dafydd asks.

I give Dafydd a warning look. We have to err on the side of caution. We can't show our hand too soon and we must keep anything not yet in the public eye to ourselves, for now, which includes the historic allegations against the late psychiatrist during his tenure at Wotton Dean.

'Yes, but—' She stops herself from saying any more.

'Look, I can't tell you what Geraint and I discussed but I can confirm that although we spoke about many things while he was here, the reason he wanted to talk to me had nothing at all to do with either of the Goldsborough's. Now, if you'll excuse me, I have things to do before it gets too dark, and I can't see what I'm doing.'

Dafydd follows as Ffion exits the door ahead of me which I grab before it swings back in my face. She bends to retrieve two potted ceramic planters from the patio and carries them into a small shed.

***

Wending our way through the scrubby brush in the grey-blue dusk, Dafydd asks me if I've ever heard of anyone with the surname 'Marshfield'.

'No. It might be a place. You saw her hide the folder too?'

'Yeah.'

A quick internet search reveals Marshfield is either a village midway between Cardiff and Newport or a residential school for boys on the site of a former military base on the outskirts of Gloucestershire.

Is that why Celyn sold up and moved to England?

I ignore the map at the top of the page and take a gander at the website which boasts luxury singular boarding rooms with lakeside views, and think it looks just like the kind of institution the Goldsborough's could have afforded to send their son.

Then I catch something that grabs my attention.

The building was established by his worship the mayor, Jevon Llewellen, but due to extensive repairs required to maintain it, closed its doors in 1996.

'Oscar couldn't have boarded at Marshfield, he'd only have been ten years old, and it says here they catered for children aged eleven plus,' Dafydd says, peering over my shoulder at the screen.

My phone rings as we reach the car.

'Boss,' comes a familiar voice, when I pick it up. 'I've got good news and bad news. Which do you want first?'

'You've found the phone and there's nothing on it?'

'I might have found the phone, but I have about six hundred other phones to sift through, and there appear to be a lot of Samsung Galaxy's amongst them.'

'I guess you'd better get cracking then.'

'Who was that?' Dafydd asks when I end the call.

'PC Meyer has a busy evening ahead checking the serial numbers of a fair few mobile phones against our victim's.'

PS TOMOS

PRESENT

The large country house owned by Celyn is set deep into the forest that borders the Wye Valley River, which cuts straight between Wales and England. There is a meadow to the left of the garden. An eighteenth-century church with headstones that veer sideways on a grassy slope to the right. And centring both is a huge monstrosity of cut stone in various colours, shapes, and sizes. The house has stood for centuries, and additions to the building make it look far from original, but the hodgepodge of brickwork and varied levels of workmanship gives the grand property a quirky appearance that, though it shouldn't, works.

All this I can only see as the house is floodlit. All along the path and the square surrounding the building there are solar-powered spotlights screwed into the ground casting the pebbled route of access in a white-blue glow.

Much of the house, including the entrance, is built from sandstone. There's a circular water fountain fronting the main doors, to the left of which are two vehicles parked in front of the double garage: a Range Rover and a classic Porche. Along with the money Celyn inherited from her husband's life insurance policy – after his killer was jailed and his death was proven in a court of law to have not been caused by her – she must be worth at least a million quid. Most probably double that, what with inflation. And it's evident by the vehicle's registration plates – private and both containing the word GOLD – that money is no object.

I ring the bell, but I can't hear it chime through the heavy oak door so I've no idea if it works. There's no letterbox to flap, so I rap my knuckles against the hard wood until I hear the unmistakable sound of a latch being deployed. The door creaks open and swings wide to reveal a rake-thin woman I don't recognise until she raises her head a few inches and I catch sight of her startlingly alert eyes. Her cheeks look pinched, her lips are thin lines framed by powdered wrinkles, and the look she gives me is as sharp as her angled features.

Emma produces her ID card. 'Detective Inspector Emma Locke,' she says, motioning to me. 'This is my colleague, Sergeant Dafydd Tomos.'

'I cun see that. I cun read you know,' she replies.

'Can you confirm your name please?'

'You know perfectly well what it is else you wouldn't be hur,' she says, irritably.

'Celyn Rossi?'

'Yes.'

'Where were you on November the twenty-first of this year?'

'Last Monday?' She frowns, then realisation dawns. 'The day Mr Fford's life was taken. Church, in the morning. I wus covering for Aisha. She serves the tea for the women's weekly bible study. Then I wus at the community centre. I volunteer there. We wur boxing up emergency aid parcels. They get sent wherever they're needed. It's a full-time job.'

'Your husband volunteered for a Christian charity too, didn't he, some years back,' Emma says.

Celyn's face turns to stone, then she smiles nervously. 'Oh, yes. That wus a long time ago, I'd almost forgotten.' Then she gives me a quizzical look and asks how we came about the information.

'I'm afraid we can't divulge that.'

'No, of course,' Celyn replies, though it's evidently hit a nerve.

'There is something we believe you could help us with though.'

'You'll want to come in, I suppose?'

'We could go down to the station if you prefer?' Emma says.

Without a word she side-steps the door, allowing us through.

As we're escorted from the atrium and down into an older part of the house that's colder, possibly due to the exposed brick walls, we pass a neo-classically designed room that I imagine is referred to as the morning room, where there is a grand piano parked in one corner, and pillars at either side of a ceiling-high glass case housing an electric guitar. 'Signed,' Emma mouths. After which is a glossy sparkled kitchen and a velvet and tapestry adorned drawing room opposite a dining *hall*, followed by a laundry room.

Celyn barely reaches five foot and probably only weighs about seven stone, but her voice is strong, and she moves like a bird, flitting through to the back of the house so fast it's a job to catch up with her.

There are no doors on any of the rooms, instead each doorway has been extended widthways to create an open partition to separate each living space, every one of which shares the same black and white painted style as the conservatory where she stops. In here, though, rather than black or white carpet or linoleum the floor is tiled like a chequerboard. Only red flowers, like those that were in vases on fireplaces and furniture elsewhere add a touch of alternative colour to the smoky glass coffee table.

She sits on a white wicker-framed sofa covered with black cushions, a sheer silver-grey throw has been folded and flung over one of the high-backed seats making the showy looking home appear lived in. She crosses her legs and pats the space beside her. 'Well, what is it you want?'

'Mr Fford acted on behalf of your husband's murderer, Roderick Penrose.'

'Is that really why you're hur?' she asks.

'He was instrumental in the success of Roderick's parole. How did you feel about that?' Emma asks.

'How do you think I felt?' Celyn replies.

'Roderick was due to be released from prison the very day Mr Fford was murdered,' I remind her.

'You think I killed him?' Celyn laughs.

'Did you?' Emma asks.

'No, detectives, I didn't,' Celyn replies, slightly amused.

'Did your son?'

'No,' comes a voice from the doorway, as a man I recognise from the image attached to the online news article I read enters the room, 'I didn't.'

'Oscar Goldsborough?'

'Yes.'

'Neither I nor my son murdered that man,' Celyn says.

'Did you cover it up?' I interject.

'No,' Celyn replies, far more seriously. 'And to think that you could insinuate something so—'

'She had nothing to do with that man's murder and neither did I,' Oscar says, interrupting his mother.

'You have any evidence to suggest the contrary?'

Celyn asks Emma and me.

Neither of us reply.

'You have access to guns?'

'Guns?' Oscar asks, with a frown.

'Mr Fford was shot,' Emma says.

I catch a surreptitious glance from Celyn to the corner of the room.

I stride over to the key-coded cabinet.

'Can you unlock it please?'

She retrieves a key from the drawer inside a desk and opens it reluctantly. Inside it there is an old hunting rifle.

'Decommissioned I hope?'

'Of course.'

I check anyway.

'This the only gun you own?'

'Yes,' Celyn says.

'Got a licence for it?'

I know she hasn't. If she had it would have come up during PC Kelly's PNC check.

'You know I haven't.'

'It was my dad's,' Oscar says. 'I've filled out the transfer of ownership forms.'

Nobody's going to give him a licence. Not even for a gun that can't fire.

It's then I notice his shoes aren't shoes at all. He's wearing slippers.

'You staying here for a bit?'

'Until I get my own place.'

'Girlfriend kicked you out, has she?' Emma asks.

She was very vocal about believing his version of events and supporting him even after he admitted cheating on her with the woman who accused him of spiking her drink and raping her in his hotel suite.

'We weren't serious.'

'You've got a kid together.' A two-year-old boy.

He shrugs, and I don't think I've ever felt like punching anyone in the face so strongly, but *I* can control my impulses, unlike him.

Celyn glares at him and he puts one hand in the pocket of his jogging trousers and declares he's late for training.

Emma steps out in front of the door blocking his exit, maintaining eye contact with Oscar as she speaks. 'Do you have any idea what your father and Roderick were arguing about prior to his murder?' she asks.

Both respond with wary expressions and an unmistakable look in each other's direction before Celyn straightens her spine and Oscar narrows his eyes. 'I was nine years old.'

'Old enough to remember,' Emma interjects.

'What about you?'

Something registers on Celyn's face, and I notice her features harden. 'Like I told your colleagues twenty-six years ago, no.'

'You think his murder had something to do with why that lawyer was killed?' Oscar asks.

'I take it by "that lawyer" you mean Mr Fford?'

'Yeah.'

Emma, sensing where I'm going with this, asks, 'Do you have any idea why Roderick might have wanted to kill your husband?'

'None at all,' she says defensively, and from her reaction I'm disinclined to believe her.

'Did you ask him?'

'I applied for a visiting order, I even went to the prison,' Celyn says in a slightly harassed tone, dabbing her eyes with a tissue she pulls from the box at the centre of the coffee table, though as far as I can see they're dry.

'When?'

'When he was on remand.'

'And what did he say?'

'Nothing. He refused to see me.'

I make an internal note of Oscar's surreptitious frown.

'You went all that way for an explanation, and he ghosted you?'

'Yes. Odd, isn't it?'

'Odd indeed.'

Stranger still that the prison governor allowed his victim's widow to visit the man responsible for making her so.

Unless she's lying.

It won't be difficult to check out her story, but do we have the budget?

'Roddy had always seemed harmless to me. Like a gentle giant. We certainly would never have had him in our house if we'd ever believed him capable of something so horrific.'

'Roddy?' Not the kind of nickname given to someone responsible for murdering your spouse.

She bristles at this but doesn't respond.

'Why did you? I mean he was a gardener, wasn't he?' Emma asks.

'A groundskeeper, actually. And, he didn't just look after the garden, he took care of the rubbish, tidied up after our lawn parties, cleared out the guttering, cleaned the windows . . . He was a keen recycler before it became common practise.'

'I meant why did he come into your home?'

'Oh, well, even groundsmen need bathroom breaks,' she guffaws.

Why is she downplaying how close they were?

'But you were friends. I mean you invited him to your tenth wedding anniversary.'

'We invited all the staff.'

'Including the housekeeper, Nancy, Roderick's

girlfriend,' Emma says.

How very Daphne Du Maurier.

'*She* was as mad as a box of frogs that one.'

'Yet you had her under your employ.'

'My husband did,' she says, correcting me. 'And she didn't go doolally until afterwards. Her mother – Irene – adopted their daughter almost as soon as she was born. Couldn't cope see,' she adds, by way of explanation.

Who would? Learning that someone you love has killed someone is bound to send anyone 'mad'.

The thought gives me pause, because aren't Sarah and I in the same boat (on shit creek without a paddle) when it comes to Chris' imminent future?

And I suddenly feel dizzy with worry.

'They had a girl?'

'Yes. They called her Carry. No, Kelly. Cathy? Kerry, or ... something.' I can almost hear the unsaid *common* at the end of her sentence, the stuck-up—

'Will that be all, detectives?' Celyn asks.

'Hold on,' Oscar says, 'Roderick is the common denominator here, right?'

I glance at Emma who reacts by tilting her chin up, motioning for him to go on.

'How do you know it wasn't him?'

'Because he never made it out,' Emma replies.

'What do you mean?' Oscar asks.

'He was granted parole,' Celyn says. 'I was there.'

'Yes, but he caught Covid-19 a fortnight after the hearing and died in ICU ten days later.'

It does make me wonder though whether discovering he'd died a prisoner might have given Roderick's daughter, reason to want to kill her father's defence lawyer as some kind of vengeful act for not having had the chance to get to know him before his release.

I make a mental note to find out her whereabouts for the week Geraint went missing.

'Are you telling us you didn't know?' It was all over the news. It would have been nigh on impossible to have avoided it. Not to mention the prison service have a duty to inform victims when a prisoner dies, to prewarn them of the potential distress caused by media coverage.

'In case you've forgotten, we've been rather preoccupied recently,' Celyn replies. Followed by her son's two pence worth. 'What with that lying slag's accusations.' Celyn's face twitches at his choice of words, but she doesn't say anything.

'He died last year.'

'Neither of them respond.

Turning our backs on the pair who stand watching us leave, Emma's phone rings with a tune that sends me immediately back to the nineties, and my mouth dries at the memory of those years. Instantly transported to Gambia, dressed in civilian attire, seated beside my comrade Mohammad, and singing along to the radio inside a helicopter above a park. Immediately before we were covertly assisted by paratroopers dressed like doctors onto the roof of a car park fronting the hospital where the president's wife and five children were being held as hostages by rebels.

'PC Coulter,' Emma says, after ending the call, explaining who she'd just spoken to and bringing me back down to earth.

I cough to clear my throat, which helps prevent the tears from forming, before I ask, 'What's he saying?'

She responds with a curious look and says, 'We'll get back to that. You look agitated. Still no news from your wife?'

'No. Which means Chris is still in custody.'

'And likely will be until . . . When was he arrested?'

'At around eight o'clock this morning.'

'So, you're unlikely to hear anything until the same time *tomorrow* morning.'

'So . . .'

'So, stop worrying about what might be and focus only on the facts.'

'Which is that . . .?'

'Ronnie Sykes, the administrator of the Facebook Group told PC Coulter that during their last conversation on the phone Geraint had uncovered information about a related matter that should he choose to pursue it, would put his integrity into question as it would be a conflict of interest.'

'So he flipped from acting on behalf of Geoffrey's victim*'s* to representing Oscar's victi*m*?'

'It looks that way. And speaking of looks, guess who wears a wig?'

'You're gonna tell me Ronnie is the mystery blonde, aren't you?'

She gives me a look that confirms my suspicion.

KERRY-ANN

PAST

I unpacked my clothes as the kettle boiled, and googled places to eat while pouring a coffee from the jar I'd brought with me. Then I called Natalia to let her know I'd arrived safely as I slurped it down from a cup I'd found at the back of a cupboard after I'd rinsed it out. I left her a voicemail when she didn't answer, as I watched the sun fall on the horizon, casting a pale glow across the deep, dark water, which I could still just about see in the dusky dark sky. I supposed she was on her commute home. Though her shift had ended half an hour before. She was likely caught up in traffic.

It began to rain heavily, turning the snow to sludge, so that by the time I'd made it from the cottage to the car I was already soaked through. There was a huge puddle in front of the door which I couldn't see as there were no streetlights on this lonesome trail, so when I stepped in it, I sprayed muddy water over the tops of my boots and up my trouser legs.

I muttered a few expletives as I slammed the car door shut, turned the key in the ignition, and whacked the heat up. The temperature gauge on the dash declared it to have dropped to zero.

I couldn't be bothered to cook. It had been a long day and I'd done a lot of driving, so I'd decided on a takeaway that was situated on the main road in Penarth. I bought fish and chips and a can of coke and while I waited, I noticed a man stood leaning against the window seat eyeing me up.

No luck mate, I'm a lesbian.

He was gone seconds before I left.

As I hurried back to the car to escape the unrelenting rain as quickly as possible, I felt eyes on the back of my head. But when I turned, expecting to see the creepy bloke from the chippy, there was nobody there.

You're being paranoid, I told myself.

The feeling didn't dissipate as I drove back to the cottage. If anything, it worsened as I sat and ate my food in front of the electric fire, replete with faux coal, and read the last few chapters of the published version of Alys Wynn's book.

DI LOCKE

PRESENT

'What else did Ronnie have to say?' Dafydd asks, as we navigate our way back down the slippery sloped lane and out onto the icy road.

'She apparently didn't come forward after the social media campaign because she hadn't yet come out as trans to her family. She was worried that making herself known to us would put her at risk of exposure by the press, thus put her in the firing line of bigots.'

'Okay, but why was she following Geraint?'

'Ah, well, she says it was to try and convince him to pursue the investigation.'

'By stalking him?'

I shrug.

'She doesn't appear to have had anything against Geraint. She said he paid for the travel and transport expenses to enable several of the women to meet with him to share their stories and offered to cover any legal fees for anyone in need, too. He told her he went above and beyond because as a boy he'd experienced something awful at the hands of someone he trusted and as he chose not to speak out, he was never able to get justice, which is why he wanted to ensure the women could.'

Had it also been why he'd chosen to become a lawyer?

'So, who exactly is Ronnie?'

'Her partner is one of the victims. She practised law many moons ago, so offered to help the women navigate the world of civil cases.'

We reach the car, skidding and tripping over frozen bracken and trying to avoid melted ice.

PC Meyer rings me while Dafydd is driving. I put my mobile on speakerphone.

'I've found Geraint's phone. The screen is badly smashed up, but it turns on, and it's not password protected so Jules' text messages – which *are* suggestive of an affair – are visible. From what I can see, in their last exchange they were arranging to hook up, but Geraint failed to show so Jules thought he'd got cold feet.'

'What do they say, these messages?'

'I'll read them out to you.' I can hear shuffling, then she says, 'Okay, the first few are similar in tone to the email exchanges between Geraint and Caz: "Saw your profile on the website, could we meet?; I'm free later; I can come to you". Then: "Forgot to tell you, you've got a spot of sauce on your shirt; my bad; Thanks for tonight; Any time; Did the waiter have a stutter?; You made him nervous; Do you think he fancied me?; Definitely." Those are on Friday the sixteenth of September. There's a phone call made on the Saturday, then on the Sunday: "I have to see you again; So soon?; Tomorrow?; It's a date; Same place?; And time if possible, got some errands to run so can get away afterwards." The following are a series of texts sent by Jules to Geraint on the nineteenth, starting just after six o'clock: "I'm here, you're not; I'm not going to wait forever; Guess you're not coming". Of course, we've no idea if they corresponded after this because Demelza saw these messages, assumed the worst, and threw his phone across the room, smashing the screen, hence how it ended up in the recycling bin.'

The texts begin as prospective client and lawyer, before sounding like old pals having a laugh, they turn flirty, then quickly go from concerned to annoyed.

Did Geraint arrive at the restaurant, apologise to Jules for being late? Did they continue their relationship – in whatever capacity that was? If they *were* in an intimate relationship with one another, did they break up, or were they still together when he was killed? Or did Geraint ghost her? And in doing so, cause her to become vengeful?

'We need to find this woman, and pronto.'

'Agreed,' both Dafydd and PC Meyer say in unison.

PS TOMOS

PRESENT

I park my car beside Emma's, and we split. After I wave goodbye to her, PC Meyer calls to ask if she's still with me as she isn't answering her phone.

'No, the DI has just left.'

'Ah, well if she's driving, she won't pick up, though she might call me back . . . I'll leave a voicemail,' PC Meyer says.

'Is it something I should know?'

'Well, those text messages between Geraint and Jules aren't the only thing I found. See, it appears that whichever one of us suggested Geraint was looking to buy a gun for his own protection might have been right. And that's not all. When I linked up Geraint's phone to the black box, I discovered something else that's gonna put a spin on things. See, there were deleted text messages between Geraint and an unknown suspect. I was able to recover them all. Make of them what you will but they look pretty dodgy to me.'

ⓧ **Received 3 November, 10.58 p.m. (unknown sender)**
YOU HAVE DAUGHTERS

ⓧ **Received 3 November, 10.59 p.m. (unknown sender)**
YOU DON'T DESERVE THEM

ⓧ **Received 3 November, 11.01 p.m. (unknown sender)**
IMAGINE IF SOMETHING WERE TO HAPPEN TO THEM

ⓧ **Received 3 November, 11.13 a.m. (unknown sender)**
MY GIRL IS DEAD

ⓧ **Received 3 November, 11.14 p.m. (unknown sender)**
IT'S YOUR FAULT

ⓧ **Received 3 November, 11.18 p.m. (unknown sender)**
YOU'RE GOING TO PAY

KERRY-ANN

PAST

A gust of wind slammed the shutter against the glass, and I jolted, spilling tea down my arm and across the pages of the book. When I stood to remove the sherpa blanket from my legs, I glanced over to the side window. There could have been a person standing out there, peering into the lounge. But with no motion-censored light attached to the exterior wall like the one I had back home it was difficult to see whether the shadow being cast was being reflected from the faux bamboo plant that stood in the corner of the unlit hallway or had been caused by something in the garden.

It was dark now, so I crossed the room towards the light switch then laid the open book onto the radiator, hoping the heat would dry the ink well enough that the pages were still readable, and carried the blanket into the kitchen to toss into the washing machine. I poured washing powder into the machine, turned the dial to 'eco', and switched it on.

A draft filtered into the room, skimming my exposed ankles, and causing me to shiver. Searching for the cause I noticed the seal surrounding the window above the sink was broken. Had somebody attempted to force the window open from outside? It was wide enough to slink through.

I shook my head. I was in a cottage alone, there were no streetlights outside, no roadways nearby, the desolate landscape hummed with silence, and I'd just been reading about the crimes that women feared happening to them the most.

A flash of lightening brightened up the sky, followed shortly by a rumble of thunder.

I turned away as a fork of lightening and a crackle of thunder drew my attention back to the door where rain pelted the heavy solid wood, alerting me to what appeared to be a cloaked figure through the panes.

A tree was my first thought.

I expected it to be an inanimate object mirrored in the glass, or even the ghost of someone who haunted the arid land stooped on the step. Though logic told me a person had come to seek shelter from the storm, to call a recovery truck to unstick their car from the sludge. But before I unlocked the door to investigate, I grabbed a meat cleaver from the drawer, just in case.

The moment I opened the door the wind wrenched it from my hand and spat rainwater at me at such ferocity I turned my face away from the sleet to dry my eyes with the sleeve of my jumper.

And froze as a cold band of steel braceleted my arm.

The door slammed shut then my assailant tugged me towards him.

The man's grip tightened as I tried to flee. He pressed a palm across my mouth to silence me and pushed me against the back of a chair leaning horizontal to the dining table, his weight pinioning me in place as I tried unsuccessfully to shove him off me.

The smell of pine needles and decay permeated the room. He'd probably spent a lot of time outdoors.

I couldn't see his face. I didn't need to. I could tell by

the sound of his breath, heavy and ruptured, that he meant to do me harm. I also knew that screaming was pointless. Aside from the large property to my left that I hadn't seen a vehicle outside of or the glow of a light from inside of since my arrival there was nobody besides me for miles.

    I stopped struggling against him. I needed to conserve my energy if I was to survive long enough to escape.

DI LOCKE

PRESENT

I arrive home to an open front door. Johnno stands behind Jaxon, one huge hand on his small shoulder, both of them waving Sophie off. The taxi does a 180° then speeds off down the road while I pull up onto the drive. The second I'm out of the car Ethan is running towards me. I bend to give him a hug. Jaxon takes the opportunity to snatch a kiss from me and I ruffle his head as I stand.

'How'd it go?'

'Good.'

'We went to swimming and eated pizza!' Jaxon squeals in delight.

'Can I have pizza?' Ethan asks.

'Sure, buddy,' Johnno says.

I mouth, 'Do we have any?' and he says, 'I went shopping earlier, after I picked Ethan up from school.'

'We wented to the park,' Ethan says.

'Did you have a nice time?'

'I gotted a new friend.'

'I've got lots of friends. Haven't I?' Jaxon asks.

'Yes, love, you do.'

Jaxon turns to Ethan and says, 'See, I tolded you.'

'Can they come to our house for a playnight?' Ethan

asks.

'We'll see,' Johnno says, as I reply with, 'Soon.'

We give each other the look all parents do when put on the spot and I know we'll both concede because the boys have us well and truly wrapped around their little fingers.

Though I breathe a sigh of relief that Sophie delivered him home without a hitch, at the back of my mind I wonder if she intends to give us a false sense of hope, so that in the future when she decides not to bring Jaxon back, we'll be blindsided.

I think back to one of my early cases involving two children who'd been reported missing by their mother after their father had failed to return them to her. It turned out that he'd taken them abroad, which as a national of the country – I forget which one – and because they had no extradition treaty in place with the UK at the time, the authorities couldn't demand he bring the child home to their mother because his actions weren't considered a criminal offence.

I glance at the back of Jaxon's head and my stomach roils at the thought of never seeing him again. And not for the first time do I wonder too, how Craig can bear to be apart from *his* son. I know he's working on himself, and his departure has a long-term purpose, but the longer he's gone the more I worry we won't see him again, that Ethan will forget who he is.

I feel an arm snake around my waist and turn to meet Johnno's knowing stare, as he squeezes me against him. His wordless affection says, 'Let me be your anchor'.

He releases me and presses his palm against the curve of my spine to usher me forwards. I reach back, offering him my hand and he places his thick fingers between my own slim ones, and we walk together into the warmth of our home.

PS TOMOS

PRESENT

I'm halfway down the street when I spot him. Sitting on the low wall separating ours from the neighbour's front garden. He's slumped forwards, elbows resting on his knees, chin drawn in. He's wearing a dark hoodie over a scruff of hair. It's not until I'm out of the car and heading towards him that he looks up, and I can see his eyes are red and his cheeks pinched from the biting cold.

'When did they let you go, son?'

'About an hour ago. I came straight here,' Chris replies.

'Let's get you inside, out of the cold, before your mother gets home from work. She'll give us both an earbashing if she learns you've been sat out here all this time. It's zero-degrees.'

'I was going to call, to let you know to expect me, but . . . I didn't know what to say.'

He breaks down then. Fat tears rolling down his cheeks and I'm reminded of the time he fell as a boy, grazed his knees on the concrete, having had the impulse to jump off the swing when he'd managed to get it to reach as high as it would go. And just as I did then, I wrap my solid arms around him and hold him tight as he rattles, sobbing into my chest. Shoulders heaving, snot staining my vest as he pulls away.

I boil the kettle as he splashes warm water onto his tear-stained face and dabs away his sorrow with a tea towel he finds folded over the oven handle. And as I add teabags to two cups, he fills me in on the day's events, his voice tremorous, eyes darting about the room.

'They made me take off my clothes,' he almost whispers in a childlike voice.

I remember how invasive it was when we had to undergo a mock arrest, search, interview, and charge during police training, and tell him so.

'Did they take your fingerprints too?' Chris asks, eyes watery.

'Yes. Mouth swabs as well, to check for DNA.'

'That's why they released me,' he says.

'On bail?'

'No.' He shakes his head. 'Without charge.'

'That must mean they've got some idea of who the sample they've got belongs to.'

KERRY-ANN

PAST

I jumped in fright at the sound of what I thought was someone's fist pounding the front door. How long had they been standing there? And, more importantly, who was it and what did they want? But when I realised it was only the thud of Alys Wynn's book falling from my lap, I bent down to retrieve it from the floor. It was dry and free of tea stains, though the page I'd been reading before I'd fallen asleep was crumpled.

I blinked away the nightmare I'd just had of having awoken from a bad dream and scrambled up, crossing the hall to enter the kitchen.

The clock on the wall read 5.43 a.m.

I pressed the lever down on the kettle to boil it just as a solid black mass slid past the window above the sink, temporarily blocking out the only source of light filtering into the room from the moon that hung low and full in the ebony sky.

DAY THREE OF THE INVESTIGATION

💬 **Sent November 7, 2022, at 11.09 a.m.**
Need to get hold of a str. Can you hook me up?

💬 **Received November 7, 2022, at 11.10 a.m.**
Sure. How soon?

💬 **Sent November 7, 2022, at 11.12 a.m.**
ASAP. How much?

💬 **Received November 7, 2022, at 11.15 a.m.**
Do me a favour.

💬 **Sent November 7, 2022, at 11.17 a.m.**
What?

💬 **Received November 7, 2022, at 11.20 a.m.**
Get me an address

💬 **Sent November 7, 2022, 11.22 a.m.**
Okay

Received November 7, 2022, 11.23 a.m.
William Maurice Parker, DOB: 08/09/53

💬 **Sent November 7, 2022, at 11.25 a.m.**
Consider it done

💬 **Received November 7, 2022, at 11.28 a.m.**
Locked and loaded?

💬 **Sent November 7, 2022, at 11.31 a.m.**
👍

💬 **Sent November 8, 2022, at 9.37 a.m.**
8b Berkley Drive, CF

💬 **Received November 8, 2022, at 9.40 a.m.**
Ready when you are

DI LOCKE

PRESENT

I'm holding a hot cup of coffee in both hands to warm them, feeling the incident room thrum around me in excitement at the news Geraint may have sought a gun, either intending to use it on someone else, or even perhaps himself and instead had it turned on him, but we can't afford to get carried away by supposition.

'What exactly did those text messages say?'

'Can you get hold of a shooter?' Dylan says.

'Actually, it says "STR",' DC Chapman says.

'Which could mean any number of things,' DC Winters adds.

'Such as?'

'In law-speak it means Suspicious Transaction Report,' Dafydd says. 'Which is a formal written document created by financial institutions used to record potentially suspicious activity. They're regarded as evidence in cases involving money laundering or the financing of terrorism.'

'Let's not forget the Short Tandem Repeat analysis, which uses DNA to distinguish between two individuals,' Dylan adds.

'Yes, but doesn't the text insinuate wanting to "get hold of" an STR?' Dafydd asks.

'Yeah, I see your point,' Dylan replies. 'Requesting one makes little sense. You'd surely ask for the reference number to retrieve or compare one against another.'

'We don't have any suggestion the twins aren't biologically related to Geraint, but Short-Tandem Repeats are also used to test a person's paternity,' DC Burtenshaw says, uncrossing her legs then recrossing them the other way. 'We know Demelza had access to her husband's phone. That's how she was able to view Geraint's text messages with Jules. What's to say she didn't also discover he'd been communicating with someone about getting a paternity test? That could also explain why she threw the phone and smashed the screen.'

Had she damaged it to avoid him finding out she'd used it, and not as she'd told us in a fit of rage over his supposed infidelity? Afterall, we only have her word for it.

'One of the first things our southern-Welsh colleagues asked Demelza, her mother Carol, and his mother Lorraine, was if the twins were biologically hers and Geraint's, as well as how long the couple had been together. Though at the time we didn't know about the texts referring to the STR, we still have no reason to doubt the twin's parentage as there doesn't appear to be a disgruntled ex, surrogate, or an adoption, and she didn't fess up to having had an affair,' DC Winters says. 'Of course, there's no way to rule out the possibility the girls aren't related to their parents without DNA tests.'

'Which I of course cannot sanction as it's wholly inappropriate, not to mention highly unlikely to have any bearing on our investigation.' So we must consider what else the acronym could stand for. 'Any other ideas as to what "STR" could mean?'

Several voices ring out simultaneously:
'No.'
'None.'
'Nope.'
'Nada.'

'So, we don't really know what he meant by *STR*, and each potential meaning of the acronym we know of are valid terms used by lawyers. However, we can confirm – thanks to the nightshift – that the day after this text message conversation took place, at around seven thirty on the night of the eighth of November to be exact, William Maurice Parker's son, Errol James Parker, was shot dead on the doorstep as he was entering his father's home in Cardiff. And that the single bullet, which entered his skull, came from the same brand of gun as those found at the scene of Geraint Fford's murder.'

Had Geraint and Errol been murdered by the same person? If they had it wouldn't be that unusual for them to have used the same firearm or at least have a preferred make and model, and so it would be expected that the bullets also matched.

The very act of firing a bullet through a barrel leaves unique individual indentations on the bullet which when recorded can be used to compare them to the grooves and markings found on the bullets from other crime scenes.

'Something else I found interesting was the cause of William's death,' Dafydd says.

'He died of opioid overdose,' DC Winters says.

'Fentanyl-laced heroin specifically,' DC Chapman says.

'The same gear responsible for all those overdoses in Newport?' Dylan asks.

'It's being looked into. By the way, how was the scan yesterday?'

'She's doing we—'

'You're having a girl?' Dafydd interrupts.

'Congratulations,' DC Winters says.

'As I was saying . . .' Dylan continues, 'Dempsey's doing well, as are the babies.'

'You're having twins!?' DC Chapman asks.

'One of each,' Dylan replies.

'Perfect.'

He gives me a wink and I smile in return.

'So, what were you saying about these deleted texts between Geraint and our unsub?' Dylan asks, indicating to the projected images on the wall.

I fill him in on the previous day's events, reiterating the information PC Meyer discovered yesterday evening, followed by the resulting inquiries the nightshift made once she'd clocked off.

'There is another possibility to consider?' DC Winters says thoughtfully. 'That *he's* the one who arranged the hit.'

'On himself, you mean?' Dylan asks, eyebrows raised.

'He wouldn't be the first person to do it,' DC Winters replies.

'To arrange his own murder!?' DC Chapman asks.

'It's been done before,' DC Winters replies.

'Yeah, by suicidal and terminally ill people,' Dylan replies.

'He'd received an Osman Warning, was being harassed by someone via text message, was self-harming, and was undergoing treatment for anxiety and depression. Who's to say he *wasn't* suicidal?' DC Winters asks.

'Alright, let's say he *did* arrange his own . . . death, who do we know that has links to both organised crime *and* Geraint?' DC Chapman asks.

The answer comes to me almost at the exact same

time that Dylan says, 'Paddy Daly.'

'Let's not get carried away peeps. While we should keep an open mind, we need to stick to the facts. And as of right now they're not pointing his way.'

'This William who Geraint gave out the address of; what do we know about him?' Dylan asks.

'Seventy years old, terminally ill, no history of prior drug use, toxicology showed no other substances in his system, autopsy revealed no sign of organ damage or injecting which rules out addiction, and his phone indicates website searches on how to mainline heroin made several weeks before his death.'

'You think Errol bought the gear so William could do himself in?' Dylan asks.

'The evidence points that way though we can't confirm that theory without the man himself.'

'Or the person who supplied him with the smack,' Dylan says.

'Which could be why the individual had Errol shot; to eliminate the possibility of police identifying him or her when Errol was eventually arrested for manslaughter having purchased the drug, thus assisting his father's suicide.'

'And you think it was one of Paddy Daly's associates who supplied the drug to Errol *and* shot him?' DC Chapman asks.

The sons of ex-IRA members and drug dealers on the radar of the NCA known to have links to foreign distributors of fentanyl-laced heroin.

'Of all the crooks Geraint has had to deal with throughout his career they seem the likeliest candidates,' DC Winters says. 'Though I doubt the person was one and the same.'

'We have zero proof linking Errol's murder to Geraint. The fentanyl-laced heroin is a circumstantial link at best. And we've got nothing concrete connecting either of the men to international drug distribution networks.'

'The other possibility is that Demelza used her husband's phone to "get hold of" a Suspicious Transaction Report to inform the Financial Intelligence Unit she suspected one of her clients, or their estate agent, broker, lender, or even lawyer of fraud,' DC Chapman says.

Once submitted she is legally obliged not to disclose the content of the report to anyone, including us, and after it's been sent only Law Enforcement Agencies have the authority to retrieve data from the Forensic Information Database Service.

'Whoever received the request for the STR – whatever it stands for – wanted Errol's address in return, which at best amounts, by definition, to "tipping-off" a suspected fraudster. Or at worst, may very well have led to Errol's murder considering the text message exchange took place on the seventh of November and Errol was shot dead on the eighth,' DC Winters adds.

DC Chapman gets out his phone and begins typing.

'Wouldn't communicating with someone in a work capacity using another person's phone violate Demelza's legal responsibility to ensure her and her client's interactions remain confidential?' DC Winters asks.

'Who's gonna know? It's not like anyone's monitoring her conversations,' DC Burtenshaw replies.

A few seconds later DC Chapman looks up, then glancing back down at the screen, repeats what the web search has thrown up. 'Lawyers can find out where you live only if it is relevant to a legal case, the ability is regulated by legal and ethical standards to ensure privacy and information is protected. Mortgage advisors, however, are allowed to conduct ID checks on their clients prior to ascertaining their affordability for a mortgage in principle, which means Demelza has access to the same platforms as Geraint, such as SmartSearch, enabling her to GeoLocate individuals, but has less stringent policies in place to ensure she doesn't abuse the privilege afforded her.'

'Want me to get on the blower to the Economic Crimes section, see if they've had any contact from Demelza?' DC Chapman asks.

If reporting a crime rather than being involved in one the information wouldn't necessarily be available to us through the usual channels.

'It couldn't hurt.'

'Depending on what they say we may have enough circumstantial proof to get a warrant to seize her electronic devices,' one of our newest recruits suggests.

'On what basis?' I ask to test her knowledge.

'Isn't the fact she may have forwarded a murder victim's address to the person who killed him enough?' she asks.

'For South Wales Police's investigation into Errol James Parker's murder it is, but there's nothing tangible connecting his shooting to Geraint's, except the brand of gun—'

'And the bullets, which, according to both their and our ballistics report, use a new cost-effective soldering technique,' she interrupts, then apologises as soon as she realises what she's done.

'Yeah, about them, what do we know?'

'South Wales Police narrowed down the bullets as having been discharged from a 9mm handgun, such as a Sig Sauer P226 or a Glock 17. Both of which are commonly used by the Royal Military and Special Forces,' DC Winters says.

I'm watching Dafydd carefully for his reaction when

I ask for his input, but his features remain professionally impassive, when he says, 'It's true that steel core bullets are preferred by the Armed Forces, because they allow for the use of high-velocity low calibre handguns. Though gunners generally use sharpshooter rifles these days.'

'I'm heading over to Demelza's in a bit, but I don't want to ask her about the STR while she has access to her laptop and phone, in case she figures we're onto her and destroys or gets rid of them,' DC Burtenshaw says. 'That's if she hasn't already done so, of course.'

'I'll inform the SIO involved in Errol's homicide; see what they have to say. As of this moment, there's nothing except supposition to suggest that the two crimes are linked because we can't find anything to connect the two men, aside from the discharged bullets having been of the same length, diameter, and even shape, going by their appearance. But I'll see if I can get the lead investigator to agree to having a warrant signed by the time you leave her place.' I smile. 'If they turn up while you're there you can act as though you knew nothing about their imminent arrival. That way Demelza won't lose trust in you.'

'What about Jules?' Dylan asks. 'Are we any further forward in finding out who she is or where those text messages between her and Geraint were sent and received from?'

'The cell phone tower pinged in the Lydart area,' DC Chapman replies.

'Where's that?' Dylan asks.

'It's a hamlet in Monmouthshire,' DC Chapman replies.

'What's in Lydart?' Dafydd asks.

'A former manor house turned conference centre, and a former boarding school turned stately home. Both are Grade II listed buildings,' DC Chapman replies. 'There's also a convent.'

'No pub?' DC Winters asks.

'Not since the early 2000s,' DC Chapman replies.

'Any houses?' Dylan asks.

'A farm owned by a Mr Tipping, which includes a coach house and stables, currently listed for sale with Savills for two point two million,' DC Chapman replies.

'Anyone in the area go by the name of Julie or Julia?' Dafydd asks.

'There's no obvious identity for Jules. But then who's to say she was in Lydart at the time of sending those texts?' DC Winters replies.

'I'm not following?'

'PC Meyer pinged the phone as soon as she got the number from those texts. The report says the cell tower that received and sent the signal was in Lydart, but that doesn't mean Jules sent the messages from there, only that her phone was there at the time that we pinged it.'

'Which was when?'

'Yesterday at 7.37 p.m.,' DC Winters replies. 'PC Meyer checked the publicly accessible Open Electoral Register last night, just in case Jules is listed as living somewhere within Lydart or the surrounding area but had no luck finding her.'

'Well, now we have a date and a timestamp as to when she *was* there, so providing she was using her real name we could get someone to ask around, see if anyone knows who Jules is or can remember having spoken to her.'

'I'll go, boss,' DC Chapman volunteers.

PS TOMOS

PRESENT

Emma is in DCI Evans' office. From the murmured discussion between them earlier I'm guessing it has something to do with budgeting. Jonesy is sniffing about the kettle like a parent in need of caffeine with his phone pressed to his ear. Something he'd better get used to feeling is tiredness now he's got two kids on the way. I don't tell him this though, no father wants to hear about the lack of sleep, shitty nappies, messy house, lack of date nights, and low bank balance while their missus is expecting. To misquote what Ms Austen might have once said, it is a truth universally unacknowledged that a man in possession of a child should not expect sleep or fortune.

According to the General Register Office Roderick Penrose and Nancy Pascoe's daughter was named Kerry-Ann. The Geometric Authentication Database they use to source their information from multiple channels (including but not limited to the UK Passport Office, The Driver and Vehicle Standards Agency, His Majesty's Revenue and Customs, the Department for Work and Pensions, the UK Prison Service, and the Electoral Register to name but a few) tells me she's been living in Cornwall for the last fourteen years. A quick Goggle search informs me she's very active on social media, promoting her upcoming release, which suggests to me that I should have heard of her. The book she's written has been quoted as 'sensational' and 'topical'. I read the description on Amazon and pre-order myself a copy, unsure what relevance – if any – it might have on the investigation.

Detouring from the project she was paid to complete, Pascoe writes emphatically about the impact that crime has on the families of those left behind, whether through imprisonment or death. *Hidden Depths* **is a genre-defying literary masterpiece allowing the reader to accompany the author on a genealogical journey, asking questions about nature versus nurture and whether true innocence exists.**

Though Kerry-Ann was not in Lavernock at the time of Geraint's disappearance (at least according to ANPR cameras in Cornwall, as well as her being the only registered driver to the one vehicle that she owns), it turns out that she will be staying within driving range for the attendance of her first book signing, on Saturday, at a small Indie bookshop in Penarth. Giving me the perfect opportunity to informally question her about her father's conviction, and whether she held any resentment towards the lawyer who failed to secure his freedom during the trial that led to his imprisonment.

DC Winters is the first to spot it. A newspaper article in *Wales Online*, published fifteen minutes ago, flagged up on HOLMES 2 as it's been written by Ffion Townsend.

It's not the headline that grabs my attention though, but the highlighted text below it, where the words 'Marsh' and 'Field' have automatically generated an alert due to the notes I added after our visit to her home.

'So it wasn't Marshfield, but Marsh-Field.'

Emma and I must both have read the title on the file wrong.

'Who is Glenn Marsh and Gina Field?'

'Glenn's the Nighthawk. Gina was his first victim,' DC Winters says. 'And sole survivor.'

'The Nighthawk . . . Is he the bloke who kidnapped and murdered all those women in the noughties?'

DC Winters nods. 'He actually began honing his skills in the nineties. That's when he took Gina.'

I sigh. So Ffion could have been telling us the truth. She and Geraint might not have spoken about Geoffrey or Liam Goldsborough.

'Are there any connecting factors between Geraint and Glenn Marsh?'

He could have had something to do with the legal team representing the Nighthawk at the time of his trial.

'Not that I'm aware of,' DC Winters replies. 'But I'm going to look into that next. Due diligence and all that.'

I've just made it to a desk parked front and centre, allowing me to interact with the entire team while I undertake my tasks, when Jonesy hands me his phone. On the screen is an address in Cardiff.

'Liam called, said someone rang the solicitor's office this morning with an update on some lab results from a BioTech company called Genomica.'

'The results of an STR?'

He shrugs. 'Says he hasn't got a clue what or who they're for, only that Geraint ordered them and that the person he spoke to about it wouldn't give him the results and seemed cagey when he began questioning them. He asked if it was possible for us to trace the caller from their phone number, which I was able to do by googling their number. I'm not sure why he didn't just do that himself. The caller rang Liam from their head office in Whitstable in Kent, but they've got thirty testing centres spread throughout the UK. This one's the closest, so is likely the lab that was used to test the sample. If it has anything to do with a case Geraint was working on Liam claims he knows nothing about it.'

He pauses for a moment then continues.

'Before he rang us though, he asked several members of his staff, none of whom recall any discussions with Geraint concerning DNA tests. There was no mention of pending test results from South Wales Police when they took his office computer. I've asked our own tech team to review the files retrieved from the hard drive, in case it has been missed, but they were unable to find anything on it concerning lab work. I've asked PC Cottrell to liaise with the remaining two. A legal secretary on maternity leave, and their legal accountant, who may have noticed an invoice from the lab added to their expenses sheet on Sage. While she's doing that can you go down to the lab and see if your warrant card will get the staff to open up a bit?'

'No problem, sir.'

'Thanks.'

KERRY-ANN

PAST

I'd fallen asleep on the sofa to the sound of skeletonised branches fingering the windowpane, squeaking, and scratching at the glass like Shiloh did when she wanted to come into the house after a day of wandering the streets. Did she miss me as much as I missed her?

    I'd slept fitfully, awaking, stiff-jointed several times in the night due to the shutter that covered the air vent in the bathroom slapping wildly in the wind, and finally to the sound of myself screaming.

    There was of course nobody lurking outside when I flung the door wide and ran round the side of the house to confront them, key between my knuckles. But the experience left me feeling shaky and unsettled and desperate to get as far away from the cottage as fast and as soon as I was able.

    Alys didn't mind. She'd already told me yesterday that she was an early riser, and that as she'd aged, she needed less and less sleep despite the lethargy the chemo had caused her. When I told her why I'd arrived so early she'd told me off for taking so long to get there.

    'There was no need to stall coming here,' she said. 'You ought to have knocked on the door. I was making my first cuppa of the day at 6.30 a.m.'

'I didn't want to scare you.'

'It takes a lot to frighten me, love.'

She put the kettle on to boil for her second cup of tea while I debated calling the police.

'Did you get a good look at him?' Alys asked.

'I don't even know that it *was* a man.'

It could have been a ghost. I can't even be sure that it wasn't my imagination.

'There's been a few burglaries of late mind, and several car thefts in the area. Whoever it was might have been hoping you'd left the keys in the door. People still do that you know, disregarding warnings of how easy it makes it for car thieves. They stick a coat hanger through the letterbox to hook it out of the lock. Did you know that?'

I recall what I heard on the radio as I drove in and berate myself for dismissing it.

'You couldn't identify him then?' she asked.

'No.'

'Well, I hate to put a dampener on it, but unless he left his fingerprints on the door handle while he was trying to open it, the police aren't going to be able to go hunting for him.'

'I know.' I sighed.

She patted my arm and offered to make me toast while I replaced the batteries in the Dictaphone and pre-set my mobile phone to record, which I used as a backup.

Ten minutes later, we sat to nibble the triangular-cut pile of salted butter and jam slathered toast Alys had placed on the centre of the dining table, and poured tea from the pot between us into china cups she told me were kept in case the queen came to visit, with a cackle.

This was in 2021, so she was still very much alive

then.

Once we'd finished slurping on our builder's-strength sugary tea Alys led me into the living room. We sat opposite one another with the still-hot teapot on the coffee table beside the pile of documents that contained her handwritten research notes.

I began by returning to Alys' revelation of the day before.

'Do you have any actual proof the Nighthawk had an accomplice?'

'No, but the police do. The DNA belonging to an unknown person was recovered from a cigarette stub found at one of the deposition sites, suggesting that someone other than the Nighthawk was in the vicinity of where one of the women were buried.'

'That doesn't mean someone else was involved. It could have been dropped by anyone, before he buried the woman there, or even afterwards.'

'Maybe.' She shrugs. 'Or maybe not.'

She hands me another file of paperwork. This one written on a computer rather than a typewriter. The pages are crisp and white and the piece of A4 topping them all is titled *The Next to Die* in bold letters.

'Writers never stop writing even when they're about to croak it,' she says, sitting back and folding her arms, wearing a smile. 'This is something I've been working on.'

'A book?'

I flipped through the pages.

'A project really. You see, it's started again. The murders.'

If the Nighthawk had an accomplice, where has he been for the last twenty years? Prison? Abroad?

DI LOCKE

PRESENT

After a bollocking off the Detective Chief Inspector for overspending on resources this month I enter a suspiciously quiet – for the time of day, at least – incident room. I glance around the space. It's like a morgue in here. Dylan is swiping right on his phone, head down, shoulders hunched, and DC Winters is absorbed in something on the screen of her computer.

There's nothing about Geraint in the newspaper article written by Ffion. It isn't even specifically about Glenn Marsh. The four-page spread lists the Worst Criminals in Welsh History – old and new – and just happens to mention the Nighthawk's serial murders.

Beneath each of the forty photographs their offences are summarised. The piece is a reportage on the apparent repeated failures of the educational, medical, and social sectors in providing care and support to the students, patients, and clients who all exhibited signs of future criminality, which Ffion deduces left the legal system to take the fall when they eventually ended up the responsibility of the prison system. The conclusion she's drawn is that those in authority are in the best position to intervene before a person goes on to commit a serious violent offence.

Something I'm inclined to agree on and not just because I work in law enforcement.

It happens, as it generally tends to do, in threes. Just after lunch, which I order to be delivered. The man on the scooter looks surprised to have found himself handing over a food order to an inspector, and then asks a series of questions I can't answer.

'Top secret, eh?' he gives me a wink, and I wonder if he knows the difference between CID and MI5.

I re-enter the building with the brown paper bags containing burgers, fries, and milkshakes to find it's bustling with energy.

Going through my emails on my phone as I trudge back to the room, I read one from DC Burtenshaw who tells me that when asked Demelza was adamant that Geraint would never exchange confidential information with anyone, and she insisted he would not disclose anything to which he was legally liable. Of course, that doesn't mean he *didn't* breach data protection legislation to provide someone with Errol's address as a favour. She wasn't told about the discovery of the text messages or their content. That'll be the job of whoever executes the warrant later.

Regardless of who it was LEAs are the only people with access to the information held by FIDS, so it makes sense that the individual worked for or with the police. It's a hard pill to swallow but misconduct within the force, though uncommon, does occur.

DC Chapman calls me the moment my butt hits my seat, having spoken to Robert Tipping, with the name of his accountant, so I hand the bag to Dylan to dish out the food. 'Julian Clements. He apparently visited Robert yesterday to discuss his business. He wouldn't specify what they talked about, but now we know who "Jules" is we can go and speak to him, find out what his relationship to Geraint was; whether Geraint was seeking financial advice or Julian was seeking legal advice. We know the firm he works for doesn't deal with Fford and Bailey, so we can count out the possibility Julian wanted to discuss Geraint and Liam's bookkeeping.'

DC Winters starts waving at me from the desk she's commandeered.

'Could you follow that up?'

'Sure,' DC Chapman replies.

I eye Dylan as I speak, who gives me a nod when I say, 'I'll call you with Julian's address after DS Jones has run some checks on the man.' I'm not sending anyone into a lion's den. 'Go grab yourself something to eat while you wait to hear back from him.'

DC Chapman is keen to end the call because 'there's a traffic build-up on the A40 due to an accident on the turn off in Raglan'.

'Boss?' Winters says, indicating for me to come on over.

The space surrounding her coats, bags, and scarves – plural – smells of vetiver, reminding me of Johnno's aftershave, and sends a spasm of longing to ripple through me.

'Yes?'

'Gina Field died seven weeks ago. There's an obituary in *The Argus*. She died at home, so there's going to be an inquest.'

'Right around the time those threatening text messages were sent to Geraint.'

I try to recall what the anonymous text messages said ad verbatim. Something about Geraint being to blame for the sender's daughter dying. Could whoever have sent them believe Geraint to be the cause of Gina's death?

'Speak to the coroner, find out how she died. And look up who Gina's next of kin are and where they live.

We may need to pay them a visit.'

The second DC Winters agrees to do just that one of the PCs, who mostly works down the corridor in the intelligence analyst's office, enters the room as though whatever she has to say is of the utmost urgency.

Our eyes lock then she says, 'You're not gonna believe this.'

■ ■ ■   👤 🔔 🏠 📢 🏃 ☀️
              HOME NEWS SPORT WEATHER

NATIONAL NEWS
WAR • COST OF LIVING • CLIMATE • UK • WORLD • BUSINESS
• POLITICS • CULTURE

—Wales—

Weather

Today	Sat	Sun	Mon	Tue
Nov 25th	Nov 26th	Nov 27th	Nov 28th	Nov 29th
-2°	-1°	0°	2°	4°

Latest

- Cardiff Cannabis club owner plans to break drugs 'stigma'
- Power cuts and travel disrupted as ice blast storms country
- Ice hockey championships to be held in London next year
- PMs plan to raise tax draws backlash from government ministers
- On the frontline: The war in the middle east
- Snow blamed for ambulance delays
- Benefit cuts causing child poverty to soar
- Over 100 people stranded as snowstorm sweeps Scottish roads
- Potholes blamed for 30% of car repair costs in this British town
- Man and child killed in head-on collision by drunk driver
- Gas prices set to increase this coming April – all you need to know
- Thousands of patients awaiting GP appointments trapped in backlog
- Murder suspect with links to Liverpool may be using fake name

Breaking

- LIVE – coverage of air strike aftermath
- Hollywood actor charged with domestic abuse – charities say not enough done to prevent violence against women and children

Local

- Major U-turn on road expansion in Valleys
- Business Fair in Swansea next week
- New installation to celebrate Nigerian art huge success
- Donors pull out of sponsorship for football club as second victim comes forward alleging rape by a player since club secured premier league status

PS TOMOS

PRESENT

The Genomica logo is emblazoned in metallic silver across a light blue swirl on a white background above the tall, wide automatic doors of the building nobody would know existed unless they were aiming for it. Due in part to the gated entrance guarded by a security team, which includes two German Shepards I'm told by the short, stocky, balding man are there to sniff out contraband. He tells me too, that I need an ID card as he loops a lanyard around my neck and directs me to where a woman awaits me holding a passport-sized photograph of moi beside my name (spelt wrong) that appears to have been snapped as I stopped to speak to security, and printed off as I traipsed the steep steps up to the topiary-adorned path that leads me into the waiting area, of which I am the only individual.

'Detective, how can I help you?' the CEO greets me.

It takes me a moment to respond as it's the first time anyone has ever called me that because I haven't yet taken my official exams.

I replicate the way my superior dives straight into her conversations with people in the hope that it will get this long, thin, snobby looking man to open up just as quickly by emphasising the seriousness of my investigation then digging for the answers I need, on the understanding that we're both exceptionally busy people.

He indicates for me to follow him through a glossy door and into a room that looks like it might be used to hold conferences.

'Our client's needs range from paternity testing to DNA comparison to assist legal inquiries, and with everything in between from genetic screening to medical diagnostics.'

'Short Tandem Repeat Analyses?'

'Yes. But it's unfortunate I cannot tell you what form of test our client required without identifying them and breaching all kinds of confidentiality clauses.'

'We know our victim contacted you, and we have information that suggests he used your services, possibly to obtain an STR, what we need to ascertain however is what case it pertained to.'

'I'm afraid I can't help you with that,' he says patronizingly, folding his wrists in front of him and smiling, sickly and sweetly. Both his words and body language are dripping with sarcasm.

'I could obtain a warrant to retrieve the report but I'm on a deadline and the department is – I'll be blunt – overstretched and underfunded, so the only alternative is to arrest you in front of your colleagues for withholding information from a police officer.'

'Pertaining to what?' he asks.

'Homicide.'

'That sounds very close to blackmail, wouldn't you agree?' he asks over my shoulder.

I glance behind me to where two security guards, the height and build of gangster's henchmen stand, blocking the doorway.

One shrugs, the other glances sideways, nose to the air, as though he couldn't care less who I was, but their false impassivity doesn't impress me.

'Ex-SAS, raised by an army sergeant and a schoolteacher.' If you think two unarmed men reliant on protein shakes and weightlifting to build up enough muscle that they don't appear too overweight to run are going to intimidate me into leaving without either you or the information I need you're stupider than you look.

I don't say that last bit, of course, I don't need to. The one who most closely resembles Lurch from *The Adam's Family* steps back as if to survey me, tilts his head to the side in invitation to come forward which I obviously don't, and raises the sleeve of his tight-fitting black polo-neck tee-shirt to display to me his skin fatigues.

'Royal Engineers,' he says, proudly.

'Respect.'

Then he loses it immediately by big-headedly banging on about all the places he's served.

'As adorable as you two are I really must be getting on ... Sergeant Thomas.'

That's when I realise who the slimy idiot reminds me of. Mr Hector, the Plaza Hotel Concierge in *Home Alone,* played by Tim Curry. It's the smarmy grin and the frog-like eyes that do it.

'It's Tomos, actually.'

I glide my phone from the pocket of my naval blue trousers, which I ironed myself – father would be proud, God rest his soul – and as though I've temporarily inherited his duplicitous mean streak, I fake a call to my superior, dropping in the words 'warrant' and 'magistrate'. I reassure her I'll see her in an hour then pretend to end the call. And praise the lord it's on 'do not disturb' as it rings silently in my hand as I return the phone to my pocket, wearing a sly smirk of my own.

In truth, my father would be turning in his grave if he was here to witness me manipulating the CEO of a large corporation into divulging protected information, but he'd be only too glad to know that it doesn't work.

I can imagine him grinning at me as I exit the building no further forward than when I had entered it and come to a stop in front of my pool car, feeling as deflated as the front tyre.

KERRY-ANN

PAST

Today's focus was to gather more information about the author, her childhood, the time she spent in college, her experiences while travelling abroad where she met her husband, and her foray into English Literature, which ultimately led to her research thesis into local crime stories, and the writing of her first book, which sealed the start to a long career as a true crime author.

'The Nighthawk interested me because he was like the bogeyman. But of course, he wasn't just a legend. Women were afraid to walk alone at night, we were all living in fear of being snatched up off the street. And the saddest reality of all is that nobody had even heard of him until he'd killed for the seventh time.'

His first victim survived.

Gina Field was just seventeen years old when he abducted her. He enslaved her in a caravan. She escaped three weeks later by using what little strength and energy she had left when he left her alone for the first time. Wrists bound behind her back, one ankle chained to the cooker door, which she tugged on until the handle snapped off, she freed herself by smashing the window above the small sink and climbing out of it and legging it into the woods. She arrived home barefoot, bloodied, bruised, and covered in her own faeces, wearing just her abductor's tee-shirt, that would be used ten years later to identify him.

But not before he'd killed seven women.

As interesting as it was to hear more about the case that had obsessed her – for her entire life it appeared – I wanted to know what Alys' relationship to her parents, husband, and children had been like. 'I need more background, on yourself.' I didn't even have enough material to start writing the introductory chapters of her biography.

'Oh, hark at me,' she said. 'When I get talking, I get carried away. I guess now I've got such little time left on this earth I can't help going over old ground. The things I thought I'd learn to live with . . . well, they niggle at me now that I'm close to the end. You see, it bothers me that the police caught him. The Nighthawk, I mean. Early on. But his solicitor helped to get him let off with just a fine and avoid jail time, which meant he never underwent any kind of psychological assessment. Had any red flags been raised early on professionals would have been able to intervene, detected some marker of future offending behaviour, maybe even prevented him from going on to murder all those women. That man, his solicitor I mean, has got a lot to answer for in my opinion, because if Glenn Marsh hadn't got away with it the others never would have been taken.'

'He was never charged, for taking Gina?' For chaining her up like a rabid dog and torturing her?

DI LOCKE

PRESENT

The news correspondent describes how the main donor of the football club, that has only recently secured premier league status, has withdrawn sponsorship since learning another of their football players has been charged with the rape of a woman. The man's ex-girlfriend. She goes on to ask what is next for the club, whose manager responds with assurance that they have the support of fans and other sponsors willing to provide funding.

She then asks if the footballer's career is salvageable after it was revealed that he'd 'forced his girlfriend to have sex with him' in the bathroom of his 'plush penthouse', insinuating that it couldn't have happened in a better place.

It's not so much a surprise as it is a disappointment that Oscar is not the only team player to have a predilection to forcing himself on women, but it angers me greatly that such an emphasis is placed on the 'huge blow his actions will have on future funding' for the club, and it sickens me that rape is still portrayed in the media as 'unwanted' or 'non-consensual' *sex*. Call it what it is, for fuck's sake.

The reporter's words hit every nerve in my body as

I repeat them, until I'm sure the tension in my muscles and the internal vibration of female rage that encompasses me is outwardly visible.

'An investigation is taking place at the request of the Association for Safety and Wellbeing in Football, as there have been several other incidents in the past two years involving the sexual impropriety of team players within the club.'

I shake my head at the news station's choice of wording. I can't blame the reporter; she's just reading from a script that was written for her by an out-of-touch – and most probably, male – producer.

'Let's hope *this one* faces repercussions,' PC Probert says.

'You mean the two that were called out before Oscar didn't either?'

'Nope,' PC Probert replies. 'Lack of evidence in both cases I believe.' She spots my empty cup and asks if I'd like a top-up of caffeine. Unable to trust myself not to scream I give her a tight-lipped nod of agreement.

Less than a minute later, she returns with a steaming cup of coffee in her hand that contains a splash of oat milk just the way she knows I like it. But no sooner have I taken a cautious sip of the scalding liquid does Dylan call me away from my desk in a hurry to see what he's found on his computer.

'Julian Clements lives and works in Chepstow with his wife. They don't have any dependents, neither do either of them have a criminal record. There's nothing online about them except he's listed on the accountancy firm's website. There are two cars registered to their home address. Both insured, taxed, and MOT'd. However, his Audi was last spotted by an ANPR camera heading west of Fishguard on Tuesday.'

The day after Geraint was murdered.

'He's done a runner.'

'It looks that way,' Dylan says.

'Contact the port, find out if he took a ferry to Ireland.'

I update DC Chapman on our findings while DC Winters appears by my side. The moment I put the phone down she tells me Gina took her own life.

'Her only next of kin is her father, Martin. Her mum died four years after her return.'

'Have you found anything that connects Geraint to Gina?'

'No,' DC Winters replies. 'Nothing. He wasn't part of the defence team who represented Glenn during the trial, and Glenn wasn't identified as Gina's abductor until he was charged with the murders of seven women. I can't see any reason for Martin to have sent those threatening text messages to Geraint unless he acted as Martin's lawyer once upon a time and failed to get him off a conviction. Though what that would have to do with Gina's death I don't know.'

'If he did it wasn't while he worked for Fford and Bailey.'

'The firm he used to work for dissolved when the owner died,' DC Winters replies. 'Even if the company's records are held somewhere we can't access them without proving we suspect Geraint of a historic crime, which we don't.'

'Geraint might not have been the one to represent him though.'

'But if Liam Bailey was his intended target, one – he's still alive, and two – wouldn't Martin have sent those threatening text messages to Liam instead of Geraint?' DC Winters asks. 'Providing it *was* him who sent them, of course.'

'What do we know about Martin?'

'Born and bred in Penarth. No priors, spent or pending. No known family in the nick. Not a named associate of anyone with a criminal conviction. No social media accounts, as far as I'm aware.' She looks me directly in the eye then adds, 'And he doesn't have any points on his driving licence.'

'He might appear squeaky clean, but he could still possess a propensity to violence. And if he *did* make those threats to Geraint by text, it suggests he has the intention to inflict harm. Which is why once he's finished the task that I've just given him I'm sending DS Jones along with you to go and talk to him and find out where he was on the night of Geraint's murder.'

THE DARK SIDE OF HORSE-RACING

Written by Clifford Siegel

One might think of The Grand National when the word 'horseracing' is mentioned. Or perhaps images of the finely attired aristocracy at Royal Ascot. Maybe even ladies wearing large parasol hats, or the excited commentary as you watch your horse thunder towards the finish line, hoping to win. But race day has far higher stakes and much deeper meanings to some within the industry than others, and whether a horse loses could quite possibly determine if their owner makes or breaks it within organised crime.

That's right, you heard me, the drug trade, arms dealing, and human trafficking all share one common denominator. And that is the need to wash dirty money, and what better way of doing it than to breed, stake shares in, rent out, or sell horses?

But before I tell you how it works, let me explain how it was discovered.

You see it all began in Dublin . . .

PS TOMOS

PRESENT

I fumble with the wrench, my fingers frozen stiff, and the nuts locked too tight. The slow loss of daylight isn't helping either, the sky dimming every minute that it takes me to change the tyre, the thick grey clouds bunched up like water-sodden cotton wool hanging over us, casting shadows of increasing length across the concrete.

I did call the Police Recovery Service as per protocol because there isn't a spare under the floor of the boot, but the man who turned up dropped the wheel on his foot as soon as he'd loosened it, so he's currently propped up against the wall nursing his painfully swollen toes. You'd have thought in his line of work he'd have been supplied with steel toe capped safety footwear, wouldn't you? I can only imagine the Health and Safety paperwork his boss is going to have to fill out once he reports the incident.

My shoulders strain from the effort of lifting and slotting on the new tyre then fixing the last lug nut in place. My forearms burn, and I'm reminded by my breathlessness how old I am, despite how young I generally feel.

'All this for something so small,' my roadside

rescuer says absentmindedly, while twirling a short slim nail between his thumb and forefinger. Blaming the offending item for having caused the flat tyre *and* his injury.

As I'd waited for his arrival, I'd sat in the car with the engine running and the heaters on full blast staring across the deserted section of the car park trying to imagine how isolated and frightened Gina had felt in those moments when she'd realised her rescuer had an ulterior motive for offering to drive her home. A deflated tyre, caused by a shard of broken glass, had led her right into the arms of a homicidal maniac.

Glancing into his rear-view mirror as he drove to the end of the road, her abductor would have seen an eight-year-old boy heading towards the abandoned fuel station, too late. His witness testimony could have proven crucial in determining where she'd last been seen. But he had no reason to tell anyone he'd passed a dark-haired man behind the steering wheel of a reddish-brown car the same shade as his mum's sofa, so police had no reason to suspect foul play when Gina's parents reported her missing and would fob off her disappearance as yet another teen having run away from home to flee their tyranny.

I wonder if that's what Eva's parents thought when they learned she'd gone missing.

I tried calling them immediately after Chris rang to tell me she'd vanished, and again once I learned South Wales Police had found her body and that she'd been murdered. But I guess they didn't want to speak to the father of the man suspected of having killed her. And I doubt they'll answer the phone to me until the person responsible for taking their daughter's life is caught and locked up.

Here's hoping it's soon.

When I get back to base Emma tells me we may just

have had a breakthrough. She then updates me on the goings on so far this afternoon.

'DS Jones spoke to a security guard at the port in Fishguard who confirmed that their CCTV camera captured Julian's car being driven onto a ferry heading to Rosslare on the twenty-third of November.'

The day after Geraint was reported missing.

'What time did it depart?'

'2 p.m.'

Eighteen hours after South Wales Police published a missing notice on their website and social media pages, and four hours after his disappearance was reported across the local news channels: online, TV, and radio.

'When I left here a few hours ago we had no suspects, now we have two.'

I tell her about my wasted journey to the biologic's lab, and she says she has an idea.

'There might be another way for us to find out if Geraint ordered a Short-Tandem Repeat test, and if so, what it was for.'

KERRY-ANN

PAST

It was late by the time we'd finished up. We'd watched the sky turn from peach and raspberry to the colour of charcoal as we'd talked about the correlation between the Nighthawk's victims and the recent murders of three women within a fifteen-mile radius of the local college, all of whom looked identical to one another and were around the same ages. It was sad and interesting, but I kept having to steer Alys back to the subject of herself. I got the sense that her deflection meant she'd had an ulterior motive all along, and rather than having wanted me to write her memoir she had instead enlisted me to find out who was responsible for the women's deaths, but I couldn't think why it was so important to her. Maybe she didn't want to leave this earth with unfinished business, or perhaps she knew something I didn't. Afterall, I hadn't yet read the entirety of her project, thus far.

I stood to leave and stared out at the blustery gale, the trees canopying the easterly edge of her lawn swaying in the wind.

Alys must have sensed I was reluctant to return to the cottage and had been prolonging my exit for as long as possible, so she suggested, due to my earlier scare, that I stay the night on the fold-out sofa-bed in the spare bedroom where her niece sometimes slept when she was little. 'Twenty or so years ago now,' she said. I also don't think she wanted to be on her own, perhaps realising that now the end was near she was likely to die alone in a big old house.

Her bed, she said, was in the living room to save her traipsing up the stairs, and in the sweeping glance she gave me I saw a commode parked beside it. The curtains were drawn, and dust motes floated down from the light fixture as she closed the door to show me the guestroom.

It smelled slightly dank and musty but that wasn't surprising considering it hadn't been slept in for two decades. Though I could tell it had been aired as there was a dead fly on the windowsill, the thinned pappus from a dandelion, and the helicopter seed of a sycamore in one corner.

***

I slept fitfully, awaking several times in the night to the sound of floorboards creaking, thinking someone was creeping across the hallway, and falling into a dreamlike state in which I wasn't quite asleep. I awoke to the unmistakable sound of metal pipes clanging.

'The plumbing's almost as old as me,' Alys said to someone I couldn't see.

I entered the living room wearing the dressing gown she'd left me at the end of my bed. It had freaked me out a bit to find it there, knowing she'd entered the room as I snored, which until she'd told me I had no idea I did. But her care and consideration towards me when she so obviously needed it herself was testament to the kind of person she was.

Natalia was seated at one end of the sofa, and it

struck me then that I hadn't heard from her since I'd texted her the night before, letting her know I was no longer in the cottage, as I'd had a fright, and that I was instead spending the night at Alys', whose address I'd given her before leaving.

I was surprised she'd travelled so far in the dark, but she said she'd left early and when I caught the time on the grandfather clock it hit me that I'd awoken far later than I'd intended.

Noticing my shock, Alys said I must have needed it, then Natalia produced from the rucksack at her feet a letter addressed to me, stamped first class and dated two days prior, which meant it must have arrived in the post the day before.

I hadn't expected the visiting order to be so quick. I hadn't quite prepared what to say to my father, despite the ease with which I could get people to open up about their experiences. I wasn't really sure how to broach the subject of my existence and his lack of presence in my life without delving into the past; the reason we'd been separated in the first place and why I had grown up without him.

But I didn't need to worry about that yet.

What concerned me was what Alys had insinuated the previous afternoon, as she'd carried a pot of tea into the dining room and placed it gently between us, which was probably why I'd struggled to stay asleep.

'I don't want to spend my last moments confined to a hospital bed. I want to die with dignity, on my own terms.'

Had I got it wrong? Was the memoir not a ruse to get me to continue her research project, but rather to ensure she had someone with her when – as she termed it – 'God came calling'?

DI LOCKE

PRESENT

I turn right at the end of the corridor and use my key fob to pass through a set of double doors before pressing the buzzer to the intercom for a section of the unit I've never accessed before. Less than a minute later a bespectacled man appears to escort me into a room lined with computers and not much else.

I must admit I haven't a clue what exactly it is they do here, except that whatever it is the crime analysts do it in bright white light that would give me a migraine if I was to spend longer than necessary in the suite they share with the rest of the tech team, and that it involves algebra and computer technology, both my weak points. What I do know, however, is that these nerdy creatures who are rarely seen outdoors despite their obvious love of UV-ray-like daylights are wizards when it comes to figuring numerical shit out, something they call 'statistical configuration'.

I don't know who I'm talking to, I don't think I've ever met any of them in person before, but they've helped us out a lot before now, and so I answer the elvish man's questions while his – assistant? – makes notes on a black-screened iPad with a pen that leaves rune-like marks on it in the colour of every type of highlighter combined.

'The results came in yesterday. We know the name of the company that completed whatever test it was and the name of the client who requested it. We were hoping that you could somehow use that information to estimate a possible date the tests took place to provide us with the crime reference number the analysis referred to. Providing of course it was a comparison between two criminals.'

'And that they're both on the UK's National DNA Database,' he says.

'That too,' I admit.

'Luckily for you, what you're asking for is relatively simple,' he says.

'It is?'

'Fifteen minutes,' the iPad-holding woman says, not looking up from what appears to be her own version of shorthand that fills the dark screen.

I frown. That quick?

'Quarter of an hour,' she says, slowly, as though speaking to a child. And I feel like one when she adds, 'We input data through the computer software program, it generates a probable outcome, we compare all potential variables to determine the most likely result.'

Seeing the confusion written on my face, her – supervisor? – tries his best to break it down in understandable terms, which is, thankfully, easier to comprehend. 'By cross matching the tests the biogenic company does against how long it takes to complete each test we can determine roughly what date Mr Fford requested the test and use that information to establish whose profile(s) on the NDNAD it was compared to.'

She nods and I smile, thank them for their expertise, and make a hasty dash, a twitch developing in the corner of my right eye from the glare of the strip light above my head.

PS TOMOS

PRESENT

Julian wasn't at home when DC Chapman went to speak to him. But his wife was. She said she hasn't reported her husband missing because she knows where he is.

'I won't be giving ye no address though,' Mrs Clements replied, according to their transcribed conversation, which I read while munching on a Crispy Crème someone kindly bought several share boxes of because it's their birthday.

'That's not a problem,' DC Chapman said. 'We've already spoken to the gardaí. His vehicle has been spotted on an ANPR camera in County Cork. He's a wanted man in a sparsely populated town in a small country. He won't get far, especially now he's on Interpol's Red List.'

For her lack of cooperation when asked where he was headed and who he knew in Ireland, she was warned she'd be arrested for obstructing a police officer in the execution of his duty if she wasn't forthcoming with the information she had, to which she piped up that Julian had fled without telling her why.

'He wasn't in bed when I woke up and some of his

clothes were gone,' Mrs Clements replied. 'As soon as I realised that he'd left I guessed he'd be at his ma's. But I don't want ye bothering the old woman. So help me god if she learns I've lost her son.'

'She lives in Kinsale, no,' DC Chapman said.

'Right, so,' Mrs Clements replied through gritted teeth.

'He wasn't there when garda searched the house less than an hour ago. In fact, his ma seemed surprised to find them on her doorstep.'

'I dare say she was. They must have frightened the bejesus out of her.'

'She told them she hasn't heard from Julian since the funeral.'

'I'm sure she hasn't. They're not close.'

'His father, no?'

'Right, so. Triple bypass. Died on the operating table, so he did. Seventy-two. Too fat for surgery.'

I swallow the last mouthful of my sticky iced bun and suck the icing off my thumb and forefinger while Jonesy calls Emma.

I can only hear her half of the conversation, but I can detect a note of relief in her voice when she reiterates it to me while I'm washing my hands in the communal sink beside the toilets.

She leans back against the wall, legs folded at the ankle, arms crossed over her waist. 'Martin wasn't at home when DS Jones and DC Winters knocked on his door, but a neighbour told them he was likely down his local boozer. There they found him, drowning his sorrows.'

They're on their way to the custody suite with him now.

'He refused to speak to them voluntarily, then resisted arrest. We're going to have to wait for him to sober up before we can interview him, but it shouldn't be long because he's not even over the prescribed blood-alcohol limit.'

In a matter of hours, the nightshift will be able to watch the live fed footage of Martin being questioned.

Back at my desk Emma points to the transcript that fills the screen of my computer due to the amount of zooming in I now have to do despite wearing such thick-lensed glasses, and asks, 'What's she saying?'

'When asked by the garda if she'd noticed any recent changes to her husband's behaviour, Mrs Clements said only the night before stood out to her because Julian was acting odd. "We were waiting for an update on the weather and caught the end of the local news. There was a picture on the screen of this man, a lawyer, who the reporter was saying had gone missing. Julian switched off the TV and walked out of the room. I had a go at him for taking the remote control with him and he apologised, came back in, and handed it to me, but his face . . . his skin had gone pale. He looked like he'd seen a ghost." At the time she just thought he had a lot on his mind. He was meeting with some banking executive the following day. But in hindsight I think they're an interesting choice of words, don't you?'

KERRY-ANN

PAST

Natalia patted me on the shoulder, squeezed it, then ran her hand down my arm to take my hand, pressing her fingers between mine in solidarity. 'It'll be okay, *you'll* be okay. And it if goes tits-up I'll be right here waiting for you.'

I smiled and she crossed her eyes and stuck out her tongue.

HMP Cardiff was a brown brick-built building that dominated the skyline. I trod along the pavement before turning into the car park that was signposted for staff only. The gates securing the main entrance loomed large as I passed them to reach the side door where the families of inmates were already queuing in a long line which snaked past the security guard by several yards.

By the time it was my turn to drop my keys into the tray and stand like a starfish for the prison officer to wave the magnetic wand in front of and behind me to check for illicit items my stomach was doing backflips.

I felt as though I'd reached the end of a quest.

I recognised him instantly as I walked into the visitors' room, where I had just two hours to learn more about the man that my mother claimed to love until the day she'd died. Google Chrome had provided me with a photograph of the man I shared half my genes with. Though I wasn't aware we had the same eye and hair colour until then as the picture had been in black and white.

He stood as though wanting to reach out and hug me. I sat on the plastic chair bolted to the floor on the opposite side of the table from the man who stole my mother's heart. He, reluctantly it seemed, followed suit.

I didn't know what to say to Roderick so was glad he broke the awkward silence. 'You look just like your mother.' He sighed, eyes watering.

'You loved her.'

'Never stopped.'

'Then why didn't she visit you?'

'She did.'

'She never brought me with her.'

'At first, she did, then I told her to stop coming, to get on with her life, focus on you. Stubborn she was.'

'I don't understand.'

'She kept coming even after I refused her visits. She'd wait outside come rain or shine. She was out there once in the snow, shivering for hours the screws said.'

'Screws?'

'Prison Officers. How'd you get here?'

'You're trying to steer me away from talking about my mother. Why?'

His eyes filled with tears again. 'It breaks my heart that we were forced apart. She was the love of my life. I never wanted . . . I did it for her.'

'Killed Geoffrey?'

'No, I . . .' His face hardened. 'I didn't want you to see me in here, to be around all this . . . negativity. I thought it best if you both moved on.'

'She couldn't.'

'No. It was a mistake. My biggest regret.'

'Do you regret killing Geoffrey?'

'No. No, I . . .'

His honest answer took me by surprise. So while we were on a roll . . .

'Why did you do it, murder him I mean?'

'Straight to the point, huh?'

I shrugged. 'We haven't got long.'

He opened his mouth to speak but I cut him off before he could start. 'I'll grab us both a drink from the vending machine first. What are you having?'

DI LOCKE

PRESENT

Having been given by the data analyst an estimated date and time the probable STR test took place, we were able to roughly match it to only one sample comparison likely extracted on the 9th of November regarding suspect X. Who, according to the crime reference number, relates to an unknown male of Caucasian origin whose DNA has been retrieved from the scenes of two murders. One twenty-seven years ago, the other just a few days ago. Both females. Both disappeared shortly before their bodies were found. Both had been tied up, starved, raped, burnt, beaten, and strangled. Just like Eva. Almost as though he'd been mimicking the Nighthawk's crimes.

Is he copying the acts committed by Glenn Marsh?

Speaking to the senior detective who is leading the investigation I discover that neither he nor his legal team have any knowledge of or connection to Geraint, but he is very interested to know why we initially believed the lawyer may have come across his suspect's DNA.

'How do you propose he got hold of it?' he asks.

I tell him we think Geraint extracted it from a cup or glass, which would have been easy enough for him to have done once the suspect – a client perhaps – had left his office.

Did someone who knew Geraint had obtained the DNA sample want to get rid of him before the results were analysed?

'I suppose that would have been a possibility, if those lab results intended for Geraint *do* refer to a Short-Tandem Repeat analysis,' he says.

I ask the detective if he's able to tell me who he gave permission to in order that the reference sample – they had acquired two decades ago from a cigarette stub – could be retrieved and tested against this other DNA profile his team collected from one of the recent murder scenes, and he tells me he signed it off on behalf of one of his colleagues at South Wales Police.

I dial her number as soon as he ends the call, just after 3 p.m.

She answers on the third ring.

A quick chat with her reveals that she ordered the analysis based on a semen sample taken from a woman who'd been abducted before her deceased body had been located.

'The DNA matched Suspect X.'

So, although the STR appears to have been a red herring, it seems I may have inadvertently come across the reason for Dafydd's son, Chris, who had been held on suspicion of murdering his girlfriend, from having been released without charge. And though the link is tenuous and likely just a coincidence, a second indirect connection to the case, I know, will result in Dafydd being removed from the investigation indefinitely. Something I know he will be upset about, but for integrity's sake I have no option but to instigate by informing DCI Evans.

'So Suspect X is believed to have murdered three women as far as you know, and has you think, abducted another?'

She confirms my suspicion then goes on to explain how Eva's phone might hold the clue as to the potential name of their killer.

'She'd deleted a dating app from her phone around the time she started a relationship with her boyfriend. One of the men on the dating app appears to have been messaging her a lot, at least according to the encrypted messaging service attached to the app.'

The boyfriend being Dafydd's son.

I thank her and end the call, then turn my attention to the TV.

Watching Martin's interview on the live feed is like witnessing a car crash in slow motion, one in which I can't intervene. It's hard not to feel sorry for the man who believes he's been robbed of his not so little girl. But none of us could possibly have guessed how he'd concluded Geraint was to blame for her suicide.

Having been shown the text messages and asked by DC Winters if he'd sent them to Geraint, Martin says, 'Yeah, I did.'

'How did you get his number?'

'I found it on the website for the law firm he works at.'

'Why did you make those threats?'

'I wanted to scare him, hurt him.'

'Kill him?'

'Yeah,' Martin replies. 'If it wasn't for him, Gina would still be here. He might not have murdered her but he's the reason she's dead.'

'The coroner recorded Gina's death as a suicide.'

'She didn't want to live anymore because of what that man did to her. She was never the same after Glenn took her. Not eating, promiscuous, taking drugs. And he might never have taken her if he'd been imprisoned all those years ago. Early intervention could have prevented him from kidnapping Gina and murdering all those women.'

'You wanted to hold Geraint to account for your daughter's suicide, why?'

It turns out that Geraint represented Glenn Marsh as a youth, and Martin blames him for the fine he received instead of a custodial sentence. His charge for animal cruelty was dropped to that of a caution. As the offence took place prior to computerisation, and it was recorded on paper while he was a minor, it was never digitised. Not that it would have made much of a difference anyway considering the caution was filtered from both PNC and DBS checks five and a half years after his eighteenth birthday.

The prosecution made the discovery and disclosed it to his legal team. Both believed it to be a precipitating factor and agreed for it to be revealed during the trial. The prosecution wanted to use it to demonstrate a callous, calculating character, the defence argued those traits proved he had a psychopathic personality disorder, hence why they suggested he plead not guilty on the grounds of diminished responsibility by reason of insanity. The jury didn't buy it, however, hence how he ended up in prison rather than a forensic psychiatric hospital. They were convinced there were other victims – dead or alive – for which he'd never been caught.

'The police never found out who Gina's abductor was. She gave a description of Glenn, and the police kept the tee-shirt she was wearing when she fled the caravan that he'd kept her in, but DNA testing was in its infancy then so there was nothing for forensic scientists to crossmatch it against.'

Biologic advances during a case review meant that the identification of a male – who'd been arrested by Merseyside police for a string of armed robberies, including a betting shop in Aberdare – carrying the same paternal DNA to that found on several female corpses matched the profile retrieved from Gina's tee-shirt all those years ago. His father's name was Glenn Marsh.

During the trial in which Gina acted as a witness, the caution for animal cruelty was mentioned, as a precipitating factor, by Geraint, who was subpoenaed to testify in court. Which is where Martin and his wife, who were there to support their daughter, learned who Geraint was. But as Glenn had been a minor at the time of the offence it could not be reported on by journalists, hence how only those present during the trial knew about it.

In a catch twenty-two scenario, had Glenn Marsh been given more than a slap on the wrist for burning and strangling a cat he might not have abducted Gina, intending to practise the very same skills on her. However, had he not abducted Gina, and sadly done more and far worse besides, he might have taken even more women's lives before he'd been caught.

Which is, in my view, as good a motive for Martin to want to kill Geraint as any other.

Loud echoic footsteps follow me down the corridor.

'Boss.'

I turn at the squeak of PC Cottrell's flat-soled black leather shoes on the linoleum entryway. She looks downcast for such an upbeat person.

'I've had no luck with the legal secretary or Fford and Bailey's accountant on the STR front.' She sighs.

'It's still possible whoever wrote those text messages was referring to a Short-Tandem Repeat but it's not looking all that promising that it involved a criminal whose profile was on the NDNAD.'

I tell her I sought the help of the data analysts who looked into potential DNA profiles on the FIDS as a last resort, and that although I wasn't holding out much hope on it being all that relevant to our investigation, what I've learned more or less confirms that whatever those lab results from Genomica referred to most likely had nothing to do with any forensic testing.

'Though there does appear to be a serial killer replicating the Nighthawk's crimes.'

I fill her in on the discovery made by South Wales Police then she asks me how Martin's interview went.

'I don't want to speak too soon but I think we may have just found our man.'

PS TOMOS

PRESENT

I shut down my computer and begin to tidy my desk, going over what I've learned as I use an antibacterial wipe to mop up the coffee stains and crumbs.

A year before his release from prison, despite never having had a visitor throughout his entire incarceration, a woman called Kerry-Ann Pascoe came to see Roderick Penrose. Shortly afterwards, he was transferred to an open prison. But within weeks he caught Covid and was admitted to a ward within the Intensive Care Department of the University Hospital of Wales, which is where he died several days later.

I wonder how her father felt being wheeled into the building he'd have known might be the last he'd ever see. Was he conscious for long, or had he needed to be sedated and monitored on a ventilator as soon as he'd been admitted, as my father had been before he'd succumbed to the cancer that had ravaged his body?

I wanted to know what Roderick and his daughter had talked about, and whether he'd ever told Kerry-Ann why he'd killed Geoffrey Goldsborough. Had he somehow found out about the allegations made against his employer? Had Nancy? Afterall, she'd been the Goldsborough's housekeeper for years, giving her ample opportunity to snoop or accidentally come across something that gave Geoffrey's crimes away, had he been stupid enough to leave anything incriminating lying about.

I swivel my chair around and stand to cross the room and deposit my wrappers in the bin when one of the forensic technician's eyes me from the doorway and asks me if I've 'Got a minute?'

'Yeah.'

'We've found some very interesting things on Julian Clements' laptop.'

Penrith House,
Fort Road,
Lavernock,
South Wales,
CF64 5UL

5th September 1995

Dr Ezekeil Conway (Director of Female Psychiatry),

I hereby give you my voluntary resignation notice, thirty days in advance as required by my employment contract.

Dr Geoffrey Goldsborough (Head of Women's Mental Health Services)

Wotton Dean Psychiatric Hospital
Saltmarsh Lane
Gloucestershire
England
GL51 4SR

5/9/95

Dr Geoffrey Goldsborough,

Please find enclosed within this envelope a cheque for the sum of £2,500, which in accordance with government guidelines is the total Statutory Redundancy Pay due to you (full calculation below).

Regards,
Pamela Kurien, Human Resources

Years (5) x weekly earnings (£500) prior to deductions = £2,500.

KERRY-ANN

PAST

I sat there stunned as my father told me how my mother had run sobbing into his arms. When he'd asked her what was wrong, she'd said that she'd quit working for the Goldsborough's. Then she explained why she was so upset. Geoffrey had offered my mother money in exchange for her silence.

What she'd discovered had shook 'Nance' – as he'd called her – to her core, and she'd run from the house to the shed at the far end of the garden to where my father was potting plants.

The letter she'd found while tidying the desktop cabinet in Geoffrey's study at the back of the house hadn't mentioned what he'd been accused of, only that the woman involved had made an allegation against him. Which in itself didn't sound good, but was it reason enough to have caused such anger in my father that he'd murdered him over it?

Apparently not.

'I crossed the lawn and went straight inside the house to confront him. Only . . .' He dropped his head in his hand, rubbed his face, looked me in the eye and said three words that chilled me to my core, 'Celyn was there.'

I leaned back against the hard plastic chair and took a moment to absorb the meaning of his words.

'You mean...?' She was there when you grabbed the iron poker from the fireplace and beat him to death, across the head, with it?

'She was in the kitchen, had entered through the back door. Forgotten something on her way out, she said. She'd overheard everything that was said between them. Your mother asking Geoffrey what he'd done to the woman, him telling her she was neurotic, that he'd been treating her for a phobia of water, but that she'd freaked out, tried to climb out of the bath, had fallen back in, had begun screeching and claiming he was a charlatan, was trying to kill her. He'd got his lawyer to write up an NDA and had voluntarily resigned from his post, to avoid a criminal investigation. He was offered a voluntary redundancy package, which I expect was their way of severing ties with him without having to go through the rigmarole of an internal investigation, that may very well have turned criminal. Said he'd been headhunted for a new position at a private hospital, specialising in eating disorders and addiction, his specialities.'

Because they knew nothing about what had allegedly transpired between Geoffrey and the woman.

'Celyn hadn't known; she must have been incensed?'

His eyes glazed over, as though he'd gone somewhere else in his mind, had returned to the past, to relive those last few minutes that would change the course of his life forever.

'She told me that they'd argued; that she hadn't meant to do it.'

'What are you saying?'

'I made a split-second decision. A bad one.'

'You covered for her! Why?'
'She was pregnant.'
'Celyn?'
'No, your mother.'
'My . . .?'

And then suddenly it all clicked into place. My mother's sudden descent into a deep depression, while she was pregnant with me. One in which the root cause appeared to have been my father's incarceration. A sadness so powerful that despite time and the medications and therapy she was never able to climb her way out of it.

'Nancy killed him. My mother murdered Geoffrey.'

And my father took the blame.

'I didn't want her giving birth in a hospital bed in a room where a screw would be standing outside the door. I didn't want you spending the first six months of your life on a mother and baby unit inside a prison. And then to be parted from her and handed over to me, a virtual stranger. It wouldn't have been fair. On you, or her. I did what I thought was right.'

He sounded genuine, but he could be lying. Was he placing the blame on my mother, who was dead and could not defend herself? I didn't know him, couldn't read him. It was infuriating.

'I'm not sorry for my actions, but I do regret not being a part of your life.'

He looked remorseful.

'I think about you every day, Kezzie.'

I frowned. 'Kezzie?'

'It's a silly nickname I gave you, in here.'

'I like it.'

He smiled, a warm infectious smile that left creases around his eyes.

There was something still bothering me though. 'Why didn't Celyn say anything to the police, tell them the truth? Why did she lie for you, for mum?'

'I made her promise not to. I told her that if she said anything to anyone, I'd tell them why Geoffrey and Nancy had argued, why she'd lost it. That I'd ruin Geoffrey's reputation. And she agreed. A little too easily if you ask me. I guess she was more concerned about her husband's legacy than anyone knowing who'd really killed him.'

DI LOCKE

PRESENT

It's almost 8 p.m. when I leave the incident room with the image of Gina Field, dangling from the cord of her dressing gown by her neck, burnt to my retinas. Martin has been drinking every day since he came home from work to find his daughter swinging above the staircase. He's grieving his daughter's death. He's been obsessing over Geraint's perceived involvement in Gina's suicide. He can't remember where he was on the evening of Geraint's murder. He's admitted to wanting to kill him. He had the means, motive, and opportunity to do so. But he hasn't admitted to having done it. And we can't prove he did.

Which is why we'll have to let him go.

We struck luck when we came upon the contents of Julian's laptop. One of the men he's in regular contact with owns a racecourse whose most recent audit by actuaries revealed he'd been evading tax. It's damning because accountants are knowledgeable on the fundamentals of business law, and although the man is not a client of his that does not mean Julian hasn't been providing him with informal advice, as a friend.

Some of the horses that race the course have been bred by Paddy Daly using studs loaned by Robert

Tipping, Julian's buddy from his university days.

Another of his mates, a Latvian-born man residing in Rotterdam whose last-known whereabouts were Canada, named Mehmet Ivanova, is one of the FBIs Most Wanted for drug trafficking. He owns a haulage company that travels the Red Sea. His last shipment, bound for the UK, was stopped by Customs and Excise in Panama. During the search ten tonnes of fentanyl-laced heroin was found on board, inside the cargo hold, by the Federal Bureau of Investigation.

The NCA have been vocal on the subject of distribution networks. And, as I recall during a conference not all that long ago, one of their Organised Crimes Commanders imparted to us – via some online training materials – how one of the popular routes of drug trafficking into the UK is the transportation of products from carriers to smaller vessels. Where the delivery to desolate (unpopular, non-touristy) beaches in Europe and The British Isles grants those involved less chance of being caught and their high-value products being seized.

This concerns me greatly.

Lavernock is the perfect place to swap merchandise. Which is why it was one of the infamous Portuguese pirate, Alfredo De Marisco's, favourite hideouts.

Did Geraint know this? Was he shot dead whilst waiting for a shipment, intending to collect evidence of Julian's involvement in his friend's illegal business dealings?

Afterall, Geraint had been in contact with Julian Clements shortly before his disappearance. Julian's university buddy, Robert Tipping, is a business associate of Paddy Daly. Paddy Daly spoke to Geraint the very day he was shot dead. He was shot dead by someone who deliberately or accidentally struck him in the stomach the first time they pulled the trigger. The person who shot him dead used the same brand of gun that killed Errol James Parker. Errol's father, William Maurice Parker, died of a heroin overdose. There's nothing linking Errol or his father to Geraint, but Colm McGinty, who we know from the Osman Warning had threatened Geraint's life, was not only the son of one of his former client's – an ex-IRA member named Fergal – but also one of Paddy's associates, a man the NCA were convinced was involved in the heroin trade. Heroin laced with fentanyl, like that found by the FBI aboard a cargo ship owned by Mehmet Ivanova, a friend of Julian Clements. A man who just happens to have departed the country the very day it was reported that Geraint's body had been found during the search for the missing man.

It seems that no matter who else we're led to all leads keep circling back to Julian.

PS TOMOS

PRESENT

I wash the dishes while Sarah dries them with the tea towel that I bought her from the services on my way back from Scotland. A souvenir reminding me of the time I nabbed that woman who was wanted in connection with the disappearance of her old college mate. Was that only two months ago? It feels like years have passed since my trek to the Outer Hebrides. She returned to Wales in the rear of a police van, while I drove the 650 miles back down to Newport in a Jaguar XF. Not my own; there's no way I could afford one of those on my salary, it was a pool car from the station's forecourt.

England, Ireland, Wales. All the other tea towels in our collection hanging on the rail beside the sink.

Hands in the lukewarm water, soap suds on my nose from our little playfight a moment ago, acting childishly, glad to have both our boys over for dinner, listening to them bicker in the living room about what to watch on our TV, smiling because it means we're all together, that despite the fact Chris is grieving Eva's murder he's no longer considered responsible, is when it comes to me.

The Irish connection.

It was there all along.

The Osman warning regarding Colm McGinty, a former IRA member, born, bred, and living in Ireland.

Paddy Daly, an Irishman, now the owner of a pub in Usk.

The fentanyl-laced heroin, believed to originate from one of his associates, in Dublin.

Julain Clements fleeing to his homeland of Ireland the day after Geraint's body had reportedly been swept up.

Not forgetting the fishing trawler spotted cruising along the coastline of the bay past the island. It was identified as having departed Dún Laoghaire three hours earlier.

I dump the towel on the worktop not realising it's wet. Sarah's always on at me for flooding the kitchen when I wash up, and she doesn't let me off the fact she has to use another from the rail to dry the cutlery, which is all that's left to do.

'Dafydd?'

'Sorry, love.'

'You've only been home an hour,' she says, rolling her eyes.

'I know, but I've gotta speak to the boss.' I plant a kiss on her forehead and dart from the kitchen.

Before I've made it to the end of the hall and stuffed my hand into the pocket of my coat that hangs on a hook beside the front door in search of my phone, she's already wheeled it down to me. 'It was on the dining table.'

'What would I do without you, eh?'

KERRY-ANN

PAST

Natalia was leaning out of the window when I reached the car wearing a frown.

'Dare I ask how it went?'

'He said he didn't do it.'

She gave me a look that said, 'Sure, don't they all say that?' and I filled her in on the conversation I'd had with my father.

'Woah,' she said, shaking her head. 'Makes total sense though dunnit?'

I reluctantly agreed.

There was a panda car parked in the lane, boxing mine in at the end which meant I couldn't turn it around. Natalia stopped her car behind the police officer's and walked ahead of me towards the swing gate. We entered the cottage together. She kept watch while I packed my belongings. It wasn't until I went to check the back door was locked that I discovered the mechanism was broken.

'Has anything been taken?' Natalia asked, while I rummaged around in my bag.

'Not that I can see.'

'Thank God you weren't here when they broke in,' she said, exhaling an audible sigh of relief.

My internal monologue completed the sentence: *Imagine what might have happened to you had the burglar found you inside the cottage?*

The copper was seated inside his car when we returned to our own, gazing at the horizon, a slice of foggy sea and sand below a weak sun visible between a crack of wall and hedge. He turned his gaze to us as we kissed each other goodbye. I'd reported the break-in to the landlord of the Airbnb who said she'd call the police herself, so there was no need to tell him.

'Ring me when you get home to let me know you arrived safely.'

I followed a couple of yards behind Natalia's car. Slowing when we reached the end of the road, I glanced up into the rear-view mirror and saw the police car advancing on us. I waved her off, turning left and watched as the copper swung right, too fast, as though he was in pursuit of someone.

I didn't think for a second, he was chasing after her.

The house was cold and quiet when I returned. The fire wasn't lit, and the TV was off. That's how I knew something was wrong. Alys wasn't in the living room though. Neither was she in the kitchen having passed out on the tiles. Nor was she anywhere downstairs that I could see. The kitchen door was locked, so she hadn't taken a tumble on the garden steps. I instinctively knew she wasn't in the bathroom, sensing she hadn't fallen into the bath and drowned herself while running it, or slipped off the toilet and injured her head and lay on the floor bleeding out. Which was why I headed straight up the stairs and into the master bedroom where I found her, the bottles of liquid diamorphine beside her on the nightstand, open, empty.

She looked as though she was asleep. But it was impossible for somebody to survive having consumed so much.

She must have been saving the bottles up. Which explained how lucid she was despite her predicament. How spritely and hungry, for someone with a terminal disease. She hadn't been taking her medication, she'd been saving it up intending to swallow it all in one go.

If it weren't for her pallor, the note she had left would have given away the fact that she was dead. She had placed it in such a way that I did not have to touch it to read it. I sat on the chair in the corner of the room, not wanting to leave her alone. While I waited for the ambulance to arrive, I thought back through our conversations, remembering one in particular which in that moment seemed to have acquired a new meaning:

'I don't want to spend my last moments confined to a hospital bed. I want to die with dignity, on my own terms.'

I had been right. The memoir *was* a ruse, but not for the reason I had thought. It wasn't that she hadn't wanted to die alone. She had wanted me to be the one to find her. But why me?

She couldn't have known how my mother had died. There was nothing on or offline naming the daughter of Geoffrey Goldsborough's so-called murderer. And even if there had been, my mother didn't share the same surname as Roderick Penrose.

I wondered if my grandmother – Reenie, as my father had affectionately called her – had felt as helpless to prevent Nancy's death or as ashamed of missing the warning signs as I did in that moment?

SIX MONTHS LATER

DI LOCKE

PRESENT

DS Tomos opens the door for me like the perfect gent that he is, and I follow him from the car and up the steps into Cardiff Crown Court. My phone bleeps with a text message notification from Dylan and I click onto it to check that it isn't urgent before turning it off and dropping it into the plastic tray.

'Another baby pic?' DS Tomos asks.

'Yup.'

I've been sent several photographs of my soon-to-be goddaughters already, each funnier than the last: all milk-drunk smiles and rude hand signals, every single one of them reminding me of Jaxon when he was small and of the fact that I'll never birth a baby of my own.

We've spoken about surrogacy, using my eggs and Johnno's swimmers, or even adopting, and the possibility of me taking some time off work to experience the joys of stay-at-home motherhood my friends and family assure me isn't all it's cracked up to be. But glutton for punishment that I am I'd like to find that out for myself.

I raise my arms and walk through the scanner, then allow the security guard to wave the wand over me, from head to toe, front and back.

I wait for DS Tomos beside the sign declaring which cases are being heard in courtrooms number one to five today. The plea and trial preparation hearing took place four months ago. Not guilty. Hence why we're here instead of inside the incident room where DS Llyons is preparing the paperwork relating to the murder of a single mother by her ex-boyfriend to send over to the CPS.

This morning marks the beginning of what I expect to be a lengthy case of I-never-did-it, despite the evidence we collated to the contrary. I have to attend today as the prosecution barrister has decided to call me up to the stand. And it is us 'expert witnesses' who will be heard first.

I can't watch proceedings until I've testified, so we separate, DS Tomos and I.

While I take a seat in the waiting area, cold because of the constantly opening and closing of the large wooden entrance door fronting the building, he heads inside Courtroom Number Three.

DS TOMOS

PRESENT

The smell of pine disinfectant and a few over-the-shoulder glances in my direction greets my entrance. I take a seat at the end of the row of benches made from the same solid wood as every other court I've ever been in. The carpet, too; thin and hard-wearing is the type used in most government-owned establishments.

Two members of the press are ushered into the gallery above us. I recognise Ffion instantly and respond to her tight smile with a nod of my head.

A prison officer enters the dock partitioned with Plexiglass, and an audible hush quiets the room. Then comes another, escorting the defendant from the holding cells below and onto a chair facing the court. And I feel myself drawn to their shuffling walk, the way the accused sits, neck bent forward, shoulders stooped, hands clasped together to hold them still, thin-limbed, and jittery, and I wonder, not for the first time, how on earth they were able to hold, aim, and fire a gun.

Everyone rises for the judge to enter the courtroom, then we wait for her to sit at the lectern before we follow suit. The jury are sworn in, then the prosecution barrister stands and glances around the room, drawing everyone's attention towards him with his silence.

His gaze is soft and sad, voice warm and gentle. 'Mr Geraint Fford, aged forty-eight, size eleven shoes, weighed sixteen stone. Dark hair, brown eyes. Collected models of classic cars, liked Mexican food, enjoyed hiking on weekends, went away with his wife and twin daughters once a year to Cornwall. Loving husband, good father, dedicated lawyer. But what this description cannot do is tell you of the devastating impact upon those who knew him in the wake of his death. He didn't try to fend off his attacker, he couldn't. He was shot at point blank range by a cold-blooded killer. The man who has brought you all here today was murdered, and it is my duty on behalf of the Crown to ensure the person responsible does not get away with it.'

His words are powerful, evoking images in my mind of lady justice with her arms outstretched, a set of scales in one hand, a sword in the other.

'That person, Ladies and Gentlemen, is here today, standing there.' He directs the court to the defendant.

We hear how Geraint's body was found and about the profound trauma experienced in the aftermath by his family, friends, business partner, work colleagues, clients, and associates.

He concludes his opening statement by painting a very visceral picture in the minds of the jury, and dare I say it the supporters of the accused, as well as the journalists, and members of the community invested in the case who are seated in the public gallery. 'The person responsible for ending Mr Fford's life didn't even have the decency to leave him where he lay. They rolled him over the edge of the island's cliffside and pushed him into the sea, so he wouldn't be found for several days.'

When he was, the prosecutor describes, much to the horror of the court, Geraint had seaweed in his hair and was coated in a thin layer of adipocere (a waxy substance similar to that of duck fat which forms on the skin of a decomposing body exposed to moisture).

As the prosecutor sits, the defendant's barrister stands and speaks of the 'dedicated lawyer's' extra-curricular activities as though volunteering his time to the 'Victims of Wotton Dean' and investigating the accusations against Geoffrey Goldsborough's son, Oscar, is a crime. A crime that put him in the firing line of a killer.

What this means of course is that just as we were unable to do, the defence couldn't find a single thing to contradict Geraint's good character. Which I dare say is why it took us so long to figure out who would have wanted him dead.

The first day of court involves witness testimonies from experts in ballistics, and blood spatter analysis, whilst an array of artifacts in see-through Ziplock bags are handed over to the jury who pass them around like unwanted Christmas presents. Included within one is the bullet that passed through Geraint's stomach which was discovered on the marram grass where he was shot, upon which some fragments of cadaver tissue remain visible on the jacket, and inside another is the mobile phone deposited in the supermarket recycling bin which contains the threatening text messages from Martin Field.

The next witness to approach the box is the lifeboatman who, along with two crewmembers were training one of their newest recruits with a practise-mission that ended with the rescue of a week-old corpse.

The accused sits, face impassive throughout. Even as the pathologist explains the injuries Geraint sustained during the shooting, followed by the cuts that covered his arms and legs from his body having been left at the mercy of the tides which threw him up onto the shore, snatched him back, then spat him out again, twice daily, for the duration of his disappearance. Which meant that while those who missed him prayed for his safe return, his flesh was being battered by the debris that lined the coast.

The defence council tries to detract from the deliberate act which led to Geraint's ultimate demise by – what, I'm not sure: suggesting his suicidal thoughts made him vulnerable to being victimised? As though the 'self-inflicted razor-cuts to his wrists' meant he was subconsciously asking to be murdered. It's the same tactic used against rape victims to portray them as sluts who secretly fantasise about being taken advantage of or suggest they seduced their perpetrators just by breathing.

His state of mind is also the subject of the medical records which are read out to categorise Geraint as depressed and anxious, potentially as a result of a difficult upbringing, and suffering from a weakened immune system and poor heart health as a consequence of the lifelong medication he was forced to take due to the medical condition that severely impacted his physical fitness.

After a short break I fill with the sandwiches I brought with me and a vending machine bottle of water – because thanks to several recent acid attacks one is not allowed to bring into the building their own drink – Emma gets to say her piece.

'What was your experience upon entering the family home?' the defence barrister asks her during his cross-examination.

'Average-sized.'

'And the environment?'

'Clean, tidy, but also lived in.'

'Homely.' He nods, circling the space between the bench and the judge. 'But it wasn't his home, was it, because Mr Fford had left. In fact, shortly before his murder he'd separated from his wife and moved into a small flat above a café in the centre of town. Isn't that right?'

She can't refute his claim, but she knows where he's heading, and that his line of questioning is necessary.

'Yes, though it was some weeks before his murder.'

'And is it not also true that his "loyal wife" Mrs Fford, had already begun to refer to herself as *Ms* Fford by the time she had reported her husband missing?'

'Not exactly.'

'She did or she did not?'

'She did refer to herself as *Ms*, but she was using her maiden name.'

'Which was?'

'Ms Boyde.'

'*Ms* Boyde?'

'That's right.'

'Not Miss?'

'No,' Emma affirms, a little hastier than intended, and I suspect she is as bored of this charade as I am.

I find the theatrics and pomposity of the courtroom dull and old-fashioned, a show put on by the state to prove to the taxpayer who subsidises it where their money goes.

The crown prosecutor stands. 'Might I ask my honourable friend to explain the point he's trying to make, my lady?'

There doesn't appear to be one, and sensing the defence's tiredness the Lady Judge calls it a day.

'We'll resume tomorrow to hear the evidence from the defendant.'

KERRY-ANN

PRESENT

Until today, I've never before been inside a criminal court. I've never even had to visit a civil court to pay a summons. I find the building and its atmosphere intimidating.

The place buzzes with nervous energy: a mixture of excitement and anticipation; nobody knowing what to expect next. Who will speak, what they will say. Take for example the person in the dock. They could be your parent, partner, child, or friend. Nobody, not even the police, could tell their sweet smile hid such hideousness.

The defendant stands, focused solely on the bench, which they approach without a hint of trepidation, keeping their eyes off the jury, and glancing down in supplication, which I suspect they've been told to do by their advocate, to give the impression of innocence. It doesn't wash with me though. I can see straight through it, now I know what secrets, what lies lay beneath such a cool, calm, and collected exterior. And I suppose one can only hope the jury see it too.

The scales so far, could tip in either direction. I can only imagine the weight of responsibility that sits on the jurors' shoulders.

SIX MONTHS BEFORE

DI LOCKE

PAST

I turned over in bed and burrowed my neck into Johnno's shoulder, inhaling the morning scent of him. Musky masculinity and a hint of the spicy aftershave he wore. He shifted forwards to snuggle against me, and gave me a half-asleep peck on the neck, leaving his lips so close to my throat his warm breath sent little sparks of electricity to fizzle across my skin.

This was my favourite time of day. When the sun had barely risen over the city and the only sound to fill the street was the chirping chorus of birdsong.

I'd received a late call the night before from Dafydd, who'd been convinced there was something connecting Geraint's murder to Ireland which had got my mind ticking and I'd ended up comparing his findings to my own, which included the fact that Liam, Geraint's business partner, had also hailed from Ireland. This had then kept me awake for most of the night and I hadn't fallen asleep until the early hours, coming to the conclusion at around 3 a.m. that if I didn't get any sleep, I'd never work out what linked everything together.

My alarm hadn't sung out yet, but it was nearing time its familiar and irritating sound would force me upright. According to my phone it was 5.55 a.m. Day four of my four on/four off shift cycle.

There were several notifications alerting me to the goings on back at HQ that the nightshift had dealt with as I slept, and which those who know me were aware I'd appreciate forenotice of. The one that propelled me out of bed informed me Julian Clements had been picked up by gardaí at a portside checkpoint where it seems he was intending to embark on a vessel routed to the Netherlands.

He was being transported to Wales by police escort on the same ferry he'd used to cross the sea, and I was very much looking forward to finding out what he had to say for himself.

PS TOMOS

PAST

Emma arrived through the doors as I was brushing biscuit crumbs off my shirt. She noticed but didn't say anything. She was buzzing to learn six garda were able to obtain tickets to board an overnight vessel to transport our suspect across the Irish sea and into Fishguard where four of our colleagues from Dyfed-Powys Police collected him in a wagon and drove him to Swansea Central Police station where he was booked in and was currently sitting in a cell waiting for his solicitor to arrive.

'They've been kind enough to allow us the use of their interview room,' Emma said.

'That's nice of them.'

PC Coulter handed me a cup of hot, sweet tea.

'Would you like to do the honours, PS Tomos?'

I took a quick glance down at the scalding liquid I wouldn't have the time to wait to cool down and drink. 'It'd be my pleasure, boss.'

'Do you mind heading on over there ASAP?'

I gave PC Meyer the half-eaten packet of Hobnobs I'd been planning to dunk into my tea and offered Jonesy the cup which he gratefully received. 'Not at all.'

I stopped off at a takeaway van on route and

grabbed a bacon sandwich slathered in ketchup and a coffee that was so weak I could taste the paper cup more than the liquid inside it. The bacon wasn't as crispy as I'd have liked either, but it did the job.

Swansea nick is a large corner building directly opposite an Art and Design college smack bang in the centre of the city most notably known for the manufacturing of steel. I was not expecting to be able to interview Julian straight away, but I was told I could because he wished his solicitor to read out a prepared statement, which basically consisted of explaining his decision to do a runner and denying having anything to do with Geraint's murder. He had of course been advised to 'no comment' his way through the entire interview but I still had to question him, starting with asking him to expand upon his statement.

'You said you did a runner as you believed you'd be next to get killed by whomever was responsible for murdering Geraint, can you tell me why that is?'

Ten minutes in and I'd already reached the pre-written questions I'd quickly drawn up before leaving Cwmbran.

'What was your relationship to Geraint Fford?
'No Comment.'
'How long have you known him?'
'No comment.'
'When was the last time you spoke to him?'
'No comment.'
'What did you discuss with him?'
'No comment.'
'When did you learn of his demise?'
'No comment.'
'What can you tell us about his murder?'
'No comment.'
'Where were you on Monday 21st of November, this year?'

'No comment.'
'You called him that day, didn't you?'
'No comment.'
'Was it to warn him?'
His jaw tightened at this. 'No comment.'
Once I knew I'd touched a nerve there was no stopping me.
'Can you name the person who murdered Geraint?'
He gave his solicitor the side-eye before responding, and it seemed to have the undesirable effect of calming his anxiety somewhat, hardening his decision to continue 'no-commenting' his way through the remainder of the interview.
'I must caution you, that if you withhold information from us, you could be charged with doing so.'
That's when I presented him with the evidence, which looked pretty damning to me.
'We have secured information discovered on your laptop which was seized yesterday. On it we found this.' I turned the A4 sized print-out over and slid it across the table, referencing it for the benefit of the recording device.
Julian's solicitor glanced from his client to me and said, 'Mr Clements and I would like a recess.'

KERRY-ANN

PAST

There was talk that another young woman was taken last night. During the press conference the detective in charge of the case informed the public that there was a serial killer on the loose, and that he appeared to be replicating the Nighthawk's crimes. She regularly used the dating app the police have confirmed the man may use to choose his victims, though they haven't yet secured any evidence to link a single IP address or name to more than one woman. They were saying they expect to find her at another of the deposition sites used by Glenn Marsh.

It makes me uneasy walking alone at night, especially round here. I reflect on my stay in the cottage, how frightening it was when I thought I saw someone snooping through the kitchen window, scoping out the place.

Then I recall returning with Natalia to collect my things and finding a police officer parked beside the cottage. The way he seemed to look through me, sending chills down my spine, watching after me as I drove away.

I never did learn why he was there, what he was doing traipsing along the footpath in the dark, or who he was searching for.

There are men like Geoffrey Goldsborough, pillars of the community who use their power and status and the privileges it affords them to do harm. When such people come under fire, they can use their position of authority to control the narrative, and quite often this enables them to avoid detection.

Like that schoolteacher who ran off with her pupil, or the security alarm fitter who burgled his customers' houses, or that custody sergeant who sexually assaulted his drunk prisoner.

My father was supposedly the exception. A man wronged by society. Let down by the education system, ignored by the health system, and assumed guilty by the legal system.

There are many men – and women – out there who've been wrongfully convicted, and that is the greatest injustice of all.

DI LOCKE

PAST

From the moment we had Julian in custody the clock had begun ticking down. We had approximately fourteen hours left to get out of him what he knew about the person who'd shot Geraint, and he was showing no sign of confessing. And why would he? He must have been scared shitless he'd be next in the firing line of whoever had held the gun.

Though we'd yet to develop a theory as to who had organised the hit and we still had no idea who had pulled the trigger we knew we were getting closer when we viewed the messages on Demelza's phone to a friend, on social media, who she'd arranged to view and buy a £10K van from, a van valued to be worth at least five grand more. Which going by their content, Geraint was paying for, with the intention of doing it up and using it to take the twins on holiday – proving future thinking, uncommon in people considering suicide. It also went some way to explain why Geraint might have withdrawn the same amount of cash. Though I wasn't convinced at first a lawyer would choose that method to buy a vehicle from someone. If, however, they knew the person they were buying the vehicle from and that person owned a respectable second-hand dealership, securing the sale of a van before listing it on their website is the kind of thing a friend would do. And having spoken to the man I was satisfied that was what had happened.

The seller, Mr Prior, had been in business for a little over three years, the reviews on his social media page were legitimate and could be traced back to their original postings on various online websites, neither he nor his staff were known to us (at least not those two we could name from the marketing ads posted daily), and the few vehicles he'd sold and which we were able to check out had passed their first MOT after having been bought and hadn't been involved in any road traffic accidents, or criminal conduct. For these reasons I didn't think there was anything necessarily untoward about the deal until I enquired about the van's whereabouts. I was unsurprised to learn that it was being enjoyed by its new owner, though when I asked Mr Prior for the contact details of the buyer he grew cagey. I wanted to know why, so I contacted the DVSA for the registered keeper's name only to learn that it had in fact been destroyed, just two days ago.

The Certificate of Destruction had been provided by a licenced scrapyard, one not too far away from the lock-up where Mr Prior claimed he kept his vehicles. We're talking about a five-year-old van in excellent condition with only half the expected miles on the clock for its age getting crushed, so I sent two of our PCs down to the woman's address to find out why she'd scrapped the van just five days after having bought it. I also wanted to know why Mr Prior had sold the van to her so soon after Geraint's death. Especially when he'd kept hold of it for several days in order for him to buy it.

It took a while to connect the dots, but it turned out that STR stood for Short-Term-Rental. The digital forensic technicians discovered this when they retrieved the search history, and using software that traced keyboard strokes, uncovered everything Demelza had ever googled. And not just on that particular phone but every device she'd ever owned since she'd had an account with the cloud storage app downloaded onto it. She'd been emailing an estate agent the day after the request for an STR was made from Geraint's phone, who it turned out had arranged the lease of Geraint's flat. It didn't take a genius to figure out the two pieces of evidence were related, but would it stand up in court as proof beyond a reasonable doubt that Demelza was involved in Errol's murder?

There was only one way to find out.

On closer inspection the estate agent's office was one of several small businesses – the others included a launderette, car wash, tanning salon, travel company, and a luxury transport service (the kind of businesses that are commonly used to facilitate the washing of money) – situated on the same street, registered to the same postal address of a company formation service. The buildings were all owned by an LLP controlled by what appeared to be a shell company headquartered in Canada whose assets were shared between an unknown number of silent partners. A money laundering red flag. One which, frustratingly, meant only the NCA had the resources to dig deep enough to scratch below the surface to expose the individual(s) behind the operation.

However, the landlord of Geraint's flat was a property tycoon who'd just sold the deeds to a new development for fifty million pounds. Having bought twelve acres of land on which he'd had a derelict school, playground, and car park knocked down and built on to contain two hundred affordable houses, shops, a sports centre, a health and wellbeing clinic, and a community hall. The application for planning permission was deemed to be in the public interest and as such, was published on the South Glamorgan County Council website. Which is how our computer experts were able to name him as one of Julian Clements' clients by checking his name against those corporations Julian had submitted tax assessments to HMRC for.

The legitimacy of his client's businesses despite Julian's association with criminals could not be a coincidence. In the same way we were unable to directly connect any illegal activities to Paddy Daly or his goons, we couldn't link Julian to anything unlawful his friends had done either. But the estate agency was the one business we were positive was a front, and the agent was the only person we could identify.

We had to find her and speak to her.

'What's her name?'

'Selina Kinsley.'

She lived in a council flat in a poverty-stricken part of town.

When we showed her the emails she said, confidently, that although she had sent Demelza the contract for the rented flat which Geraint had signed for she hadn't taken part in the conversational exchange via text message. 'I deal exclusively with the administrative side of sales and leasing. I don't quote properties, list them, or take bookings for people to view them. My manager does, Jamie.'

'Surname?'

'Peterson.'

Whoever had used Geraint's phone to exchange William Maurice Parker's address for details of the flat Geraint subsequently moved into, had told Errol's murderer how to locate the man prior to him being shot. Which meant that although we were still no closer to finding out who'd killed Geraint, we could prove the person – we strongly suspected to be Demelza – had been in recent contact with Jamie, and that *he* must know who the mystery owner of the estate agency was and would also be able to confirm or deny that Demelza had been the individual who'd texted him.

At least that's what we thought.

I called the SIO in charge of the investigation into Errol's murder and gave him a rundown of all the information we had. He replied that he was on his way down, agreeing that we could now confirm the two cases we'd been working on separately were connected. Then I texted DC Burtenshaw asking her to put the kettle on.

On my way. Call Carol, ask her to come pack an overnight bag and collect the kids. We need to ask Demelza some questions.

Case Notes re. Errol James Parker, taken on Monday 28th November 2022 from convo with Dtv Sergeant Armand of SWP

Errol, 34-year-old mixed-race man.

Son of William Maurice Parker: bookmaker, and Eliza Jane Parker: homemaker.

Brother of Amanda 'Mandy' Moore, who is married to Joseph 'Joey' Moore. They have two children: Robin and Danielle.

Joey Moore's father, Samuel, is serving seven years in a Vancouver prison for drug offences: possession of a controlled substance (Fentanyl) for the purpose of trafficking.

Joey has no surviving siblings (his only sister died of a rare heart defect at two years of age).

Eliza died of blood cancer when Errol was eighteen years old.

At the time of his death, Errol owned a guitar shop in Cardiff.

Forensic accountants seeking potential reasons for his murder randomly selected several of his personal financial records from different tax years and used data analysis to assess them for inconsistencies and discrepancies to identify abnormal income and expenditure patterns, anomalies, and trends. Half of them indicated fraudulent activities, which included: company misrepresentation by altering (distorting) figures to falsely report data.

Errol uses the same accountant as the estate agency. The guitar shop is in a row of buildings lining the same street, owned by the Toronto-based LLP.

PS TOMOS

PAST

On the outside Demelza was a respectable wife, mother, daughter, and friend. She had no criminal record, neither had any of her immediate family, she'd never been in debt, her business was legit, and she didn't seem to have any dodgy pals, so how did she become embroiled with the employee of a murderous criminal?

The request for an STR made using Geraint's phone and the search history on her laptop for a Short-Term Rental put her squarely in the frame and made us question if *she* was what connected Errol's murder to Geraint's.

While DS Armand of South Wales CID interviewed her, she sat rigid, back against the seat, arms folded, defensive.

He showed her the emails, which spanned several years, that suggested her relationship with Jamie was comfortable and that there was an element of trust there. Leading me to suspect they knew each other personally. Well enough to ask her to break the law, and to trust her to keep her mouth shut if she ever discovered what had happened to Errol as a consequence of providing Jamie with his address?

'You're looking at serving fifteen or more years in prison for acting as a principal offender by aiding the murder of Errol James Parker.'

After several questions referring to Errol's murder DS Armand changed tactic.

'The toxicology test came back on your husband. There was no sign of an overdose. Geraint didn't swallow those pills, Demelza. Did you get rid of them to make it look like he had?'

She shot him a look that caused my skin to prickle because it was the first reaction he'd roused out of her.

'Did you empty those pill packets, so we'd think he'd taken them, to throw us off the scent, because you knew he was dead, either because you killed him yourself or you know who did?'

'I don't see the relevance of this line of questioning,' her solicitor said.

DS Armand ignored him. 'We checked your phone records. You didn't try to call your husband after he left your house, despite how worried you told us you were for him. Instead, you went straight to PINGing his phone. Why?'

'I really don't see how these questions are relevant to your investigation,' her solicitor repeated.

This did nothing to dissuade him.

'Did Geraint find out you'd had a part to play in Errol's murder? Did you or someone else arrange to have Geraint killed to make sure he wouldn't blab?'

Emma hit a button, and the recording switched to the other live-fed footage, where situated in another interview room, further down the corridor, had sat Jamie Peterson, the manager of the estate agency, who was facing the same sentence for his part in the commission of the crime.

They both knew the person who'd ordered the hit and quite possibly who had carried it out, but neither of them was willing to talk, though the evidence against them was stacking up.

Only . . .

The phone that Jamie Peterson had used to respond to Demelza's request for an STR was unregistered, the chat system on it was likely encrypted, and it had no doubt been destroyed immediately after his conversation with her. The computer Selina had used to email Demelza the rental contract for Geraint to sign used a VPN, had a clean search history as far as criminal activities were concerned, and we couldn't tell which other members of staff did or did not have access to it.

It felt like we were going around in circles.

DCs Chapman and Winters paid a visit to the property developer, Tristan Newell, except after that conversation it felt like we'd hit another dead-end.

The screen blinked as Emma clicked onto another folder containing the recording of Tristan's interview.

He spoke with a West Country accent, but I detected a slight Southern Welsh twang likely due to the fact he was born in Glastonbury and schooled in Chepstow but had been living in Cardiff for the past fifteen years, at least according to the DVSA.

'I don't know who owns the agency, only that the woman who deals with my properties is nothing short of professional and helpful,' Tristan said.

'How many do you rent out?'

'One hundred and forty.'

'That's a lot. How does someone get hold of enough money to afford to own that many homes?'

'I bought my first house with a twenty-five-year mortgage. Paid it off working three jobs in fifteen years. Used the money from the sale to buy three more outright, which I fixed up and rented out while I slept in a camper van on my mother's driveway. After slumming it for a year I'd saved enough money to buy another property to live in while I focused on setting up my own property development firm, and I used all my dividends to buy more houses, mostly derelict or abandoned, and all of them needing a lot of work doing to them. Which isn't a problem when you've got the money and know-how.'

'How'd you go from earning a couple hundred thousand pounds a year to fifty million?'

'This piece of land came up for five hundred thousand, with planning permission. I sold my house to buy it. That's how confident I was that once built on it would be worth more than I could ever have dreamed possible. And it was worth every moment sleeping in a portacabin on a building site for the past eighteen months.'

I had to respect the dude for working hard for what he believed in. He deserved to retire and live off the profit for the rest of his life. Especially considering he turned out to be an angel in disguise. Tristan Newell with his polo shirt, slim-fit jeans, white Ralf Lauren trainers, fake tan, and swagger.

'She calls herself La Matriarca. It's Spanish for The Matriarch.'

'Who?' DC Chapman asked.

'The boss.'

'You know this how?' DC Winters asked.

'Spent some time in Portugal.'

The two detective constables took it in turns to question Tristan.

'I mean, how'd you know the nickname of the woman who owns the estate agency?'

'Oh, I see. Well, she's the woman who manages my properties. Only those I haven't bought through them of course, to avoid a conflict of interest. I know, it's a bit *Queen of The South*.'

'Could you explain to me what you mean by that?'

'It's a series on Netflix. Very good if you're into the drug-lord drama stuff. She was like a female Pablo Escobar. Oh sorry, you meant the owner of the estate agency. What can I tell you? It's human instinct to make assumptions. We all judge based on first impressions, right? Only, she doesn't look like the kind of person you'd expect to hide behind a pseudonym, you know? Too . . . proper. Not mumsy at all.'

'When was the last time you saw her?'

'In the office, at about the time I signed over responsibility for forty of the newbuild's. They were completed last month.'

'Would you be able to describe to me what she looks like?'

'I can do better than that.'

The dictionary definition of the word: matriarch, is a woman who is the head of the family. A person of influence. A leader. I imagined her as a mother, perhaps someone of middle-age. Unfortunately, that didn't really narrow-down our pool of suspects, which is why I was incredibly thankful that not only was Tristan able to provide us with a date as to when she would have been captured entering the premises but also that the estate agency's shopfront was within the parameter of a council-owned CCTV camera.

Emma paused the video, and it stopped on a frozen image of Ms Fford's face.

As I stared at the suited woman with dark hair and heels, I had to admit that when compared to the picture in the Wikipedia entry for the hit TV show, her resemblance to Teresa Mendoza was uncanny.

VISITATION ORDER

By agreement of the governor, Warren A. Brodie, you are granted this order of visitation. All visits must be booked by 2 p.m. the day before any planned visit. Visits are 2-4 p.m. Wednesday, Saturday, and Sunday. You <u>must not</u> bring any contraband (mobile phones etc.) onto the premises (including the car park) and you <u>must</u> bring photographic ID and proof of address to gain entry into the facility.

Visitor:
Miss Kerry-Ann Pascoe of:
Trevithick Court
Falmouth
Cornwall
England
TR5 1CL

Inmate:
Mr Roderick Penrose
HMP Prescoed
Coed-y-Paen
Pontypool
Monmouthshire
Wales
NP4 0TB

KERRY-ANN

PAST

The police arrived before the ambulance. I was already giving my statement to a female constable when the paramedic stepped through the front door. He ran straight upstairs to where the other – male – constable was stationed, to confirm Alys was deceased. Then traipsed back down again, ten minutes later, and stood in the doorway of the living room making notes on an iPad while the constable read my statement back to me and asked me to sign it.

I watched from the living room as someone in a white suit wearing shoe coverlets with a mask on their face, a camera hung round their neck and a small plastic case held in his gloved hand go up the stairs. He came back down the staircase ten minutes later holding his plastic case under his arm and carrying three small see-through bags that each contained Alys' suicide note, what looked like an address book (to compare against the note to ensure she wrote it, and I didn't unalive her then frame her murder as a suicide?), and medication she'd been prescribed. In his other hand, pressed to his ear, he held his phone. I heard him tell whoever was on the other end of it that he'd photographed, dusted, and swabbed the room and that he was now on his way back to wherever it was he'd come from.

The female constable gave me a penetrative look as she spoke. 'We'll need you to come down to the station so we can take a sample of your DNA.'

'When?'

'As soon as possible,' she replied. She must have seen the anxiety gnawing at me as I sat in the armchair biting my lip because her face softened then and she added, 'It's just a matter of precaution.'

Because Alys had died at home, and they needed to eliminate my fingerprints from those found on the bottles of diamorphine she'd necked.

I gave her a nod of understanding.

The undertaker arrived to collect Alys and take her to the funeral home. We left the house, each in our own vehicles, shortly afterwards.

My fingerprints were scanned, the inside of my cheek was swabbed, and I allowed them to cut a small section of hair from the back of my head at the root.

An hour later I was back on the road, having spoken to my editor and explained the reason for my early return home.

Natalia greeted me at the gate. She must have recognised the sound of my engine as she was stood waiting for me to leave the car before I'd even applied the brake, to help drag my roller case up the steps. She enfolded me in a huge hug the second I'd closed the front door behind us. It was one of those embraces where you're aware how emotionally stiff you are but appreciate the melting togetherness of someone else's comforting warmth as they meld themselves to your curves.

When she withdrew from me, I suddenly felt unmoored and gazed into her crystalline eyes, which immediately made me feel buoyed. I pulled her hips towards mine and pressed my mouth against hers, sliding my tongue in between her lips, demandingly.

She'd left for Wales in the early hours of that morning, had driven through the snow in the dark to deliver the Visiting Order to me and had taken me into Cardiff to meet my father in prison, because she knew how much it would mean to me to have her there. She'd followed me to the cottage in Lavernock to collect my things, so I wouldn't be alone inside the building that I'd fled in the night. And then she'd travelled all the way back to Cornwall again, intending to get some shuteye, as she had to work the following morning. She couldn't have been that long home when I'd called to tell her Alys had taken her own life and that I'd be returning later that same day.

It was almost dusk by the time I'd parked up outside. She must have been bone tired, but still she pressed me up against the wall and buried her face into my neck. Her bite caused my skin to tingle. One hand cupping my jaw, the other under my jumper. Running her fingers through my hair, kneading my breast.

It had been days since I'd felt her body rubbing against my own, the heat of her skin touching mine. I brought her hand down to where I needed her and tightened my grip on the back of her neck as she pushed two fingers into me.

DI LOCKE

PAST

Switching off the monitor I eyeballed the room. 'Thoughts?'

I had to question if Demelza intended to divert our suspicion away from the estate agent by putting the onus on Geraint acting shifty, claiming she thought he was having an affair, so we wouldn't dig too deeply and uncover the name of Selina's manager or that of the woman she and Jamie worked for if we did. The woman we now knew must have ordered whoever shot Errol to pull the trigger. Because the Mendoza lookalike was none other than her mother-in-law, Ms Lorraine Fford.

PS TOMOS

PAST

Marked in red, the route from Cwmbran to Lorraine's house on the enlarged map filled the screen in front of me. It was a newbuild on an estate just outside Cardiff. DS Armand had just been given the task of organising and leading an arrest team to bring Lorraine into the custody suite so she could be interviewed in relation to Errol's murder. And I had only just that minute received clearance to read the letter Yoshida Healthcare had sent to Geraint, which Carol had collected from her deceased son-law's landlord and provided us with much-needed context to understand the genetic testing carried out by Genomica. When the two PCs who'd been tasked with speaking to the manager of the scrapyard came strolling through the door of the incident room, smirking.

'What has you both looking like my neighbour's cats after they've shit on my lawn?'

'The van, Serge,' the younger of the female constables said, short, with cropped hair, and wearing the shiniest black shoes I think I've ever seen.

'What about it?'

She eyed her colleague who turned to me and said, 'Why don't you come and see for yourself?'

I followed them outside to where the 'pure grey' Volkswagen Transporter was parked.

'The VIN plate under the bonnet matches the number plate of the van that's in the photograph Mr Prior sent to Demelza.'

I pointed to the van. 'What about the plates that are on it?'

'Cloned from an identical van registered to an address in Liverpool,' she replied.

'And that's not all,' the taller of the two constables said, pulling out a small evidence bag from the tray inside the door of the patrol car she drove to and from the scrapyard in, exposing the back of her hand where a flower tattoo had been partially hidden by the sleeve of her white shirt. 'We also found this.'

It looks like a piece of clingfilm.

'What is it?'

'A strip of pallet-stretch shrink wrap made from low density polyethylene. It was on the floor in a corner of the van. It's the kind of material used to package stacked items in a warehouse, or to secure products on board a shipping container. Unusual in a non-commercial vehicle, we thought. There were some minute granules of cream powder dusting the carpet beside it, too, so we carried out a rapid drug identification test using what little of the substance we were able to collect, and it was positive for heroin. We estimate that if the van was fully stocked you could easily transport a ton of the stuff.'

'Where's the owner of the scrapper.'

'Osian was non-comp over us seizing the vehicle, so the arresting officer had to taser him. He's with the doctor in the custody suite.'

Non-compliance suggests guilt. But over what? Failing to crush a car he'd declared destroyed or running a drug trafficking operation?

'What did they arrest him for?'

'Assault. He spat at me, sir.'

'Have you filled out an incident form?'

'Yes, sir. Witnessed by a member of the responding unit.'

I gave her a nod.

Being the owner of the Authorised Treatment Facility, or ATF as scrapyards are termed, meant Osian could be taken to court for providing a false declaration of destruction to the DVSA. We could also do him for obstruction as he lied to us about the van having been destroyed, when in fact he'd stuck a set of cloned plates on it intending to dupe us into believing it to be another van entirely. What we couldn't do was prove why. We could speculate based on the evidence, but we didn't have enough heroin sealed inside the see-through bag to charge the man with possession.

'Who's guarding the lock-up?'

'A PS Kavanagh and three of her colleagues.'

I know her well, she's an exceptionally committed Police Sergeant.

They might not have had enough heroin to charge him for possessing it, but the few particles found gave Kavanagh et al the power to search the premises and seize anything that could have been related to the sale of opiates, without the need for a warrant.

'The woman who brought the van to the scrapyard . . .'

'Bronwen Ingram, doesn't exist, Serge. And the address written on the V5 is made up.'

'We need to pull Mr Prior in, get a description from him of the woman he sold the van to; see if matches the E-FIT PC Cottrell is going to try to drag out of Osian,' the other PC volunteered. 'That's if they weren't both lying, of course, and there was in fact no such woman at all.'

'Happy to do that, Serge.'

'What about the owner of the van in Liverpool, whose plates were cloned?'

'Elys Whittaker. Twenty-nine years old. Lives alone. Drives a "matte black" Chevrolet Camaro. PNC-clean. No associations.'

'Address?'

'Court Park Drive, number—'

'She's heading towards Nantwich as we speak,' the long-haired, sharp-eyed constable interrupted her colleague before apologising.

Pixie cut smiled in return, and they shared a momentary look that caused me to suspect they were a little closer than workmates.

I nodded in appreciation of their hasty response in adhering to procedure.

'We believe she's on her way to Cardiff. She seems to make the trips down from Merseyside on the regular, going by the ANPR hits on the Chevy.'

Yoshida
Innovative Healthcare

Mr Fford,

I write to inform you of the results of your genetic testing through Yoshida Healthcare Ltd.

Analysing the blood samples you provided, our geneticist confirms you have tested POSITIVE for BRCA1 mutation, which as you are aware from our discussion is associated with the potential development of certain cancers.

As a result of this information, I would like you to call us to arrange an appointment with one of our genetic counsellors so that we can discuss possible lifestyle changes you could make to positively influence your risk factor.

Dr Gaurav Kapoor

KERRY-ANN

PAST

I awoke with a sharp pain in my neck, having slept with my head in the crook of Natalia's arm. With my eyes half squinted shut I found her cheek and gently kissed her while I reached over to check the time on my phone. As I turned, she moved with me, so I ended up straddling her. I swept her hair behind her ear, leaned down, and whispered, 'Stay in bed.'

She groaned and pulled the duvet up and over her head, cocooning herself beneath the covers while I slid my feet into my slippers.

I flung my dressing gown on, wrapped it tightly around my waist, then headed down to the kitchen. The kettle boiled while I cracked eggs into a pan of milk. I was about to carry up the tray, containing two cups of coffee and two plates of scrambled eggs on toast, when I spotted the folder tucked neatly into my roller case in the hallway where Natalia had left it.

I hadn't packed it. Alys must have. Before she'd ended her own life. Which meant she'd wanted me to take it home, because she'd known I'd need it to finish her story.

DI LOCKE

PAST

It all began to slot together once we realised where Elys Whittaker was heading, because going by her movements she'd been distributing drugs from one end of the country to the other for at least the past twelve months, which was the maximum length of time ANPR camera footage could be retained.

Tracking her wasn't difficult. We only had to follow her customary routes while she drove the vans. Plural because while (the original) one was stationed at her address in Liverpool, according to Merseyside Police, the other(s) (yes, it turned out she had at least two more 'pure grey' Transporters bearing the same cloned plates as the one we had in our possession) were captured on ANPR cameras in two different areas of the country. One was spotted as far north as Edinburgh, while another, just four hours later, was caught in Plymouth. Neither of the vans had ever been seen travelling between, meaning they must have been kept somewhere local to the area in which they frequented. Unless the van (not the one which remained parked beside her house) had entered a black hole, it was scientifically impossible for the vehicle to have made what should have been a nine-hour journey in just less than half that time, and all without the driver stopping for a rest. Which was how we knew there had to be another person involved.

It would have made far more sense had Elys drove only as far as the meeting point to swap vehicles with whoever before travelling to her next destination. And perhaps she did, except for that one time when the van had appeared in Scotland while simultaneously having been seen in Devon. But it only takes one slip-up to draw the attention of the police, and once we had her on our radar, we weren't going to let her out of our sight.

Which was why when the Camaro was located in South Wales, two different vehicles were deployed to join Elys on her journey to Cardiff. While the two pool cars that had followed her from Nantwich through Wales returned to the forecourt of Cheshire CID's headquarters in Warrington.

She couldn't have known we had her under surveillance, even if someone had informed her that we'd nabbed one of the vans – because wouldn't she have hidden the one on her driveway if she did? – so the officers tailing her were able to trace her all the way to the nail salon that sat between a shop selling handbags and a taxi company. Just a few yards left of the late Errol Parker's former guitar shop and a couple of buildings down from the estate agency to her right, owned by Lorraine.

She was entering the rear door with four holdalls filled with bank notes when they cuffed her.

PS TOMOS

PAST

We couldn't locate the two other Transporters with the cloned plates. Elys was probably organising their disappearances during one of the three phone calls she made while she drove down to the nail salon, which we found out by talking to the staff that she was the owner of. As well as the time stamps telling us she'd made the phone calls during her journey through Cheshire, one of the numbers she'd rung turned out to be helpful in determining who she had working for her. His name was Javon Tindale, a Londoner who was known to us, and had prior convictions for drug dealing, with links to the southwest. And another of the callers we couldn't identify, as the phone was unregistered.

    We knew above her on the food chain there would be someone responsible for loading and unloading the vans with the merchandise that needed to be picked up and dropped off, another organising the logistics of the swaps, then you had the person responsible for transporting the product into the country, another ensuring it arrived at its destination, and someone buying it from whoever oversaw its production. And at the top of them all was the head of the operation, who sat in luxury somewhere ordering everyone about from the other end of a phone.

The original Transporter, that had been sitting on the driveway of Elys' average-looking Liverpool home, was swabbed inside and out by a specialist CSI team working on behalf of Merseyside Police whose verdict was that the van had been used to transport large amounts of heroin, going by the traces of the substance detected on the passenger seatbelt, the driver's window switch, and the handle of the sliding door on the left-hand side of the vehicle. That meant we could prove at least two of the – four? – vans had been used to move drugs.

A search of her house revealed nothing obviously untoward. There were no hidden stashes of money, no extravagant purchases, she didn't own a second home, she wasn't renting out a storage facility, and she didn't take a lot of trips abroad, so it was difficult to see how she benefitted from ferrying drugs around the country. She seemed, on the outside at least, to be a family-oriented woman, a single mother of two with a close circle of friends, some she'd known for decades, who again appeared nothing but wholesome. But then there was that other phone number Elys had dialled on her way to South Wales. One of the team recognised the last three digits.

'Name's Scott Fford.'

Geraint's uncle, the one who lives in Merseyside?

'Lorraine's brother?'

'One and the same.'

. . . I'm walking back from the grocery shop when one of my sources, a former freelance crime photographer who was around during the Nighthawk's reign, calls and arranges to meet me the following day. I hadn't expected him to respond to my voicemail, so I'm feeling lucky.

A lot of time has passed since he worked for the local paper — he's with a national now — but he tells me he still has all his original photographs, which he says he'll bring with him, as he's got something to show me.

The next morning I'm sat opposite him in a glass-fronted café round the corner from the train station, close to the centre of town. The wind is so strong the pavement sign blows over and skids onto the road. An elderly lady wheeling a shopping trolly bends over to pick it up and gets hit by a cyclist. A man with his hands full of loose oranges runs across the road to help her up. Kai, the photographer, bolts up from his seat and out of the café. The wind snatches the glazed wooden door from his hand and slams it hard against the wall, causing the picture frame beside it to fall onto the table below, landing on a freshly poured tea, causing the cup to break in half and leaving a puddle of steaming liquid to drip onto the lap of a young woman who cries out in pain.

This chaotic scene reads like a piece of fiction, but truth is stranger than and is evidence of how one single event causes a ripple effect. Which is, ironically, how I came to be there in the first place.

Kai photographed the images he'd taken on his Nikon — back when he'd been sent by the paper that he'd sold them to — and emailed them to me the day before we were due to meet. My grandson had to borrow my computer for his homework that day, so I'd used the library to upload and view them.

The slim woman with mid-length hair lay inside a body bag underneath the cover of a tent, out of view, several yards away from where he stood snapping shots of the tape that had been wound around the barks of two tall oaks. Bindweed covered the overgrown grass, and nettles stung his calves as he knelt to take the picture.

The colour version was no clearer than the black and white one that had been printed on the front page of the *South Wales News* article. At least not at first glance. But on closer inspection it was obvious there was one major difference. In the far right-hand corner of the image that had been sent to me there was no cigarette stub, and on the published copy there was. Just like all the other images taken that day by photographers employed by various newsprints.

'The photographs are time-stamped,' Kai says. 'That cigarette stub appeared halfway through my photography session. That's why there's two, almost identical, pictures. Only one was taken at the start of my shoot and the other was snapped at the end.'

'There was at least a dozen or more men on the scene that day, treading through the wooded grove, any one of them could have dropped it.'

And it certainly looked as if that was what had happened. Until Kai had flipped through the 216 photographs that he'd taken with his digital camera to choose the money shot; the perfect image to adorn the news piece that would catapult his career. And realised he'd captured the hand holding the cigarette in another photograph he'd taken earlier.

He was married. He wore a gold wedding band on his finger. But that's not all that was visible. The cuff of his jacket matched those of the other two officers of the law stood behind the police cordon.

KERRY-ANN

PAST

Natalia's hand on my shoulder startled me. 'Oh, sorry. I was about to bring this up.'

'Don't worry Miss-head-in-a-book, I'm up now.' She smiled and took a seat beside me at the table.

I was still standing, leafing through the pages of Alys' project, scouring the material I hadn't managed to read before Alys had passed away and my subsequent return to Cornwall when I came across something interesting.

'Huh.'

'What is it?'

I explained what had happened during my stay with the author, reiterating what I'd learned about the connection between the recently murdered women and how Alys had initially believed the Nighthawk had operated alongside someone who'd disappeared when Glenn Marsh had been arrested. Thinking the man had then reappeared after having spent twenty years elsewhere – prison or abroad the most likely scenario – before he'd begun killing again.

'Why did she think that?'

'A cigarette stub was found close to where one of the women's bodies were dumped. The DNA extracted from it didn't match Glenn but did belong to a man. From that she developed a theory that Glenn had an accomplice. Although to still be operating now he'd have needed to be a young apprentice back in the mid-nineties. Glenn was in his late thirties when he was caught. But then Alys thought it made more sense that the cigarette stub was just an incidental finding. It might have already been there. It could even have been flicked onto the ground by a Scene of Crime Officer – which is what CSI were formerly called – who'd failed to secure and eliminate the contamination of the area. She even considered whether a member of the press may have been responsible. There were crime reporters from TV and radio present. Any one of them could have been smoking.'

'That's plausible,' Natalia said.

'I thought so too, especially when she brought my attention to the recent kidnapping and subsequent murders of three female victims, which the police have now confirmed to the media echo those of the Nighthawk. Their bodies tell a similar story of enslavement that mimics the crimes of Glenn Marsh, suggesting we have a copycat in our midst.'

'That makes sense,' Natalia said.

'Except that it would be impossible to replicate each and every detail, because certain aspects of the crime – the manner of death or the way the body is displayed for example – are withheld from the public. So how would the killer know those things without access to such information?'

'Unless he'd been there,' Natalia said, peering down at the line of text above my index finger.

Identifying the uniformed man had uncovered the offending litterer. The constable who'd wasted police time by leading forensic specialists to analyse a cigarette stub one of their own had dropped, and probably adding countless hours of unnecessary investigatory work to the murder inquiry, as detectives assessed whether another person might also have been involved.

The officers didn't need to remember who their colleague was, there had been a record of every member of the force who'd been there on that specific day. The police quickly put an end to the idea the Nighthawk had an accomplice and lay to rest any notion that the cigarette stub belonged to him by admitting the incompetency of their colleague. Something I don't think they would have done had it not been for Kai.

'I wrote about the cigarette stub in the Nighthawk.'

'Your debut? I don't remember reading such an entry,' Kai says, questioningly.

'My editor wouldn't allow me to include it, because of the ongoing inquiry by the Police Complaints Authority — that's what the Independent Office for Police Conduct were previously known as — so it was never printed in the final version you can buy in shops and online today. But had I been allowed it would have dispelled a lot of unnecessary speculation.'

After my conversation with Kai, I reached out to the retired detective who'd been in charge of the investigation to see if there was anything he'd like to add, considering it was his colleague who had smoked the cigarette then thrown it onto the ground, just metres from where a murdered female lay. It would be an informal chat, I told him, as I hadn't even been commissioned to author another work of true crime since my diagnosis. When we spoke, I let him know that I was now conducting research into the recent spate of kidnappings and murders inspired by the Nighthawk. I also let slip what I'd found while scouring Kai's images; the ones that hadn't been used to adorn a newspaper article and comparing them to the ones that had.

If the raw copies had been edited prior to printing, the police would have discovered this by checking them against those taken by their own forensically trained photographers to eliminate the possibility they'd been photoshopped. The former inspector, who occasionally assisted in homicide investigations despite his retirement told me their crime scene photographer had also captured the culprit and reassured me the constable had been reprimanded for skipping basic crime scene security and containment procedure by contaminating it.

'He referred himself to the PCA for compromising the integrity of the crime scene. He was given additional training and has continued to serve the public for more than two decades, even bagging himself a promotion.'

If my oncologist hadn't chosen that moment to call me, I wouldn't have had to end our conversation so abruptly. The cancer had already been graded terminal. I was waiting to discuss potential treatments, not to prolong the inevitable, but to make the end of my life a little more bearable.

'Can you come in tomorrow to discuss options with a palliative care nurse?'

'Sure, what time?'

Analgesics and antiemetics was the nurse's recommendation, to ease the pain and sickness caused by the tumour obstructing my bowel and the cells that had spread from my cervix to my bladder, my right kidney, my liver, and stomach. She later added Lorazepam, a benzodiazepine.

I took one at night, to ease the crippling anxiety brought on by the impending end to my life and to aid my nightmare-fuelled sleep. I was less restless, more sedate. But also, more focused and determined: not to lose my mind to the liquid euphoria the NHS had prescribed me; to keep my wits about me; to finish this godforsaken project; to use my medication sparingly.

I left the café just as it began to drizzle, leaving my face shiny and the Hermès scarf, wrapped loosely around my neck, damp. I chewed on the detective's words as I made my way to the bus. My eyesight wasn't what it was, and the medication made me giddy, so I'd given my car to my granddaughter who was learning to drive, accepting I no longer had any need for it. She'd promised to take me out in it for a spin once she passed her test. I hadn't the heart to tell her I would no longer be alive then.

DNA profiling wasn't standard procedure until the Nighthawk was caught, almost a decade after the cigarette stub had been found at the site of where he'd dumped one of his victims. Prior to this, the police used blood typing and fingerprinting to distinguish between suspects. But as it was winter, most people were wearing gloves, so fingerprints were out of the question, and of course there was no blood on the cigarette stub, so all they had was saliva.

Salivary gland chromosomes are not only used to identify a person's sex, but also the amount of white blood cells present, which enables the police to determine an individual's blood type. This allowed the police to confirm the cigarette had been smoked by a man, and that it did not belong to Glenn Marsh.

But without testing the constable's saliva they couldn't compare it to the Type A (RhD Positive) sample retrieved from the cigarette stub, so how could they have known for definite that it had belonged to him?

DI LOCKE

PAST

We had three members of the same family in custody, but it looked like we weren't getting anything out of them that day.

It was clear that Demelza wouldn't talk and had chosen to remain loyal to her mother-in-law, which risked a lengthier prison sentence and a few years longer away from her twin daughters. We weren't able to persuade Lorraine to tell us what her connection to Errol's murder was either and she seemed content to know that her granddaughters were being taken care of by their other grandmother, Carol, which suggested she also didn't intend to speak and was comfortable with the fact she wouldn't be returning home for some time. Scott refused to cooperate, too, and when questioned wouldn't explain why Elys had called him; though one look at their phones was enough to confirm they were in a close personal relationship. Neither would he tell us where he was going when officers found him. We could guess though, that he'd been planning to visit his brother, Luke, in Spain. Because he was heading for one of the Canary Islands – a known tax haven – according to the one-way flight ticket he had on his person, when we found him stood in the lounge of Cardiff airport clutching his passport in one hand and a suitcase in the other. He hadn't tried to scarper when he spotted us though. His decision must have had something to do with his sister-in-law's father.

We told him we'd located Derwen's fishing trawler off the coast of Holyhead. He wasn't on it, but Scott didn't know that. As soon as he heard the man's name the impassive expression on his face froze.

Beneath the lobsters he'd trapped and stored in boxes of ice inside the cargo hold below deck a couple of Police Dogs working for North Wales Police sniffed out fifty kilos of smack under the fishy stink of Derwen's fishing vessel.

We'd guessed, not all too wildly, that as he was a lobster catcher there was a connection between Derwen and his in-law's criminality. It was the Irish trawler which had passed the same bay his son-in-law's body had been thrown up onto, which had given us cause to consider it. We already knew there was a link concerning Ireland and narcotics so had predicted there might be an association between Derwen's fishing career and the importation of heroin. I wouldn't be surprised to learn this meet and greet Demelza had attended in the hotel where she'd met Geraint all those years ago was actually some gangland boss' birthday party either. At least not after what else we discovered.

The Spanish Police were unable to find Geraint's uncle Luke inside his €15M southwestern Majorca mansion, replete with spiral staircase, infinity pool, and a garage full of flash cars. But it was pretty clear to us how he earned his money. Especially considering the amount of it that he slept on.

'How much do you reckon is there?'

Dafydd leaned forward and squinted at the image

of the master suite inside Luke's luxurious abode that filled the screen of my laptop, where there were bed-shaped money stacks he estimated to be a 'shitload'.

Confidential
Received 27th November 2022

National Security Intelligence Report

ORGANISATION and OFFICER	South Wales Regional Prison Intelligence Team Prison Intelligence Officer Priya Kaur	PLACE/DATE/TIME OF REPORT	HMP Parc 27/11/2022 1.03 p.m.
INTEL SOURCE or INTEL REF NO	1102(7)/D	REPORT URN	22BTRS-1102

SOURCE EVALUATION	A Always Reliable	B Mostly Reliable	C Sometimes Reliable	D Unreliable	E Untested Source
INTELLIGENCE EVALUATION	1 Known to be true without reservation	2 Known personally to the source but not to the officer	3 Not known personally to the source, but corroborated	4 Cannot be judged	5 Suspected to be false

	Permissions			Restrictions	
HANDLING CODE To be completed at time of entry into an intelligence system and reviewed on dissemination	1 May be disseminated to other law enforcement and prosecuting agencies, including law enforcement within the EEA, and EU	2 May be disseminated to UK non-prosecuting parties	3 May be disseminated to non-EEA law enforcement agencies	4 Only disseminate within origination agency/force. Specify internal recipient(s)	5 Disseminated Intelligence Receiving agency to observe conditions as specified below

REPORT

Covert Human Intelligence Source (name classified) overheard Solomon King (aka Mad Dog), D.O.B. 07/09/2001, of Berry Hill, Caerphilly, bragging about having 'gat someone' for 'nicking P's' (paper money/bank notes). The original offence for which he is imprisoned is for the murder of a fellow gang member, JP (Johnathan Paulson). All associations and area links were reviewed by the team upon acquiring this intelligence and it transpires that shortly before he was remanded in custody (where he is currently awaiting trial) he travelled to Cardiff. On that day, a man named Errol James Parker was shot and killed on the doorstep of his home. The two men share an association with a female named Lorraine Fford, of Penarth, who is presently under the investigation of Gwent Police, who are acting on behalf of South Wales Police, in relation to his murder.

Subject Name: CHIS (Bloggs) SP09	DOB: 7/09/01	Evaluation		

OPERATION NAME/NUMBER:	S		I		H

Op Spec Pen Park West	A		I		I

DISSEMINATION TO: Operational Command Unit XS21
RISK ASSESSMENT FORM COMPLETED? YES
(Record location of form prior to securing) Held within Central Intelligence Unit for Prison Security (CIUPS)

PS TOMOS

PAST

Having updated us on the reported intelligence contained within an SIR – commonly termed a 5x5 by law enforcement – received yesterday, detailing the overheard conversation of an inmate temporarily imprisoned inside HMP Parc while awaiting categorisation after having been sentenced, DS Armand was able to verify the information disclosed therein and charge Solomon with Errol's murder.

Sol, as he preferred to be known, upon learning he'd be facing an additional minimum of fifteen years in prison on top of the fifteen he was already less than a few months into serving, decided to turn informant himself and named Lorraine as the person who'd actioned Errol's murder. In exchange he'd have been offered either a lighter sentence or a financial dividend. This meant he'd now be moved to HMP Parkhurst's Prisoner Protection Unit on the Isle of Wight, where all the supergrasses were safely housed and whom only senior officials allowed to work on the unit would be able to identify.

Along with the mobile phone evidence we'd secured that proved Demelza had located Errol on behalf of Lorraine, both women could now be charged with conspiring to kill the man and were due to appear in front of the magistrate in the morning.

That wasn't all he discovered either. In fact, I'd dare say that was even the half of it, since it became apparent that Sol and the racecourse owner's accountant, Shazia Hussain – suspected of committing accounting fraud, enabling the man to evade corporation tax for decades – was being represented by none other than the very same hotshot lawyer who'd been seated beside Lorraine during her interview.

DS Armand was going to update us on his findings once he'd spoken to Sol, but it appeared likely the accountant, and perhaps even the accountant's lawyer, worked for the same criminal organisation as Geraint's mother and uncles.

The incident room was fairly quiet for a late afternoon; a lull in the workload had left a collective hush to descend over the team. Emma had been called away half an hour earlier. Someone had apparently been waiting in reception for her. I thought it might have had something to do with what she'd told me about her stepson or even the boy's biological mother, but I didn't like to speculate.

While everyone busied themselves, albeit beneath a hood of almost soundless concentration, I was conducting research on our suspects, delving into their backgrounds, looking for connecting threads, which had enabled me to weave together a pattern.

It turned out that Luke was ex-military. Having served seventeen years in the Special Forces undertaking covert operations, he spent nine of them travelling back and forth to deployments in Afghanistan and Iraq from airbases in Qatar and the United Arab Emirates before becoming an Expert Protection Officer for a personal security firm that provided close protection services to, amongst others, senior military and government personnel, in the UK and overseas. It was during a sabbatical in Cyprus that I suspect he hooked up with the wealthy older woman he was engaged to marry and who just happened to be the daughter of a man who owned a pharmaceutical company headquartered in Arizona, that amongst other things sold fentanyl to its US suppliers, who in turn exported the product to Europe.

From what I'd read online the majority of fentanyl was manufactured in China and delivered to Mexico where it was either imported to the reputable buyers who'd ordered it or the illegal traders who often stole it, and where it was cut and diluted and mixed with heroin then transported into the US and sold to distributors who move it north into Canada or East to Spain, France, and Britain. The traffickers use ingenious ways to get it past customs without detection. Often by reforming the powder into pills and selling them in packets marked as other medicines to disguise them so they can be delivered by unsuspecting couriers.

'Guess who buys their lobsters from the company Derwen works for?' DC Chapman asked.

I drew my attention away from the unread emails in my inbox but kept my eyes on the screen of my computer.

'The restaurant chain Carol delivers seafood to?'

'Hole in one,' DC Winters added.

'And guess which Northwestern European country both companies bank with,' DC Bishop asked.

'Luxembourg?' Another tax haven.

'We have another ace,' DC Winters replied.

I spun round in my seat to look at her. 'How did you find that out so quickly, and at this time of the day?'

'I asked one of our Financial Intelligence Analysts

to book a table at the Anglesey restaurant,' DC Chapman replied. 'They use your debit card to approve a 0.00 booking transaction fee to verify your identity. Which of course won't lead back to us as the card used is specifically designed to leave no technological trace. I also ordered a crate of their finest shellfish to be delivered to the B&B down the road from where I live as a gift to the owner who recently lost her husband. Both purchases revealed the address of where their own transactions are processed. Although it's an online bank, they're required by law to have a registered postal address.'

'Nice one.'

'Want to know something else interesting, DC Winters asked, answering before I could reply. 'They have the same bank account.'

'So one person owns both companies?'

'Not one, no,' DC Chapman replied. 'More like one hundred.'

DC Winters nodded. 'The restaurant chain and the fishery are owned by a holding company.'

The same Canadian-based LLP that collects the income generated through criminal enterprise from the 100-plus small businesses in South Wales, some of them located on the same road in Cardiff, according to the NCA, one of which was owned by Lorraine Fford. Not forgetting the guitar shop that had previously been owned by Errol Parker, before whoever took it over did so; something we needed to establish. And, of course, Elys Whittaker's nail salon.

'So the money filters out of one company and into the other, creating an internal laundering system so as not to raise flags elsewhere.' Which in theory seems like a ingenious idea, except like a house of cards, when you make one wrong move the entire deck topples down.

I read the 'About Us' page on their website.

The Blue Lobster Shellery prides themselves on exporting their freshly caught shellfish to wholesalers, fishmongers, hoteliers, and restaurants throughout the UK and Europe.

Allowing couriers, like Carol, to distribute fentanyl-laced heroin alongside their catch.

'We need to speak to Carol,' DC Chapman said.

'She's got the kids. It's a school day and it's cold out, so they'll be at home now I should think,' DC Winters said.

'Where's home?' DC Chapman asked.

Neither Demelza, Scott, nor Lorraine would talk. We couldn't rely on Elys, who was intent on protecting her boyfriend by keeping quiet. Osian was likely frightened of losing his credibility with Mr Prior – who had either ordered him to scrap or fake scrapping the van – if he spoke to us. The man himself was giving nothing away. Javon, a mere drug runner, wasn't going to risk pissing off the organisation they all appeared to be working for. And so, we had nobody left to lean on. Except Carol.

We still hadn't located Derwen, so we had Carol under surveillance hoping she knew where he was and would reveal his whereabouts to us.

I checked with the UCOs, or Undercover Operatives as they're fully titled, to confirm Carol was at home before I told DCs Chapman and Winters her address. I looked them both in the eye and added a word of caution after I gave it them. 'We need to play this carefully. The twins are with her, so we don't want her to feel cornered. Tell her what you know but don't accuse her of anything.'

We wanted her to think we suspected Derwen had been roped into working for his in-laws out of a sense of loyalty, and that we sympathised with Carol, believed she must have felt obliged to help them out too. When really, that couldn't have been further from the truth.

They left just before Emma walked into the incident room, followed by a burly bloke who looked like a bouncer and a woman who had the same stature as my wife, who lifted weights for fun. Both crowded the doorway as they stepped into the room together, causing everyone to look up from their desks.

She introduced us to the two smartly dressed individuals then allowed them to take over the unexpected late afternoon briefing. Which in itself was unusual, because I'd never known – in all my years of working within the police force – a senior officer to allow anyone of the same calibre to directly brief their team, least of all Emma, who was the last person on earth I'd have expected to do so. Not because she didn't like to defer to others and preferred to be in charge, but as she was especially controlled and knew how to reiterate, explain, expand upon, and summarise important information so expertly there was never any need.

The guy reminded me a little of a movie character. You know, the workaholic cop with an ex-wife and a missing daughter which he blames for his drink problem. He was bold and brash, but he did a good job of having us all enthralled within seconds.

He and his colleague, on behalf of the International Criminal Police Organization, had been working a joint investigation into largescale money laundering that crossed the borders of several countries, beginning in Asia, and concerned multiple UK-based companies.

'Do you know what Julian did before he set up his own accountancy firm?' Agent Vaughan asked nobody in particular.

'He worked for the British Embassy,' Jonesy said

confidently, making it sound as though he was hobnobbing with diplomats and ambassadors and the like while supporting relations between foreign defence investors, which was about as far from the truth as you could get. 'He was a Staff and Personnel Support Officer for the finance section of the administration department within the military,' he added.

Agent Vaughan nodded then expanded on his explanation. 'His role was to facilitate in the transatlantic trade of firearms. He retired in 2003. But for eleven years he undertook various assignments, including in Iraq. Though he was, for the most part, being flown backwards and forwards from an airbase in the Kingdom of Saudi Arabia to Afghanistan, alongside a man named Eduardo Cortes.' He ended with an upward inflection as though asking us a question, though what he'd said was posed as a statement.

'Geraint's dad?' I couldn't disguise the note of surprise in my voice. 'They worked together?'

Agent Cheng gave me a nod and continued. 'After their last stint they both went their separate ways. Eduardo stayed on in the military for a number of years, working for the Trade Division of the US Department of Defence in Alabama, assisting with the importation of firearms, before moving to Maine. Where he now lives a quiet life on the coast inputting data on endangered marine wildlife observed by protected species researchers on behalf of some environmental agency. While Julian returned to the UK and set up his own accountancy firm. There was nothing in our files linking the two of them until Special Agent Beddoe, working for the Transnational Organized Crime Division of the Federal Bureau of Investigation based in Panama, discovered a vessel owned by a man named Mehmet Ivanova attempting to cross the Red Sea with ten tonnes of heroin on board.'

'How did you link Mehmet to Julian?' Jonesy asked.

'He had the man on speed-dial.'

And if it wasn't for Mehmet's arrest that morning as he attempted to enter Italy using a fake passport, the Toronto resident, who was being held within a supermax-security cell inside a Federal Detention Centre the INTERPOL officers stood in front of us couldn't name to protect his location, wouldn't have been offered and turned down a plea deal to name the primary operator and founder of the holding company that invests his profit in exchange for a lighter sentence.

'So you're saying that not only did Geraint's dad serve alongside Julian while stationed in Saudi Arabia, but this LLP is directed by the person Mehmet works for and who he refuses to identify. Have I got that right?'

'That's correct.'

'Do you have any idea who this drug lord that traffics large quantities of heroin from Afghanistan to Wales might be?'

Agent Vaughan didn't get a chance to reply. The moment he opened his mouth, Emma's phone rang, interrupting us.

She answered it on the second ring.

'Yes, speaking . . . Okay, I'll see you there . . . About half an hour.'

She finished the call then turned to us and said, 'A Mari Wynn is waiting to speak to me at Cardiff nick.'

The late great Alys Wynn's daughter. The woman who wrote *The Nighthawk*. What does she want?

KERRY-ANN

FIVE DAYS LATER

I was nervous entering the indie bookshop, heaving the heavy satchel laden with hardback copies of my memoir, ready to sign. I was greeted affectionately by the staff who immediately asked if there was anything they could do. I didn't think it would take me long to set up, so I said, 'No, thank you. I think I've got it covered. You've done more than enough just letting me be here.'

One of the women hovered uncertainly by the shelves containing the newly released paperbacks. 'I could pour the drinks?' she asked, nervously.

'Oh, yes, please. I almost forgot about the refreshments.'

She seemed buoyed by this, so I let her get on with it while I unfolded the rolled-up poster under my arm.

'Did the cake arrive on time?'

I was afraid I wouldn't have the strength to carry fifty spare books plus everything else, so had the individually packaged tea bags and cupcakes topped with miniature books bearing the cover of my own made from icing delivered direct to the store yesterday.

'Oh, yes,' she replied. 'And they look delicious.

Almost too good to eat.'

'You're welcome to have one yourself. I expect there'll be loads left.'

Her face beamed.

My fingers were still stiff and aching as I pressed each edge of the enlarged image of my book cover into the four corners of the stand that backed the pasting table that was ready for me to decorate. I unwrapped the wipeable tablecloth my publisher had provided between the edging and smoothed it over the rectangular-shaped wood until there wasn't a crease visible. I opened the first of two large cardboard boxes, each of which contained twenty-five copies of the gorgeously new-smelling books, and fingered the pages, delighted by the fragrance of my own success. I stood and turned to place them one at a time on the table in a domino-affect arc when my forehead almost connected to the chin of a tall stocky man who appeared to have been leaning over the table in search of – me?

'Sorry to have made you jump,' he said. 'Just wondered if I could have a quick word with you before the cavalry arrive.'

'About what?'

'Your conversation with Geraint Fford. I'd like to know what you spoke about.' He said this as he tapped the copy, he'd brought with him and held in his hands.

My throat dried and my pulse quickened.

'You're . . . a copper?'

Not the one who was creeping around the cottage though.

'I work for CID. I'm investigating his murder,' he replied.

'Oh.'

My heartrate slowed again.

I thought I'd given a rather detailed description of

our discussion in the book. There was a lot I didn't write about though. Things I couldn't tell this – detective?

Geraint told me how he'd been the one to help get Glenn Marsh off a custodial prison sentence for animal cruelty which he believed in hindsight was for Glenn to practise his skills in deprivation, starvation, and neglect which he used as torture devices against the women he kidnapped. And that he'd regretted it every day since.

'Who are you?'

He introduced himself as Dafydd Tomos, said he was an off-duty police sergeant. I looked him up and down, and knowing what the press are like, demanded to see his ID. Satisfied he wasn't a journalist, I indicated for him to take one of the seats that reminded me of those hard plastic backache-inducing school chairs I was forced to sit on for six hours a day as a child.

'I spoke to him about my father.'

Geraint told me that he felt partly responsible for those women's deaths. It caused him a lot of emotional distress over the years to the point that he even contemplated suicide. Though he never admitted to having acted on those thoughts.

'What was he like? I mean, how did he seem to you?' he asked.

'Quiet, but not timid. He seemed to find it easier to listen than to talk. I guess that's something that makes a good lawyer. But it's also something I'm better at doing, so I found it weird.'

'I suppose being a memoirist isn't much different. You have to find a way of telling someone else's story.'

'I guess you're right.'

'Have you been keeping up with the news?' he asked.

'If you mean, have I read what the media are saying about Geraint's family, then yes. But if you want to know if I was aware of who he was or where he came from, then no. I didn't know anything about that side of things. In fact, I felt a little blindsided when I found out. I mean, he never came across as the kind of bloke to be involved in anything shady.'

'You didn't think he was?' he asked.

'No, but he must have been, right? I mean he was a lawyer for Christ's sake. He was in the perfect position to get his parent's pals off whatever charge they were arrested for. Why'd you think they paid for him to go to a private school and a top university? They needed him.'

Or you could say they used him. It wasn't like he'd have had much choice but to follow in their footsteps, is it? Being brought up by criminals, I suspect he felt right at home working alongside them day in day out. Either way, he was no doubt on their payroll.

'Did he say anything to you that you didn't use in your memoir? Something that could help us to understand him better, or that could assist us with our enquiries?'

I was careful with my reply.

'I pick and choose what to write obviously, but no, I don't think anything he said could help with your investigation.'

'It must have been hard for you to learn that your father was a murderer, to hear him excuse his crime, and blame your mother for it.'

His question caught me a little off-guard, I didn't think Geoffrey's murder had anything to do with Geraint's, but I guessed being a police officer wasn't much different to being a lawyer or memoirist either. Our inquisitive natures can often lead to clues we don't know we need that inadvertently enable us to move forward.

I studied the bookshop. A couple of people had wandered in from the high street, but I doubted they knew who I was or had come in specifically to buy a copy of my book for me to sign, I was no bestselling celebrity.

My father was dead, and so was Geraint, so I figured it couldn't hurt to tell him what really happened.

DI LOCKE

PAST

Speaking to Mari Wynn was not high on my list of priorities but it was almost the end of my shift. The duty night team would soon begin to filter into the incident room, and I'd have to handover to the DI – a highly regarded gent who I both respected and admired – so I decided to pay her a visit on my way to check in with DC Banks, who only today had been given a date for his return-to-work interview with HR. A necessary element of bureaucracy that infuriated him.

I indicated for Agent Vaughan to continue, to tell my team what he'd told me thirty minutes ago, while I put my coat on to leave.

'Your man was shot with a fifth generation Glock 17. Although they're more commonly used by the military they're also sometimes used by militant forces. Cartels and terrorist organisations, for example.'

'Geraint was not a drug lord or a terrorist,' Dafydd quipped.

'No, he was not,' Agent Vaughan said. 'But he most certainly knew someone who was.'

Colm McGinty's father, Fergal.

PS TOMOS

PAST

I kept my ears on Agent Vaughan, while I scanned the intel I'd just filed. 'Luke, which airbase was he stationed at?' I asked the team.

'Luke?' Agent Vaughan replied, seemingly unbothered by having been interrupted mid-flow and believing I was aiming my words at him.

'Luke Fford, Geraint's uncle. He was in the military. He served in Afghanistan and Iraq. There are two airbases, one in Qatar and the other—'

'Al Minad,' Agent Cheng cut in. 'In The United Arab Emirates,' she added. She glanced up at her superior, and he stared down at her, impressed. 'The one in Qatar is in Al Udeid. Which is where Julian and Eduardo were based.'

'I don't recall coming across the name Luke during our inquiries,' Agent Vaughan said, thoughtfully.

'You think he worked with Julian and Eduardo,' Agent Cheng said, matter-of-factly.

'I think it was through her brother that Lorraine met Eduardo.'

'What if it was? How does Luke relate to your investigation?' Agent Vaughan asked, not unkindly.

'He owns a mansion in Tenerife, where he kept over

ten million dollars in cash, until Spanish Police raided his home. He's . . . *dating* a woman whose father owns a pharmaceutical company.'

'You think the two of them provide the fentanyl used to cut the heroin that was found on Mehmet's carrier,' Agent Vaughan said, confirming my own thoughts. 'I'll speak to our contacts in the MOD. Find out what I can about Luke's deployments. See if he ever worked with either Eduardo or Julian. Though if I'm honest, I find it highly unlikely. Covert Ops are just that. I can't see how he'd have been involved in anything discoverable.'

KERRY-ANN

FIVE DAYS LATER

During my prison visit, my father had told me how my mother, while cleaning, had come across the correspondence from Wotton Dean Hospital, detailing the terms of agreement for Geoffrey's departure. 'Unethical practises', 'misconduct', and assurance that the former psychiatrist would 'no longer be pursued for investigatory purposes'. His beloved had then combed the house for further evidence, so that she could out the psychiatrist. The plan backfired however when Geoffrey found Nancy rifling through his documents in the study, and she confronted him. She asked him if Celyn knew. He said no. She threatened to tell his wife that he'd lost his job, that he'd been behaving improperly with the women under his care, if he didn't. He refused, of course. She spun round and tried to leave, intending to tell her employer. He held her back, wanting to stop her. She shoved him, but it was like trying to move a brick wall. She was scared. He was angry.

That much is true.

My father enters the story here, when my mother ran over to him, distraught, telling him what she'd found, about the argument she'd had with Geoffrey. He wanted to confront the man himself, over what he'd been accused of, but most importantly for having upset his pregnant soon-to-be wife.

The police sergeant knew this, it was what I wrote in my book. But there were some things I'd omitted.

I'd assumed my father had entered the house, challenged Geoffrey on my mother's findings, and they'd fought, which had left Geoffrey dead. Because he'd led me to believe that he'd bumped into Celyn – who'd returned because she'd forgotten her purse – as he was exiting the rear door that led through the kitchen and out into the vast gardens. That she'd not only overheard the argument between Nancy and Geoffrey, but also the altercation between Geoffrey and my father, and consequently they'd decided it would be mutually beneficial to him and Celyn if Roderick were to take the blame for Geoffrey's murder, to protect the late psychiatrist's legacy, Nancy's reputation, and my future.

But that's not what happened.

He was stunned by the scene that greeted him, but he tried not to think as he wiped the handle of the poker to remove Nancy's DNA from it, then held it as though intending to strike someone with it to add his own fingerprints to the weapon. Then he trod in the bloodbath surrounding Geoffrey's body to ensure his footprints marked the carpet, to implicate himself.

As he did this, he turned to find Celyn staring down at her husband's body, her face pale, eyes unblinking, seemingly too stunned to speak, holding the phone in one hand and the receiver in the other, her blouse and skirt saturated in blood.

'I've called the police,' she said. 'They're on their way.'

He begged her to let him take the blame, wanting to protect his wife from a life sentence, prevent me, his unborn daughter, from growing up without my mother. He thought he was doing the right thing. How could he have known Nancy's guilt would destroy her fragile mind?

She saw him gazing at her clothes, said, 'I tried to revive him.'

He had no reason to doubt her.

'Roderick thought my mother had killed Geoffrey and took a split-second to decide to cover for her. He had no time to think, the police were on their way, blue lights flashing, sirens blaring. It was only as he took in Celyn's calm demeanour and thought back to the way Nancy had approached him that he realised he'd reacted before asking anyone any questions.'

Why hadn't Nancy told him she'd pulverised Geoffrey's head in? Warned him in advance of what to expect before he'd entered the house?

Why had he automatically believed Nancy had murdered Geoffrey? What had Nancy said to lead him to believe she'd killed him?

Why weren't Celyn's clothes blood-soaked? If she'd attempted mouth to mouth resuscitation on her husband, shouldn't her face, hands, and clothes be saturated in blood? Why did she look instead as though she'd been merely lightly sprayed with claret?

'"*You* killed him," he'd said. Celyn had stared back at him. "No," she'd replied. "You did."'

'That's why he ran. That's why we, the police, found him hiding out on Sully Island,' PS Tomos said. Where he sat all night, shivering, until the sun began to rise, teeth chattering, muscles stiff, lips blue.

I Nodded in confirmation.

'He found my mum waiting under the oak tree. She saw the blood on his hands and shoes and assumed he'd got into a bout of fisticuffs with Geoffrey. When he explained what had happened, she became hysterical.

I think that's what broke her.'

He told her to go home, said when the police came to speak to her that she had to play dumb. She refused. 'Damn it, Nance, do as I say.' He'd never spoken to her like that before, never once raised his voice to her or ordered her to do anything. 'They're going to arrest and charge me with murder. I'm probably going to get life. She cleaned her DNA off the poker before I got mine all over it. That bitch is never going to admit what she's done. She's not going to allow anyone to separate her from her son for anything. She said if I don't confess, she'll tell the police you did it. You're not going to spend the next two or three decades in prison. I won't have it. Do you hear me? You have to look after that baby for us both.'

She stood there open-mouthed as he crossed the garden, hopped over the hedge, and followed the narrow country road down towards the public footpath, which eventually widened out onto the hiking trail that split into two, one route leading towards the cottage I'd stayed in last November. It was hard to believe six months had passed since I'd first visited the bay in the bleak, stone-cold, snowy midwinter. And I had begun writing what was supposed to have been Alys' memoir, which had incidentally turned into my own. He chose the other path, which led out onto the narrow winding road and crossed the beach to the island.

He wasn't framed. 'He set himself up.'

To fail as a father, and to die as a prisoner.

'Have you told anyone else this?'

I knew what he was thinking; that had I reported what my father had told me to Geraint, he would have questioned Celyn, and that would have put her well and truly in the frame for his murder. But Geraint's killer had already been arrested and charged and was locked up based on irrefutable evidence discovered at an address in Pontypool, so I didn't think it was relevant.

But the truth was, 'No,' I hadn't.

DI LOCKE

PAST

My breath fogged in front of me as I crossed the car park. There was a light smattering of what I thought was rain on the windscreen, but it turned out to be interior condensation which had frozen onto the glass. Shivering, I started the car and switched on the heater to demist the windows. It took ages to dispel the glistening water droplets, which I had to wipe away with a cloth, and the blast of hot air did little to rid the perpetual chill I felt beneath my jumper.

The streets were surprisingly quiet on the drive over to Cardiff nick, but as I drew closer to the city centre the traffic halted and I sat for forty minutes staring at the Christmas lights hung between the shopfronts which shimmered as they swayed in the chilly breeze.

Mari was a tall, wide-framed woman with a tough demeanour and a hard set of eyes that latched onto me as soon as I entered the room.

'The desk sergeant told me you asked to speak to me, specifically.'

I sat in front of her, directly opposite the vulnerable witness suite attached to a play area containing toys, boardgames, jigsaw puzzles, and books, that was separated by a lateral opening door. It was where minors could be supervised while we spoke to their guardians.

'That's right.' She spoke in a direct manner I respected. 'You're in charge of the investigation into Geraint's murder.'

'Yes, I am. Do you know something that could assist us with our inquiries?'

'There's this woman, her name's Kerry-Ann Pascoe. She's written a book about her father, Roderick Penrose, who was imprisoned for murder. It's being released this Thursday.'

I remained tight-lipped, allowing her to fill the silence. Mainly because I had no idea why she wanted to talk to me, and because of that I had no idea what to say to her.

'Well, that's not what she was supposed to be writing. She was commissioned to author my mother's memoir, explore her life's work and how she balanced her writing career alongside bringing up a family.'

She paused for effect before continuing.

'Kerry-Ann came to stay with my mother, last year, at the house. Thought she was being . . . watched, so she'd fled the cottage she was renting in the early hours. She was the one who found her. There was no doubt about it, my mother had saved up all her medication. But she wasn't a cruel woman. She'd never have wanted Kerry-Ann to find her, not after everything that poor woman had been put through. That's how I know my mother's death wasn't intentional, at least not by her own hands.'

She took a moment to compose herself, adjusting her position on the seat before taking a long inhalation then continuing. 'Sure, she might have planned to swallow those pills, the note she left was certainly written by her, but she wouldn't have done it then.

She'd have waited until the time was right, until she'd said goodbye to everyone, before she acted. Alys was a strong woman, a fighter. She fought cancer like a soldier, taking on the battle despite knowing she'd already lost. Unlike the alcohol.'

'Her death was ruled a suicide.'

'Someone killed her,' Mari said. 'I know they did.'

She went on to tell me that at the time of her death Alys was thirty-six years sober.

'She quit drinking a fortnight before she discovered she was pregnant with me. My first words were Bill and Bob. The first book I read was AAs Bible, otherwise known as The Big Book. I blame my mother for my sweet tooth, having spent much of my early years drinking tea and eating biscuits at the back of a church. Do you know, she never missed her weekly home group meeting for as long as she lived. It was her sponsor who read out the eulogy at her funeral.'

I was wondering what this had to do with Alys' death when she added, 'My mother didn't have long left to live, but the time she did have she chose to spend it with a complete stranger. Something that, at the time, I didn't understand. But writing was what she lived for, and she was convinced the Nighthawk had an accomplice. She used to talk about it all the time. And then the bodies of those women you keep hearing about on the news started showing up in the same exact locations as the Nighthawk dumped his victims, and she suddenly changed her mind. She began to suspect he had a copycat. She kept saying that whoever he was must have known exactly where to dump his victims because he knew each of the Nighthawk's deposition sites, and that knowledge could only be obtained by someone who'd been present at every one of them.'

'Couldn't he have got that information from the

public domain, just as she had?'

'She had contacts. Police contacts. When she wrote *The Nighthawk* there were less stringent policies on what the police could discuss with the press. There was one uniformed officer, I can't remember his name, but he was here a lot. My father didn't like him, said he got a bad feeling about him.'

Barely taking a breath between words she went on to say, 'During the last conversation I had with my mother over the phone she told me she planned to give Kerry-Ann a folder containing this project she was working on, where she drew comparisons between the Nighthawk and this unknown man who's carrying out these crimes today, using her previous research. My mother had gone back over her original unedited manuscript, and the list of contacts she'd used to pen her first draft, and came across the details for a photographer named Kai, who apparently had snapped a picture of this copper . . .'

Mari went on to tell me that he was caught smoking at one of the crime scenes. Got in trouble for contaminating it by dropping a cigarette stub on the ground. Apparently, it was cold, so everyone had been wearing gloves. Except the image captured him without them on. Of course, back then they could only distinguish between a person's blood type to identify and eliminate suspects, so they tested the saliva on the cigarette stub against Glenn Marsh's and concluded that it hadn't belonged to him. But they'd never compared the sample to the constable.

'I've read Kerry-Ann's book. I managed to wangle a proof copy from the publisher to review in advance of its publication. In it she's written that she spoke to Geraint to get a legal perspective on Roderick's trial. She hasn't written the entirety of their conversation but I know my mother also told Geraint that after speaking to Kai she thought that a copper was responsible for killing the women today in the same way the Nighthawk murdered his victims all those years ago, and that she believed the police knew who he was and were protecting him, what with him being one of their own.'

That's when it hit me. It wasn't just the military who used Glock 17s. The Home Office provided them to certain members of the police force, too. Aside from the occasional use of long-arms the self-loading pistol was their go-to firearm.

If this man had killed Alys in order to shut down her investigation, then who's to say he didn't also shoot Geraint for asking too many questions? And that Kerry-Ann was still alive, could be explained by the fact the book she'd diligently researched, written, and submitted to her publisher was about her father, and didn't have anything to do with the Copycat Killer.

'Hypothetically speaking, how would he have got inside Alys' home? Got her to take all those pills?' There was no sign of forced entry or a struggle, and after hearing about Kerry-Ann's experience up at the cottage I couldn't imagine Alys allowing a copper into her home without a fight.

'The front door locked from the inside by yanking up the handle, but if she'd been expecting someone, Kerry-Ann perhaps, she might have left it unlocked, meaning anyone could have just walked in. And the morphine was in liquid form; easier to swallow. She told me it tasted sweet. She took a lot of sugar in her tea. Anyone could have poured it into her drink, and she wouldn't have noticed. She hardly used the stuff; didn't want to, not with her past addiction to alcohol, so she didn't have a tolerance. Hence how, I suppose, she'd managed to save so many bottles of it up. It wouldn't have taken much to cause her to overdose.'

I wasn't convinced. It just seemed like a lot of trouble to go to, and it wouldn't have been quick. Though, unlike shooting someone it didn't leave a mess and was quiet, less conspicuous.

'I found this when I emptied the house,' she said, reaching down into a large handbag at her feet and handing me a notebook. 'She used a different one for each of her projects. I think these are the people she wanted to speak to about what she was working on when she died.'

I flicked through it quickly. The pages were filled with names, addresses, and telephone numbers. Some had been crossed off. I expected those that weren't hadn't been contacted yet. There were a few journalists, and a couple of detectives. I recognised one of them.

'Mind if I take this?'

'Keep it. It's no use to me.'

PS TOMOS

PAST

I had been looking forward to going home and spending some time with my family when the chief called me into his room.

Facing DCI Evans I felt like a schoolboy who'd been sent to the headmaster's office, or as though I'd gone back in time to my days in the Special Forces and was sitting across from my captain.

He had to decide whether to keep me on the case or let me go. Nothing I said or did would be enough to change his mind. My powerlessness at the situation gnawed at me, somersaulted my stomach and left my mouth dry.

I did as I'd been taught by my therapist and counted backwards from 100 in numerical digits to still the compulsion to tap my foot against the thin carpet in a nervous attempt to calm my racing thoughts.

'During your time with us you've been a valued member of the team. Old-school but without the misogynistic shite.'

I felt my chest tighten and my palms sweat.

'Sir I—'

'See, this is what I'm talking about. You're respectful, to everyone, not just your superiors. You're diligent too. Always offering to hit the road before being asked to, regardless of how far you have to travel. And above all else, you're a natural leader. Someone who our constables can look up to, secure in the knowledge that they're in good hands. Which is why I'm hoping you'll return to us when you pass.'

'Sir?'

He must have seen the confusion on my face because he added, 'You're off to London two weeks Monday for your National Investigators Exam. I'm giving you the next fortnight off to study, so you'd better bloody ace it.'

KERRY-ANN

FIVE DAYS LATER

The book signing was a success. I sold all the copies I'd brought with me, and the shop almost ran completely out of stock.

I hadn't expected the police sergeant to stay; hours had passed since I'd revealed to him why I was reluctant to include my father's story in my memoir. I couldn't be sure it was true, although I felt it was. Neither could I tarnish Celyn's name on the basis of a few words spoken by a convicted murderer, regardless of the fact that he was my dad.

When PS Tomos asked me what I was working on next, I lied, said, 'Nothing.' Partly because it was still a work in progress; the DNA extracted from the cigarette stub found at the deposition site where one of the women was located all those years ago matched the semen found on one of the more recent female murder victims, though the man it belonged to was still unknown, at least to the general public. But also, because I wouldn't have written it at all if it wasn't for Alys who'd begun writing the story in the first place. And whose last words to me on the subject were: 'I want you to finish it. But you can't use your own name. I don't want you putting yourself in danger.'

SIX MONTHS LATER

DI LOCKE

PRESENT

I don't need to be here today, but I thought I might as well see the trial through to the end since I've already heard both Kai and Ffion's testimonies. The thing about criminal trials, however, is that in much the same way as a police investigation, you never know how they will go.

I'm not counting on a lengthy argument from the defence, they don't really have anything tangible to refute; only a couple of timeline inconsistencies that just as the defendant's barrister can't prove neither can the Crown Prosecutor disprove. I'm hoping for an admittance of guilt to save those relatives, his friends, colleagues, and associates who are in attendance the emotional distress of having to sit through hours of denial and self-pity, or whatever the defendant wishes to excuse his actions with, so I'm slightly taken aback and majorly pissed-off when he tries to make out that he's been set up.

His defence means there is no need to cross-examine him. He doesn't have to come up with a reason for the existence of his DNA, because none had been found at the scene of Geraint's murder, and as he has confessed to having been close to the area at the time Geraint was shot, he comes across as a reliable witness. Especially considering he was able to provide the court with a relatively valid explanation: a receipt for a coffee-to-go purchased on his way to visit his sick mother in the nursing home she resides in. This meant the chance of securing a conviction was very much up to debate, despite the evidence against him, because his defence team weren't required to seek an alternative suspect. Their only job was to add an element of doubt in the juries' minds as to whether he was the culprit.

Chapter One

'It began as most legends do, with a tragedy. There was of course a hint of truth to the story, but no one today knows which parts are fact and which have been created or embellished throughout the centuries, but what I can tell you is that the Nighthawk is real. I know because I've seen him.'

That's how it starts, her introduction, the travel guide.

'Seen him how?' an elderly gentleman pipes up.

'His ghost.'

He nods, apparently satisfied with her explanation.

Great! She's a kook.

She talks us through the history of the chapel ruins on the island, which can only be accessed on foot for one hour, during extremely low tide, because at all other times it's completely submerged underwater.

The Nighthawk in this instance is the Norman pirate, Alfredo De Marisco, who originated from Portugal. He invented the skull and crossbones flags that have become a popular symbol of pirating in the western world, and today, tend to be used to adorn children's birthday parties in the form of bunting.

The tide surrounding the island is one of the most volatile, and often, during the eleventh century, in bad weather and before the existence of lighthouses, marooned seafarers would find themselves struck through the stomach and the captain pinned to the bow with a blade, while the Nighthawk pillaged the quartermasters and sailors on board to plunder the cabin of their ship if it had the misfortune to bank there.

The flag back then put people off thwarting his plans. Today they alert the neighbours to the impending doom of raised voices high on sugar and of a balloon drifting into their back yard and landing in their pond threatening the lives of their fish.

As I trace the boggy mudflats, I breathe in the salty sea spray, captivated by the majestic stone ruins of Saint Twrogg's while the guide delivers a haunting sermon on the destructive forces that led to the abandonment of the chapel that's rarely visible above the surface of the Bristol Channel.

'The Great Flood in 1607 which took the lives of hundreds of people, killed livestock, destroyed homes, and ruined working folk's livelihoods was followed less than a hundred years later by the Great Storm of 1703, which did much the same to a vaster population and a wider expanse of land. Each sudden rise in the levels tore layers off the marshland and caused the rocks surrounding the island to crumble and sink. And between both was the most turbulent time in British history. We're talking political unrest, civil war, famine, plague, and, of course, the witch trials.'

This seems to draw the attention of one of the five tourists I'm visiting the cold, damp little island with.

'Witch trials?'

'Yes.'

''Ere, in England?'

'Technically this island belongs to Wales . . .'

Then comes a discussion on the possibility of a referendum, a debate about the pros and cons of Wales departing the UK, having not only its own parliament but also laws, and becoming an independent country altogether. I leave them to argue amongst themselves, drawn to the rotten wood of what appears to be the skeletonised keel of a wrecked ship that's coated in limpets and juts out like black teeth from the quicksand.

'Ah,' the guide says, coming to stand a few feet behind me, having noticed my intrigue. 'That's the old bones of one of the ferries that used to transport people from Aust to Beachley. They stopped the service in 1966 when the Severn Bridge opened, enabling people to cross the Severn Estuary from Avonmouth to Chepstow.'

The remains of the slipway could just as easily belong to the tall wooden posts used to tie nets to trap lobsters, like the ones I saw when I visited that most ancient and sacred of islands just off the coast of Swanbridge Bay, in Lavernock.

It was windy that day. The scrubby grass that coated Sully Island was puddled from the rain, and the waves crashed against the craggy rocks, as high and mighty as if the world was about to end.

Well, it had for one man at least.

Twenty-five years before, in a six-bedroom house with a circular drive, hidden behind a row of ferns, half a mile inland. Where a man was brutally slain. A man my father was convicted of killing.

1

DS TOMOS

PRESENT

Ed's presence hasn't gone unnoticed. From the very first day of the trial, which I felt compelled to witness seeing as it concluded my first murder investigation since qualifying as a Detective Sergeant, the press have spent as much if not more of their word space reporting on how he's dressed, where the suit he's wearing today was purchased, and who he has seated beside him as he stares vacantly at the accused. They've photographed the vehicles he's arrived in and those he's left in, each practically identical (sleek, black, German, SUV) though always bearing a different registration plate. Born from immigrant parents, and brought up in poverty, it's clear that his wealth and the luxury in which he is accustomed does not come from counting marine birds.

    I'd be lying if I were to tell you it did not come as a shock to learn that his chauffeurs and who looked to be his bodyguards were in fact being paid by legitimate means. Namely, a very generous pension from the MOD, which topped up his wages nicely, and allowed him to rent a lighthouse on the coast of Maine and invest in bitcoin, which he'd recently traded for something called Non-Fungible Tokens, which Emma mispronounced 'non-fungus thingamabobs' one time much to the amusement of the team and must forevermore live with the nickname Mushroom. Because despite the hard tenacious exterior she portrays, she is just like you and me underneath; she gives as good as she gets when it comes to banter.

The FBI had completed a thorough investigation of Ed's finances after it had come about that he'd been in a relationship with and had borne a son to a British narca. During which they'd found no evidence he'd had anything even remotely to do with the largescale trafficking of drugs. Though his mushroom token investments sure as hell were questionable.

There are still people filing into the courtroom when the defendant is brought in.

'All rise,' says the bailiff, once everyone is seated.

The Prosecutor for the Crown gives his closing statement, in which he paraphrases his opening speech before summarising the trial as though we weren't all here sitting on aching behinds for three days to reach the inevitable unanimous verdict that we wait with bated breath to hear.

It is the defence's opportunity to give their final statement, then the foreperson announces that the jury find the defendant, 'Guilty.'

Chapter Two

The wind whips my hair about my face as I traverse the winding pebbled footpath across the shallow water that stretches from the café and along the shingle to the island. Broken shells nip at the toughened skin at the heels of my feet, sandals slipping on the rocks, freezing water heavy with seaweed that knots itself around my ankles, and which I have to untangle and kick away as I plod along.

I have three hours to explore the last known geographical location of the Nighthawk, dusty with sand and riddled with tall, wild grass. Once I've made it to the peak, where I have a one-hundred-and-eighty-degree view of the hamlet of Lavernock to my left, Swanbridge Bay to my right, and straight ahead the untameable sea – the pirate's hunting ground – I inhale the briny saltwater, eyes on the two distinct and equally fascinating islands in the distance: Steep Holm, considered to be part of the county of Somerset, where the remains of a Roman watchtower sits embedded amongst the wild peonies; and Flat Holm, decidedly a part of Wales, and where the seafarers mission building – that still stands – was used as a sanitorium to treat cholera in the late nineteenth century.

There is a natural causeway built into the vertical cliffs framing the shoreline of Sully Island, where a man is already perched like a bird on a telegraph pole, rod in hand, casting his line out to the waves, hoping to magnetise something edible to feast on tonight. Right where, I expect, my father fished while he slept on this isolated patch of the Vale of Glamorgan during his time on the run.

2

KERRY-ANN

PRESENT

A whole life tariff.
 That's what the judge sentences him to.
 Without the eligibility for parole.
 He cries.
 Like a fucking baby.
 Good.
 But then he glances up as he wipes his eyes with the back of his hand. I catch his gaze and our eyes lock for a moment. And I wonder, did my dad cry?
 And I have to get out of here.
 It feels like someone has thrown a lasso around my chest and is tugging on it.
 My vision tunnels.
 The faces surrounding me blur into one.
 I'm gasping for air as I reach the wide tiled entrance.
 I burst through the heavy wooden automatic doors and suck in a huge lungful of strawberry and kiwi tasting air, thanks to the dreadlocked man in a sharp button-down navy-blue suit running up the steps with an e-cigarette between his lips and a vaporous mist following along behind him.
 Then I spot a familiar face, and my pulse slows, and

my limbs feel looser, lighter.

Natalia can't hide the concern that creases her brow as she approaches me.

'What happened in there? What's wrong?'

How can I explain it to her if I'm unable to comprehend it myself? How when I looked into the defendant's eyes, I saw only a fearful desperation to be believed. And that the only other person who'd ever looked at me in the same imploring way was my father. A man who claimed to have been innocent of the crime for which he was convicted.

'What if they've got the wrong man?'

Not that anything could be done about it now anyway. Afterall, the Criminal Justice System relies on facts not feelings, and science doesn't lie.

Does it?

Chapter Three

Despite the name, Nighthawk's, known formally as Nightjar's are not nocturnal, nor are they birds of prey. They're most active at dusk and dawn. They're well-camouflaged and can survive in most habitats that include a variety of eco-systems, such as meadows, cities, forests, islands, mountains, swamps, and beaches. They migrate from south America to Europe and can be found in the southernmost parts of the UK during the summertime. They eat mosquitos, grasshoppers, beetles, flies, and wasps while in-flight. They often mate when abroad and are territorial. An old wives' tale suggests they drink milk from the teats of goats. Folklore has it that the Nighthawk is the bird of the devil and that if you spot one outside your home you've been hexed. And it doesn't seem so fantastical when you consider that sightings of the bird in a particular area tend to rise in correlation with cursed luck, which includes personal tragedies, natural disasters, and high crime rates.

Take Sully Island for instance, where Nighthawks are often spotted by birdwatchers. For several hundred years Swanbridge Bay thrived as a port. From the late 1800s until the 1960s the area was popular with tourists. The height of the area's popularity though would have been the fifties, when day-trippers were able to travel by train using the Taff Vale Railway extension from Penarth, Cardiff, Barry, or the South Wales Valleys to fish for cod, paddle in the sea, buy an ice cream from the beachfront café or tea from the refreshment kiosk at the manor house, and a family could stay in a caravan at the Spinney Holiday Park. But once the railway line was shut off and the coastal road blocked off the visitors dried up, the café closed its doors, and tourism moved west to Porthcawl, The Mumbles, or Tenby.

Legend has it the semi-detached cottages that

once housed the local fishermen and their families, and which was converted into a restaurant and public house respectively, got its name The Captain's Wife from the theft of the captain's wife's remains, which were kept inside a jewellery box within the captain's cottage, during a burglary.

It's not *her* ghost that haunts the bay though.

SIX MONTHS BEFORE

DI LOCKE

PAST

Agent Vaughan called me as I headed back to my car. His contact in the Ministry of Defence was able to rule out Luke's association to Julian due to the fact he had served as part of a counterterrorism unit within the Special Reconnaissance Regiment, which had nothing at all to do with finance or administration. To be certain though, he'd compared the dates, times, and locations of Luke's deployments to Julian's, which confirmed they hadn't even been in the same country as one another since they'd become adults. There was also nothing linking Luke to Eduardo until his sister, Lorraine, had made him an uncle with the birth of Geraint, so they hadn't known one another as children either.

What we were not expecting however was to learn that prior to Eduardo's deployments to Afghanistan, Qatar, and Arizona respectively, the specific branch of the AGC he was sectioned in were directly responsible for supplying arms to the Irish Defence Forces during the Troubles. Which I imagine would not only have caused friction between Eduardo and his son, due to Geraint's involvement in defending members of the terrorist organisation his father had armed their opposition against, at the start of his career. But I suspect it also would have created conflict between Geraint and his clients – some of whom were former Provos: that is the Provisional Irish Republican Army – had they somehow learned about his father's role within the British Army.

Though this information was concerning, it was what else Agent Vaughan's contact was legally able to divulge that had me worried.

'Geraint's father was one of twenty personnel who were instrumental in arming people like Fergal McGinty and Douglas Daly with ammunition.'

Had Eduardo ever come across them? Had they formed an alliance? Had he struck a deal whereby he'd arm them with guns and grenades in exchange for drugs? Did Colm McGinty have a problem with Eduardo, and as a consequence put a hit on Geraint's head? Is that why Detective Inspector Bridges had sent him an Osman Warning? Was Eduardo the Kingpin who Mehmet refused to name and who Agent Vaughan was prohibited from identifying until they were captured?

'How?'

Agent Vaughan went on to explain how the IRA procured their small handheld gun armoury.

The route they travelled began in New England, where they were made. The guns were then packaged and transported across the United States to their New York distribution centre where they would be exported across the world – Saudi Arabia and Japan being their biggest buyers. So how had they ended up in Belfast via the port of Southampton using money funded by financiers in Toronto, Canada?

It was during transfer to Spain or Holland that some of the smaller shipments were rerouted to the UK on board European vessels, including fishing trawlers.

Either by pay-offs or theft from the British Army's surplus stores – that were meant to be destroyed when BNLR. 'That's Bought but No Longer Required,' he tells me. Which resulted in rifles, revolvers, and pistols getting into the hands of the IRA. The US Department of Defence discovered what was happening pretty fast, however, so a Texas gunsmith living in New Hampshire began arming the Provos directly with Lugers, using London gangs to transport them to Ireland. The only ammunition of which they could use was made in a munitions factory in Torfaen, South Wales. The same factory that provided over half of the UK's defence organisations with projectiles. And who Eduardo and nineteen other personnel were responsible for organising the sales of. Which meant they were indirectly involved in the accruement of missiles through illegal trade. A serious crime that defied international laws and would have resulted in a hefty prison sentence had they not been doing so on behalf of the British government.

'The Government Arms Promotion Unit employs army personnel to demonstrate and sell weaponry and other equipment overseas to enable companies to get rid of surplus stock. The UK Defence Industry hires around 100 individuals to do this, saving the MOD billions of pounds each year. Eduardo and Julian were two such people.'

South Wales, UK.
New England, US.
Saudi Arabia.
Belfast, Ireland.
Toronto, Canada.
Spain.
Holland.

Every single one of those geographical locations were somehow involved with our investigation. Which is why I could be forgiven for starting to think the obvious; that Geraint's murder somehow had something to do with his father's military career, rather than his mother's involvement in the murder of Errol Parker.

I ended the call and noticed the time on my phone. I'd better get a move on if I wanted to beat the rush-hour traffic on the one-way system that was the B4236 that led to DC Banks' modest abode.

PS TOMOS

PAST

I was halfway home when I got the call. Emma sounded frantic and with the radio on and the heater blasting out hot air I had to pull over and cut the engine so I could hear her better. It was by pure luck that I'd already turned off the main road and onto the side street nearing home. Where, I expected, Sarah was stirring a mouthwatering vegetarian chili, as she'd promised to do for tonight's meal. I could imagine it simmering on the stove as I turned the heater down and the radio off.

'. . . present at the deposition site where one of the Nighthawk's victim's bodies was located. And it just happens to be the very same locale where the cigarette stub – now thought to belong to Glenn Marsh's unknown accomplice – was discovered.'

She sounded out of breath.

'Sorry boss, can you repeat that, from the beginning, I didn't quite catch what you said?'

I could hear her inhale deeply before she replied.

'Ray, DC Banks, wasn't there. According to his wife, he's at work.' She slowed her words. 'She knows nothing about the diabetes. He's been leaving the house at 7 a.m. sharp every morning, and getting in at different times every evening, so she'd no reason to suspect he was up to anything. Of course, she immediately jumped to conclusions thinking he was having an affair or had done something to have got himself suspended, so to put her mind at ease I told her about my conversation with him the last time I saw him, at the hospital, before he was discharged.'

She took another breath before continuing.

'You remember, in the car park where he collapsed, I offered to call his wife, but the paramedic said she'd do it? But in the ambulance, Ray said he'd do it himself once he'd been assessed. I thought he was worried about his diagnosis, concerned it would impact his authority to use a firearm, but she suggested he might not have confided in her because he'd seen how sick the diabetes had made *her*. She rang him, in front of me. His phone was off. And it got me thinking . . . about what Mari Wynn had told me when I spoke to her this evening.'

I heard the *bleep-bleep* of a car door's central locking, followed by a rustle, and asked her where she was.

'Ponthir.'

She carried on. 'Mari thinks her mother was murdered, by a copper. She admits Alys was suicidal but doesn't think she'd have allowed Kerry-Ann, a practical stranger, to be the one to find her.'

'Kerry-Ann Pascoe? Roderick Penrose's daughter?'

'Yes. She'd been staying in a cottage in Lavernock while she wrote Alys' memoir. But she got spooked, thought she saw some bloke leering at her through the windows, so she turned up at Alys' much earlier than usual one morning and ended up spending the night there. Her girlfriend, Natalia, showed up too, apparently, to support Kerry-Ann, who was due to visit her father in prison the following morning. After the visit, Natalia followed Kerry-Ann back to the cottage to collect her things. There was a copper there when they arrived. He didn't speak to them, and according to Kerry-Ann she instantly wondered if he was the man who'd been hanging around the cottage. She reckoned he tailed Natalia's car, so she decided to follow them. Only when he noticed Kerry-Ann behind him, he drove off. When asked where he left them, she said she didn't know the name of the street, but that she passed the police station in Penarth a minute later. When she returned to Alys' she found her dead. Alys had written a suicide note and had been saving up her pain medication. The verdict of the police and the coroner was that she'd taken her own life.'

'So what makes Mari think someone killed her mother? Or that the person who did it was a copper?'

'She was writing about the Nighthawk's copycat and as part of her research she spoke to a photographer who was around at the time of the original killings and who had captured a picture of a PC smoking a cigarette at one of the deposition sites where one of Glenn Marsh's victims was found.'

'And you think the constable was DC Banks?'

'Not only did he used to live close to Penarth nick, but he also worked there right up until he aced his National investigator's Exam in March. And he's an Authorised Firearms Officer. Which means he has both access to and knows how to use guns.'

I heard her car engine start up.

'You think he faked a diabetic episode?'

She replied to the sound of her foot pumping the accelerator. 'I don't think it's a coincidence that he got ill just as soon as we inadvertently came across a link between Geraint and Glenn's crimes. Besides, his wife is diabetic. It wouldn't be difficult for him to get hold of a vial of insulin. And having seen her do it he'd know how to inject himself. If he got the dosage right, he could get himself hospitalised without risking his life or arousing suspicion. And he smokes. Lord knows I'm always harping on at him to quit.'

I *thought* he was a smoker.

'I'll get on the blower to the records department, see if there's anyone at South Wales Police Headquarters who can trawl through the files, find out if he was present at any of the Nighthawk's deposition sites.'

'There's no need. I've already spoken to the SIO leading the investigation into the Copycat's killings. He read the Operation Nighthawk files as part of his inquiry. He recognised Ray's name straight away. He was there alright, guarding the scene where the cigarette stub was found. But that's not all. Guess when he decided to train as a detective, sell his house, and transfer to Gwent CID?'

I had to wrack my brain to recall when the first of the Copycat Killer first struck.

'March 2020.'

During the first of the COVID-19 lockdowns. When people were expected to stay indoors unless absolutely necessary and when criminals took advantage of the decreased risk of their crimes being witnessed.

KERRY-ANN

FIVE DAYS LATER

As much as I love the country that I was born in I couldn't wait to return home. Partly to put some distance between myself and South Wales, which I now seemed only to associate with murder: Geoffrey Goldsborough's, the Nighthawk's victims, and now the Copycat's victims, but mostly because I missed Natalia.

In the year since my visit to Lavernock we'd got engaged. On the highest cliff point of Land's End, facing the Atlantic Ocean, she knelt on one knee and proposed. I said yes without a moment's hesitation.

Since her promotion from waitress to sous-chef she'd been experimenting with food and had taken it upon herself to do all the cooking. Something I didn't mind but meant we'd often have to buy ingredients on a whim, dependent on what she fancied eating that night. Seconds after I'd walked through the front door, I was being herded back out of it again and into her car for a trip to the supermarket.

We'd not long got in when we learned the police constable who'd been snooping around the cottage that I'd been staying in last year had been arrested. Natalia hurried into the kitchen and placed the bags she was holding onto the dining table then headed into the living room and switched on the TV. It was a habit we were both afflicted with; to increase the noise level inside the house as soon as we'd closed the front door behind us. I suspected it was due to us both being only children and growing up in quiet households. We'd obviously missed the name of the man but had caught the smartly dressed presenter right at the moment that he was introducing us to a crime reporter who began discussing the scene behind her in so much detail it was clear she didn't know any more factual information about what had led to the warrant or what the police had found inside the man's house than the viewer. Although it was clearly enough to charge him with murder.

Natalia returned to the car to collect the largest items of our shopping trip from the boot, which included a crate of canned soda, a five-litre bottle of laundry detergent, and a twenty-four pack of toilet tissues. Alone in the room, I watched as the man was escorted in handcuffs from a suburban home, past a group of press officers who were snapping pictures, shooting video footage, and bombarding him with questions that had he replied to could have been given as evidence against him in a court of law.

Back in the TV studio, the presenter described how it was believed the former member of the police force was responsible for the death of the late great true crime author, Alys Wynn.

I was caught off-guard when her name was spoken and dropped the carrier bag containing eggs onto the carpeted concrete floor.

Natalia had chosen that moment to re-enter the room, and so she reached down to inspect the damage. 'Didn't lose a single one,' she said, bewildered.

I think she was expecting me to remind her that was because I was the one who'd told her to pack the egg box on top of the other light goods. But catching the stunned expression on my face, she quickly realised something was wrong.

'What is it?' she asked, finally registering my eyes had been magnetised towards the TV screen.

I stood there, slack-jawed, unable to compute what I was hearing.

'Is that...?' She pointed to the professional-looking photograph they'd chosen to display of a much healthier Alys, which filled the right-hand side of the screen, and I nodded my head in confirmation.

She took my hand and squeezed it. Following that with a slow shake of her head.

'But, how?' I eventually gasped. 'I found her. She'd left a suicide note. Her bottle of medication was on the bedside table beside her. There was no sign of a break-in when I . . . let myself in.' I tore my gaze away from the TV and stared at Natalia as realisation dawned. 'She left the door unlocked! Anyone could have entered the house.'

'Not anyone,' she said. '*Him.*'

The same man I'd seen in the chip shop. Who'd been creeping around the cottage the day we'd returned to collect my belongings. And who'd tailed Natalia's car from Lavernock to Penarth police station, until he'd spotted me following him, the day we left.

DI LOCKE

PAST

My first impressions are usually right. I knew Demelza was aware of more than she was letting on, from the very beginning of my investigation. I also knew that whatever she was holding back from telling me would make her look bad. And I was right. She'd given Errol's address to her mother-in-law, a woman who just happened to work for a cartel.

Lorraine hadn't thought twice about paying Sol to shoot a man to death for daring to encroach upon her boss' territory, as was the duty afforded her, what with her being one of the senior members of the organisation. Which we knew thanks to Sol's decision to talk, and we were grateful he liked the sound of his own voice, because once he opened his mouth he didn't seem to want to stop.

But nothing, and I mean this sincerely, could have prepared me for the discovery of the all-black 9mm Glock 17 in DC Ray Banks' car.

Executing the warrant had not only resulted in the finding of the same brand of weapon used to kill Geraint but had also led CSI to the needle-punctured vial of insulin located under the driver's seat, wrapped inside a piece of tissue which had Ray's fingerprints all over it. Corroborating my theory that he'd made himself sick in order to evade police capture as soon as we'd learned Geraint had represented a teenage Glenn Marsh.

Had he fled because he knew it wouldn't be long before we connected the Copycat to Alys? But if that were the case, what possible reason would he have to do so unless he'd killed her? And wouldn't killing her imply Alys knew something she shouldn't? Which is exactly why we believed Geraint had been murdered.

Because he was one of ours, Gwent CID weren't allowed to continue the investigation. And as he'd previously worked as a constable for South Wales Police, in Penarth, there were only two other Welsh forces who were able to continue where we'd left off and Dyfed-Powys Police were the closest in terms of geography.

Due to the potential for further corruption, the case was transferred to a higher-standing Detective *Chief* Inspector Hutchins. And it was him who'd come to the same conclusion as us. Which is that the only plausible motive DC Banks had for killing both Alys and Geraint, was if he was the Nighthawk's Copycat Killer.

PS TOMOS

PAST

When the DNA sample retrieved from the cigarette stub found at one of the Nighthawk's deposition sites was retested by the Forensic Review Support Section, on the request of the SIO heading the case involving the Copycat Killer, the Chief of Operations confirmed that although it matched the semen sample extracted from one of the Copycat's victims, which was registered to a profile held on the UKs database, there was no way of determining the name of the person to whom it belonged. To find out if the man had ever lived and/or worked abroad, they ran the unique numerical digits through the International DNA Database, accessible through INTERPOL's automated secure global police communications system, known and used by law enforcement in seventy-seven – and counting – member countries as the DNA Gateway. But they didn't get a hit on that either.

The Copycat Killer's crimes bore a striking resemblance to those committed by Glenn Marsh in terms of the method he'd used to incapacitate, abduct, and torture his victims. The type of victims he'd chosen (young adult female, slim-framed, dark hair, pale skin). And whoever he was, he had close access to crime scenes, allowing him to monitor them and enabling him to keep abreast of our developments.

But while DC Ray Banks had the means, motive, and opportunity to kill both Alys and Geraint, if he was the Copycat Killer, we had nothing but circumstantial evidence to prove him responsible for either of their murders. Even having the same shoe size as the partial footprint found, and a pair of Nike Air Max trainers with the same tread as the pattern left in the snow was deemed of limited value.

However, in his position of authority, he could easily persuade someone he was trustworthy. He was physically fit enough to overpower anyone who weighed less than he did and didn't know any self-defence moves. And he had access to both insulin and a Glock 17, both of which he'd admitted, during his interview, to have stolen.

He could, as he'd claimed, have been self-medicating with his wife's prescription for the diabetes he knew he had and didn't want to admit to having, seeing how the disease affected his wife. Just as he could have forgotten to hand his gun back in before leaving the shooting range due to 'brain fog', despite such security checks aimed at preventing people from being able to do just that.

But I wasn't buying it. Which is why we were wholly reliant on obtaining a sample of his DNA.

KERRY-ANN

SIX DAYS LATER

It took the police just twenty-four hours to secure a charge and it seemed that once the Crown Prosecution Service had given them the green light, they had him bang to rights. When I read the statement that they'd released online it looked as though Detective Constable Ray Banks was going to be spending the rest of his natural life behind bars. Of course, they couldn't divulge how they'd come to the conclusion but when they said 'forensic evidence' it could only mean that his DNA matched the profile extracted from both the cigarette stub left at the scene of one of the Nighthawk's crimes and the semen swabbed from one of the women believed to have been killed by the Copycat, so I was annoyed but unsurprised when I heard on the televised news at lunchtime that the 'Killer Cop' – as they'd so originally named him – had denied all charges.

He'd be putting his victim's families and friends through further unnecessary turmoil. Why couldn't he just admit what he'd done, and tell the police where the woman they still hadn't found was? It wasn't fair on her only surviving relative – her father.

Which got me thinking about Gina Field's dad, and

then my own. And I started doubting his innocence, which made me feel guilty.

Tears stung my eyes, but I blinked them away.

Natalia put her arm around my waist and drew me towards her, pressing her cheek against mine.

I breathed in her fresh salty perfume that reminded me of the sea and turned my face towards her.

'Let it all out,' she said, so I did.

SIX MONTHS LATER

DI LOCKE

PRESENT

I feel eyes on the back of my head. I've felt the tingling all day. When I told Johnno about it, he said I might have an iron deficiency and suggested I book myself an appointment with my doctor. But I can't help but wonder if this is the exact same feeling Kerry-Ann felt while Ray was hovering around in the shadows watching her.

It has crossed my mind more than once that there may be another Nighthawk wannabe waiting to take over from the Copycat Killer, and I have wondered if he's following me. I also realise how ridiculous this sounds which is why I dare not voice my thoughts to anyone.

The pub is just as I imagined. Day-drinkers stood around the bar, a group of men studying the comings and goings of patrons near the front door. The constant hum of a generator placed on the external wall near the back door, left open to allow smokers the use of a small square patio they call the beer garden.

'No guesses as to why you chose this place.'

None of us are in the mood for a celebratory drink seeing as we lost one of our own team while HMP Long Lartin won another inmate from the force.

The woman serving today has no idea who I am. But one quick glance of DS Tomos and recognition ignites in the eyes of the tall, tattooed, shaven-haired bloke built of brawn who stands beside her serving a customer a pint of bitter.

'Finally decided to try one of our locally brewed beers, have ye?'

I shrug, say, 'Why not,' and Dafydd orders me a pint.

I take a sip, to quench my thirst, and it leaves a conflicting taste in my mouth.

We weren't able to stick anything on him. But we will, one day. And today, it's our turn to remind him that we're watching his every move, and that when he slips up, we'll be right here waiting to catch him. Yesterday, it was DCs Bishop and Burtenshaw. Tomorrow, it'll be DCs Chapman and Winters.

We split in the car park. Behind us, the River Usk smoothing pebbles, heard but unseen in the dusky Spring haze.

The air is warmer now, the birds chirping a tune in the trees above me as I walk to the car.

The drive is as busy as ever, but I roll the window down and inhale the scent of roses as I near home.

Next-door's bin is overflowing as I stride up the path. The stench of rotting meat and the sight of several small maggots wriggling about on the tied top of a black bag greets me right before I push open the door.

The house is unusually quiet. Jaxon's eyes sparkling as he looks up at me from the doorway of the living room, and says, 'Eefan gonded wiv his daddy.'

My stomach drops.

Then I hear a scream, high-pitched and excited. And my heart pounds as I race down the hall towards the open back door.

Ethan, perched almost six feet above ground, sits on

Craig's shoulders wearing a huge smile on his face.

Both stop and stare at me for a second, then Johnno appears from the side of the house carrying two paper plates containing steaming hot dogs, with two thin lines of tomato and mustard sauce down the lengths of them.

I've never seen Craig's eyes so bright, his skin so clear.

He reaches up to remove Ethan from his shoulders and I notice his arms look fuller. He deposits Ethan onto the ground and opens his mouth to speak, but before he can say anything I've run towards him and latched onto him fiercely.

He stands straighter and he's put on weight, and he smells so . . . clean.

The tears come then, hot rivulets sliding down my face. I don't realise he's crying too until I feel his shoulders shaking. The movement reminds me of the day I found him, just eight weeks ago, seizing on the bathroom floor from alcohol withdrawal.

I stiffen. And he must feel it because he pulls back. I look up at his watery eyes, and he has that same no-nonsense gaze he gave me the day he demanded to take the rap for the bag of cannabis I had in my pocket. The very reason he was given a police caution, and I was able to join the force in the first place. We evened it out though, when I stood in front of him and took the blade meant for his stomach from the lad who he owed weed money to, which pierced my womb.

That's not the reason I can't have kids. During a routine internal scan of my uterus, to determine the extent of the endometriosis that was being blamed for my infertility, my gynaecologist found signs of Pelvic Inflammatory Disease. A swab test later revealed I had undiagnosed chlamydia; thanks to a bloke I'd been dating.

I realised while he was away, detoxing, learning to live soberly, that I could no longer blame myself for Craig's police record, that it wasn't this alone which affected his job prospects. I wasn't responsible for his alcoholism, any more than I was at fault for not realising our mate Jimmy was dying of the very same disease.

Life is what *you* make it, and I intend to spend every day of mine thankful for what I have.

DS TOMOS

PRESENT

The animosity coming off Chris as I step through the front door is almost physical. He stumbles towards me and strands so close that I can smell whatever cheap spirits he's been drinking. His gaze is unfocused, features devoid of emotion, his body language tells me he's rearing for a fight.

This stranger is not the boy I got up in the night to feed. Who I taught to ride a bicycle without stabilisers. Who, as well as his older brother, stayed by his mother's side day and night, after the car accident that caused her to lose the use of both her legs. This young man is not my son. He is an imposter. But as much as it kills me to see him like this, I understand it. I just don't know what to do about it.

He's drinking too much and too often.

'Life. Life! What about hers?' he spits.

Eva's.

He sat alone throughout the trial, at home, too afraid of making a scene to be there in person. I attended every day of court for him, so that I could return home each day knowing he'd be here waiting for me, to tell him about the day's events.

He wobbles against the wall, then bounces off it and

into the armrest of Sarah's wheelchair. 'Sorry, mum,' he slurs.

Instead of replying she gives me a look that says, 'Tread carefully,' but I don't think she realises how many violent drunks I've had to deal with in my line of work. Predicting the behaviour of a pissed-up pissed-off twenty-year-old is no more difficult.

He looks at me, glassy-eyed. 'How could you not have known?' he slurs, face distorted as though he's about to cry. 'You must have seen the signs?'

I take a step back, allowing some distance to form between us but he moves towards me, snatching it back up again.

'It's not your father's fault, Chris.'

His mother's voice snaps him out of whatever he's thinking, and he jumps as if her words are the crack of a whip.

He glares at me for a moment like he wants to hit me, but the old Chris reappears briefly. The one I wiped the snotty nose of. And who I allowed to paint my face, so we'd sport matching bruises when he almost broke his nose during a school rugby tackle. He releases a sob that sounds like he's held it in for far too long, then he darts down the hallway and out into the night.

I move to chase after him, but Sarah stalls me with a gentle hand to my stomach, which feels softer, and glancing down, I notice is getting a tad podgy.

'I'll go.'

She is gone for no more than a minute and returns alone.

'He'll come round. He just needs time.'

'Where's he gone?'

'Back to the flat.'

The one he's renting now that his Halls of Residence are a traumatic reminder that the one night he allowed his girlfriend to walk back to her room on the other side of campus on her own is the night her killer chose her as his next victim. It is something that will haunt him forever.

I know because I've carried the weight of Mohammad's death for almost as long as I served in the Armed Forces.

'He's right though, isn't he? Maybe I'm not cut out to be a murder detective. Maybe I'm better off leaving CID completely. Or even taking an early retirement from the police force. They say once you lose it, the ability to see past your own nose, it's time to go. Maybe this is *my* time.'

KERRY-ANN

PRESENT

Sea foam sprays against the rocks edging the cliffs. Each thunderous wave smashing against the rough grey stone and whipping up the surf. The wind whispers nonsensically into my ear.

I turn away from the double-glazed doors that lead out onto the veranda.

It was Natalia's idea. 'A holiday will do us both some good,' she said. So here we are. Well, here I am anyway. She's in the kitchen making us a Greek salad. My favourite.

To date *Hidden Depths* has sold over half a million copies. The friends I've made in the book industry tell me this is excellent for a debut. Though it doesn't stop me from doubting myself and thinking that I could do better. This, my editor tells me, more than being published, or even receiving my first one-star review, is what makes me an author. This internal desire to beat my own achievements is also what propelled me to finish writing Alys' incomplete project into the Copycat Killer – Ray Banks' – crimes.

I've spoken to Detective Inspector Emma Locke and Detective Sergeant Dafydd Tomos to get their interpretations of the investigation for my second foray into true crime. Only this time I did things a little differently by borrowing the title, *The Nighthawk,* and using the pseudonym, Louise Mullins, just as Alys wished.

SOUTH WALES TIMES

IN THE DOCK: Look who's been in court this week

A round-up of recent cases heard in Cardiff Crown Court (Reported by Isabel Da Silva, Tue 11 July 2023, 8.07 a.m.)

Jayden Pring
26, of Arlighton Heights, pleaded guilty and was sentenced to serve twelve months in prison, suspended for two years, for driving whilst disqualified.

Connor Derrick
44, of Wentloog Avenue, fleeced thousands of pounds out of vulnerable people for building work he did not complete. He was ordered to pay back £60,000.

Ravi Hussain
37, of Pencoedtre Lane, burgled a disabled pensioner at knifepoint. He has been jailed for six months.

Lorraine Fford (67, of Lisvane Road), **Demelza Boyde** (45, Cliff Hill), **Jamie Peterson** (32, Prince Charles Close) Each given seven-year prison sentences for conspiracy to commit murder.

SOUTH WALES TIMES

INQUIRY INTO DOORSTEP MURDERER'S DEATH

(Reported by Sian Conelly, Fri 11 August 2023, 9.01 a.m.)

Solomon King, aged 21, of HMP Parc, died from hanging inside his prison cell in December 2022, shortly after the governor had arranged for him to be transferred to a high-security prison. He had been found deceased by a prison guard.

King had been expecting to be sentenced to a further fifteen years in prison for the murder of Errol James Parker, who'd been shot dead on the doorstep of his home in Cardiff. A sentence that he would have begun serving once his current sentence for murdering father of four, Mattheu White, had been served. But King, believed to be a hitman working for a drug gang, took his own life the day before he was due to be transferred to HMP Parkhurst, on the Isle of Wight.

During the inquest, the coroner concluded that it was Solomon's own association to organised crime which ultimately led to his death. And during his final statement the coroner made it clear that, 'Every person of authority involved in his incarceration positively contributed to Solomon's safety and did everything in their power to protect him.'

This comes after several inmates' deaths at HMP Parc this year which are currently being investigated by the Prison and Probation Ombudsman, sparking concern amongst the family and friends of those within the prisoner population as to whether there may be a common denominator.

SOUTH WALES TIMES

COUNTY LINES DRUG GANG LEADER GUILTY

(Reported by Kyle Wever, Weds 25 October 2023 at 9.01 a.m.)

■■■

Loading images . . .

Last month we reported that several members of an organised crime gang responsible for the countrywide distribution of Class A drugs were each given jail terms for their part in the operation, which included convictions for: possession of a Class A substance, money laundering, and fraud.

Elys Whittaker, Scott Fford, Luke Fford, Derwen Boyde, and Julian Clements were each given minimum prison terms of five years. While Carol Boyde was handed a suspended sentence. Others suspected of being involved continue to be under the investigation of a local police drug task force. And several more have been tried in their prospective countries. Namely Mehmet Ivanova, from Holland, and Greek Cypriot Zara Demetriou.

Today the lead operator, Colm McGinty, responsible for organising the trafficking of heroin into the UK, has been found guilty.

McGinty, the son of a former IRA member, Fergal McGinty, who was imprisoned for the bombing of a Belfast pub during the Troubles, will be sentenced tomorrow at the Central Criminal Court in Dublin.

The heroin McGinty is responsible for bringing into the country was laced with fentanyl and is suspected to have caused the deaths of twenty-eight adults since it hit the streets of South Wales, due to its deadly strength.

The Next to Die, DI Emma Locke: Book 5 coming soon!

A year ago, one of Detective Inspector Emma Locke's colleagues was convicted of multiple counts of murder. Today, he appears to have struck again. Only it can't be him, can it? Not if he's in prison. So who is emulating the Nighthawk's Copycat? Supposing there even is one.

CONTACT NUMBERS

If you are experiencing suicidal thoughts, please talk to someone. The Samaritans were a lifeline to me, many years ago, and they continue to support people going through difficult emotions. You can call them free on: 116 123.

AUTHOR'S NOTE

Other than Lavernock House there are no other properties on the headland of Lavernock besides St. Lawrence's church and the rectory, but the desolate landscape surrounding them seemed like the perfect spot to build one. And so, to the right of Fort Road between the car park and the holiday village where Sully Island rests on the Bristol channel between Weston-Super-Mare and Swanbridge Bay I've erected an imaginary croft called Bwthyn Golygfa Ynys (Island View Cottage).

At the end of Fort Road, to the left, there is a footpath backing the dense hedgerows, where, if you were to walk or cycle its length for about a mile, you'd find one of the UK's Royal Observer Corps monitoring posts in Penarth, with a view of Ranny Bay. To the right, if you were to cross the shingle beach while the tide was out, you'd be able to slip through the woodland and follow the uphill path to the nuclear bunkers of Lavernock Battery, overlooking St. Mary's Well Bay.

The place really is as picturesque and hauntingly quiet as I hope I have portrayed it to be in this novel. But I think the only way to give this hidden cove justice would be if you were to see it for yourself: https://en.wikipedia.org/wiki/Lavernock

ALSO BY LOUISE MULLINS

DI Locke Series:
#1 The Secrets I Keep
#2 The Lies I Tell
#3 If I Can't Have You
#4 The Nighthawk

Death Valley Series:
#1 Lucky
#2 Lost in America
#3 In Her Shadow
#4 Beneath the Surface
#5 Silver or Lead
#6 Highway to Hell

Standalones:
Scream Quietly
Damaged
Why She Left
The Perfect Wife
One Night Only
What I Never Told You
Buried Sins
Love You Gone
Love You Dead
Love You Bad

Historical:
The House of Secrets
Lavender Fields

ACKNOWLEDGEMENTS

As always, I owe huge thanks to my long-suffering husband, who acts as my sounding-board throughout the writing of each novel and helps me to figure out the ending of every one of them.

First and foremost, I have mentioned at the start of this novel, the exceptionally talented true crime author, Kathryn Casey. If you haven't read any of her books yet, you must.

Lisa Cutts and Roger Price, thank you so much for answering my questions relating to police procedure. Your guidance made this a better book.

A special mention must go to the real Surjit Parekh. Who is not actually a pathologist at all, but is in fact a huge support, a phenomenal blogger, and someone I am proud to call a friend.

Family Liaison Officer, Detective Constable Burtenshaw's surname is also borrowed, with the consent of a very good friend of mine, Jessica Louise.

Amanda Kelly, AKA Warrior Woman, also makes an appearance as a Police Constable.

And, last, but by no means least, Kevin Crocker, who is also not a doctor, but I daresay would make a bloody good one – no pun intended.

Many others have also helped me along the way. Without their support I never would have continued doing what I love. So a big shoutout must go to:

Kerry Watts, Maggie James, Caroline Cole, Helen Phifer, Katy Johnson, Rose McClelland, Christine Stephenson, Livia Sbarbaro, Alyson Read, Lynda Checkley, Deb Day, Tina Baker, Ruby Speechley, Donna Morfett, Sharon Rimmelzwaan, Zoe O'Farrell, Joy Wood, Terri-Ann Metcalf, Claire Sheldon, Linda Regan,

Vered Nita, Lucinda Berry, Kimberly Belle, Caroline Mitchell, Cate Holohan, Miranda Jewess, Awais Kahn, and Janice Hallet.

And finally, thank YOU, for reading this book. It is only because of your loyalty that I can continue writing.

Please do leave a review if you can. Telling others what you think about a novel can help massively in boosting its visibility.

Louise Mullins writes full-time using the experience she gained from a career in the field of forensic mental health, working with offenders and survivors of serious crimes.

To keep up to date with her latest releases you can find her on Facebook, Twitter, Instagram, Threads, and TikTok as: @mullinsauthor.

Fortress specializes in the publication of crime fiction.

Printed in Great Britain
by Amazon